REBECCA TREE

A POLITICAL DYNASTY UNRAVELS

TREE
for PRESIDENT

MICHAEL ABRAMSON

Acknowledgements

It took a village to raise this book.

For all the patient early readers:

Thomas F. Cook, Jon Gingerich, Carrie Wharton Priest,
Barbara Zolot, the late Jay Colton,
the late Thomas A. Nesbit Jr., Janice Willett,
Cabell Smith, Penny Street.

To the habitués of Greenpoint Brooklyn's
Word Bookstore, where writers' groups rose up out of the
store's basement space: Dean Strober, Nathaniel Kressen,
Vinny Senguttuvan, Sonya Patel, Christina Parrella,
Jessica Sarles-Dinsick, Taylor Tobin, Maria Pedone.

And a special thanks to Krista Madsen,
Maryann Calendrille, Bonnie Britt, and Sonya Grayson.

For my wonderful wife, Erika Jakubassa,
the smartest person in my room,
who will always be my brightest star.

Part One

Chapter 1

White House State Dining Room
Washington, D.C.
Eight p.m.

Sam Tree, the president of the United States, was about to die.

Sucking on his first oyster, a Peconic from Long Island's Great South Bay, Tree's lips smacked from the mollusk's ocean kiss. His face flushed, fleshy pink cheeks speckled with red. In his veins, free fatty droplets looked to relocate.

Next was a Raspberry Point from Prince Edward Island, plump and creamy, it tanged his palate like the melony musk between the legs of his favored brothel duo, the "Uzbekistan Express." Fatty droplets now sped through arterial shunts to their destination of choice, the president's brain stem.

The third oyster was a Glidden Point flat from Maine. Tree's sucking came to a halt as his throat went into reflexive alert. Like a locomotive thrown unceremoniously into reverse, spit flew from his mouth. The Glidden Point Flat tasted of a high-tided mussel, its brain too primitive to have fled dehydrating ground. The president's countenance of pleasure disappeared, and a foul odor commandeered his mouth; he spat noisily into his linen. His brain's pathways began to inflame.

Incensed, he vacuumed in the fourth with a loud slurp, a Moonstone from Point Judith Pond. It was pedigreed by the terminal moraine, a species of oyster birthed at the end of the Ice Age, flavored by mineral rich water, a taste seasoned with a relish of stone and iron. Tree's eyes bulged momentarily as the Moonstone pirouetted through his esophagus, rotating south to his stomach.

The guest of honor, the Chinese premier, Sun Jian, sat on the dais next to President Tree. Jian shook his head briefly before his neck drew inward like a panicky turtle in retreat. Inside Tree's brain, C-reactive proteins slammed out of control.

Tree abruptly pushed his plate away; his left eye twitched, and his head shook as he stood. With his gait out of balance, he approached the podium. His eyes turned the two teleprompters into four. He felt a shallowness of breath.

Tree had just begun his remarks when the First Lady, Ashley Tree, seemed to detect an ominous slurring of speech. She watched in disbelief as her husband's knees buckled, his speech broke apart. For a brief moment, an unearthly wail emanated from deep in his throat.

The president dropped the folio holding a hard copy of his prepared speech. The palm of his right hand shot up and smashed into his left eye. Taking a lurching step away from the podium, he fell forward like a dead weight, his head slamming into his main course, a plate of steaming Double Pleasure Live Whole Sea Bass.

A team of Secret Service medics, supervised by the president's physician, frantically tried to revive the leader of what had once been the most powerful and respected nation on earth. Twenty minutes later, a doctor paused and looked at his watch. He recorded the president's time of death for posterity: 9:28 p.m.

Chapter 2

Airspace Over the Arabian Desert

The moon, with a waxing crescent, dipped below the horizon line of the desert sands. The stars illuminating the cloudless night blossomed with fresh intensity.

Forty thousand feet above the surface of the earth, a custom-built hydrogen powered Learjet, carrying a solitary passenger, streaked through the sky.

Beijing to Boston.

Rebecca Tree, President Sam Tree's only living sibling, sat transfixed in the plane's executive cabin, searching the night sky as a spectacular meteor shower concluded.

Below stretched *Rub al Khali*, the Empty Quarter, the world's largest sand desert, one of the least hospitable places on earth—scorching hot, aridly dry, and unyielding.

Each year she arranged her global business trips to coincide with the celestial event. The April Lyrids, named after the constellation Lyra emerged from a point near Vega, the fifth brightest star in the night sky.

The beauty and the force of nature humbled her, moved her.

The meteors, in her mind, became proxies for lost loved ones; sadness chilled her bones as fragile memory traces raced through her mind.

She remembered a famed story from Japanese mythology of celestial exiled lovers, each year on the seventh night of the seventh moon crossing the Milky Way on a sky bridge of magpies for a wondrous reunion.

The lovers' tears fell as raindrops that night all across Japan.

* *

Dressed in jeans and black Keds, Rebecca wore a Giant Monkey Frog T-shirt. Under the image of a grotesque-looking Peruvian amphibian perched precariously on a tree branch, the shirt's slogan read "Licking This Frog May Make You Crazy." She had purchased the shirt twenty years ago when the *Phyllomedusa bicolor* species was endangered. Now it was extinct.

She sat in the pitch-black cabin for an hour after the meteor shower ended before reluctantly switching back on a bank of computer screens and state-of-the-art satellite communications systems. Some of the screens displayed 360-degree panoramas of the cockpit; two offered comfort during turbulence by showing her the pilots' faces. The manufacturer created this modification to help Rebecca fight off panic attacks, which sometimes came with flying. If left unattended, her brain would work itself into a frenzy imagining how it must have been for her parents, how rapid their descent, and how instant their demise upon impact. Or worse: the possibility it went slow.

She became lost in thought as her mind reviewed the complexities of her life.

She was the granddaughter of America's most powerful politician; her older brother was the president of the United States. A successful inventor and businesswoman, she was also the sole voice of rebellion within the Tree family.

As the older of the Tree twins — by six minutes — she felt a responsibility to protect her sister Allison, in life as well as in her death. Rebecca had unfinished business with the Tree dynasty; unanswered questions remained which needed to be addressed.

The public knew little about Rebecca Tree, and she did her best to keep it that way. As CEO and chairwoman of the Argyle Group, a private equity company with a small minority stake owned by the Tree family, she managed a substantial concentration of global wealth, successfully turning around an old-line fossil fuel conglomerate into a global leader powered by sustainable technologies.

In addition to their investment interests, her family's male bloodline had built a formidable and controversial political dynasty. Her grandfather, Merewether Tree, served seven terms in the United States Senate until he retired at the age of eighty. Her great-uncle William, the younger half-brother of Merewether, and a congressman, rose to the powerful chairmanship of the House Ways and Means Committee, and then served as Secretary of the Treasury, until retiring after two heart attacks.

Merewether and William were often called Big Tree and Little Tree—fondly by their supporters and bitterly by their enemies. Last and least came Rebecca's brother Sam, disdainfully nicknamed Baby Tree, whose rise to the presidency paralleled the nation's increasing dysfunction.

The male Trees had created a political brand—the Millennium Populist Party. With moral certitude, they proclaimed their belief system, an ingenious blend of economic populism and religious fundamentalism, to the wreckage of a badly divided electorate.

Rebecca reached back under her left shoulder blade, and started massaging a thick, jagged line of scar tissue, acquired, she had been told, from a childhood fall. It had been there for as long as she could remember, seated like a button with direct connects to memory fragments as rare to her as the Dead Sea Scrolls and just as fragile.

An incoming cellphone call disrupted her, and she began talking to a private investigator named Oswaldo Lemus.

"Your grandfather has built an impenetrable wall of secrecy around his estate and the nearby town," Lemus said.

"So, no information of value?"

"None, *nada*, *rien*. I've had four of my most charming, good-looking agents trying to make friends with the locals."

"And?"

"None of the locals have been inside your grandfather's mansion. Apparently the town suppliers—the butcher, the green grocer, all of them, signed confidentiality agreements with your grandfather's steward. We can't even determine how many pounds of meat, or fruit, or any item for that matter are delivered each week."

"Geez Marie."

"Their delivery vans stop at the main gate, a mile from the house. Everything is unloaded there and put inside an electric van bearing the insignia Hillock-Hill Ranch, Home of Senator Merewether Tree, Retired."

"Is the type in gold leaf?"

"Ha. No, it gets worse. There's a reproduction painted beside the text of a portrait of Senator Tree, which must be his official portrait. Arms folded, American flag behind him, bookcase on right and globe of the world on left."

"Stop, this is making me sick."

"Look, he either has a great deal to hide. Or he's extremely paranoid. Or both."

"I'll put my money on the 'both' theory. I don't know what to do about this anymore," Rebecca said, her voice filled with undisguised frustration.

"Rebecca. We go way back, you and I. Can I tell you what I think?"

"Yes. I wouldn't be able to stop you in any event."

"Ok. Stop looking, at least for the moment. We have failed to uncover any useful information about your twin."

"Let me think about it."

"Becky, I love you like a sister but don't hire me again unless you are willing to dig into the weeds and break some legs."

Rebecca slumped in her seat. Closing her eyes, she tried to fight off a wave of despair. Trying to fill in the huge blanks of this meager story was all she had of her sister, and it was too hard to let that go.

* *

Agitated by the conversation with Lemus and unable to sleep, Rebecca opened her laptop and typed an email to her Chief Operating Officer, Fatima Massiri:

Fatima, I'll be back in the office late tomorrow morning. The attached notes are the proposed claim amendments discussed yesterday with our Chinese attorneys on the micro wind turbine patent. More when we speak in person. She paused for a few seconds. *Beijing can be lovely this time of year. Not even thirty million cars can destroy the Summer Palace Garden and the Temple of Heaven. Best, R.T.*

A flurry of incoming calls on her cellphone interrupted Rebecca's thoughts. She had assigned distinct ring tones to the names in her address book. One was the opening riff of Billy Strayhorn's "Take the

A Train" and promised a friendly caller.

But it was another set of tones—the ominous chords of Richard Wagner's *Tristan and Isolde*—that began to abrade her ear. The ill-omened chord was reserved exclusively for the few living members of her immediate family and their associates.

With the second jarring Wagnerian call, without looking at the caller ID, she opened the back panel of her cellphone and removed the battery, throwing it into one of the many pockets of her orange messenger bag, which she always carried for both its sentimental value as well as the practical.

She was determined to have some peace. The plane's engines hummed like a low-frequency kitchen blender, helping her to slide towards sleep. The night sky, led by the Milky Way, began to dim, and Rebecca was soon in a forest, now a young child seeking a tree to climb.

Her mind churned into the nightmare that recurred often to plague her:

> *A familiar oak tree. A pine needle carpeted forest. She searches for secret messages from her dead father. The big house fills the background. The wind carries a sound of distant crying, and a plaintive voice calling out like her sister.*
>
> *She runs towards the house; a heavy pine door opens into a cavernous kitchen. Logs burn in a cooking fireplace—pig roasting on a spit. Flames grow. Sparks fly. Smoke. Muffled whimpering. Her sister is tied to a chair, arms and legs bound, mouth stuffed.*
>
> *She runs to her twin and unties her. Allison, fully free, still moaning and crying, picks up a kitchen knife and turns toward Rebecca . . .*

Suddenly she is awoken as the plane hits a patch of turbulence. The lead pilot's voice came over the intercom. "Sorry Becky, the jet stream just slammed us. No warning. It should be okay now. We just received a request from Homeland Security that a government number is trying to call you, but they think you are blocking it."

"Thanks," Rebecca groggily replied, trying to shake herself out of sleep and to distance herself from the fears the dream triggered. "My phone is off. I'll turn it back on."

Rebecca becomes fully awake although still disorientated. Trying to normalize, she returned the battery to her cellphone, which began chirping with a backlog of voice mails. Before she could look at the messages, the phone blared its harsh Wagnerian tone. WHITE HOUSE displayed on her phone. She answered the call.

"Rebecca Tree here," she said, her voice armored.

"This is Sherman Knight," a nervous voice declared. "I'm assistant to Henry Hess, President Tree's Senior Advisor. I'm afraid I have bad news for you. It's about your brother Sam."

Rebecca froze. Her history with her brother had been Cain-and-Abel poisonous. As she recovered from the unexpected jolt, she put Knight on hold as she flicked her finger at the Firefox icon on her laptop. A CNN homepage flashed with a banner announcing: PRESIDENT SAMUEL TREE DEAD AFTER COLLAPSE AT STATE DINNER. As Rebecca continued to read, a second screen popped up. V.P. GEORGE JENKINS BAYOU TO BE SWORN IN AS PRESIDENT. Nearly motionless, she nudged her phone's hold button.

"Do they suspect foul play?"

"No, cerebral hemorrhage."

God's will, Rebecca thought. She had long ago given up hope that her brother might change or show the slightest small sign of caring for her—it was not meant to be. Rebecca worshiped a loving, forgiving God, but Sam being called to account at such a young age came as no surprise and stirred in her no remorse. Sam had attempted an unspeakable act of sibling abuse towards her nearly thirty years ago; fortunately for Rebecca his attempt failed and he had never asked her forgiveness.

Within moments, the *Tristan* chord jolted her again. She pressed the green receive button. "Rebecca Tree here."

"Rebecca!" It was her great-uncle William Tree, as she knew by the ringtone. "Your damnable brother has managed to die."

"Yes, Uncle William. The White House called me a few minutes ago." She stumbled for a second, trying to achieve a full state of clarity. "Please give my condolences to Sam's widow and the children."

She paused. "I'm en-route back to the United States from Beijing and expect to land in Boston about five a.m." For a brief instant she debated what to say next. "I'm due in Stockholm the day after tomorrow."

"Well, change your plans, my dear grandniece, and now! You have to be at this cursed funeral the day after tomorrow."

"I don't know whether my schedule will allow me to come to Sam's funeral," Rebecca said as her voice stiffened.

"What do you mean?" Tree yelled. She moved the phone away from her ear. "He was your brother . . . your only living sibling. And this is not a simple funeral but an affair of state and an important gathering of power — political and financial."

Tree, met with silence, shifted into a stutter. "You . . . you . . . don't forget your obligations as chairwoman of Argyle. Sam was a limited partner. There are family issues to be discussed." His voice rose to a threat. "I have a message for you from your grandfather."

Rebecca felt a chill rush through her body. "Which is?"

'Be there!'

Rebecca felt as if a surgeon's knife had just made a capricious cut. Without waiting for a response, Great Uncle William hung up.

Chapter 3

Rebecca's plane lifted off into the pre-dawn light from Wayfarer Ketch, a private aviation terminal north of Boston. Her heart raced, and her ankles numbed, as a painful cramping grabbed her calf muscles while her mind filled with thoughts about the tragic Tree family history.

The only fact she had ever known about her parents was their loss—that they died in a plane crash before she and her sister reached two years of age, too young for her to remember them. The few hazy memories she had been confusingly entwined with faded snapshots from dreams, of a life with her twin sister that ended when Allison died at age four. Now her brother Sam had passed; the numbers of her family continued to dwindle. But it wasn't Sam's passing that caused this psychomotor reaction and reflexive sense of longing. It was Allison, always Allison.

Rebecca clutched a comfort locket around her neck. As the view of distant Boston receded under her plane's wing, she tried to distract herself by surfing the news channels. She began with the three major American networks but bypassed each one as their lead stories highlighted her destination that day, the funeral of her brother, where she had a front row seat reserved in a history for which she wanted no part.

She focused on a BBC special titled "Update: Global Climate Report." The first segment examined the degradation of world food supplies, as many developed nations employed immigrant guest workers to hand-pollinate crops; despite the herculean effort, most experts predicted irreversible global famines in the near future.

A narrator opined, "Half a million low-paid Mexican workers are all that stand to protect America's food supply. Agronomists now believe California's fruit could become as rare as caviar in post-Tsarist Russia.

"Adding to America's woes is a rampant lawlessness that is sweeping through the border states of New Mexico and Arizona. Hate crimes are on the rise, often directed at the same field workers who are preserving America's food supplies. Vigilante groups flying the banner of 'America First' are making daylight attacks in armed SUVs against immigrants. When night falls, whole towns are reportedly coming under the control of a shadowy group known as 'Native Force.'"

The narrator's voice continued, shifting to concerns about sea levels. "Two feet of rising waters are tipping the course of America's history. Parts of Florida's Palm Beach County have surrendered to the sea, while still prosperous cities, like Boston and New York, have privately financed seawalls and pumping stations, creating mammoth construction projects employing ant-like armies of workers. The Army Corps of Engineers have tried to fortify the Potomac Basin, protecting the nation's capital. It is still leaking—badly."

A bolded text message from Fatima flashed across her television's monitor:

BECKY, TURN ON CNN NOW.

Rebecca switched channels and the screen filled with a photograph of herself, a commissioned portrait retouched to minimize her facial freckles.

Slamming down her fist in anger at her image being broadcast, she grabbed the remote to turn the monitor off but hesitated. Instead, she reached into her bag for a hand mirror and a canvas cosmetic bag and began awkwardly working foundation makeup into her freckles as she continued watching the news show.

Although Rebecca's image of herself had been stamped in puberty, tall and gangly, skin hyper-pigmented with spots, and soda-bottle bottom bifocals to correct eyes that had crossed at age five—God's will, according to her domineering grandfather—she understood that the world perceived her grown-up persona in a different light. Now thirty-seven years old, she stood a full six feet, with erect posture and a determined stride. Her fiery red hair dramatically set off against a canvas of what now registered as sparkling freckles, as the result of a recessive gene on chromosome sixteen. With high cheekbones, a narrow nose, flush lips, she presented a striking image. Her brown, almond-shaped eyes, surgically uncrossed at age twelve, shimmered when she smiled.

"A family saga is unfolding at President Tree's funeral, with the imminent arrival by private jet of his only living sibling, Rebecca Tree, a businesswoman. Ms. Tree has managed to keep herself out of the public eye during President Tree's term in office. We go now to our Boston Bureau Chief, Sonya Coughlin. Can you give us some more background?"

"Thank you, Arnold. Yes and no on the background. Ms. Tree has a reputation as a fiercely private person, and her friends and associates are very protective of her. What we know is that she runs a privately held equity company, Argyle, which invests, manages and builds out global alternative energy businesses with cutting-edge technologies. She doesn't give interviews and photographs of her are scarce; beside her official portrait we have on screen now, our bureau has only a few pictures of her playing soccer, which seems to be a passion of hers."

"She spent three years in the Army," the anchor Arnold Olden interjected, "part of which was spent in combat zones in Saudi Arabia, but these details of her service seem sketchy."

"Hmm," Coughlin said, "sketchy often means army intelligence or special operations. In addition, she is a graduate of Balliol College, Oxford graduating with honors in mathematics."

"Interesting," Olden said, "we will provide our viewers with more details about Ms. Tree as they become available."

Rebecca muted the volume and angrily bold-texted Fatima. HOW DID THEY GET THIS STORY? DID MY UNCLE PUT THIS OUT? I'LL WRING HIS NECK.

No, your pilots had to give Andrews traffic control the manifest, Fatima texted. *The press monitors all private aviation coming into the funeral.*

DANG. I should have figured that out.

Rebecca turned the volume back up.

"There is a lot of speculation centering on Rebecca Tree's relationship with Sam Tree, as well as her grandfather Merewether Tree and his political party, the Millennium Populist Party. Our White House correspondent, Nick Byers, is standing by with an update."

"Thank you. We have just run Rebecca Tree's name through all the White House databases, particularly the visitor's log. She has been to the White House only once, as a three-year-old; her grandfather had taken her and her twin sister Allison, now deceased, to meet the president and the vice president. There is no record of her attending the inauguration of Sam Tree three years ago."

"I guess she isn't interested in the family business."

"You got that right. Muttonheads," Rebecca said, yelling at the screen as she removed the batteries from her remote before tossing them into a recycle bin.

As her plane descended into Andrews Air Force Base, Rebecca's phone began playing the dark chords from *Tristan und Isolde*. She stared at the caller I.D., WHITE HOUSE at 7:45 a.m.; WH at 7:50 a.m.; then again at eight. Next came HENRY HESS at 8:02 a.m.; 8:05 a.m.; and at 8:10 a.m.; followed by WILLIAM TREE. Ten minutes later, at 8:20 a.m. the tones began again. She juggled the phone in her hand, and hit the red decline icon, refusing all calls.

Better they tyrannize my voicemail, she thought. She focused her attention on a screen showing her pilots expertly manning the controls and reminded herself to breathe.

Her plane landed and rolled to a halt. Rebecca fortified herself for her reluctant participation in a ritualistic event, the burial of another member of the Tree family.

* *

Rebecca descended her plane's steps at Maryland's Andrews Air Force Base, grateful to plant her feet on solid ground again while longing to be anywhere else in the world but here. A Secret Service agent escorted her into a long black Cadillac limousine that drove her past a Marine band's drums and bugles that played *Ruffles and Flourishes*.

Ushered directly to the First Family's limousine, Rebecca saw her great-uncle William standing a short distance away. He flinched when he saw her and turned his gaze away. Perhaps he had spent all his ire screaming at her over the phone yesterday, Rebecca thought.

Tree's face had lengthened over the years; his skin had leathered and random patches of tufted hair crowned his beady, unsmiling eyes. As he aged, he had taken on the vulture-like appearance of his older half-brother.

"Different litter, different wife," went one of the well-known nasty comments about the pedigree of his sibling, made by Rebecca's grandfather, the family patriarch.

George Jenkins Bayou, Sam Tree's former vice president and now the newly installed president of the United States, stood next to William. Nearly eighty years old, Bayou's hands shook from the Parkinson's disease that wracked his body. Despite what the public had been led to believe, the inner circles of power all knew that Bayou's health was rapidly failing.

Old conspirators never die—they busy themselves at state funerals.

The rear window of the First Family's limousine lowered, and she heard the weak and plaintive voice of the newly widowed Ashley Tree call out, "Rebecca, I'm so glad you're here." With swollen, reddened eyes looking out of the opened window, she brushed her funeral veil away. "Please sit with me."

Rebecca got into the back seat and slid over so she would be close to Ashley. She hadn't seen her in person for more than ten years but remembered her having a generous smile and a ready laugh. Now she was surprised by how much her late brother's wife had aged. Once a top-ranked tennis player, it looked like she had gained fifty pounds in marriage. The few television clips that Rebecca had seen of Ashley didn't show the wrinkles prematurely creasing her face. A tell-all biography described her as a churchgoing cheerleader who got straight A's and had made a pledge to remain a virgin until marriage.

"Ashley, I'm so sorry for your loss. I wish I had been able to spend time with you and the children."

"It's not your fault. I know Sam kept you away from us." Ashley's voice bristled. "Sarah and Patrick were so excited by the holiday presents you sent them . . . a small moment of happiness in the house and your gifts were always so thoughtful but Sam always found a way to spoil it." Ashley let the funeral veil slip back over her face.

Rebecca was taken aback by Ashley's intensity. Through the veil the widow's right eye twitched, and one hand palsied.

"Are you okay?" she asked, clasping Ashley's shaking hand.

"No, not really," she paused, shaking her head.

"Do you want to talk about it?" Rebecca asked.

"No," Ashley responded before looking away and going silent. The inside of the limousine felt like a small cave, cold and claustrophobic.

Rebecca gazed across the tarmac where she spotted William Tree now heading for the First Family's limousine. She braced herself. Ashley's eyes followed and at the sight of him, she grabbed hold of Rebecca's wrist.

"Your great-uncle went ballistic when I sent the children to stay with my parents instead of bringing them to the funeral," she whispered.

"I don't understand . . . why did you send them away?"

Before Ashley could answer, the rear door opened, and William Tree's aging but still trim and tall frame swung nimbly into the back seat.

"Well, Rebecca," he said. "I'm so pleased that you took time from your busy schedule to attend your brother's funeral. I see you even got some news coverage."

Tree spoke mostly using only his lower lip; his upper appeared clamped in place. His mouth made a twisted pucker as he uttered each sentence, forcing a whoosh of air out with each word.

With a seemingly sympathetic gesture, he turned to Ashley. "Ah, my dear, how are you faring?" It was a question not seeking an answer, and he continued blithely. "I know what a difficult time this must be, to be widowed so young, to face such an emotional day without the love and support of your children."

Ashley shot him a look as cold as an iceberg.

Rebecca licked her lips; they tasted bitter like dandelion greens.

Tree, a veteran of pontificating to an empty chamber, ignored the women.

"It surely is a trying time for us, as well as for the nation," Tree said. "Perhaps we might arrange a quiet family reunion after the funeral."

The car now filled with a suffocating silence as neither of the women responded. Rebecca looked out through the one-way privacy glass window of the limousine at the accouterments of the state funeral. Mimicking the tragic final chapter in America's Age of Camelot, a lone black stallion, wearing the traditional backward boots, led the entourage. A procession of limousines, packed with sour-faced politicians, financiers, and mostly lesser heads of state, formed slowly across the tarmac. A twenty-one gun salute and the Air Force band playing "My Country 'Tis of Thee" wrapped up the pre-funeral niceties. Slowly, the cortege moved off the airfield and crossed from Maryland into Virginia, toward its destination, the United States Capitol.

Half-talking to himself, Tree remarked, "Look at the crowds. So many people coming out to pay their respects. With the help of the good Lord, the Tree family will always be America's first family."

Rebecca didn't respond, knowing that the crowd counts came up sparse, mostly government workers pressured to attend.

Ashley composed a reply. "Yes, Uncle William, I'm sure Sam's memory will always be cherished by a grateful nation." The edges of her words flicked out like a switchblade.

When the procession left Virginia and wound its way through the streets of Washington, Tree, a petulant sneer locking his lips, lowered the outer one-way glass and proffered half-waves to the crowd. Halfway up Constitution Avenue, protesters appeared in numbers that overwhelmed the mourners. With large black X's painted on their foreheads and wearing black shrouds over faces and shoulders, the dissident citizens multiplied faster than the security forces could contain them.

Finally comprehending that the faces on the street no longer appeared friendly, Tree stopped waving. As the outer window went back up, he muttered, "Godlessness is becoming rampant." Disgusted, he glared at the protesters swelling around the motorcade.

Rebecca read the dissident signs, stamping them into her memory. BRING ALL OUR TROOPS HOME seemed to be the most common. She especially liked a well-dressed passel of gray-haired ladies who wore

"Grannies for Peace" buttons pinned to their lapels.

My mother would be near their age. She might have stood this day with the Grannies.

Rebecca wished she could be outside the car.

An elderly black man with a full head of white hair, his chest and sleeves wallpapered with a collection of protest buttons that spanned decades, strutted close to the phalanx of Secret Service agents surrounding the First Family's limousine. Rebecca had to stifle a laugh as she spotted a prized antique button in his singular trove, TOMATA, POTATA, U.S. OUT OF GRENADA.

The car carrying the First Family quickly became the focus of the protesters' attention. Signs painted in bold black letters proclaiming WILLIAM TREE; WAR CRIMINAL formed part of a vivid tapestry of accusations along with SAM TREE IS IN HELL NOW and AMERICA IS DEAD-GOD HATES YOUR PRESIDENT. Blood-red hues highlighted the most derogatory placards.

William Tree stared at a placard that proclaimed GOD IS AMERICA'S TERROR.

"Americans died to protect our liberties, and these animals take to the streets and march like brown shirts," he said. "If I had been president, I would have known how to deal with these idiots and traitors."

Ashley Tree's eyes darted from one window to the next. Rebecca reassured her, "Don't worry. We're not in danger. Just a few more blocks to go, and we'll be on the Capitol grounds."

"So many unhappy people in the country," Ashley said.

Suddenly Rebecca heard a loud bang near the car, and a few seconds later, another even stronger. Thick black smoke filled the air; panic rippled along the edges of the crowd. An odor of gaseous fumes seeped into the limousine. Ashley screamed.

Rebecca pushed her down on the seat and covered her with her body, trying to quiet her own racing heart. For a moment she flashed back to a desert battleground, seeing the blast hitting the armored Humvee, watching bits of flesh and machinery fly.

"Stay calm," she said. "This limousine is better fortified than a tank."

Fortified. It didn't save his life or the others.

"What's happening?" Ashley started to cry. "I can't take this."

"I don't know. It's going to be okay," Rebecca said, trying to portray calmness. Her stomach churned as she too vividly recalled the last body she had covered, two decades ago in a war zone. He had died in her arms taking with him their dreams of a loving future.

William Tree cursed loudly, "Deviant dogs, Bolshies, maggots."

The limousine slammed to a stop, and the rear door flew open. Two more Secret Service agents, their faces covered with thick black soot, leaped into the passenger compartment. Four others clambered onto the specially designed running boards, one of them rapidly tapping three times on the driver's window. The driver responded to the taps and the limousine of the First Family broke out of the motorcade, swerved wildly, and accelerated to high speed. Rebecca got a glimpse of the horse-drawn casket carrying Sam Tree, its lead horse reared up, its handlers struggling to restrain the animal as they raced ahead.

Protesters began throwing things. They sounded like soft, squishy objects, probably rotten fruit, often accompanied by louder sounds as empty soda cans pinged off the car's roof. The limousine sped the last few hundred yards to a staging area just off the Capitol steps, to secured grounds away from the masses.

The moment the First Family's limousine stopped, a furious William Tree shot like a torpedo out of the car. He appeared to be looking for someone in authority to exact an unspecified revenge on the anarchists, atheists, and evildoers who had dared to inflict such indignities on him.

Rebecca remained in the limousine with Ashley, trying to calm her.

"It's over now," she said.

"I was terrified. Look at my hands, they're shaking."

Rebecca held on to Ashley's hands trying to warm them.

Ashley looked liked she just got off a runaway roller coaster, seemingly struggling to force a weak smile.

"That ride down Constitution Avenue was . . . just . . . awful," she said, managing to put some strength back into her voice, "but it did my heart good to see your pompous great-uncle . . . deflated."

"Welcome to a Tree Family funeral," Rebecca said.

A few seconds later a tap came on the car's window, and Rebecca rolled down the window with the push of a button.

"Mrs. Tree, Ms. Tree," a Secret Service agent said.

"What happened back there?" Ashley plaintively asked the agent.

The agent wore dark sunglasses and her shortly cropped gray hair dated her. "Our apologies. It appears that an overloaded truck in the photo-pool blew its engine and clouds of diesel fumes and smoke blasted out. Thanks to that and the protesters, we are now half an hour ahead of schedule. The State Department's chief of protocol would like to sit privately with you to go over some last-minute details, and the Secret Service deputy director would like to speak with you, Ms. Tree."

Rebecca looked at Ashley, who nodded and said, "I'll be okay . . . and please, you will come to the service?"

"Of course," Rebecca said, as she left the limousine.

The agent led her to a command station in a double-wide mobile trailer parked next to the Capitol steps. On the office door near the back, a nameplate, next to a Secret Service seal, read "Caleb Toussaint, Deputy Director."

Toussaint came from behind his desk upon seeing Rebecca enter. A smile broke through his deep-set, sad eyes. He carried two hundred and forty pounds of muscle on his six-foot-four-inch frame. A tightly napped salt and pepper head of hair crowned a high forehead. Toussaint had a broad nose and a military-style mustache set against coal black skin; he walked with a pronounced limp, a legacy from a desert battle-ground. Toussaint and his wife Camille were the only friends Rebecca had in Washington though they still were more inclined to shake hands than hug.

"I'm sorry about your brother, although I know there was no love lost there," Toussaint said.

"I don't want to talk about Sam. I haven't seen you or Camille since we dedicated the new memorial stone for Jackson."

Toussaint's son Jackson, a fellow officer in a specialized Army intelligence unit stationed in Kuwait City, had been in a Humvee directly behind Rebecca's jeep convoying from Riyadh through Free Saudi when insurrection fractured the kingdom. On a road outside Al Duwadimi, a buried explosive device hit his vehicle, instantly killing two soldiers and seriously wounding him. Despite cries from her team to stay down, Rebecca had pulled Jackson from the Humvee and dragged his nearly lifeless body just out of an enemy's sniper's range, but not before taking one bullet in her upper thigh. Two hundred yards away a pinned down team of medics could not reach him in time. He died minutes later in her arms leaving her with a dying wish she still honored.

"Yes," Toussaint said sadly, "it's been two years since Jackson's dedication ceremony."

"I know," Rebecca said, struggling to pull herself back to the present, ". . . it has been too long. How are you and Camille doing?" Rebecca asked, her heart fumbling awkwardly inside her. Rebecca felt unnerved at Toussaint's greeting smile when she had entered the room; the smile traveled through her like a substitute embrace from the lost son.

"It's still hard, but we're starting a memorial project named for Jackson."

"That's great," Rebecca said, her eyes momentarily taking in photographs hanging on the wall behind his desk.

Toussaint's husky voice had a rich, baritone quality. His tones came out deep, measured, soothing with a compelling authority, not an "eat your spinach" kind of voice. But talking about his son was too difficult, Rebecca thought, as it was for her.

"It'll be a health clinic as well as a recreational center for inner-city kids," he said.

"A health clinic?"

"I'll be coaching them in basketball, and giving them an occasional inspirational lecture."

"My basketball is lousy," Rebecca said, "but any other kind of help, just call me." Rebecca thought wistfully of Toussaint on the basketball court with adoring young faces looking up to him, as he mentored their game. No doubt he would be reaching into his pocket for money to buy some of the kids new sneakers.

"Thanks, I might take you up on it."

She knew him long enough not to dwell any longer on Jackson. "What's happening on the streets? It didn't look all that critical, until that truck caused such panic."

"Money for wars and more bailouts of Wall Street, but nothing to replace a truck for the Parks Department. I've had enough. I am going to take early retirement next year. I want to spend more time with my wife," he said, leaning forward and rubbing the knee on his bad leg. "I'm sixty-two years old. I've done my share. Do you promise to come to dinner soon? Camille's been asking about you."

"I think I'll have a break in about two weeks. I'll call her to confirm."

She looked again at the photos on the wall behind Toussaint's desk. The first, from the old *Life Magazine*, pictured a skinny little kid, Toussaint's grandfather, marching with Martin Luther King Jr. in Selma; the second showed a young man, Caleb Toussaint, lying wounded in a ditch outside of Al Bayda in Yemen. The third picture was one she knew well; it was Jackson at his college graduation. His proud eyes warmed the room. Wearing a graduating robe and mortarboard, he held his diploma in one hand, a mischievous glint emitting from soft, sparkling brown eyes. He wore a bright red bowtie, no doubt asserting his non-conformity. He directed a full smile and a thumb up at the camera's lens.

She tapped at her locket with her fingertip as if it were the outer shell of her aching heart and looked at her watch; it had already been such a long day. "Can you drive me to Mount Vernon? The burial service starts in awhile, and Ashley Tree asked me to be there."

* *

Rebecca and Toussaint entered the cemetery through a side entrance and walked up a narrow footpath ascending to a hill commanding a view of the gravesite, Sam Tree's final resting place. Under umbrellas, a few hundred mourners huddled. A cold, hard rain had swept away the day's earlier blue skies and grayness now covered the graveyard.

Rebecca stopped in a grove of birch trees and watched the assembled crowd of dignitaries.

"Are you ready to join them?" Toussaint asked.

Rebecca looked away, pulling up the collar of her coat tight around her as a chill came into her bones.

"Tell me Caleb. I forget. How many in your family?"

"An older brother and two younger sisters."

"How often do you speak to them?"

"My sisters every week. My brother maybe once a month."

"Sounds like a real family. It has been nearly thirty years since I last saw Sam. And I only have spoken to him once since then. Let's stay here. I'll mourn, if I can, from a distance."

They watched the funeral in silence.

For Sam, she had no loving memories. A shameless exploiter, he and his operatives defeated the incumbent president, Maria Sanchez-Smith's re-election bid by capitalizing on the political disarray into which the country had fallen and, for good measure, planting a sordid and fabricated story impugning Sanchez-Smith's sexual orientation. By the time the facts had emerged, Sam had ascended to the highest office of the land.

Not long after her sister's death, Sam's cruelty toward her began.

"Allison isn't dead," he would say with the smirk inherited from their grandfather. Rebecca's refusal to answer his taunts seemingly spurred him on. "You spotted-face monster, she's living in an underground jail half a mile from Granddad's mansion. Sometimes when I stay at his house, we go and feed her scraps from the table. And if there are no scraps, we give her cat food."

Rebecca's body would tighten, and she broke into a cold sweat whenever he came near her.

As time went by, she began to spend more time locked in her bedroom, finding solace in the books she read and the imaginary worlds that reading helped her travel through. She indulged herself in fantasy adventures with her lost twin: Rebecca and Allison as pirates on sailing ships, as scientists on expeditions down the Amazon looking for endangered species, as child soldiers in Union Blue fighting beside their father in great Civil War battles.

She became sickly and couldn't hold down food though no one noticed. Her grandfather was never there, and her grandmother lived mostly in her sick bed. She had no one to turn to and her tears, books, and imagination failed to protect her against Sam's bullying. Shortly after her fifth birthday, her eyes crossed, leaving her unable to have both eyes aim at the same point in space. Without thick corrective glasses, she would see two of everything; her world doubled but not in a good way. She felt more and more miserable as other kindergarteners began to taunt her with names like "four eyes." She took their insults passively, as her body weakened. Then one day she found a book in the library, the story of a polio-stricken child with a partially paralyzed left leg. Everyone said the child might never walk again. The little girl, less than twenty years later, became celebrated as the world's fastest woman by winning three gold medals at the Olympics. Her name was Wilma Rudolph.

Rebecca read and re-read her book. Rudolph had loving parents, tireless in finding therapy for their daughter in the segregated South. Next to her bed she kept two biographies of her new heroine.

One day exploring the woods around her grandfather's estate, she saw a small red fox at the top of an open field, sitting and seemingly staring at her. She began to walk toward the fox until it turned and ran toward the shelter of the woods. Rebecca went after the fox, going as fast as she could, until, gasping for breath, she fell down, rolled on her back and stared up at the sky. She was exhausted, but the emotional heaviness she carried lifted slightly. Now feeling encouraged she went and ran in the woods every day, slowing getting stronger and faster. She told herself she could be like Wilma Rudolph.

Within a year she felt strong enough to begin to teach herself how to fight back.

In her seventh year she had grown two and a half inches and towered over the boys at school who had previously taken delight in tormenting her. One day she saw two boys, out of sight of the teachers, bullying a new student, Stephen Spurgeon, the son of a well-known preacher who had recently moved to Colorado. Rebecca ran over, stepping between them, and as an instinct prevailed, she pushed the first boy hard and made a threatening fist gesture toward the second. To her surprise, both bullies ran away.

Her brother Sam became her second challenge. Out of respect for their dead mother, both Sam and Rebecca, escorted by nannies, attended Catholic Mass every Sunday. While her brother fidgeted in the pew, Rebecca listened, transfixed by the word of God spoken each week by Monsignor Hargrove. She began to memorize the scriptures.

After a few more of Sam's ugly gibes, she would use the newly acquired weapon in her small but growing arsenal, a Biblical quote.

"Someday the Lord is going to have a day of reckoning with you," Rebecca said, her finger wagging angrily in Sam's direction.

Arise, O Lord; save me, O my God: for thou hast smitten all mine enemies upon the cheekbone; thou has broken the teeth of the ungodly.

The quote silenced Sam, at least for a moment.

Then, when she was eight years old, Sam made a clumsy but menacing attempt to rape her. He pinned her to her bed, holding her wrists down, and pushed his right knee between her legs. Rebecca managed to arch her back and free her left hand. She grabbed a small glass vase from the nightstand and took a wild swing. The first blow only glanced off the side of Sam's head, but it caused Sam to lose his grip, allowing Rebecca to wiggle herself free.

"You four-eyed, speckled-faced bitch," Sam screamed in fury, spit spraying from his mouth.

Because of the venom in his tone, an instinct intervened to ensure that Sam never attacked her again. She aimed the second blow perfectly, with good force; the resulting gash in Sam's neck required stitches.

Within a week, her grandfather had packed Rebecca off to a Swiss boarding school specializing in troubled children of the global rich.

Chapter 4

Several hours after the funeral, Secret Service agents escorted Rebecca into a bunker-like conference room in the White House, the walls filled with darkened closed-circuit monitors and world time-zone clocks. The room felt airless.

Double-doors opened behind her, and she heard the disconcerting sound of Henry Hess's voice. A former three-pack a day smoker, emphysema was slowly killing him. "I'm so sorry about your loss. Sam was . . ."

"Save the hot air for the next speech you ghostwrite," she said, cutting him off. "Why am I here? Make it brief. I have a company to run."

Hess, adviser to generations of Trees and considered the political genius of his time, ignored her outburst and threw a thin folder onto the conference room table. "Read it carefully. I'll be back in fifteen minutes for your response."

The folder exuded an ominous stench. A White House security tag used for classified documents had been attached to ensure it never left 1600 Pennsylvania Avenue undetected. Even before reading it, she knew it would be a masterpiece of manipulation and a blueprint for her family's determination to maintain political power. She didn't need to read more than the first few paragraphs to confirm her suspicions. Rebecca was being asked to take up her fallen brother's sword to head the Millennium Populist ticket in the upcoming election after George Jenkins Bayou's caretaker term expired, to continue the Tree dynasty by becoming the next president of the United States.

She skipped the next ten pages and went to the summary. If she refused to do their bidding, they threatened to use their voting shares to strip her of her position as CEO and Chair of the Argyle Group.

Rebecca needed to calm herself. She returned to a thought that had obsessed her as a child, one that spurred her early interest in science: the literal meaning of her name. A tree acts as a sponge for carbon dioxide that reduces pollutants by filtering the air and replenishing the earth's oxygen. Tree roots held soil together preventing erosion. A perfect mission statement from God and/or nature, the young Rebecca had always thought to herself. At twelve years old, she started to sign her name Rebecca tree, with a lower-case t, until her teachers berated her, refusing to accept her test and essay papers.

Now it struck her what a strange lineage she had inherited; the Trees cleaved to power, control, and money; they put solar panels on their roofs and servants recycled their bottles, all for good public relations while their companies and political party never hesitated to decimate the earth for profit. In what seemed to be an act of despair, they looked to her, not a natural ally, to maintain their empire.

The doors behind Rebecca opened, and Hess's raspy heavy breathing filled the room as he painfully pushed air out of his damaged lungs.

"I'm not interested in your plan," Rebecca said as her voice stiffened like branches in an ice storm.

"Before you make a final decision, your grandfather wants to speak to you," Hess said.

No one had said anything about the reclusive Merewether Tree being in Washington. "Has he finally come to pay his respects?" Rebecca asked in alarm, as her body torqued, her legs kinking under her chair.

"Well, he's not quite here." Hess pushed a button under the desk and a one hundred inch screen dropped down at the far end of the room. As its rear-projected image flickered on, Rebecca knew that she had been blind-sided. Her grandfather's face cascaded across the screen, each pore grotesquely magnified. He circled over the room like a bird of prey.

Inner-circle Washingtonians referred to him as "The Magpie." His brown left eye had the softness of a cadaver's with a residue of chiseled charm. But it was his virile blue right eye that projected a fearsome frigidity, striking dread in all who dared to oppose him. Partial paralysis had set in on the blue-eyed side, leaving him with a droopy eyelid. Nearly bald, with a few wisps of hair sprouting from a high forehead, his brow creased deeply. His nose fell like an elephant's trunk flapping over a small mouth while his chin competed poorly for prime real estate.

"Rebecca, my dear, it's so lovely to see you," Tree said. He directed his blue-eye at Hess, "Get out of here. I need some private time with my granddaughter."

Hess made a quick retreat.

"It has been too many years, my dear, since I last saw you." After Hess had closed the outer door, Tree fixed a sharp right-eyed stare at her. "You're certainly no longer the ugly duckling playing in my yard. Quite handsome you've become." His words slid out sticky like treacle.

"Where are you? Why didn't you come to your grandson's funeral?"

"I'm home. I hope you like my state-of-the-art broadcast system."

"It's lovely, I'm sure."

"Anyway, I don't do funerals. Except for my wife's. When she died, I promised I'd only attend one more funeral—my own."

"How gracious."

Ignoring her comment, Tree continued. "I wanted to see you. My doctors told me it's best not to travel too much."

"What do you want from me?" She fought to keep the tremor out of her voice. She felt like a Seeing Eye dog in training, deliberately brushed by a car, left physically unharmed, but always in terror of the shape, the form, or the car color of the attacker.

"You read our proposal. So you know very well. Don't you think it'd be a splendid idea for you to be president?" Tree turned his head slightly so that the not-quite-dead-yet brown eye dominated. His tone softened.

"Unlike your . . ." Tree clogged his next word as if he had banged a bare toe in a night-darkened hallway, "brother Sam . . . you're quite a clever one. Done well. Served your country in combat, built out an investment company far further than I'd have imagined."

"Why would I even consider such an offer?"

"Now, now. No need for a war. Maybe we can reach an understanding—you and I. Let's talk a bit."

Talk a bit. Her mouth tasted sulfuric like a rotten egg.

* *

The last time she had spoken with her grandfather intimately she was seven years old. Great-Uncle William, Merewether's younger half-brother, his wife Jane, and Rebecca had made a two-hour drive through the Rocky Mountains to Tree's mansion. Being an orphan was bad enough, Rebecca had thought then, but her aunt and uncle, Great, Grand or otherwise, made her feel like a castaway, shuttling her from Merewether's mansion to their Denver home when the grandparents no longer wanted her. Both houses seemed like prisons, but she preferred living in her grandparents' home surrounded by forests. Of the few vague memories she had of her grandfather, she recalled the dominant emotion of fear. She was afraid of him, though his outbursts, usually in anger but often comical, made him less of a wax figure than the others.

When she had lived at her grandparents' home, she had found a carton filled with Charles Dickens' novels, illustrated editions for children; like a squirrel hiding nuts, she shallowly buried the books in a box in her "secret park," a natural opening in the center of a nearby wood's thick brush. Rebecca then imagined herself to be a female version of the orphaned Pip in *Oliver Twist*; her grandfather became Mr. Bumble, and she used to laugh, in private, at his pomposity. Assigning a character for her great-uncle was more challenging until she found the smug and self-righteous Pecksniff in *Martin Chuzzlewit*.

In a vivid memory of a Christmas past, the family, all the living Trees, totaling less than half a dozen without her grandfather's bedridden wife, sat uncomfortably around a dining table, large enough for forty, set with heirloom silver and china. Servants scurried about. The meal started with cold salmon wedges encircled by Pacific oysters, followed by a salad, and a main course of spit-fired goose stuffed with apples and prunes. The aroma of roasted chestnuts and truffles, which garnished the fowl, perfumed the room, intermingling with the sweet saffron from a side platter of roasted potatoes. Dessert came as a pair. The adults enjoyed a plum pudding pregnant with dates, raisins, and cherries crowned with Christmas holly. It smelled of nutmeg, ginger, and cinnamon soaked in "Looey Catorce" (so-called by her grandfather) cognac. For the children, Lu, the cook, had baked her own favorite, Alabama pecan pie. Rebecca remembered being allowed in the kitchen; Lu's warm hand, the color of dark chocolate, guided her tiny fingers on a whisk as they beat fresh cream. Lu drizzled in sugar and vanilla extract. A fire, which frightened Rebecca, had blazed fiercely in the kitchen's hearth.

Merewether Tree, the alpha male — ambitious, self-confident, competitive, and always opinionated — dominated the holiday table. When he wasn't extolling his accomplishments, he would break out into an off-key ditty. "Chestnuts roasting . . . Jack Frost nipping . . . Yuletide carols." It was the one day of the year he was never mean.

After dessert, a childhood ritual would begin. Her grandfather would disappear for a half an hour. Rebecca would then be ushered into the great man's study where a fireplace with birch logs popped. A Christmas tree stood flush with antique ornaments, candy canes, and stockings. Well-wrapped gifts circled the base. Grandfather Tree sat on the couch donned up in a Santa Claus suit.

"Ho, ho, ho," he exploded with a belly laugh. Suddenly he acted warm and tender. He tweaked his granddaughter's nose and spun a verse by a famous poet. "We were very tired, we were very merry." Rebecca had yearned for this moment all year, and it became an isolated but treasured memory. She would follow his line with, "We had gone back and forth all night on the ferry," which earned her a tickle.

They sat together on a small couch; Rebecca positioned on her grandfather's left side, his brown eye gazing out at her fondly as he stroked her hair, speaking softly, asking questions. She felt wanted, even loved for that short hour. By the end of each holiday, she begged to return and live full-time in his house, complaining that her aunt and uncle regarded her like a stranger, treated worst than their employees' children.

"We'll see," Tree would say, his tone too formal for a child to understand. "Maybe next year. Perhaps next Christmas. It's difficult having children here. Your grandmother's not well, and I have obligations to serve my country as the senior senator from Colorado, which keeps me traveling nearly non-stop."

Next Christmas never came for Rebecca. Before her eighth birthday, she had been exiled to a boarding school in Switzerland. For the next three years, every month she wrote a letter home about school, filling each letter with news of her accomplishments. Each month, a beautifully engraved envelope arrived in response, from the office of Merewether Tree, United States Senate. The postmark read Washington D.C., "Our Nation's Capital." Her heart soared as she opened the fine linen stationery; minutes later she would be reduced to tears. The text of each letter read as nearly identical.

Your grandfather is pleased with the progress you are having with your studies. He hopes you will continue to do such excellent work. As for your request that he visit you in Switzerland, his schedule does not have an opening until next year. You are, as always, in his prayers. A different woman's name but always with the same title — *Special Administrative Assistant* signed each letter.

And then next year's opening in her grandfather's schedule always became the next year again.

On her eleventh birthday, Rebecca stopped writing letters home.

* *

Rebecca knew what would follow next in the White House bunker. Her grandfather could fry a soul faster than a short-order cook. He would sauté her on one side and then when he felt her table-ready, he would flip her over to finish grilling and seasoning her.

She heaved a deep sigh. For a moment, she became the seven-year-old perched on his Christmas-postured knee, her outer defenses breached, her fort's moat too shallow, archers retreating from their parapets' posts.

"Perhaps you'd join me," Tree said. "I believe my old eyes spy an excellent port on your sideboard."

She took the bottle and poured herself a glass.

On the video screen, Tree lifted a flared sipping glass. He moved his hand making a toasting gesture toward the camera.

Rebecca returned his gesture, muttered an appropriate salutation, and put the glass back on the table untouched.

"Against your religion to take a little drink?" Tree asked, "I'd be a little nicer to me. We're family, and after all, family comes first."

"Since when?"

"My dear, I understand that perhaps I wasn't always there for you."

"Try never."

"Not true. You know, we're a lot more alike than you think. You've got the Tree Family steel in your spine."

With his last remark, she rose up in her seat. "And you're trying to claim credit for that?"

In her hand she held Hess's folder; it burned at her fingers. She slammed it on the table, blood rushing to her face.

"How dare you. Why do you to try to bully me? You didn't have the votes to stop me six years ago from becoming Chairperson of Argyle. Where would you get the votes now to depose me if I don't run for president, as your rotten little plan threatens to do?"

"Now, now," Tree said. "I know we haven't seen eye to eye for a long time. But it's best to hear me out."

Rebecca closed her eyes.

"Trans-Siberian Oil and the Russian government want Argyle," Tree said. "Nothing personal, just business. They've offered the American partners a pretty penny for our shares."

"You barely control fifteen percent," she said.

"Yes, but they say they can get another twenty, maybe twenty-five from some of your investors, in France and Germany."

Her eyes widened with horror. "You're insane. They'll never sell to the Russians."

"Grow up, Rebecca. Everyone has a price. I understand the Germans and French are currently negotiating options."

"I don't believe you. You're making up this whole story."

"The Russians are offering a tempting sweetener. They will increase the pipeline flow of natural gas into the European Union. Your investors, no matter how loyal they are to you, will not be able to resist their governments' pressure. Call your good pal, the recently retired Chancellor of Germany. I wouldn't be surprised if she was unreachable . . . for the next few days."

"You, you're a son- . . ." Rebecca held her tongue. He wasn't going to force her to swear. "That's still not enough shares."

"True, but the Chinese, your old school pal Ling and his partners, have thirty percent."

She began to scream. "He'd kill himself before he betrayed me."

"I quite agree with you on that point, but the Chinese government might kill him first. They're not bleeding hearts like some of us. Executing their young? No, they wouldn't think twice. They're desperate for Russian oil as well as natural gas."

Rebecca went silent. A wave of nausea churned through her stomach. Without a good option, she suppressed her rising panic and began to analyze his power play. Sadly, it contained a rationale that went well beyond Tree's normal range of deceptions. She despised the Russian ruling oligarch families; none were more corrupt and tyrannical than the family of the chairman of Trans-Siberian gas, Popov Zhuralev, whose hired thugs murdered dozens of his striking workers. His central committee allies used their huge oil and gas reserves and a potent legion of nuclear missiles to beat up the weaker kids on the block.

Rebecca tried to recompose herself, when her grandfather launched an unexpected diversion.

"I've also sent you a present. A token of friendship, you might call it. Hess left it in the drawer of the sideboard."

"What is it?" Rebecca's felt like she was filling with crushed ice flecks from her stomach to her throat; perhaps she should have had a sip of that port.

"I think you might enjoy what I brought for you. Open the drawer." His blue eye leered at Rebecca. Looking satisfied with his work, the short order cook now applied the seasoning.

Rebecca opened the sideboard's drawer and took out a thin package.

"Open it," he demanded, with an imperious tone in his voice.

Her hands trembled as she tore off the plain brown wrapping to reveal a heavy piece of construction paper with yellowed edges. Her eyes took in a familiar shape, drawn with a child's hand, of her grandparents' house in Colorado.

The lower right edge of the image was signed, "Ally T."

"It's quite genuine, my dear."

She stared at him in horror. "My whole life, I begged for a memento of my sister—a photograph, a scrap of paper, anything. And you claimed that Grandmother, in a fit of grief, burned everything."

Rebecca touched her locket—a singular present from her grandmother—which she never took off. Logic told her that it was her grandfather who had hidden and destroyed heirloom memories. *Why?*

Tree smiled at her benevolently; his smug countenance a clear signal. He must believe that now he could control and contain her rebellion and carry out Hess's neatly typed political plan.

Her heart, pumping loudly, sought a weapon, something that could reach into the video screen and kill him now. It would be a just revenge. But her heart locked in combat with her mind: *I can't kill him. I must turn his evil against him, somehow. I will. I'll find a way.*

With her grandfather himself beyond her physical reach, for the moment, she dug for some form of counter-attack.

"Grandmother told me some strange things when I used to visit her sickbed. I was still a child. I didn't understand what she meant, but I remember the words."

"What are you saying?" a suddenly startled Tree replied.

She turned to his wide-screen face with pointed intent. "Grandmother said that God will have no mercy on your soul. She talked about Judgment Day—your Judgment Day!"

"Now, now," Tree's voice rattled, his eyes narrowed, and a look of uncertainty swept his segmented face. His neck teeter-tottered like an unattended seesaw in a high wind. Finally it settled on the brown-eyed side. "Take a couple of days to digest our little talk. Let's continue our chat, say the beginning of next week. Take my advice, my dear. Think a bit on it. No need for the Russians to come along and destroy all your good work. I'm sure the partners would accept a new chairperson of your choosing."

His neck oscillated, his face turned right. "Perhaps I can find some more drawings for you. Maybe even a photograph. And whatever Grandmother Tree told you, well . . . in her last few years . . . let's just say she wasn't quite right. I believe that God will look kindly on my life and the great work I have done. Why I'll do just fine on Judgment . . ." Tree's voice trailed off.

Even though her grandfather had raised the stakes considerably, a rattled deathbed phrase on Grandmother Tree's parched lips rang in her ears. "Seek justice," she had whispered emphatically to the seven-year-old Rebecca. Her whole life she had puzzled over what the old woman meant. *Justice for herself? For her grandmother's sufferings? For her twin? Or perhaps seek justice for the world?*

She needed more time to think. Today her grandfather volleyed the first shots of a battle, but the war needed to be waged on a field of her choosing.

Affecting a voice of icy calmness, she fought to maintain a defense. "I believe today is a day of mourning. We're both good Christians. Your grandson's body is barely cold. You'll not have my response for a week." With that, she spun on her heels and left the room.

She had put on sunglasses to hide her stressed eyes. Her Secret Service funeral escorts, four men in black suits, waited for her as she left the White House grounds.

"Ms. Tree," an agent said, "we have instructions to escort you back to the airport," gesturing toward a waiting limousine.

She looked into a beefy face framed by an old-fashioned crew cut. "Please, just leave me alone. I'd rather take a taxi."

"Ms. Tree, with all due respect, we have an obligation to protect all relatives at a state funeral. You're the sister of the deceased." Following the protocol for grieving relatives, the agent reached for her elbow.

"Please just leave me alone," she said repeating herself as she pushed his hand away. "I'll take that taxi at the corner."

Taken by surprise, the agent took a step back. "I apologize," he said, lowering his voice almost to a whisper. "Ms. Tree, I'm just doing my job."

Rebecca softened slightly. "It's been a difficult day. Just let me take the taxi. Your vehicles can convoy, if you have to. Okay?"

"Yes," said the agent, "that'd probably be fine. Let me call it into Command," he hesitated. "You know, we sort of met once before."

"We did?"

"I was in an operational intelligence unit. My advanced martial arts class started just as yours ended. My unit had twenty-four soldiers. We sat on the bleachers as the instructor demolished the outgoing class, your class, one-by-one in training."

Rebecca managed a small laugh as she remembered being helplessly flipped in practice combat.

"How many of your class came home?" she asked, looking more closely at the agent.

"Twelve of us came back whole—physically at least. Six flew as cargo in flag-draped coffins. And six came back in pieces."

"I'm so sorry. War does unimaginable things."

Rebecca looked closer at the agent's face, as his Secret Service mask momentarily slid away, revealing warm eyes that resembled another soldier in her life from long ago. Then her eyes met a solid gold wedding band on his finger. Rebecca bit her lip.

"Yes, I hope I didn't disturb you," the agent said.

"No, not at all. Well, nice to meet you again."

Chapter 5

"Homeland Security has put all aviation in the northeast in lockdown," the pilot's voice came on over the intercom. "They think they will be able to work through it all in the next hour."

"What is the problem?"

"Their computer system got hacked again."

"Alright. Let me know when there is a status change."

Rebecca sat in the back of her plane, hunched over like a child, studying Allison's yellowed drawing. The image of the old house appeared illustrated in two styles. The bottom was sturdy, regular, unexceptional, with even lines demarcating the brickwork. But the second floor lacked routine, the bricks no longer even, the upper floor windows skewed with the roof jagged, nearly tilted. She remembered that Allison loved drawing, and she was always conscientiously precise.

Why does the upper floor become irregular?

She thought of the last year she still lived with her grandparents. The big Colorado house, just below the timberline, with the two wings referred as the East and the West by her grandfather—the Senator, everyone called him that. The residence's staff, mostly the descendants of Hungarian refugees, who had fled the tanks of Budapest, treated him as a demigod, the great post-cold-war warrior.

She remembered her nearly prison-like isolation during that time, chauffeured to a small private school down-mountain, allowed to play only once a week with Reverend Spurgeon's son, Stephen. From the school library she took out pre-approved books; sometimes her only friend Stephen took out unapproved books for her.

Once a month she had been taken to the East Wing to visit her grand-mother, resting weakly on her sickbed. Three doctors arrived, regular as clockwork the first three days of each week. She nicknamed the one, who always knelt down and spoke kindly to her, Dr. Monday. One day she memorized the labels pasted to the vials on the old woman's nightstand, identical prescriptions with the three different doctors' names at the bot-tom: FOR ANXIETY, TAKE TWICE A DAY; FOR STRESS, TAKE THREE TIMES A DAY AFTER MEALS; FOR INSOMNIA, TWO TABLETS AT BEDTIME. Each bottle had the same imprinted line: MAY CAUSE DROWSINESS.

Body odors, pungent and bitter mixed with the smell of oint-ments, rock oil and tiger balm, which filled the room. A four-poster bed of heavy mahogany sat with intricate carvings draped by gold tap-estry woven in a florid pattern. Propped up by a platoon of pillows, Grandmother Tree's arms stretched out, bony and thin, beckoning Rebecca. She spoke in a low voice; her prune-wrinkled face still had traces of a once-vibrant beauty aided now by a slur of powdered blush against each sagging cheek.

Rebecca climbed onto the bed, over an assortment of hardcover books with un-cracked spines, fighting the malodors that caused her stomach to churn.

"Closer, my dear. My voice is weak . . ." Grandmother Tree's parched lips opened. " I wish . . . I could have done more for you . . . and your sister . . . I used to live on memories of better times," she paused, searching for words. Her eyes blinked, and her jaw clenched. "But now I can no longer forgive him."

"What are you saying, Grandma? I don't understand."

"You will someday. I'll make sure you do. After your father died," she continued in starts and stops.

"Please, tell me something about my father, a story . . . any-thing . . . please, Grandmother."

"Maybe another day, when I feel better."

"Why did they have to die? No one will ever talk to me about the plane crash, or their lives before. All I know is that they are gone."

"Not now," said Grandmother Tree, her voice dimming.

Rebecca fought back tears.

The old woman now seemed unaware of Rebecca's presence and began to commune with herself in whispers. "How he snapped at me . . . so mean and vicious . . . honor and cherish? . . . just words, one night he left me helpless on the floor." Her voice trailed off, her lids nearly closed now. "I might have died. There will be a Judgment Day."

Suddenly her eyes flew open; perhaps deep in her mind a memory rewound and a moment of lucidity replaced stupor.

"Rebecca. How lovely of you to visit. You're a smart girl. You have a good heart. Study hard, be a good Christian, love God. He will watch out for you," she paused, her lips moved, but nothing came out. Her body trembled, her eyes shut, and a nurse rushed over, taking a pulse. One of the Hungarian nannies grabbed Rebecca by the collar and dragged her out of the room.

Grandmother Tree lived six more years, confined to her bed as she slipped further into a demented state until she finally passed one night in her sleep. On Rebecca's twenty-first birthday, letters began arriving nearly once a year, written by her grandmother when she was still coherent. A San Francisco-based lawyer, the executor of her estate, had sent them over the course of a decade and a half.

The letters read like a tragic novella, with short, joyful openings, before descending into darkness and despair. Catherine Tree née Baxter, a San Francisco debutante, whose wealthy father controlled vast areas of timberland in the Northwest, graduated from St. Olaf's College in Northfield, Minnesota, with dreams of becoming a doctor until Merewether Tree came courting. At twenty-four, freshly graduated from the University of Colorado's law school, the tall, craggy-faced youth with intriguing eyes had ideas and ambitions. His charisma drew in his classmates, young men and women wanting to coast in his orbit.

The courtship lasted two years. With her father's death, Catherine, the only child, inherited a sizeable estate. She married Tree, moving to Colorado, where he persuaded his new wife that he, as her husband, needed to invest her inheritance. Oil and gas exploration boomed in

Colorado, and Tree played his first hand a little late, at the top of a cycle. He began drinking heavily and his wife's will to fight her domineering husband slipped. Tree became embittered by his wife, who for two years had failed to prove fertile and bear him an heir. Then he went into politics and acquired money, which went straight into his private accounts.

At last Catherine Tree became fragilely pregnant. After nearly nine months of being confined to her room by her delicate health, Nathaniel, Rebecca's father was born. Merewether was obsessed with his young son. He stopped drinking and masqueraded himself as a good husband.

Puzzling allusions filled the letters; Catherine Tree sacrificed greatly for Nathaniel, she loved the boy as if . . . the pen would often drop off mid-sentence, the thought left uncompleted. Then this beloved boy, Nathaniel, and his wife crashed into the snow-filled Spanish Pyrenees, and the narrative unraveled.

* *

As Rebecca looked out the cabin's window, she could see the planes snaked in a long line on the tarmac still waiting for air traffic control clearance.

She remained distracted and lost in thought as she replayed a jumble of conflicted chapters in her life. Suddenly Rebecca was startled as she felt a bee bite like sting come off her fingers. Looking at her hand she realized that she had rubbed two fingers raw 'worry beading' her locket's chains. She paused and opened the locket's two chambers, in which two images reposed, icons of dead loved ones — in one chamber a vignette photo of her parents with their arms wrapped around their twin infants, and, in the other, the beaming face of the man she had loved and lost to war, Jackson Toussaint. They were her most cherished earthly possessions

She briefly closed her eyes and softly recited a prayer of her childhood: *Unite us together again in one family, to sing your praise forever and ever.*

The pilot's voice came back on over the intercom. "Becky. Air traffic control told us to queue up for takeoff in twenty minutes. Is that good for you?"

"Yes, thanks. Sorry it became such a long day for you. Are your families okay with your being gone so long?"

"Everyone is good," the pilot, Janet Scanlon said. "My mom is staying over with the kids."

"Great. I'll be ready to go soon. Make sure you add two more vacation days for yourselves," Rebecca said.

For the next fifteen minutes she lay on the floor of her plane going through a routine of six yoga poses designed for stress relief. Starting with a downward facing dog, ending twenty minutes later with a child's pose. She then got back in her seat and let the pilots know that she was ready for takeoff.

Rebecca then punched her time zone watch. Germany was at the start of its business day; it was time to find out if her grandfather was bluffing. Picking up her cellphone, she pushed UTH, which brought up two entries for Ulrika Tripp-Hertzen, the former Chancellor of Germany, who was now the senior partner in EU Investments. She pushed the first entry, UTH CELL. After six rings, it went into voicemail.

Annoyed, she pushed the second entry, UTH WORK. Frau Stroebel, Hertzen's English-speaking secretary, answered at Tripp-Hertzen's office. "Ah, Ms. Tree, I'm sorry Frau Hertzen isn't available. I'm holding all her incoming calls for, let me see, the whole day. Can she get back to you?"

Rebecca wanted to smash the cellphone. "It's important. I need to talk to her today."

"I'll make sure she gets your message," Stroebel replied with a stiff Bavarian accent, each 'r' felt like sandpaper scraping on skin.

Tripp-Hertzen and Rebecca had done business together for more than a decade. Rebecca felt a wave of betrayal and self-doubt sweep through her. She looked again at her at her time-zone watch. In Beijing it was already afternoon the following day.

She pushed LING-CELL.

Albert Ling had graduated at the top of Rebecca's class at Harvard

Business School and became her trusted business partner. Born into a dynastic family of great power, his great-grandfather, the chief engineer of Red China, had been a favored party cadre of Chairman Mao. The fires of the People's Revolution sparked the Ling's business empire, but the family's party protection now fatigued as it reached its fourth generation. At any moment, it could pass its 'sell-through' date.

"Rebecca, I've been worried about you," Ling said upon answering. "Are you okay?"

"Yeah, peachy," Rebecca said. Ling would understand each word; they created long ago a coded system for urgent situations. "I was thinking about the raven's bridge. Do you still remember the poem?"

"Let's see," Ling said. "Moments of tender love and dream. So sad to leave the raven's bridge."

"Great memory you have. Are you still writing poetry?"

"Always my hobby. Maybe I'll write one after work and send it to you, if you like. The poem might be able to reach Boston in a couple of days."

"That would be great. I've got to go."

She needed to talk about the threat of an Argyle takeover with Ling face to face. The 'poem' would take off on Ling's jet before the end of the week. After hanging up, she sent an encrypted email marked URGENT to her private secretary, Gilad Levine.

Fatima had taken her parents and younger brother on a vacation to a Costa Rica rainforest and wouldn't be able to access a secure link.

Gilad—I'll be in the office around 8 a.m. Need the following: Pls. alert the security tech to set up for a series of AV teleconferences. I need to talk to: Lord Hare, Tripp-Hertzen, and Jake Schutz at Schutz, Woods, and Fast. After that, I'll want to speak to Ling in his Beijing office. Thanks. RT.

Chapter 6

Before her plane began its descent to Boston, an unsteady Rebecca changed into a blue silk business suit with a double-breasted jacket and stockings of the same color. Underneath the suit, she wore a white T-shirt with an animated iridescent green frog perched on the T of bold type proclaiming TREE HUGGER. At Wayfarer Ketch, a solar-powered water taxi waited to transport her to Long Wharf, where Argyle Group's world headquarters stood, a three-story eighteenth-century restored warehouse with three additional floors built of angular glass and steel. The building's entrance sign said Building 117. An ad hoc seawall guarded the water side of the building.

When she arrived, her secretary greeted her as she stepped from the water taxi. With a full head of gelled-back jet black hair, soft brown eyes, an aquiline nose, and a ready smile that offset a double chin, Gilad Levine chubbily filled out a gray two-piece business suit brightened by red suspenders.

"Good afternoon, Ms. Tree."

Rebecca smiled and took Levine by the arm. Holding his arm reassured her that she was walking on solid ground. "Let's take the stairs up to my office."

"Sure," Levine said, as he sucked in his breath.

The building had one elevator, and company policy encouraged workers and visitors to use the stairs. Employees who walked or bicycled to work received incentive bonuses. Never owning or wanting to drive a car, Rebecca usually bicycled to work but in inclement weather she used public transportation. Electric share-cars filled two back rows of the parking lot for needed trips around town. On weekends, employees could sign up and take them on outings to nearby Cape Cod. The basement of Building 117 housed a swimming pool and a full fitness center with three personal trainers. The cafeteria served a standard range of cuisine, as well as specialized diets as required for employees. A separate, full kosher kitchen cooked for six employees.

Levine grimaced as they started up the steps. "The AV room is ready. The outside tech is there, and he ran all the security checks."

"Did you get hold of Tripp-Hertzen?" she asked as they completed the first series of steps.

"No luck on that one," Levine said. "Lord Hare is on stand-by, waiting for your call."

"Great," she said, as they started the second floor. "And the law firm?"

"Same thing. They're on stand-by." Levine's breath began to labor.

"And Ling?"

"He's available after 3 p.m. Whew . . . our time. Sorry, I'm still not in shape."

Rebecca gestured with her finger, like a mountain climber pointing to a summit, as she pulled Levine's arm, coaxing him up the last steps.

"You're doing fine. How's your weight?"

"I just broke under two-twenty last week . . . And I can keep my heart rate at 130 for forty-five minutes," he paused slightly, "on the stair climber."

"Terrific. You're more than halfway there."

* *

Rebecca interviewed Levine to be a personal assistant after he graduated Phi Beta Kappa from Brandeis. He wanted hands-on experience before continuing to business school. Each year, Rebecca received hundreds of applications from top students graduating elite Boston universities. She paid salaries comparable to the large, publicly held New York firms like Goldman or Morgan, but being privately held offered a more informal, collegial environment. Argyle, under

Rebecca's tutelage, gained a reputation for blazing new trails in cutting-edge future-orientated investments. Elite business school graduates regarded it as a solid, blue-chip, progressive company not known to speculate or leverage desperately. When she had interviewed Levine, who had been on a shortlist of three candidates for the job, her last question seemed to startle him.

"How much do you weigh?"

Levine's face flushed, and his eyes flashed disappointment. "I'm two-sixty. It's a struggle. It's in my DNA."

Rebecca stood.

"Thank you for taking the time, Ms. Tree," Levine said, assuming the interview had concluded. "I appreciate it."

She stared at him for a few seconds, as Levine's DNA reference tugged at her heart. The contents of her genetic spiral terrified her. "When can you start?"

His resume and recommendations were among the strongest she had seen; but more, to the point, his warmth instantly endeared him. Rebecca also sensed in him deep loyalty.

"You're kidding, wow. Tomorrow. Today if you want." Levine beamed like a young boy given his first baseball glove.

"Come Monday. And bring your gym clothes. Ask for Fatima; she'll get you started."

* *

Rebecca and Levine, now sweating, reached the top floor. As she swept into her private office, Levine said, "I sorted the mail. Junk mail is in the red box, patent office and patent attorneys' correspondence is in another . . ." He reeled off the contents of six boxes ending with, "the last box has personal mail and invitations."

"Okay, give me an hour. Then, let's see, it's almost one p.m. Let's do Lord Hare at two. Give London a heads up."

* *

Rebecca looked at her desk calendar and noted with sadness that next week would be the anniversary of the death of her best friend from college, Annie Forsyte. She wistfully recalled the day she had met Annie outside of the All Souls College Library, where she had awkwardly locked her new, used bicycle on a full-to-capacity bike rack.

When Rebecca reemerged from the library, she saw a young woman in a short skirt and long stockings with roses tattooed on the fabric, pacing around the locked bikes occasionally kicking the tire of Rebecca's.

"Oh, I am so sorry. You can't get yours out?"

"Why did you lock this? It's not worth stealing."

"I paid twenty-five quid for it yesterday."

The young woman roared with laughter. "Are you a tourist? The bike you bought isn't worth five shilling. Look at it. The back wheel is out of true, the derailleur is bent, and it won't shift. You must be daft. Are you first year?"

"Yes." Rebecca said, looking at her new acquaintance's eccentric bicycle, with half-size wheels, a super-high seat post, a honk horn on the handlebars, and a thrift shop plaid plastic luggage bag now perched on a rear rack.

"How much did you pay for yours?" Rebecca said, with a teasing tone.

"Nothing. A gentleman admirer built it out of parts. We're English; we recycle everything. What are you supposed to be reading?"

"Math and physics. You?"

"Botany and biology. And I'm a genius," the woman said, rolling her eyes like a circus clown.

"Great," Rebecca said, with a laugh, feeling that she might be lucky her first week and make a friend at Oxford. "My name is Rebecca Tree."

"Tree? You should be in my department doing dendrology. Me, I do all plants not just the wooded ones," the woman said extending her hand, after taking some tools out of a small bike bag underneath her seat. "I'm Annie Scargill, of the NUM Scargills, just warning you in case you're a Tory."

"What is the NUM?"

"I can see you're not a Brit, not that I didn't already know that from your accent. National Union of Miners; my grandfather ran the union and went to the mat with Maggie Thatcher."

"I hope he won."

"No, he lost. Sadly. But enough of dreaded politics. Let's fix this underprivileged bicycle you overpaid for and then we can ride over to Simon's on Cowley Road, and you can buy me some fish and chips for all the trouble you've caused me. I've been stuck waiting here for nearly an hour.

"And," Annie said, taking an old-fashioned pocket watch out of a man's vest she wore under what looked like a well-used frayed tweed blazer, "then we need to be at the Duke of York to tip a start of semester pint with my mates. I can audition you for my new best friend. See if you have any remote and highly unlikely chance of passing muster," Annie said, with a wink and grin.

As Annie made some adjustments to Rebecca's bike, she began to stare at her feet. "Those shoes, they have to go."

"Hey," Rebecca said, "some new best friend you might be. My bike is no good; now you're starting in on my shoes?"

"No," Annie said, trying to reconsider. "They are a bit Audrey Hepburnish. If you're free Saturday, we can go to the flea market and update your look a bit."

From that day on, Annie and Rebecca were inseparable.

Rebecca took the small stack of mail out of her personal in-box and looked them over one by one, mostly invitations for upcoming charity events in Boston. She knew she wouldn't go, but she would send checks to many of them.

Rebecca started to open a letter from a favored charity when she spied another envelope that roiled her. The postmark, from Poplar, Colorado, more than a month old, bore an engraved return address: "Senator Merewether Tree, Retired, Hillock-Hill Ranch." The address read Rebecca Tree, The Argyle Group, Boston, Massachusetts, with no street address or zip code.

How many people no longer use zip codes? How arrogant, or maybe it's something else.

She dwelled on the last thought for a moment before opening the letter. *A greeting card?* It was the same shape, but Christmas, and his annual machine-signed holiday card remained a half-year away.

She pulled the card out of the envelope. Not a greeting card; the outside brazenly embossed with ornate gold letters.

"From the desk of Senator Merewether Tree, Retired." Two lines scrawled under the opened fold.

"Rebecca, I have been re-reading Argyle's annual reports. I think it's time to think about higher profit margins. — M.T."

She tore the card quickly, then methodically into halves, then quarters. A shredder beside her desk sucked the torn pieces into its maws as her mind conjured up a piranha devouring fresh catch.

A grim-faced Rebecca took the elevator down to Building 117's sub-basement. When she had become chairwoman of Argyle she had the elevator reconfigured with a skylight capping the shaft, and a glass ceiling on the cage to allow some light in. The doors opened to an array of electronic inspection devices. A camera scrutinized her before a robotic arm pushed out a scanner. A bossy, mechanical voice said, "position right eye at biometric plate." She hated that voice. *The Chinese needed to program more human-sounding speakers.*

"Thank you, you're cleared for entrance." A final Americanized afterthought piped through the machine: "Have a nice day." Rebecca wanted to kick the machine so hard it would never speak again.

The outer doors opened, and she walked down a corridor, entering a securely cocooned communication room, walls covered with deflection devices to keep out inquisitive listening devices. Two technicians, one in-house and another from an outside security firm, hunched over a computer, re-running a final test. Rebecca put her hand on the shoulder of the in-house technician, Denis Rodriquez. He looked up from his work, a smile flashing across his face.

"Hi, Rebecca. Great to see you."

Rebecca asked all employees to call her by her first name. Only Gilad Levine couldn't manage the informality.

Rebecca took a small package out of her vintage orange bike messenger bag that she acquired twenty years earlier and handed it to Denis. "I brought you and your wife a present from China, something for the baby. Open it when you get home. It will bring good luck."

"You shouldn't have, this is fantastic. My wife will be so happy.

Can you still come to the christening?"

"I've got it scheduled. I wouldn't think of missing it."

After shaking hands with the outside security technician, Rebecca asked, "Are we ready?" Looking at her watch, she drummed her fingers on a wall panel, breaking into a light sweat as the walls seemed to close in on her.

"We're re-running a final encryption synch with London. They're standing by; you're ready to roll in fifteen seconds. We'll go to the backup security room to keep validating the encryption, and leave you alone. Any problems, just press the red button."

"Right, the easy button," Rebecca said, taking out a small linen handkerchief to wipe her hands dry. "Okay, let's get this going."

The technicians left the room. When she pressed the transmit button, the image of her English colleague, Lord Anthony Hare, appeared behind a desk in another secure room. A message ticker-taped across the screen's bottom: "Transmitting. Receiving in London, England. Time 13:34.27 hours. Respondent now being requested to press input code for a final synch."

For the next sixty seconds pulses of light and random numbers flashed over Hare's face until a green light lit. CLEARED.

Rebecca spoke first. "Sorry to be calling you so late, Anthony."

"You look stressed," Hare said. "Are you okay?"

"Me? No, I'm good." Rebecca said, trying to quiet the grinding of her teeth. "Have you heard from Ulrika?"

"I've tried to get hold of her for three days, but no luck. She left me a message, but I sense she's not looking to chat."

"Do you know what's going on?"

"No, but my secretary's been getting phone calls from Skronikov asking for a meeting. He won't say what it's about."

"The Russians are trying to put together a hostile takeover of Argyle."

Hare thundered to his feet. "No, that's outrageous. Do they have any shares tendered?"

"Ulrika's acting like a seller. And probably my grandfather."

"Your grandfather? Is he cabbaged?"

Rebecca had to think on that. After a pause, she replied, "He drinks, but I don't know how much. He's the instigator, not the main problem."

"He's not a good egg."

"Our friends the Russians are the blaggers," she said, recalling the rich Cockney language of Hare's upbringing. "They might blackmail the Chinese and try to get them to nationalize Ling's shares."

"Bollocks to that! No way will they ever get the English shares. Over my dead body."

"Right, I think I can stop them. I needed to be sure of your backing."

"Rock solid . . . not to worry."

"I appreciate your support."

"Something else I needed to discuss with you."

"What is it?" Rebecca asked.

"You asked me at our last Argyle meeting to see if your mother or her family had any role in the rebirth of the Northern Ireland conflict."

Rebecca felt herself go tense. "And?"

"Same dead end when I had it looked at five years ago; same dead end when I had it looked at ten years ago. Same narrative as before: your mom was born in Londonderry, sent at the age of two to live with an aunt in Boston after her mom died. And her father ran a cabinet-making shop. Information about him is pretty thin, so that is suspicious."

"So what do you think?"

"Look, amendments to the Good Friday peace accords mandated that all British intelligence files on Northern Ireland stay sealed for eighty years. And then the Irish are brilliant about not talking."

"And you don't think it is strange to send a two-year-old out of the country?"

"From a war zone with bullets flying and bombs exploding? No. She was sent somewhere safe. You need to think about letting this go."

"I know," Rebecca said, with resignation. "I've pretty much come to that position. Even the detective agency I work with is telling me to back away for now. And my grandfather. He refuses to tell me anything."

"Thanks for your help," Rebecca said. "I'll get back to you as soon as possible . . . Oh, Anthony, put on some security for yourself and your family until we see how this possible hostile takeover plays out."

* *

As she headed back to her office, a text messaging beeper in her pocket began to vibrate. She pulled it out and unfolded its display screen.

URGENT . . . Suspicious activity in the currency market. I'm heading for your office . . . Pomeroy.

McAllister Pomeroy headed Argyle's currency trading department, her old job. The world seemed to think that Rebecca inherited the chair of Argyle, but nothing could have been further from the truth. Before she graduated Harvard Business School, all the major investment firms in New York and London made lucrative job offers, but she wanted a privately held firm that needed fresh blood. Argyle's currency trading unit existed mainly to hedge the company's foreign holdings against monetary fluctuations. She case-studied Argyle during her last six months of business school; in the end, she felt like a kid looking for money in her grandfather's pockets. Merewether held a significant — though not majority — stake in Argyle, and was treated as an important stakeholder. Everyone opposed the idea but her.

The head of Harvard Business School argued that she belonged in New York or London; he considered Argyle second-tier. When he pushed her, she told him she wanted to be a 'fifth columnist,' subsequently retracting it as a poor joke. He snorted and told her to read Freud on jokes. Later she learned that her grandfather wrote the then Chairman of Argyle, expressing displeasure at the prospect of his granddaughter working for the firm. The Chairman took it up with the employment committee and wrote back to Tree that internal compliance rules forbid his vetoing their unanimous recommendation.

Rebecca subsequently managed, over the years, to have her allies in Arabia and China buy down a portion of his ownership interests.

Pomeroy skittered into her office so fast Rebecca looked down at his feet, expecting a skateboard.

"A little turmoil in the markets?" she asked.

"A lot. Our computer program picked up what looks like an orchestrated accumulation of currency options about ten minutes ago. It started small, but the graph lines quickly spiked upward."

While Pomeroy spoke, Rebecca tapped on the glass top of her desk, hitting the near right corner, bringing the glass alive with the LEDs of an embedded remote. A sixty-inch carbon nanotube multi-screen dropped from the ceiling; BBC Financial filled the main screen, with CNN, MSNBC, Wolf Global, and Al Jazeera in smaller screens along the bottom.

"How are our positions?" she tapped again, dropping another screen with a dedicated currency ticker. She tapped once more, and a personal computer rose from within her desk, its massive screen breaching like a submarine breaking water.

"We're making money. Quite a bit. We went short . . . at the time." Pomeroy grew hesitant.

"Of my brother's death?"

"Right."

"You made the right trade. Nothing to be apologetic about."

"And our computers jumped first on top of the suspicious trades," he said, his teeth softly clattering like a baby shark. "We beat out Goldman's computers by almost ten seconds."

Rebecca smiled. Goldman outsourced their technology to Bangalore while Rebecca insisted that M.I.T. do Argyle's. It cost her ten times as much, but it had just paid for itself one hundred times over in that ten-second gap.

She looked at Argyle's trading page. The screen wasn't the right size, too big for her reading glasses, causing her bared eyes to squint.

"Look at it now, McAllister. It's steamrolling. Something's afoot." Pomeroy came from behind the desk and leaned over her as they stared at the numbers of free-falling markets flashing across the screen.

As they spoke, the M.I.T. computer-trading program auto-piloted Argyle capital reserves into global exchanges, and profitably rode the downward direction of the market. Rebecca felt puzzled at first but turned quickly to anger as it became more obvious to her: players in the markets were front-running private knowledge, and most likely conducting illegal insider trading.

"What do you want to do?" Pomeroy asked.

"Let's stick to our playbook. We're not speculators. Tell the traders to start unwinding their oldest short positions concurrently with their oldest long positions."

"Boss, this is low-hanging fruit. If monkeys are playing in the markets, it's not our responsibility."

"No." Rebecca's face reddened. "I'll only say this once. Reduce our exposure. Calmly. And our compliance department should write-up an S.E.C. potential insider trading alert. Something fishy is going on."

"Right, I'm on team," Pomeroy said, as he picked up his cellphone and speed-dialed his assistant. "Ballard. I know . . . Right, steady rudder. Unwind all of the September contracts, and then the Julys' . . . Tell them to be tidy. Spot on. I'll be back to you in five or less."

One of Rebecca's mini-screens began to blink. A CNN breaking news banner strobed wildly. SOURCES REPORT THAT JOHN SPENCER WILL ANNOUNCE A RUN FOR PRESIDENT.

"Oh, my God," she said. *Is John Spencer running for president?*

By proclaiming an evil conspiracy by the Mexican government planning a full-scale invasion of illegal aliens intent on taking over the Southwest, Spencer had catapulted into American politics as a fundamentalist populist leading a virulent anti-Hispanic movement. The recent election of the militant Emiliano Ramos as Mexico's new president had created a bonanza for Spencer, giving his movement, spurred by talk-radio and the Internet, fresh momentum. With four other deeply divided political parties already splintering voters, he had nearly won the Arizona governorship in the state's last election and had recently tried to mainstream his movement, sidestepping the issue of armed vigilantes and dumbing down his message.

Would he have a chance to become the next president? And who was behind him?

"Rebecca," Pomeroy, who had remained looking at the screens, said, his voice sounding tense and agitated, "the equity markets are getting savaged. Everything is in free fall. What do you want to do?"

Rebecca rubbed her eyes with one hand as she repetitively twirled gathered strands of hair that had fallen down her cheek. She felt sick, uncomfortably warm. She opened a small refrigerator, filling a cup with crushed ice that she spooned into her mouth. Images of anti-immigrant vigilantes riding SUVs with assault rifles roiled through her brain. Clearly, the markets thought a racist, independent party candidate had a shot at winning a national election.

"Tell the traders to unwind all their positions," she said, turning back to Pomeroy. "I want them down to zero exposure within three days or less. And then we'll run silent for awhile."

Pomeroy opened his mouth, but Rebecca's face steeled.

"Right, zero. Run silent. Run deep . . ." his voice trailed off as he picked up his cellphone.

Chapter 7

Back in the sub-basement's secure communication room, Rebecca waited to be patched into Ling in Beijing. Events were spinning out of control: the fate of the company she had built hung in jeopardy, a demagogic racist had announced a run for the presidency, and a cherished friend was in personal danger.

The blustering image of John Spencer gnawed at her. She imagined him as a crow, the black cat of the sky, waiting to swoop in on defenseless prey. Two years ago, President Sam Tree's Supreme Court nominee Robert Coyne had managed to get confirmed. Election reform laws made one last turn of the screw as it became legal for unlimited, unaccountable monies to pour into any candidate from any source. Large special interest corporations, a corrupt labor union, even a foreign government could funnel money through straw men. The court ruled that all campaign contributions equaled free speech and couldn't be restricted.

Ling's image appeared onscreen, wearing a vintage Harris Tweed jacket, a royal blue button-down collar shirt, and a red Ascot twisted around his neck. He wore wireless spectacles on his well-tanned face, which harmonized with his gelled, perfectly parted hair.

He bowed like Charlie Chaplin peering into a camera lens, and then waved. Rebecca knew he was upset; typically he continued this silent comedy routine until he got her to giggle.

"What's the matter? Charlie doesn't look up to speed."

"Yup. My pilots faxed Beijing-to-Boston flight plans for tomorrow. Beijing International's flight control bounced it back within an hour. It came back with a 'No Fly' stamp."

Rebecca's hand shot up and clamped momentarily over her mouth. She mashed her teeth, straining to calm herself, until she finally said, "I'm worried about your safety, and . . ." she paused, "your family."

"The family flew a few days ago to Paris to visit relatives," Ling said, forcing a wink out of a pained face. "Hold on a minute," Ling said, as an aide came up to him, handing him a note.

Rebecca watched with a growing feeling of dread, as the two men whispered a brief exchange. By the time the aide left the room, all the color had drained from Ling's face.

"I have to leave now," he said, his voice terse. "My aide got a tip from a source in the Chinese Intelligence Agency. By the end of the day, I'm told they'll put my offices in lockdown, and they'll hold me under house arrest."

"Oh God, no," Rebecca said. "Tell me what you want me to do?"

"I got your encrypted email earlier with the details. Speed up your plan to outmaneuver the Russians. Buy your grandfather's shares. If you need more capital, I have it parked offshore."

"Yes," she said as her body shuddered. "I'll get the shares. Hold tight. It might take a week before this plays out."

Ling opened his mouth to speak as the transmission cut off; the screen went white, and the audio washed away in static. Rebecca's stomach plunged like a malfunctioning elevator through a skyscraper shaft.

Chapter 8

Seeking Advice

Adrenaline, the body's go-to drug in times of flight or fight, pushed Rebecca up the stairs to her office. She often thought those were the only two modes she lived in—from planes to battlefields—and that her blood must run clear as her neurotransmitters produced a pure chemical excitement.

In her office, she began making phone calls to contacts she had in the State Department and national security agencies to see if they could help protect Ling. Failing to receive any assurances, she reached out to the Chinese Ambassador to the United States, but he refused to take her call. Finally, she reached his Third Deputy.

"Let me be very clear, Under Secretary Hom. Argyle now has twelve solar cell factories in Guandong Province. We employ nearly twenty thousand Chinese nationals, pay them top wages, give them child day-care, medical insurance, and provide long-term employees with higher education opportunities for their children."

"Yes, Ms. Tree, the Chinese government has the greatest respect for your enterprises. But while we welcome your business, we will not allow foreign nationals to influence our internal affairs."

"That's fine. However you want to say it. I'm just saying that if I start to feel unwelcome in China, I will shut those factories down overnight and move them to Vietnam. And all the machinery as well. Read our contracts; they have the relevant provisions with appropriate guarantees from the International Monetary Fund. I don't want my internal affairs meddled with either. Do you understand my position?"

"Yes, Ms. Tree, I will convey your concerns to my government."

"You do that," Rebecca said, as she hung up. *Mealy-mouthed functionary.*

With little left that she could do for the moment, Rebecca decided to leave the office early and go for a run along the Charles River before her scheduled dinner with Harvard President Emily O'Brian and her husband, Lucretia Fironznia.

First she sent an urgent text message.

"Are you in Boston today?"

"Yes," came a quick response.

"I need to talk to you. Meet me in an hour at our usual spot."

* *

She wore long black runner's pants, with a tank top underneath an official looking U.S. Army nylon jacket. She ran alongside the Charles River, straining against a brisk wind.

She took measured, determined breaths with each step, an occasional twinge radiating off the scar tissue left by the bullet extracted from her thigh by an Army surgeon after Jackson's death. She accelerated her pace.

She believed her message to the Chinese Under-Secretary would not be treated lightly. They wouldn't dare harm Ling, she thought, but they could make things very difficult. If she accepted her grandfather's proposal, it should make the Chinese back off. *But,* she thought, *what did Merewether want?* She had gone head to head with him over Argyle, and she had prevailed. *Was this a second round for him? Why would he want me in the White House? I would never accept his agenda.*

But what if this was an opportunity for her agenda to flourish? She could become more powerful than her grandfather, discover truths long denied her. She began to feel the stimulation of the challenge, a chance to turn the highest office in the land into a positive force.

Restore rationality, she thought. *A slogan for a campaign button?*

A tall bulked-up man stepped out of the shadows of a grove of river birch trees as Rebecca neared the end of her route. She sprinted the remaining yards directly towards him, and now slightly out of breath, said, "Thanks, Oswaldo, for getting here on such short notice."

"I assume it is important, so I rearranged a few things."

"It is," Rebecca said as she caught her breath. She couldn't help but stare, startled, at Lemus every time they met. A knife scar ran along his face, beginning from the outside corner of his left eye, meandering down his cheek, hooking under his chin, and finally running back up to his lip.

"I want to hire your firm, hire you."

"Again? I thought my methods make you nervous."

"They do. But this is an exception."

"What do you need to be done this time?"

"John Spencer. I need him investigated. Someone has to dig in the weeds."

"Can I ask why?"

"Nope."

"I don't know. You know I have some complaints about you."

"What did I do now?"

"Some of our old platoon members are suspicious of you."

She knew Lemus from her specialized Army intelligence unit; he too had been in the convoy the day Jackson and two other soldiers died. After the first explosion, he established a sniper position and saved four fellow soldiers and probably her life as well.

Long before he went to war, he acquired his dramatic facial scar.

A single Pentecostal mother in New York's East Harlem raised him. Gangs controlled the streets, and the Latin-Kings initiated him by throwing him onto the southbound tracks of the East 116th St. stop on the Lexington Avenue line. But before they did that, they carved up his face.

"For the last five years, some of the platoon members, the seriously wounded ones from the day of the attack on the convoy, get monthly checks from an offshore foundation no one has ever heard of. They think the money comes from you."

"I am not familiar with the matter," Rebecca said, forcing a formal tone.

"You're a natural. Are you sure you're not considering a political career?"

Rebecca roared. "Sit down with me for a bit on that bench over there. I need to talk to someone I trust."

Rebecca took Lemus by his elbow and guided him to a bench away from the jogging path.

"I miss you, Ozzie. How is the family?"

"All good. Nydia is still teaching and loves it. We just bought some land outside El Yunque."

"The rain forest in Puerto Rico? Great."

"We plan to build a house there after the kids leave the nest. You need my shoulder to cry on?"

"Yes. You're right about politics; my grandfather wants me to run for the presidency."

"Your grandfather is crazy and smart as a fox."

"Why?"

"Hey, this is dysfunctional America. Anyone can become president. So it might as well be you. You'd make a lousy president—and, believe me, you can take that as a compliment—but you'd be a dream compared to the gang of thieves so far declared . . . except . . ."

"Except what?"

"Any president that doesn't kowtow to the racist nativists will become a target for assassins. I have good sources in the Secret Service—besides the attempt the public knows about to assassinate President Sanchez-Smith, at least two other attempts on her life failed."

"Well that's a good way to get me to do something: threaten me. Listen I have to be somewhere soon. Will you help me?"

"Sure," Lemus said, pulling something from his pocket resembling a flashlight. "Here, take this. It opens to display a message screen and keypad. It is coded and encrypted. If I have information I will pass it to you or if you need to contact me in a hurry you can use it to reach me."

"You can send your bills to my home address."

"Your money is no good. Going after a racist hate monger like Spencer will be a labor of love. Donate my fees to a worthy cause. Maybe some wounded warriors."

"Jerk," Rebecca said, with a grin, as she fist-bumped his arm. "I'll talk to you later."

* *

Rebecca, wearing blue jeans and a T-shirt with a picture of a camel adorned with a mortarboard, robe, and thick eyeglasses captioned in block letters GRADUATE CAMEL, sat on the kitchen floor at Harvard's president, Emily O'Brian's house, rubbing the stomach of the family's golden retriever, Frankie.

"Frankie's getting a little heavy," Rebecca said.

"Blame my over-the-top husband. He refuses to buy pet food like any other citizen; instead, he blends organic vegetables — yams, carrots, green beans — with chopped meat, vitamin C, and fresh garlic. Big deal, he's head of a divinity school, and I lose every argument. 'No cans for humans, no cans for animals.'"

"Poor Frankie," Rebecca said, as she rubbed the dog's ear with one hand, and scratched his stomach with the other until his tail started wagging uncontrollably.

"Frankie's lucky he doesn't get his teeth flossed twice a day," O'Brian said. "Your face looks drawn."

"You think? Maybe I should come by and have my dinners with Frankie. Should I change into something better than this? I brought extra clothes in my messenger bag," Rebecca said.

"No, you look fine. Are you playing tomorrow? Your suspension is up."

O'Brian coached and played goalie for Back Bay Boston, a women's soccer club that competed in an amateur all New-England league. An art history graduate of Radcliffe, she qualified once for the United States women's Olympic team as the second goalie.

"I'll be there," Rebecca said. "It'll be a welcome relief. I'm still sorry about the fight with the Maine forward."

"You've played with us for ten years. You never lost your temper before. Do you want to talk about it now?"

"No, if you don't mind. Who's coming for dinner?" Rebecca asked.

"You know how my husband is," O'Brian said. "This dinner discussion about your political future became one of his projects."

"Maybe I shouldn't have told you about it," Rebecca said.

"Nonsense, you need to confide in someone. But I should warn you,

Lucretia and I don't share the same opinion about this idea of you running for president."

"Let me guess: you're against it, and he thinks it's a smashing idea."

"Exactly," O'Brian said with a chuckle. "Nothing personal."

Rebecca laughed. "That's the agenda for this dinner, to debate the merits."

"Merits? There is nothing meritorious in politics. Three out of the last seven presidents have had articles of impeachment filed against them. Two proceeded to trial. And now we have seen the unthinkable—a billionaire real estate developer became president, and then his long-time crony, a corrupt St. Louis mayor, makes a deathbed confession detailing a sordid trail of real estate bribes, and the flaunting of building department regulations. Now a whole nefarious gang sits in a federal prison. I read that the guards have nicknames for the cells—Oval Office, Cabinet Room, War Room, and Treasury Department."

"I guess this dinner wasn't your idea," Rebecca said, taken aback by her friend's intensity.

"I love Luke, but he is delusional when it comes to the real world. Never marry a theologian. They live in bubbles. Sometimes he's so optimistic I'd like to choke him." O'Brian picked up a lid on the stove. "I can finish here, Luke's waiting for you in his study, and I believe he's got Randall Wilson with him. Harriet Ogden, from the law school, is expected shortly."

"Oh good, I've heard great things about her."

"And Tucker Richards will be here later. He's being interviewed by the BBC."

"Richards, he's a wild one. He knows, I hope, this conversation is off-the-record."

* *

Lucretia Fironznia was the only child of Italian missionary parents, Dean of Harvard's theological school, a progressive Catholic, and confidante of the Pope, Porfirio Gutiérrez, the former Archbishop of San Salvador. When Rebecca entered the study, Fironznia was engaged in an animated discussion with Randall Wilson. Both men stood to greet her. Rebecca knew of Wilson by reputation but had never met him. A huge man, half a foot taller than Rebecca, with a full head of poorly managed hair, he had bushy, lupine eyebrows that arched and a craggy face. His hand felt rough as a bear's paw when she shook it.

"Do you know Randall's writings?" Fironznia asked Rebecca.

"Yes, I read both volumes of the *Roosevelt Dynasty*. I found it spellbinding. The chapters on Eleanor Roosevelt's childhood shocked me. A gripping story. Quite a family."

"Well, you have quite a family yourself."

"I'm afraid the Trees are hardly Roosevelts."

"Rebecca," Fironznia said, "do you know that Randall once started working on a biography of your grandfather?"

"Yes, I refused a request to be interviewed. I think Professor Wilson sent me a letter about ten years ago. I'm sorry I wasn't able to be more helpful."

"Quite all right, Ms. Tree," Wilson said. "At least you sent me a polite and thoughtful letter, more than most people did."

"What happened to your book?"

Wilson's shoulders shook, his head pivoted momentarily like a tennis spectator, and his eyes widened with exclamation. "Tonight's fully off the record?" Wilson said.

Fironznia laughed after he finished swilling port around his mouth. "*Omerta* is practiced better at Harvard than in my native Sicily."

Wilson recounted his story of attempting to write about Merewether Tree, then a sixth term United States Senator. As a Pulitzer Prize-winning biographer, Wilson approached his usual sources about a Tree biography, but they quickly dried up. He persisted for months, but no one would talk on the record. Then he received a call from Tree's secretary, inviting him for a visit at the Senate office building. Tree had welcomed Wilson into his inner sanctum like a long lost friend, offering him a glass of sherry and a cigar, inquiring of his guest's writing career and family. A half-hour had passed before Wilson moved to the subject of the visit. The Senator shook his head indicating that he had no interest. Wilson persisted until Tree agreed to answer a few questions, off the record. On the third question, Tree, his face livid, rose from his desk, and told Wilson in no uncertain terms to leave his office and not to dare think about any book.

"What did you ask him?" Rebecca said.

"I asked him if the death of his son, your father, had changed his political perspective. Without saying it directly, he threatened me and promised dire consequences if I continued to pursue my project."

Sounds just like him.

"If you had been able to write a biography of my grandfather, what do you think the flap copy would say?"

"Good question," Wilson said. "Let's see. 'For better or worse, Merewether Tree did more than any man to shape America's post-Cold War global destiny. In his first two terms as a United States Senator, he made a lightning-fast rise to power and earned a reputation as a deal-maker, reaching across both sides of the aisle. Seen as promising presidential material, he failed twice to secure his party's nomination. As a major architect of the fall of the second incarnation of the Soviet Empire, it is believed that he subsequently enriched himself with lucrative business deals. The second half of his Senate career marked his split with the party that nurtured him, the Democratic Party. In reaction, he started his political party, the Millennium Populists, which disingenuously proclaimed themselves anti-Wall Street. They promised voters full employment through massive public works projects while emphasizing strong religious values. Through what his enemies declared 'divide and conquer' tactics he tried but failed to get his half-brother William elected to the presidency, later succeeding in placing his grandson Sam in the Oval Office. Now in his eighties, he has not been seen in public in the last five years, but is believed to continue to exercise substantial political and economic power.'"

"Impressive flap copy," Rebecca said. "You know more about my grandfather than I do. At eight years old, he sent me abroad, and I didn't see him again until I was twenty-two. And I've only seen him a few times in the last fifteen years; the last time was by videoconference when he asked me to run for president on his party's ticket."

"The few people who would talk to me," Wilson said, "described him as a man who grew more bitter with the years, and more ruthless as he exercised his considerable power."

"And the source of this power," Rebecca asked, "besides his political base and his financial fortune?"

"My theory is that he was adept at acquiring information and knowing how to use it to cement allies and intimidate those who dared oppose him."

"What kind of information?"

"He was close to three FBI directors. I think they shared files with him."

"Blackmail?" Rebecca said.

"I can't prove it, but that seems likely."

And now he is trying to blackmail me, Rebecca thought.

* *

Tucker Richards, one of Harvard's most controversial and flamboyant historians, joined the party as the dinner neared completion.

"Ah," Richards said, "this group looks, by definition, to be conspiratorial. And I'm told that every word is privileged, and I should expect to roast in hell if I divulge the contents."

"It could be worse, especially for you, my dear friend," Fironznia said. "But let me update you. Professor Ogden has just finished giving us a cram course on the Patriot and Sedition Acts and executive power."

Harriet Ogden, the Miles Rose Professor of Constitutional Law, authored a seminal work entitled, *Who Killed the Constitution?* In her mid-fifties, she had been New York City's District Attorney before coming to Harvard. Black curly hair and velvety brown eyes framed her round face and plump cheeks. She wore thick silver Hopi Indian bracelets on both wrists with spider figures etched into them.

"I was born an optimist, but the last decade has worn me down," Ogden said. "The unintended consequences of these acts and the assertions of executive privilege are terrifying."

"But you see no hope of reversing these trends?" Rebecca said.

"Not much. When your brother Sam got his Supreme Court nominee confirmed, I felt democracy stood under a death sentence. It has been six to three against abortion, six to three against habeas corpus, six to three against environmental protection, six to three for corporate interests, six to three for no campaign finance limits. Sadly, the list goes on."

"Six to three!" Richards bellowed out. "I'm sorry, but who fought them? 'No one' is the correct answer. Where were the feminists when they eviscerated Roe vs. Wade? Where were the civil libertarians when they gutted due process and upheld preventive detention?" Richards rose up from his chair, holding a crystal wine glass in his hand. "There is nothing left to toast in America, but I can recite:

First they came for the Socialists, and I did not speak out—
because I was not a Socialist.
Then they came for the Trade Unionists, and I did not speak out—
because I was not a Trade Unionist.
Then they came for the Jews, and I did not speak out—
because I was not a Jew.
Then they came for me—and there was no one left to speak for me.

"Whoa," Rebecca said. "There must be some solutions."

"The answers are not pretty," Richards said, "my colleague, Professor Ogden is correct in her book. The Constitution is killed, or at best, it's hooked up on life support, and there are people in America who just want to pull the plug."

"But the country could push back," Rebecca said, "new leadership could emerge. It has happened before."

"Yes," Richards said. "'Yes, we can' became 'Yes, we could,' and then it became 'Yes we could have.'"

"And who do you blame?" Rebecca said. She felt a constriction in her chest as if she had eaten ice cream too quickly. She made a small cough. "The preacher or the choir?"

"I blame," Ogden interjected, "the choir. The people thought change would be a one-day event; they would go to the voting booths, and everything would end happily. They sent their chosen general into battle but they didn't volunteer to enlist long term."

"I disagree," Rebecca said. "Great generals prepare their troops properly for hard battles. 'Victorious warriors win first and then go to war while defeated warriors go to war first and then seek to win.'"

"Sounds like you're rising to the fight," Richards said.

"No, Sun Tzu just came to me." Rebecca, and most of her fellow trainees had memorized the book, *The Art of War*, in the Army's counter-intelligence school.

"Let me explain what would happen if you took up your grand-father's offer and ran for the presidency," Richards said. "First, your opponents would ignore you, and then they would marginalize you. They'd call you a puppet candidate."

"A puppet?" Rebecca said. "How interesting. A name I've never been called."

"And if you gained any traction, which is unlikely, your opponents would strew your path with banana peels." Richards beamed with delight as he took great pleasure in his description. "And if you slipped, no one would pick you up."

"I have learned never to let anyone intimidate me," Rebecca said. "And plenty have tried."

"Rebecca would make an excellent candidate," Fironznia said, "look at her track record, in business, in environmental leadership. She has high ethics, believes in God, and she served her country on the battlefield."

"Sweetheart," O'Brian broke in, her voice filled with frustration. "It won't work. Even if she won, they wouldn't let her govern. It would be hopeless."

"What do you mean?" Rebecca said, her demeanor shifting to defense. "I'm sure I could govern. I run a huge business, and I'm told I do that quite well."

"No," Ogden broke in, "I think what Emily means is that if you became president, and sent your cabinet nominees to the Senate, you wouldn't get them confirmed."

"Why?"

"You might get minor posts confirmed like Commerce, Labor, or Education,"

O'Brian said, "but as to State, Defense, and Attorney General — forget about it."

Richards rose back up from his seat. "If this monster John Spencer is elected president, which he might be, what do you think he'll do? Tell her, Harriet. We've had this discussion."

"Spencer," Ogden said, "would never get an Attorney General or other powerful cabinet posts of his liking confirmed by a divided Senate."

"So what would he do?"

"I'm afraid he'd use the emergency powers invested in the Executive branch by the last Patriot Act to appoint his cabinet."

A chill swept through Rebecca. "Are you serious?"

"Deadly serious. The country is on the brink of the greatest threat to its survival since the Civil War."

"And you think Spencer could be elected?"

"Yes," Fironznia said, "and we're all terrified. And I'll tell you the academic world's dirty little secret. We all have sister universities in Europe, and we buy beautiful apartments in cities like Berlin, where we can escape if things get too bad here."

"It's a perfect storm," Richards said. "The American Empire could go into political collapse."

Rebecca looked around the table. The room went silent.

"Someone has to stop John Spencer," Rebecca said, passion rising in her voice.

Emergency powers, she thought, trying to digest the implications.

Chapter 9

Merewether Tree appeared onscreen, formally dressed in a business suit and holding horse reins as he sat in a white riding carriage upholstered in red velveteen. Behind him, the sun dropped over the mountain range west of his estate.

"Hello Rebecca, I thought you might enjoy the setting sun with me before we discuss business."

The image had the feel of a *carte-de-visite*, a photograph shot on a painted backdrop in a nineteenth-century photographer's studio. The setting sun lit his hair, but the angle seemed askew, and his posture tilted backward.

"Perhaps we should talk in my office," Tree said. "More privacy, you know." The screen went momentarily black, and then Tree reappeared behind his office desk, the background behind him no longer book-lined, as in their previous conversation. Now logs crackled in a stone hearth.

Tree belched loud guffaws. "State of the art. Some big Hollywood animation studio installed the whole deal. Cost a pretty penny, but it paid for itself in six months. Consulting fees."

"Very impressive. My compliments," Rebecca said.

A very old boy with his toys.

"Anyway," Tree said, "Have you made a decision?"

"Perhaps," she said, keeping her voice measured. Her grandfather had broadened the battle; Rebecca had people to protect.

"Were I to entertain your offer, I have some terms."

"Of course. "

"First, how much did the Russians offer for your shares?"

Tree pursed his lips, twisting his head, as his camera lens zoomed in, until the screen filled with his blue-eyed side. He held up his right hand, curled it into a tight fist, then bared his alabaster teeth and unfurled his fingers one at a time. One . . . two . . . three . . . four. At five, he fully rotated his hand and thrust it toward the lens. Then he started again with the left hand: six . . . seven . . . eight . . . nine . . . ten. Now he held both hands flat out at the screen with the tip of his thumbs hooking his nose hairs.

"Ten billion?"

With his face in a full leer, he flashed his index and middle finger once, cackling like a hyena.

"Twelve billion?"

Tree narrowed his eyes leaving his mouth agape. His bleached dentures dominated the screen.

She gulped at the figure, a bit inflated, though not by much. "Alright. I'm going to buy you out."

"Hmm," Tree said, "you have that kind of money?"

"I'll get it. But I'm family. So I'll take a ten percent discount."

"This is business. The price is fair."

"OK. Final offer, take it or leave it." Rebecca said. "I'll match that number less five percent. Yes or no?"

"Alright, five percent for family."

Rebecca had lines of credit from banks in North America, Europe, and the Arab Emirates. If needed, she would post her shares, with Ling's as collateral. "If we agree to all terms, the first drafts of the contracts will be transmitted to you in a few days, and the deal must close within twenty days."

"That'd be fine," Tree said, as a drop of spit departed his lower lip and rested on his chin. "Anything else?"

"Yes, this is all contingent on your facing off the Russians and getting assurances that the Chinese will keep their hands off Ling and his family."

"And you'll run?" Tree asked.

"Yes, only if I have ironclad guarantees for Ling's safety. I want the Chinese ambassador or his first deputy to come to my office and tell me to my face that Ling will be left alone."

"I'll take care of that."

"What do you expect from me?" Rebecca asked, gulping as she realized she had set this in motion, something too big to fathom in a quick video conference.

"William and Hess will take care of organizing the party bases. They'll furnish you with speechwriters, the requisite staff, and adequate funding. Of course, you'll have to play nice. Your privacy will go out the window and you'll have to give up your no-interview stance."

"And beyond my religious convictions, are your party people going to object to ideas of mine they might not find compatible?"

"Of course they'll object, and I might side with them."

"I can't support the death penalty."

"Ah yes, that little misunderstanding you had with your brother."

It wasn't a misunderstanding; an innocent woman executed is called murder, Rebecca thought. "Yes, that misunderstanding."

"Honest difference of opinion," Tree said. "Not a problem. I'll have Hess drop it from the platform. Your job is to run . . . to win . . . You're a Tree . . . I expect no less of you." Tree's head tilted further back, and his sloganeering lips seemed to reach for the ceiling. "By any means . . ." he began to mutter, "sacrifice the few for the sake of the many."

The screen went black again. Rebecca sat there unmoving, stunned. A moment later, Tree re-emerged with a new background, the original, the book-lined study. "Damnfangle. I pushed the wrong button," he said. "I have some advice on how you should handle your opponents."

"Of course, Grandfather. You're the expert."

"Never mind that. Just listen. The damn Democrat. What's his name."

"Senator Yaled?"

"What kind of idiotic name is that?"

"I think his grandfather is Lebanese."

"Christian, I hope."

"Stop with the editorial. What's your advice?"

"The pompous hyena fancies himself a legislator. His track record speaks for itself. He's been in the Senate for thirty years, and you won't find one major bill with his name on it. Go after his record."

"Okay, what about Wyeth, the Republican?"

"He should have been a painter like his grandfather. Hess can give you a dossier on him. He's corrupt as a skunk."

"As a skunk, what does that mean? Never mind, don't tell me, and I don't want any dossiers. I fight my own battles, on level playing fields."

"Have it your way. Watch out for Withers."

"The Constitutional Party candidate?"

"Yeah, the one with the terrible hairpiece."

"I can handle him. What about John Spencer?"

"Stay away from Spencer. He can't win."

"I don't understand. He seems the most dangerous guy in the race."

"That might be. But he doesn't have the money to run the distance. Henry Hess has a handle on all this. Follow his advice. Spencer won't be able to run national TV ads in the month before the election. He'll fade. If you go after him now, he'll be able to raise more money. Trust me, dear. No one knows this game better than me."

Trust me, Rebecca thought. *No way,* swallowing the sour taste talking to her Grandfather always created in her mouth.

"Anything else we need to discuss?" Rebecca asked, hoping he might say something, anything personal. She had mostly given up hope a long time ago for some emotional family connection, except, in truth, deep down in her soul the yearning never left her.

"No . . . not now. First stop, connect with Hess and announce yourself to the party." He turned his ominous eye toward the recording camera.

"All right then. Goodnight, Grandfather."

Chapter 10

West Wing of White House
Washington D.C.

"My dear Rebecca, I'm so delighted you've returned." With an unlit cigar dangling out of his mouth, Henry Hess stood propped on a column just outside the main entrance to the White House.

"Get rid of that cigar. You know I hate them, and you're not supposed to smoke."

"Sorry, I smoke when I'm nervous."

"Well, if you live less, you'll have less time to get nervous," Rebecca said. "In any event, I need to depart D.C. airspace by eleven p.m. I don't want to be rushed. I'm expected in Amsterdam for a meeting."

Rebecca had arrived at the White House to negotiate final conditions with Hess, who, expecting a deal, had already scheduled a video conference to share her decision with the party faithful.

"I was a bit concerned; you left our last meeting white as a sheet."

Rebecca's tone quickly silenced him. "I'm not here to discuss my health. You're looking for a business deal to save your skin. So let's skip the small talk. Is that bunker you call a conference room available?"

A few minutes later, Hess sat at a table with a neatly stacked pile of position papers nearly obscuring his face. Rebecca refused to sit; instead she paced around the table, her hands in rapid animation as she spoke.

"I've reached an understanding with my grandfather. I'm prepared to accept your offer, with several additional conditions."

"Which are?"

"I'll campaign on my schedule not yours, and I don't want any of your managed events with handpicked audiences. I'll do all that's required with jumping through the media hoops and everything else."

"Is that it?"

"No. Here's a big one. You'll leave me alone. I'll work with the staff you provide, but I don't want to be henpecked by you or my grandfather. Not while I'm campaigning, and not if— *big if*—I win."

"Your grandfather briefed me," Hess said. "I've been empowered to accept certain additional conditions, and I do. So if you have no objection, let's proceed to your video conference with the party hierarchy; we should start shortly." He looked at his watch. "We have a fifty-state hook-up with nearly a thousand people participating."

Rebecca moved to the head of the table and remained standing, towering over the seated Hess. Thinned pure white hair dropped off his head, and muffed the top of floppy ears, which framed his elongated face. Dyed jet-black eyelashes dominated a pair of beady bright blue eyes. He had a long nose, which widened at its nostrils like a river racing to the ocean.

Rebecca wore a soot black power suit with a short skirt and matching sheer black stockings for the occasion. Underneath the suit jacket, she wore a man's black linen shirt over a T-shirt that proclaimed SAVE THE TURTLES; gold hoop earrings framed her face. She wore the boldest, shiniest red lipstick that she could find, all slightly risqué as intended. She felt like she was playing dress-up, emboldened by a costume. She wished Annie were here to help her navigate what to wear for this strange new world she was entering; she felt clueless.

The conference room lights dimmed, and the wall of monitor screens flickered on. From a side door, her great-uncle William entered the room silently, seating himself at an empty place along the length of the table as a slew of faces appeared on the monitors, all of them men, the leaders of the Millennium Populist Party. One by one, they recited a litany of condolences for Sam Tree's demise and offered their support for her candidacy. As she listened to the desperation in their platitudes, she knew they had no other prospective candidates. Their one asset was their fanatical base of voters, who come Election Day, would drive through hailstorms, march through snowdrifts, and brave tornadoes, all to exercise their franchise and vote for whomever their party presented.

As she listened, her pent-up rage turned to resolve. *He who knows when he can fight and when he cannot will be victorious.* The wisdom of Sun Tzu's ancient words silently mentored her. When the men finished, she looked directly into the camera and spoke, parsing words with great care.

"Gentlemen, thank you for your thoughts and prayers at this difficult time and thank you for the service you performed for your country during trying hours. Next week, we will need to start anew. I accept your offer to pick up my brother's fallen sword. God willing, we shall retain the presidency and carry forward the work of the Tree family and the Millennium Populists."

She imagined a mythic sword, self-propelled, hurtling out into space and boomeranging back to earth, slashing at these corpulent men who had used their power so cruelly.

Carry forward, she thought. *These men had created a nearly endless loss to carry forward. The books needed reconciliation—not in accounting, but in spirit, like a penance or confession.*

A sense of relief appeared to flood the faces on the monitors, coupled with the repressed smiles of greedy expectation. To Rebecca, their hopes seemed delusional, as if they could return to the salad days of Big Tree and Little Tree when their world behaved like a giant slot machine fixed to hit jackpots with each pull of the lever. Be loyal. Line up. Get rich.

"I thank you for your support and continuing help," Rebecca concluded. "Goodbye for now, and God bless."

As much as she resented being put in this absurd position by her family, she took some solace in now self-certifying herself as a 'fifth columnist'.

The video monitors flickered off. Not missing a beat, Rebecca turned to her uncle and said, "If you wish to campaign for me, Uncle William, I can't stop you, but I won't appear on the same stage with you, except at the inauguration."

Her uncle blanched. She turned matter-of-factly to Hess, who handed her a folder.

"This outlines our campaign strategy and the party platform, the recently revised version," Hess said. "And here is a list of three you might pick from for a vice president." She glanced at the names not recognizing any.

"I would pick Aldo Peña. He might be able to loosen up the Hispanic vote boycott. Good to think strategically," Hess said as he tapped his index finger on his forehead. "I'll meet with you again at the end of the week to flesh this out."

Silently, Rebecca nodded, taking off her hoop earrings and putting them in her suit jacket pocket.

Chapter 11

Rebecca moved quickly, arranging for Argyle to buyback all of Merewether Tree and his associates' shares, before resigning her position as CEO. She nominated Lord Hare to be the new chairperson, and the partners confirmed her choice. Most of her shares Rebecca had collateralized to secure the buyout of her grandfather's; she gifted her remaining shares to a cross-section of environmental and children's rights foundations with a sole proviso that the shares could never be re-sold.

She rented a small warehouse space in South Boston and hired several Argyle employees granted a leave of absence. Her friends from Harvard set up a research network involving a dozen universities who churned out high-end research and position papers.

Rebecca then established a website and made a very low-key announcement of her candidacy. The announcement played as a sidebar on the network news the next night. Most newspapers ran the story below the fold. One tabloid summed it up best: REBECCA WHO? Las Vegas bookies offered gamblers three-hundred-to-one as the betting line on the new candidate; they claimed they had no takers.

After three weeks of campaigning following Hess's playbook — a traditional menu of photo opportunities, town hall meetings, and interviews more suited for entertainment audiences — Rebecca polled in the low single digits at the bottom of the pack. More disturbingly for her, the America First Party candidate, John Spencer, polled second with twenty-one percent of the vote. The vigilantes allegedly associated with him had gone to the ground; Spencer brazenly argued that he was the candidate best suited to restore law and order to a battered nation.

In less than a month, the first candidate debate was scheduled to take place in Boston. Rebecca grew nervous as she tried to digest the "issues" briefing books provided to her. For the first time in her life, she had trouble concentrating, as if she had crammed for a test that promised nonsensical questions. She slept poorly, if at all. The morning before the debate, she noticed that she needed another notch on the belt holding up her blue jeans.

* *

"Ms., just so you know, the area you are sitting in will be closed off in an hour or two."

Rebecca looked up from a bench outside the University of Massachusetts' Clark Athletic Center to see a young Boston police officer wearing wire-rimmed spectacles with longish blonde hair peeking out from under his cap. He wore a button that said BPD COMMUNITY AFFAIRS. Its logo bore a smiley face.

"For the debate?"

"Yup. We have to put up barricades. They expect protestors."

"Who will they be protesting?"

"Probably everyone. Political candidates are pretty equally disliked in Boston," the officer said with a boyish grin.

Rebecca pushed up her bike goggles but kept her helmet on as the conversation created a distraction from her glum mood.

"Which candidate will attract the most protestors?"

"John Spencer, no doubt. He is despised here," the officer said, putting his foot up on Rebecca's bench and taking a drink from his water bottle. From a small side pack, he took out a fresh bottle with a label proclaiming Beantown Water and gave it to Rebecca.

Boston community affairs officers verbally engaged each citizen they encountered and offered water, city maps, and a list of locations of emergency services.

"Thanks for the water. What about the other candidates? Will you watch the debate?"

"Nah, I am on overtime duty till a few hours after the debate. My girlfriend seems interested in it. She'll tape it for me."

"What does she think of the candidates?"

"Not much. But she wants to see Ms. Tree—she is partial to women candidates. I sort of agree with her on that—but Ms. Tree, it's nice that she lives in Boston, but WIN, PLACE, no way. SHOW, even that's a long shot."

Rebecca looked at her watch. "I have to go. You've been very kind."

"My pleasure," the officer said, tipping his hat. "Do you need any other information? Nearest cash machine? Where to queue for half-price theater tickets? Tonight's catch of the day at Fisherman's Wharf?"

Rebecca laughed jovially. "No, I'm good." She waved back at the officer as she began to wheel her bike away. Then she thought for a second and stopped. "Yes, one thing. Where is the nearest stop for the Cambridge bus?"

"Two blocks away, on the other side of the Athletic Center. But you can't take your bike on the bus."

"I know. Thanks again." Rebecca walked a block toward the bus stop before doubling around to the back of the center, where she locked her bike to a rack before heading for the Cambridge bus.

* *

The morning after the first debate, Rebecca, wearing her bicycle clothes, gazed out her office window as the rising sun poked through a storm-blackened sky. She heard Fatima's familiar knock on her office door.

"Come in."

"Lots of people looked for you after the debate," Fatima said as she rushed into the room carrying a stack of folders.

Fatima Massiri had straight, jet-black hair, and wide brown eyes the color of raw sienna. Her skin, unblemished, shimmered a light olive color, and her aquiline nose gave her face intensity, like the gaze of a young falcon.

Rebecca remembered the time she met her.

Fifteen years ago, Rebecca had returned an urgent message from

Emily O'Brian, the Associate Dean of the Harvard Business School.

"Hi Rebecca, thanks for getting back to me. I need your help with something."

"Sure, if I can," Rebecca said as she peered through a small telescope aimed at a woodpecker's nest perched on a tree outside her dorm window.

"Do you know Fatima Massiri, a first-year student?"

"I don't know her. I've seen her on campus. She is very striking, and I hear she is brilliant."

"She is and she's a lovely person. Her father just got swept up in an FBI dragnet of a Brooklyn mosque. We are trying to help her, but the government is using a Patriot Act provision to freeze out lawyers for thirty days. Fatima is distraught."

"Oh, I read about that. It sounded like total overreach to me and counter-productive. But what is it that you want from me?"

"You are still on ready reserve. You have contacts. Can you see if we can do anything to help her? It's crazy; her father served five years in an Egyptian prison because he advocated for democracy."

"Can you email me all the details that Fatima has? If her family checks out okay, I could try calling in a favor or two. Ask her to meet me tomorrow afternoon at Herrell's Expresso in the Square. Let me see what I can do."

* *

"I know about your father," Rebecca said right away as she sat down. "I might be able to help."

"How," Fatima said warily.

"I spoke to someone who shared information about your father's problems."

Fatima's face turned crimson. "You don't have the right to snoop into my family business."

"I have a security clearance. I need to vouch for you, so I need to ask you some questions."

Fatima stared coldly at Rebecca. "If you're trying to recruit me, then I don't want your help."

"Absolutely not. We need to go through this." Rebecca paused, but Fatima just stared at her so Rebecca continued going over details of a narrative that she would need to confirm. "You're Egyptian-born. Your parents taught at the University of Cairo. They advocated for democratic reform in Egypt."

"My father's life isn't your concern," Fatima said, angrily standing up, looking as she might go.

"Look, Dean O'Brian asked me to try and help you." Rebecca tried to suppress a smile; she didn't want to telegraph her delight at Fatima fighting back. "But that's not why I agreed to do this. I risked my life doing counter-intelligence; I saw people dear to me killed in senseless wars; now I see xenophobic civilian governments using mass arrest tactics which disgusts me and only makes us all less safe."

Fatima remained standing for a moment, but then reluctantly sat back down. She clamped her eyes momentarily before saying, "Ok, I'm sorry. I'm so upset my brain has stopped."

"You have every right to feel that way," Rebecca said, reaching to softly put her hand on Fatima's shoulder.

"We need to finish this bio. I need to make some calls on your behalf. Ok? I will do what I can to get him home."

"Yes," Fatima said, her voice sounding heavy from exhaustion.

"After your father's release from an Egyptian jail, your family emigrated to New York, but despite their degrees, they could only find work cleaning office buildings until they saved enough money to open a twenty-four-hour deli in Brooklyn. You became a *wunderkind* in the New York public school system graduating first in your class from an elite high school, Stuyvesant, and then you went on to Harvard on a full Bloomberg fellowship.

"Two days ago Federal agents came in the middle of the night and took your father away; he is now held in isolation. Your mother is beside herself for fear that you may be snatched next."

"I thought America had a constitutional government."

"I'm not here to debate politics," Rebecca said.

"Then why are you really here?"

"I have knee-jerk reactions when I see anyone bullied. Maybe it's a character flaw. I was bullied badly as a child by my brother."

As she regarded her, Rebecca realized how delighted she was to have made her acquaintance.

"Give me your contact information. I might be able to wrap this up in a few hours. And I'll do my best to make sure your family isn't bothered again."

"Ms. Tree . . ."

"Call me Rebecca."

"Thanks, I don't know why you're doing this, but . . ."

Fatima couldn't finish her thought, so Rebecca got up, handed her a slip of paper with a phone number on it, and said, "When you graduate, call me, if you like. Who knows? Perhaps we might work together."

Nearly two years later, Rebecca sat in the corner office she occupied as the supervisory trader in Argyle's currency department. Her cellphone trilled a friendly tone; the display read FM. Rebecca had programmed Fatima's number after the day they met, hoping someday she would call.

"Hi, congratulations, I understand you finished first in your class, and I heard that you left the number two student miles behind you."

"Still spying on me?

"Sorry, it's a bad habit. Will you forgive me?"

"No . . . maybe . . . yes."

"Great. Has the bidding war for you started?"

"No war, yet."

"Oh, come on. Goldman and Credit Suisse must be after you."

"Funny that you should ask. I've had several rounds of interviews, but no actual offers. I think they can't get past my hijab."

"Never mind. I'll keep thinking you have big offers."

"Why?"

"I want you at Argyle. I'll start you at this year's Harvard MBA median base and add twenty percent for your class rank, and then add another twenty percent because you speak Arabic."

"Hey, that's twenty thousand higher than last year's class top offer."

"Is it not enough?" Rebecca asked, chuckling.

"No, it's a great offer."

"And all the usual perks and bonuses."

"Whoa, hold on," Fatima said. "What's my job title? Whom do I report to?"

"You'll report to me. I need a bi-lingual Arabic speaking analyst to follow the currency markets."

"How many weeks vacation do I get?"

"Two weeks the first year."

"Make it three."

"Done deal?"

"Deal."

"Great, expect a formal offer in the morning. I look forward to working with you."

Fatima went on to become Argyle's most incisive Middle Eastern analyst. When Rebecca rose to CEO and Chair of Argyle, Fatima became her chief operating officer. Rebecca hired many brilliant people, but Fatima had an uncanny ability to intuit her boss's thought processes and was bold enough to call her out on them when she thought Rebecca might be wrong.

* *

"How did you manage your vanishing act?" Fatima asked. "You're in trouble, Becky."

"Do you have someone who can do a first draft of my throw-in-the-towel speech?"

"Sure. Lots of people would love to write it, but I don't think you can quit."

"This is too hard for me. What was I thinking? I'm in way over my head."

"I told you this hare-brained idea would only lead to heartbreak."

"So, let me cut my losses and quit."

"Quitting is not an option for you. You would regret it for the rest of your life."

"What do you want me to do? I've been publicly humiliated. John Spencer called me a spoiled trust fund baby and the Wolf Global moderator cut me off from responding."

Fatima uttered a short, nervous laugh. Rebecca swept a stack of papers off her desk and slammed its surface with her fist.

"What the bloody h . . . devil. Why are you laughing at me?"

"I'm sorry. Look, this debate was a disaster, no doubt, but in a way it humanized you."

"Humanized me? I came across as a complete idiot."

"Not entirely. If you can stand it, you should look at the morning papers." Fatima drew the *Boston Post* from a stack she carried.

DEBATE OBSCENITY FROM CANDIDATE TREE? Rebecca's face adorned the front page, distorted in disbelief, frozen in a mega-mouth shark pose. Underneath a second headline read: DID SHE SAY 'F . . . ING A . . . HOLE'? TURN TO PAGE SIX FOR THE LIP READER DEBATE.

"I didn't say that."

"What did you say?"

"Freaking idiot. Spencer is a freaking idiot. Look at him," Rebecca said, taking out her sketchpad where she had an unfinished caricature, which portrayed Spencer with a face like a badly peeled potato and ears beaten into cauliflowers. He wore state trooper sunglasses perched on a nose that ski-sloped into pinched lips. His big bushy eyebrows marsh-grassed straight up and joined a thick carpet of hair, which domed his head pony-tailing back down his neck."

"Is that what you were doing when you were bent over your podium? I thought you were taking notes, but you never reemerged. Very cute. Save it for your presidential library. Lots of us have been working non-stop to try and save you from making a fool of yourself," Fatima, said her voice pitching up. "Forget about your cute little hobbies: caricatures, planning bird watching expeditions, goofy T-shirts, and forays to guard hatching turtle eggs in Nicaragua. You need to commit yourself and stop just going through the motions. Else I quit."

"You don't like my tees?" Rebecca's feelings were hurt but not so much that she couldn't find her sense of humor. She got up from her chair and came up to Fatima putting her hand on her shoulder. "You're right. Forgive me. Help me get back on track. Please."

Fatima pointed to Rebecca's chair. "Sit down and listen. And then listen some more. You need to take stock of the good news/bad news bind you're in."

"Okay, lay it all out for me," Rebecca said, as she slumped back down into her chair cradling her head in steepled hands.

"You know the bad news. You made a poor choice to get involved in politics. You're not well-suited for it."

"And the good news?"

"The pollsters you refused to meet with ran fresh numbers after the debate."

"Great, and my mid-single-digit rank is now in the low-single-digits, and heading toward zero."

"Yes, with male voters, but there have been some signs of life among women voters."

"After last night?"

"Yes, they didn't like the way the other candidates and moderator pushed you around. Many of the women viewers took it personally— more turned off by the male line of attack than by your abysmal performance."

"So what."

"If the field stays the same, and if you could make a decent come-back in the second debate, the next president will win the office with less than thirty percent of the vote. As impossible as it seems, you might be able to get to that percentage with a coalition of women, young voters, and environmentally-minded Evangelicals."

"I hate this."

"So why did you do this? I told you not to do this."

Rebecca hesitated for a long time before getting out of her chair and turning to look at the morning sky as Boston Harbor began to brighten.

"I thought I had a mission, to destroy John Spencer. But so far I've failed."

"A reporter after the debate passed me a confidential folder on Spencer."

Rebecca turned and stared at Fatima. "What's in it?"

"An uncompleted story on his nefarious activities with his cohorts."

Rebecca silently went to her wall safe and pushed her thumb on the access pad. The safe popped open, she withdrew a folder, returned to her desk and began thumbing through it. "Does your folder mention an offshore bank account in Grand Cayman?"

"Yes."

"Does the account in your folder have a number?"

"Yes."

"Are the first three digits 756?"

"Let me see. Yes, but I have five digits. 75643," Fatima said, as an incredulous look swept her face.

Rebecca tossed the whole folder in the air, and then clapped her hands as she smiled for the first time in days.

"I hired an investigator to check up on Spencer," she said. "He has an informant who has been supplying information, but it hasn't been complete enough to use. It must be the same person providing your reporter. Now the account has five digits, which means whoever is taking a bribe in the Caymans is giving more information. There are a few more dots to connect, but this could be a shortcut to knock Spencer out of the race and hopefully, out of politics."

"Whoa. Hold on Rebecca. Even if you knocked Spencer out of the race, then his votes will probably go to Withers, the Constitutional Party."

"Not much of the lesser of two evils."

Rebecca turned toward the window and squinted her eyes in the direction of Bunker Hill. Americans lost the fight that day, she told herself, but more significantly, the myth of British invincibility shattered.

"Wait," Rebecca said, turning back to face Fatima. "Did your pollster geniuses get any response to the debate segment about voter suppression?"

"Yes," Fatima said, "that was your one strong moment in the debate, and it played well with African-American and non-boycotting Hispanic viewers. But most of the Hispanic organizations are supporting a vote boycott. The pollsters predict that fewer than twenty percent of Hispanic voters will vote in this election cycle."

Rebecca paused briefly, carefully framing a question. "Is anyone in your network close to Marie Sanchez-Smith?"

"Maybe, why? Why would she talk to you? She hates the Tree family."

"I am not the Tree family. See if she would consider taking a meeting with me. And tell her that I voted for her in the last presidential election."

"Did you really vote for her?

"I certainly didn't vote for my brother."

"Looks like you're becoming quite the politician after all."

Rebecca glared at Fatima but said nothing.

"Do you still want a resignation speech written?"

"Yes, but maybe I'll save it for after the second debate."

Chapter 12

Ministry of the Lord Church
Nashville, Tennessee

A glass-domed arena the size of four football fields, the Nashville-based Ministry of the Lord Church, occupied the largest edifice in North America solely devoted to the worship of God. A surrounding one hundred acres parked thirty thousand cars, with room for five thousand recreational vehicles. More than ninety thousand worshippers traveled each week to hear the Reverend William Spurgeon, Rebecca's godfather, preach the gospel.

The Ministry served as the destination church for believers regionally, nationally, and internationally. On Thursday nights, chartered jets arrived from Asia, Europe, and South America, their passengers whisked away to Hotels of God, owned by the Ministry, where ardent believers paid top dollar especially for the higher-floored, "Closer To Heaven" suites. Often they brought children of marriageable age, and through a fee-based service, unions "made in heaven" were arranged and ultimately performed with full bridal services at a chapel attached to the amphitheater.

There was never a gray day at the Ministry. Cranes raised giant lights at the first sight of a cloud, washing the faces of the faithful with a heavenly incandescence. When Reverend Spurgeon himself appeared on stage, bursts of rainbow-like light pulsated through the glass roof.

Full broadcast services reached a global audience of over twenty million.

Sunday service started at nine a.m. Two young preachers — one male and one female — warmed the crowd. Backed by a two-hundred-person choir accompanied by an all-female Christian heavy metal band, they suffused the hall with the spirit. As excitement mounted, lights dimmed on the audience and stage. The choir hummed an incantation, and the pulsing of the crowd became palpable.

Soon, a single spotlight began roving around the arena, then a second. The lights searched the crowd, paused, wavered, and then finally honed in on a fixed spot center stage. Like moths attracted to a lone porch light, waving hands of the mesmerized stretched toward the illumination.

"Praise the Lord, Jesus is in the house, our Savior, Jesus Christ — the second coming is near."

The crowd went seismic when three hundred pounds of Reverend Spurgeon, aglow in a perfectly-positioned spotlight, began his signature move, a fervent dance step, pushing down on his right foot, flexing his knee, flinging his right arm out before ending in a half-bow. He then repeated it in reverse, left foot down, knees flexed, left arm out, finishing with another bow. The crowd roared as he skirted the edges of the stage, around the pulpit, dancing now with his back to the audience, finishing with a twirl to face the assemblage, continuing his godly shuffle at an ever-rising pace.

"Praise the Lord!"

His pulpit resounded with state-of-the-art microphones that fed into a powerful amplification system though even in a power outage every syllable he articulated would still ring clear.

"In Jesus' name. Today is a day of Redemption. We are here to celebrate the Life of Jesus, His sacrifice on the cross. Jesus died for all of us; His life is the power of love and speaks to the importance of devotion. But today, I don't plan to give a sermon. Instead, I have a special treat for you, a visitor — and one that I think will make both the Lord and all of you happy. The sister I'm about to introduce you to started memorizing the Bible at the age of five. One cold January day, on my first world revival tour, in the headwaters of the Rhine River I baptized her at the age of ten. Her faith in God and our Savior's love is a powerful force in her life. It's my great pleasure to introduce you to my beloved goddaughter, the next president of the United States, Rebecca Tree."

The choir sang, "Praise the Lord, Sing Hallelujah."

Rebecca wore a flowing white ministerial robe, red hair cascading over her shoulders. To the crowd's delight, she clumsily attempted a version of the Reverend's shuffle, pushing down her right foot, flexing her knee, her right arm out, then same with the left, finishing with a bow.

The already lathered crowd loved it though Spurgeon appeared to feign a look of outrage. As she finished her spin, Spurgeon joined in, holding her hand. The duo briefly danced a "Jesus Loves You" two-step with an energy and synchronicity that suggested God himself served as the choreographer that day.

Rebecca then took her place behind the pulpit, and looked to her right, seeing the proud gleam in her godfather's eyes, a rare source of approval she recalled from her childhood. The spectacle of such a giant over-the-top church didn't phase her since she'd seen the seeds of its potential in Colorado. Reverend Spurgeon pushed his church to its standing-room-only limits in Denver, finally moving his family south to this megachurch property. As an innovator, she had to respect its success; as a faithful person, the more the merrier, especially since the outwardly apolitical Spurgeon ran a global network of highly respected evangelical charities focused on aiding displaced refugee families.

She beckoned the crowd to be quiet. The house lights dimmed and then brightened; now, she could see the crowd as far more nuanced than some of their chants. Her eyes scanned the hall and the discordance of signs being held up surprised her. GOD IS GREEN, paired off with CHOOSE LIFE:YOUR MOM DID, PRAY FOR DIVERSITY and THE REPRIEVE: GOD'S CLIMATE POLICY

Rebecca's legs shook. She knew she had to put aside her discomfort at being cast in a public role and put on a convincing performance. Seeking strength, the words of Martin Luther King, Jr. surged through her: *I have seen the Promised Land. I want you to know tonight that we as a people will get to the Promised Land.*

On the pulpit, she had placed two different sermons, one written for her by Henry Hess's staff, and another she had struggled with for the last week. She hated them both.

Standing on this stage was too difficult for her.

In her life, if she mentioned God or religion to most friends she could see their eyes glaze over. Mainly she kept those thoughts to herself and in a way, they weren't very expressable in the first place. Every Sunday, no matter where in the world she found herself, Rebecca tried to find a quiet, small church with a service she could participate in or even just an empty sanctuary where she could spend some time praying for her lost loved ones.

He sets on high those who are lowly, and those who mourn are lifted to safety. Job 5:11.

She had believed that God had made her a promise as a child to step in where others failed her; with it, Rebecca began a path to pursue knowledge as well as to protect the birds and small creatures she found in the woods. God had her back, she had told herself, and she could do the same for others who may need her.

But then Jackson had been wrenched from her, and later her best friend Annie; she went through a difficult period of hating God for taking them from her. She tormented herself with questions for which she could not find answers. If God had her back, why did he take her parents, her twin, and, ultimately, anyone in her adult life she allowed herself to love? For several bitter years, she only went inside a church to take God to task directly. Finally, she began to soften, telling herself that life will never be fair or make sense, and thought of all the charitable work on behalf of others that people of faith often do, and she came back slowly but firmly to God and the religion she had adopted in her late teens.

Putting aside her printed copies, she looked out into the audience of the gathered faithful and began to extemporize.

She took a deep breath, briefly touched the locket under her robes, its gilded casing now worn smooth with her compulsive rubbing, some of its gemstones missing, and began with an incorrigibly weak voice.

"Over three hundred years ago, across England, in every town and every church a great debate raged. History might record it as one of the most bitter disputes of all times, and one which religion played a crucial role."

"Speak up!" Someone shouted from the back. She leaned closer to the microphone and continued, louder, looking to find a solid footing.

"The issue that day was slavery which I am sure we would all now agree is an incomprehensible evil.

"The anti-slavery forces numbered only a few, but they remained resolute in their commitment and faith. Many of them identified as Claphamites, a small group of English evangelicals led by William Wilberforce, intent on stopping England's involvement in the slave trade and in slavery itself.

"The Claphamites fought their battle within the English government proposing in the House of Commons and the House of Lords bill after bill to abolish the slave trade. Defeated time and again, they continued their campaign throughout England. Armed only with tools of persuasion and moral belief, their manner was civil, non-violent, and respectful.

"It took thirty years, but they prevailed.

"I was seventeen years old, just starting my undergraduate years at Oxford, in England, when I read a history of the Claphamites; I became so moved that I visited their church, Holy Trinity Clapham, which still stands, and became a member." She had found her voice but would she lose the crowd? She needed to fast forward this to the here-and-now.

"Today we are challenged by similar, sometimes identical issues that faced our fellow evangelicals in the nineteenth century. Slavery, and indentured servitude is sadly rearing its ugly head in many parts of the world. In our country, too many young men and women, are ripped from their families and communities and put into an ever-expanding prison system for non-violent first offenses

"Born-again men and women, led by Claphamites, evangelicals of a similar faith to ours, fought against slavery, debtor's prisons, even cruelty to animals; they did not hesitate to fight for unpopular positions.

"This is our mission — to do God's work, to help our neighbors, to disagree with open minds and express ourselves in civil discourse.

Rebecca paused as she scanned the crowd, hearing competing murmurs of approval and disapproval that swept different sections. To her left, her eyes took in the first three rows occupied by handicapped congregants, some able to clap, while others just stared.

Her eyes focused briefly further back in the hall at a young man in the aisle, perhaps an injured veteran, wearing sunglasses, and a baseball cap with strangely straight black hair dropping down to his cheeks. An oversized anti-war button was pinned to his jacket. He sat on an American flag cushion in a well-decorated wheelchair with custom wheel covers, pinwheels embellished with stars and stripes. Behind him a woman stood, dressed similarly to the young man, except with straight white-blonde hair below her baseball cap.

Reverend Spurgeon coughed loudly off to her side to reel her back in, and she resumed.

"As an evangelical, as a Claphamite," Rebecca said, trying to find her thread, "my mission is to do all I can do to stand with citizens around the world to fight to protect what God gave so generously to us. Only a great loving God could have inspired our natural earth, abundant in woods, rich soils, and species so diverse.

"I know many of you believe that God will handle the climate issue; after all, volcanic eruptions during the last decade have given us an extraordinary reprieve, unexpectedly lowering the earth's temperatures."

Rebecca could hear restless murmuring from the crowd rising in unfriendly shouts from one side.

"God put us on this great earth to do his work. We cannot reach out to him for temporal salvation; that is our responsibility. If God, in his infinite wisdom, gave us a reprieve then I believe it is his intention is to give us some extra time to heal our planet.

"Reverend Spurgeon has kept me informed of the wonderful work this congregation did to help our brothers and sisters who suffered so greatly when hurricane Deborah devastated North Florida last year. God would be pleased to see you reaching out to people who represent a rainbow of colors and many religions. I believe this is God's plan; the gates of heaven are open to all who do good works."

She could see that some in the crowd looked perplexed, a few shaking their heads and pointing fingers. Others nodded in assent, and a good portion of the crowd clapped. On the periphery, a few began to walk out.

Spurgeon pushed himself to the podium, seized the microphone, his voice roaring like thunder. "You're in God's house today. Rebecca has a valid point; we might not all agree, but we've never censured in this congregation. Hear her out. Praise Jesus, for all his bounty."

Spurgeon handed the microphone back and stood at her side, softly clapping his hands, swaying his body, eyes closed, energizing the audience.

When the crowd quieted, Rebecca said only, "Thank you and God bless." Sweat broke out on her brow while a chill passed through her body.

The choir started up again as Spurgeon shuffled up to Rebecca, arms outstretched, grabbing the microphone, starting a chant, while dancing in a circle with her.

"Hallelujah, Praise the Lord Jesus," Spurgeon said. "Prepare yourselves to fully accept God, and like this beautiful young lady just said, go and do the Lord's work in your communities and for your nation."

Spurgeon then leaned over, whispering into her ear. "Well done, brave lady. I hope you picked a good political strategy. I think the contribution plates might be a bit thin this week. Some of the more conservative old-timers look unhappy. The 'reprieve' debate is just too hot to handle at the moment.

"Maybe if you fail at the Presidency, we could form a little joint venture in the religion business. Perhaps it's time to modernize my mission, franchise, go solar. . . ."

"We'll see," Rebecca said, smiling with the relief of knowing that she did her best.

"Now, my dear. Do you wish to walk the aisles with me? It's my custom. The crowd loves it, and I'm sure they'll be doubly enchanted by your presence."

"I would love to," Rebecca said, as she looked nervously at her watch, "but I have an important meeting in Indianapolis in three hours. I'd better head to the airport."

* *

Two hydrogen-powered SUV's carrying Rebecca and a candidate protective unit began pulling out of the Church of Lord parking lot.

A grating noise, low bass notes, began to vibrate Rebecca's chest cavity.

Looking out her window, she observed a white van with Arizona plates being held by a church security officer in order to allow the motorcade to pass. In the front seat, she could make out the outlines of two shaved heads and a bone-thin couple with shoulders rocking, who appeared to be singing and clapping to the sounds of heavy metal born again rock, seemingly throwing their faces holy roller style upward to God.

Rebecca thought about commenting on the couple to her Secret Service escort agent, but she quickly became amused by a new distraction.

An elderly man with a nearly pure white head of hair crossed her line of vision driving a horse and cart half loaded with scrap metal.

The side of his wagon had a logo, crudely painted, proclaiming: CHRISTMAS COMES EVERY DAY. Underneath the logo, in smaller letters were written Samuel Winthrop Christmas, Proprietor. Proudly Recycling Greater Nashville for thirty years.

Piled on top of the cart, Rebecca could see a shiny new wheelchair folded up.

Chapter 13

Ex-President Maria Sanchez-Smith
Indianapolis

"How much further to Indianapolis?" Rebecca asked the driver.

"If the traffic stays this light, no more than forty-five minutes."

"Thank you," Rebecca said, turning to Fatima sitting in the back-seat next to her.

"How much time do we have with her?"

"Not we. You. No one else is allowed to be in the room. Ten or fifteen minutes, maybe she will give you twenty, but don't count on it. She has oral arguments before the Supreme Court in three days."

"It's amazing what she did in the last case."

"Gonzalez versus New Mexico?"

"Yes. Finally, the Supreme Court stopped these unconstitutional deportations by state governments. It's the first time in five years that this court came up with the proper application of justice."

* *

Maria Sanchez-Smith sat behind her desk surrounded by piles of legal briefs, barely looking up when Rebecca entered the room. She raised an index finger indicating Rebecca needed to wait as she then gestured to a chair for her to seat herself.

After a few minutes, Sanchez-Smith got up from behind her desk and moved towards the window of her office overlooking the city's main square.

"In 1864, two hundred African-Americans marched out of the town square in Union uniforms to fight for their country and to abolish slavery. Most of them died in battle. The same year arsonists burned the town's only African-American church. Freed slaves sheltered there described waking up to glass shattering and rooms filled with smoke. They fled for their lives. The few soldiers who returned after the Civil War had little or no opportunity.

"Now nearly two centuries later, I, a former president of the United States, spend most of my days and many sleepless nights trying to get fair treatment for Hispanics who continue, despite pockets of opportunity, cleaning the toilets and tending the gardens of privileged classes." Turning to face Rebecca, Sanchez-Smith said, "So what can I do you for you, Ms. Tree?"

"I want you to consider supporting my candidacy for the presidency."

Sanchez-Smith's eyes appeared to widen in disbelief, and a laugh rumbled out of her throat as she shook her head back and forth.

"Look, Ms. Tree, I can't blame you for your family, and I am not bitter about losing to your brother, but I remain outraged about the unpleasant effect it had on my family. The accusations of your brother's operatives nearly destroyed my marriage and caused devastating pain to my children."

"I am sorry. Sam Tree was a bully. He bullied me as a child, and he bullied anyone who got in his way. The last time I saw him, I was eight years old."

"Even if, for some unforeseen reason, I could put aside my feelings about the Tree family, I have to tell you that, so far, you're a terrible candidate.

"I don't understand why you are running for the presidency. There are life and death issues involved here; until the courts finally agreed to overthrow blatantly unconstitutional laws, hysterical xenophobic politicians had mass-deported nearly two million Mexicans, Muslims and Africans. It is heartbreaking; children have been ripped from their parents and placed in orphanages, which must feel like concentration camps to them.

"Do you appreciate what is at stake here?" Sanchez-Smith took a folder off her desk and angrily slammed it down in front of Rebecca. "Look at this; it sickens me."

Rebecca opened the folder and almost gagged. There was a cartoon of an obese man who appeared to be Mexican sitting on a chair made of cactuses with a noose around his neck. Another image portrayed an Arab man with white robes and a grotesquely hooked nose holding a dagger in one hand and sticks of dynamite with a lit fuse in the other. Two wrist-bound virginal looking blonde tweens with a look of pure terror on their faces sat at his feet.

"Who produces this?" a badly shaken Rebecca asked.

"We don't know. We think people associated with John Spencer, but we can't prove it."

"I know some people who might be able to find out. If you are willing, give me any leads you have. Surely you know that I am opposed to these deportation policies and any form of racism. They are un-American and, for me, un-Christian."

"Then damn it. Speak up, open up your pretty mouth, and use the formidable brain that I've been told you have. If you believe in what you just said to me, then make your voice loud, no make it *deafening*, and be clear."

"I will. I promise," Rebecca said plaintively.

"You were awful in the first debate," Sanchez-Smith said, her tone relaxing. "You had a look on your face, I don't know if it was boredom or fear, but you clearly didn't want to be there."

"I didn't want to be there. Who would choose to share a stage with these buffoons? If I had to share a lifeboat with them to get off a sinking ship, I would prefer taking my chances alone in the sea."

Sanchez-Smith eyes appeared to warm slightly at Rebecca's last remark and her head tilted slightly indicating some curiosity.

"So how are you going to resurrect your candidacy? If your heart rate were to go as low as your poll numbers, you would be clinically dead."

Rebecca roared with laughter, and now felt some hope that she could win Sanchez-Smith over. Her poll numbers had inched up, albeit at a snail's pace. She regained some ground since the debate though still stuck in fifth place, still in the low-single digits.

"Look, I let myself get bullied in the first debate. I was slow to respond. It won't happen again. Believe me, I know how to fight back. I won't be 'flat-lining' in the second round."

"I don't think that is going to lift you out of the cellar."

"Well, eventually I am going to win you over to my side, and that will be huge."

"Ms. Tree, I am starting to like you a bit, but this isn't reality to me. I have to prepare for my Supreme Court case," as she taps one of the stacks of dog-eared paperwork practically fencing her in. "I am sorry, but I don't think I can help you."

"Wait, President Sanchez-Smith. There is something I might be able to do to help you."

"I don't think so."

"What if I could drive a fatal stake into John Spencer's candidacy?"

"How?" Her eyes lit up.

"I can't share that, yet. Wait till the second debate. Could you answer my what if?"

"If John Spencer is driven out of the race by you, I might consider taking a closer look at your candidacy, but no promises. Also, I understand Aldo Peña is on your short list as a possible VP. If by some remote chance you become president, I would be more inclined to consider you if I someone I trusted played on your team."

Chapter 14

Second Debate
October 7

"Good evening. This is George Edgardo, reporting for ABC News, from San Francisco's Moscone Convention Center, where the second presidential debate has just concluded. We have expanded our post-debate coverage to a full hour with extensive excerpts.

"Let's start with Marla Pazer of the *Washington Post*.

"Marla, your thoughts?"

"I am in a state of shock, pleasant shock I must admit. Rebecca Tree, who put in an abysmal performance in the first debate, came out swinging at all her opponents, as well as the press corps. Ms. Tree had a great night."

"But Marla," Theodore 'Tug' Cabrera from CNN interjected, "I grant it that Ms. Tree certainly showed cleverness tonight, but for most Americans she is an unknown quantity. For those few Americans who will bother to vote in the upcoming election, she is just another Tree in the forest, and the country has seen enough Trees."

"Yes, Tug," Pazer continued. "Tree or no Tree, she spoke to the issues, presented a well-rooted critique of the American political system, and offered a vision of the future that made sense."

"Sense," Cabrera said. "More like nonsense to me. She is off with the fairies. 'Well-rooted?' A twenty-second-century America where corporations ignore shareholder value, where we all live in tiny ultra energy-efficient houses selling excess energy back to the utilities? Am I supposed to go back home after a hard day's work and spend two hours on an exercise bicycle producing electricity for my TV to watch Friday Night football? I don't think so."

"You're lucky to have a house. I guess you are paid enough to build on stilts. Over two million American have lost their homes to rising waters from global warming in the last decade."

"Didn't heavenly induced volcanic activity solve our global warming problem? I'll keep my ninety-eight-inch plasma TV and my six thousand-square-foot house, stilts and all, thank you very much."

"Men never change. It's pathetic," Pazer said, her voice rising. "Two months ago, I went to a party at a beachfront mega-mansion on Long Island. They bragged all night about whose house had the bigger house stilts. I think you guys need to get away from your fixations on size."

"All right," Edgardo said, clearly agitated, "We are veering off-course here. Your debate on house stilts might be more appropriate for a pre-dawn Saturday morning home-improvement show. Let's move on, if we can.

"Our senior political analyst, Willard Thomas, is joining us now on a satellite feed. Willard, can you give us your take on how tonight's debate might affect the current presidential race?"

"Before the debate," Thomas said, "the Las Vegas bookmakers increased the day-to-day odds that Ms. Tree would soon drop out. The odds of John Spencer winning the race went up steadily during the same period. Now, as they say, all bets are off."

"So, is Rebecca Tree tonight's winner?"

"Yes, she won the debate, but decreased any remote possibility of becoming president."

"I don't understand."

"Simple. If the sensational charges she made against Spencer are credible, then the primary benefactor will be Constitutional Party candidate Ron Withers. Perhaps Ms. Tree could run third if she gains momentum out of this debate performance, but she can't hope for much better."

"All right, let's play a clip from the beginning of the debate."

"The American political system, well represented here by two sitting United States senators, has failed the American people," Rebecca said.

"The dismantling of all controls over campaign finance has made politics a pay-to-play game, resulting in the enrichment of politicians and the impoverishment of the people."

"It takes years to master the legislative process and to refine the skills needed to bring significant legislation to a floor vote," said Senator Yaled. "Ms. Tree has none of these skills, and certainly no experience in governance. None of us like to spend as much time as we do raising money, but I can assure you, I always vote for the best interests of my constituents."

"Perhaps, but the best interests are influenced, usually drastically, by the best contributors," Rebecca said.

"Perhaps Ms. Tree has a better suggestion on how to run our political system," said Senator Wyeth.

"As a matter of fact, I do," Rebecca said. "It's not a difficult fix. Simply triple the salaries of all the members of the House and Senate."

"What!" said Governor Withers. "Well, I can see that Ms. Tree likes to spend the people's money lavishly."

"Triple their salaries in exchange for full disclosure and a robust system of self-regulation," Rebecca said. "No contributions from special interests, no secret meetings, no revolving doors into high paid lobbying jobs or seats on corporate boards upon retirement."

"The American people don't have a trust fund, in case you didn't know," said Governor Withers. "And the Supreme Court has long decided these issues."

Ah, there's the trust fund right hook again. She swallowed her desire to respond since this would only get messy: she did not live on Tree money but it did provide the start-up capital for her campaign.

"Yes, primarily in *Citizens United v. FEC*, where the Court removed restraints on political independent expenditures by corporations, associations, or labor unions. In addition, *McCutcheon v. FEC* lifted restrictions of aggregate contributions by wealthy donors, but that has nothing to do with self-regulating, which is what I am talking about," Rebecca said.

"The Congress of the United States costs the taxpayers a billion dollars a year in salaries, staff, and benefits, while, according to several business school studies, more than a hundred billion dollars a year is given away in unnecessary tax breaks, subsidies, and mismanagement. Congress' refusal to allow Medicare to negotiate drug prices costs the taxpayers twenty billion dollars a year, and that's just one example. Spending an extra two billion dollars to force them to work honestly and exclusively for their constituents seems like a good deal to me."

"About half a dozen exchanges on the issues similar to this one came up in the debate," Edgardo said. "Has Ms. Tree proposed innovative solutions to problems that have vexed the American system? Marla, your comments please."

"I thought this exchange was dynamic. Who would have ever thought to pay these legislative failures more money to make them behave?"

"This is crazy," Cabrera said, "this will never happen. We know that. All her nutty ideas and ten bucks will get you is a coffee and a donut."

"Tug's idea of helping Main Street America is to let them eat donuts. I loved her food stamp proposals—totally brilliant."

"Let's go to that excerpt," Edgardo said, "it is one of the debate highlights that is trending on Twitter."

"Ms. Tree," began A.J. Cohen, the Debate Moderator. "You said earlier that many of the domestic problems that face Americans are solvable. Can I put that comment to the test?"

"Please do," Rebecca said.

"The American taxpayer spends over one hundred billion dollars per year on its food stamp program to help alleviate poverty, but many critics see the program as a failure," Cohen said. "How would you solve this problem?"

"Sure," Rebecca replied. "Food stamps need to be restructured to maximize their effectiveness, and their overall costs need to be reduced, which can be accomplished in several ways. The government needs to build out a premium food stamp program where recipients commit to a card only usable for healthy foods, which would also have associated programs that promote cooking skills and micro-farming. The end result is one in which each recipient has a better chance of actually feeding their family, as well as creating a means to step out of a cycle of poverty. While the premium program will cost more initially, the cost reductions achieved by having fewer sick, while helping impoverished citizens move into micro-industries where they can then become tax-payers, will be a benefit to our society as a whole."

"Marla and Tug. Your comments?"

"Well," Pazer began. "This innovation thing is fascinating. Only one American president had been granted a patent, which would be Abraham Lincoln. Ms. Tree has, I believe, over one hundred patents naming her as inventor or co-inventor. I think it makes an interesting concept: an entrepreneurial president who looks to innovation to solve problems. She threw out a half-dozen ideas tonight, which, at a minimum, are worth a serious look. And, if you are watching social media, you'd know her ideas have caused a bit of excitement."

"I can assure you," Cabrera said, his voice filling with contempt, "that Rebecca Tree is no Abraham Lincoln. Besides, Lincoln's invention was a cockamamie idea — to lift boats over shoals and obstructions in a river."

"For once, I agree with my esteemed colleague. Especially since the Chinese invented river locks in the first century."

"All right. Enough," Edgardo said. "I grew up in a house where my father always taught me to save the best part of the meal for last. So, we will conclude with what has been christened the 'Smackdown in San Francisco' between Rebecca Tree and John Spencer. Let's go to the clip."

The moderator directed a question to Spencer. "You're considered by many a divider, and others have accused you of being a racist. What steps would you take to heal our divided country, if elected?"

Looking into the camera lens, Spencer offered what appeared to be a well-rehearsed answer. "Restoring law and order to our beloved country, particularly our troubled border states, would be a positive step to begin the healing process. I believe that's the message that our good citizens, fed up with anarchy, are sending to Washington."

"And as to the racism charge?" the moderator asked.

Spencer theatrically slammed his fist down on his podium. "These scurrilous allegations are but a sham. With God as my witness, I harbor no ill will toward any man, but by the same token, I am proud and American-born, and we need to take care of our own first."

"I would like to respond to Mr. Spencer," interjected Rebecca.

"Yes, Ms. Tree," the Moderator said. "Please, your response."

"Neither God nor the American public, will be Mr. Spencer's witness this day," Tree said, her eyes daggering into Spencer. "I have watched Mr. Spencer's recent speeches and the careless liberty which he takes in his Biblical references. I believe his gospel to be a shameful version, written by a devil, not a disciple, and Mr. Spencer spews a doctrine of hate across our great land. If Mr. Spencer wishes to quote a higher source, then he might consider serving a gospel, which speaks of love and tolerance."

Spencer's face went red. His knuckles tightly gripped the podium's edge, turning greenish-white.

"Ms. Tree, how dare you attack me," he spluttered.

"I believe I speak a truth that most Americans feel in their hearts."

"I serve my country by defending it. And I serve my God," Spencer bellowed.

"No sir," she replied. "You serve only yourself, running, with surrogates, a multi-million dollar business that sells hate books, hate music, and hate websites—that's your currency. You have a well-stocked inventory of products to attack our fellow Americans of a different skin color."

Spencer stepped around his podium, his face purple, one eyelid caved, the other in a full twitch, and began to scream at Rebecca, a tone of desperation seeming to flood into his voice as if he had fallen without warning into a pit of poisonous snakes. "You're a devil . . . a liar. If you weren't a woman, I'd . . . "

Rebecca appeared serene as she leaned her right elbow on the podium and cupped her chin. She seemed to savor the moment; she squinted and flashed an icy smile at Spencer before making a summoning motion at her opponent with her left hand.

"If I weren't a woman, you would do what?"

Chapter 15

Lord Trippington
Dallas, Texas

Four days after the second debate, an all black 797 emblazoned with the logo of Trippington Air landed at Dallas/Fort Worth International Airport. The main cabin's usual configuration of one thousand seats was modified so that only one throne-sized seat remained in the middle of a massive horseshoe-shaped desk with six embedded computer screens.

Lord Trippington sat hunched over a screen whose dedicated monitor displayed a label: Calorie Tracker. He watched as five years of data scrolled by, showing his average caloric intake by year, by month, and by week.

A sidebar displayed the measured volumes of inputs as well as the weight of urine and solid waste matter that passed out of his body.

A graph display drew intersecting lines tracking the caloric intake against the waste removal.

Ten years ago Lord Trippington weighed four hundred pounds. At six-foot-four-inches tall, he now weighed one hundred and forty pounds. An extreme calorie restrictor, he never ate more than eleven hundred calories a day.

Trippington had built a research lab near his global headquarters in Coventry, England where he spent millions investigating the lifespan of mice grouped by their caloric intake. With five years of mice research under his belt, he began similar studies on dogs, cats, and rhesus monkeys. After animal rights activists had exposed the cruelty of the studies, the English government banned them, and Trippington secretly built a new lab in the Philippines.

A few minutes after landing, the senior partner of Stryker Coldwell, his lead American law firm, came on board.

"So let's make sure I understand your analysis," Trippington said. "It is your opinion that if Senators Yaled or Wyeth are elected, we will not get any new Supreme Court justices appointed favorable to our case."

"Yes, Spencer is with the program if he manages to stay in the race and Withers is on our side."

"And well-provided for by us?"

"I can't speak to that, but I wouldn't dispute it."

"And this silly girl? Sam Tree's little brat sister."

"We don't know enough about her. But I wouldn't count on her. She seems unpredictable."

"Have we invested any money in her campaign?"

"Not my bailiwick. You need to talk to your political people. I can only speak to the legal cases that you are concerned with and what might happen to the Supreme Court if there is the expected vacancy."

Trippington looked at his watch. "I have to be at a meeting with our U.S. and global news editors in an hour. I'll get back to you on the legal cases."

* *

Trippington had bought, in foreclosure, the Bank of America Plaza, Dallas's tallest skyscraper. He rebuilt it to its original specification adding the intended twin tower and a hotel.

The building headquartered Wolf Global, his conglomerate of local and regional newspapers, over fifty television stations, cable and satellite providers, and six of the top ten most visited websites in America. Astute contributions to corrupt politicians had bought him exemption after exemption to media ownership rules, which had been originally designed to limit the kind of octopus control Trippington now had on information flow.

For years, white shoe law firms in his employ had beaten back dozens of lawsuits attempting to dismantle his media empire, but one case, brought by a determined rural Mississippi sole practitioner, had persisted and it now appeared on track to reach the Supreme Court within two years.

In a large conference room on the top floor of the skyscraper, over fifty senior Wolf Global news editors had assembled. Many of them had flown overnight from news bureaus around the world. Trippington entered the room wearing a black parachute jumpsuit, and black sneakers, his face partially obscured with thick black eyeglasses and his head shaved. Behind him, an aide carried a bottle of spray disinfectant and several sterilized, sealed hand towels.

The managing editor offered his hand to Trippington, who ignored it.

"Thank you all for assembling on such short notice for this emergency meeting. You are the best-paid, seemingly most intelligent group of journalists ever brought to work together in one organization. I used to have a high opinion of you all, but, unless you execute a quick turnaround, I would advise most of you to seek other employment."

"Nobody could foresee the outcome of the second debate," said Carruthers, the managing editor.

"Your ability to foresee is why I pay you big bucks. Foresight gets you huge bonuses. I can foresee that, as of now, there will be no yearly windfalls coming your way. Forget about your summer beach house, your new mistress or boyfriend, your next E-class convertible."

"What do you want us to focus on?"

"We had two good horses in the race — Spencer and Withers. This skinny hotheaded lady has probably knocked out Spencer."

"We have our best dirt diggers working on Rebecca Tree."

"If you can't find the right dirt, then make sure you make it up. Nothing works better than an artfully constructed lie to obscure the truth. We trolled Sanchez-Smith. Hold on," Trippington said, as he summoned over an aide with whom he had a whispered exchange. "Did your security team search all these idiots?"

"Yes, no cellphones, no hidden tape recorders. Plus we swept the room twice for listening devices."

Turning back to the now ashen-faced journalists, he said, "Go back, and dig deeper into Yaled. He is half-Lebanese. Must have some terrorist relatives. Wyeth is clearly a 'poof'. Find some of his wife's friends. She must cry on someone's shoulders.

"Dig into Tree's military record. Army intelligence, probably all made up. No, better. Maybe she tortured a few people in her time. Looks just the type. She's not married, and we've treated that with kid gloves. Take the gloves off. No results. Then no jobs for most of you.

"Am I understood?"

Trippington walked out of a silent room, as his aides handed him sanitized towels and spritzed disinfectant on his black parachute jumpsuit.

Chapter 16

Aftermath of Second Debate

The tabloids had gone apoplectic in the days after the debate. A tight shot of Rebecca, eyes bright, fingers beckoning her opponent from the lectern, ran under the headline: BRING HIM ON, TAUNTS TREE.

Millions watched the clip online, and local television affiliates followed the post-debate debate for nearly a week. Talk show hosts used the event as fodder for a month. Overnight, Vegas bookmakers dropped the odds on Rebecca to eight-to-one, and many took up the bet, enough to lower the odds to five-to-one by the following day.

The New York Times published an editorial entitled "Standing Up to Demagoguery," stating that "Rebecca Tree created an exemplary profile in courage among a field of candidates who have failed to take a principled stand against the blathering rabble-rousing of John Spencer. This paper did not take Ms. Tree's candidacy perhaps as seriously as we should have. No matter the result of the upcoming election, this country is in debt to Ms. Tree for her courageous outing of Mr. Spencer."

Rebecca was awoken very early the morning after the debate with a long encrypted text from Oswaldo Lemus on the messaging flashlight he had provided her.

Becky, did you happen to read about this terrible cable and phone service outage that shut down large parts of Phoenix last week? It took them 24 hours to get it all untangled. They even had to call in outside contractors. Arcadia, Arizona got hit badly.

John Spencer's home was in Arcadia, Arizona.

They had to call in outside contractors, how interesting, Rebecca thought.

Rebecca had much to be pleased about that day, save for the hounding from Merewether Tree. All morning he called her office, demanding a video conference. Later that day, she relented.

"Why did you do that?" Tree, as his face filled the screen, began jabbering wildly. "Have you no sense? Hess has crafted a careful plan, which step-by-step will give you a small plurality on Election Day, enough to be president. Now you've gone and energized Spencer's base. This won't work. Spencer needs to draw enough votes from the other candidates to give the presidency to you."

"Why Grandfather," she said, mimicking his stern tone, "I thought you, more than anyone, would be proud of me."

Tree's face blackened like the sky before a sudden storm. "This is politics. You need to control everyone's interests, not destroy them. This isn't in the playbook."

"I threw that playbook out." In her mind, she popped up an imagined umbrella over herself. "Do you want to write a new one? I'll read it with great interest."

Rebecca then hung up.

* *

After the second debate, the traffic on Rebecca's website surged, small donors flooding the site contributing mostly donations of five, ten and twenty dollars. The network, born in the halls of Harvard, spread virally across America's campuses. She no longer needed Tree family money to run a robust campaign. Her favorable numbers polled higher, while Spencer's plunged, with sixty percent of the electorate now interested in giving her a second look.

Wolf Global quickly mounted their counterattack: promoting stories questioning Rebecca's family values, her military service, and her sexual preferences. But the attacks became counter-productive as many segments of the electorate, previously apathetic, became increasingly offended and irritated with the tone taken by the Wolf Global correspondents and started taking Rebecca's candidacy seriously.

Spencer's numbers continued to collapse. A few weeks later, *The Washington Post* published an investigative piece substantiating her accusations. Sources, not forthcoming before the debate, suddenly deep-throated to the *Post*'s reporters, revealing that Spencer and his business associates had sponsored and profited greatly from websites that promoted "I Hate Hispanic Heritage Month." They sold images of Mexicans hanging from crosses and sniper rifles with racist caricatures of blacks, Hispanics, and Arabs displaying through their scopes.

Two weeks later, Spencer dropped out of the race. Still in last place, Rebecca no longer polled single digits. She gained headway with the voters while acquiring new enemies.

Chapter 17

Campaign Gains Traction

"Congratulations Becky," Fatima said, as she got up from a desk at Rebecca's chaotic Boston campaign headquarters. On the floor boxes of campaign buttons and posters overflowed. Two exhausted staffers played ping pong on a red, white and blue table with a slogan painted on each end, RESTORE RATIONALITY WITH REBECCA TREE. Dramatic black and white photographs displayed on the walls, each portraying a family of an animal species near extinction including Javan Rhinoceros from Vietnam, Cross River Gorillas from Nigeria, Black-Footed Ferrets from North America, and Polar Bears from the Artic.

In the background, speakers played out Rebecca's newly adopted theme song picked by Gilad Levine, a die-hard country western music fan. The plaintive nasal twang of Willie Nelson sang *Living in the Promised Land*, its lyrics a welcoming tribute to immigrants, "the tired and weak," promising to "make them strong," here in America, where they could bring their foreign songs, and "we will sing along."

"Did I do something right?" Rebecca said, as she glanced at the polar bear poster, a mother bear with three cubs wrapped in her folds, with the slogan underneath SAVE MY FAMILY.

"No, I did. I just got off the phone with Sanchez-Smith's chief of staff. We have a speaking slot for you at National Association of Hispanics convention next month."

"I thought they weren't going to have any presidential candidates speak as part of the vote boycott."

"I am a great persuader."

"You should run for this job."

"Seriously, Sanchez-Smith and the association's executive board are more than pleased about your takedown of John Spencer and . . ."

"And what?"

"Wolf Global's attacks on you pushed her buttons."

"How do you know all this?"

"Her chief of staff went to my high school. One class under me. Over the years, I did a few small favors for her. We've been talking a lot on the phone."

"You never told me that."

"When they write my biography, it will be entitled *The Tree Whisperer.*"

"You're funny — sometimes." Rebecca said, as a grin of satisfaction spread across her face. "What else do we have scheduled?"

"Well, since you 'kneecapped' Spencer, we've been flooded with blue chip invitations," Fatima said coyly pulling a stack of printouts from behind her back.

"You mean I don't have to go to any state fairs and pretend to eat fried Snickers on a stick?"

"No. It's arugula all the way from now on. First, Asra Farres wants a one-hour interview on CNN. Prime time. And they will promote it big-time."

"Is she doing the other candidates?"

"No, that's the best part. They all have refused."

"Intriguing. Can we put anything off-limits?"

"Maybe, a small carve out."

"No Sam Tree questions. It's not fair to Ashley and her children. And no demeaning tabloid love-life questions.

"Okay. Let me negotiate it? And then . . ." Fatima grinned and did a drum beat with her fingers, pretending to fumble with an envelope.

"Let's see. How about the Ebenezer Baptist Church?"

"I can't speak there. It is hallowed ground. I am not worthy."

"True. Speak, no, but you told me once that singing in their gospel choir was on your bucket list."

Rebecca came from around her desk and embraced Fatima in a long hug.

"Are you serious? That would make me so happy. You have no idea. I sang in my school choir but nothing like this. They've won the world gospel competition the last three years. That's amazing. I love you for doing this."

"*Tree Whisperer*," Fatima laughed softly, her finger to her lips.

* *

The church lights dimmed, and a spotlight ellipsed the curtain. As the draped fabric opened, the Ebenezer Baptist Church choir, led by famed Choirmaster Horton Johns, sang the first stanza of "Amazing Grace." A wave of surprise swept through the rows; amongst a choral sea of mostly black faces, a tall redheaded woman with a mass of brilliant freckles stood proudly in the mezzo section. Worshippers in the front rows took out their cellphone cameras and memorialized the scene, and the next day, a slow news day, many newspapers around the world ran the quirky image on their front page, giving her campaign some additional traction. Within a week, Rebecca's polling numbers inched up several points, finally moving her out of last place, closing in on number two.

A week later, Rebecca addressed the National Association of Hispanics, held at the Apostolic Church of Faith in Dallas, Texas. Fatima had learned that the executive board had debated lifting the planned election boycott depending on Rebecca's speech and Sanchez-Smith's blessing. Rebecca knew the magnitude of this moment and she grabbed it. She delivered the speech in Spanish, bringing the crowd to its feet at the end when she recited a verse from the poet Jose Marti:

Cultivo una rosa blanca	*I cultivate a white rose*
En julio como en enero	*In July as in January*
Para el amigo sincero	*For the sincere friend*
Que me da su mano franca	*Who gives me his honest hand*
Guantanamera, guajira Guantanamera	

At the end of Marti's poem, stage lights dimmed as a singer offstage belted out "America the Beautiful." The woman perhaps most revered by Hispanic-Americans, Maria Sanchez-Smith, appeared on stage, holding a single white rose for Rebecca. Since the second debate, a few alternative media publications had been speculating wildly on the possibility that the former president, who had been brutally defeated in her re-election bid by Sam Tree, might in fact now endorse a candidate named Tree.

Sanchez-Smith whispered a few words in Rebecca's ear; Rebecca smiled widely.

"Rebecca Tree is an extraordinary woman," Sanchez-Smith said, addressing the crowd. "She has great compassion and is blessed with a vision for an America where each of us, black, brown, red, white, can build a bright future. As we know all too well, our country is wracked with division. Ugly forces are at work, led by malcontents frustrated with their lives' shortcomings. They compensate by targeting people of color, mainly our brothers and sisters who have come to El Norte seeking a better life.

"I have listened to all five candidates in their first debate. Fortunately, now thanks to Ms. Tree, the field has narrowed to four. The choice has become clear for me; only one candidate has the courage and principals to stand up against the forces of division that threaten our people.

"I urge all of you here tonight, and all of you listening at home, to join me on Election Day to vote for Rebecca Tree. As for me, I have cleared my schedule for the duration of the campaign to join Ms. Tree in her quest for the presidency."

Sanchez-Smith waved farewell to the crowd as she began to leave the stage but stopped halfway. She pivoted back to the microphone to join the chants erupting from the first few rows of the hall.

"VOTA, VOTA!"

The whole audience joined in, and the chant quickly swelled into a deafening roar, new chants added along the way.

"VOTA! VOTA! VOTA!"

"TENGO GUSTO DE SANCHEZ-SMITH!"

"AHORA NO BOYCOTT!"

"SI VOTA!"

"TENGO GUSTO DE SANCHEZ-SMITH Y REBECCA!"

Chapter 18

Interview on CNN's Hot Seat

"This is CNN's Asra Farres, the host of tonight's *Hot Seat*, with a one-on-one interview with Rebecca Tree, who has suddenly and unexpectedly emerged from the back of the presidential candidates' pack into a contender."

Turning to Rebecca, Farres said, "Before we begin, I would like to compliment you on the beautiful outfit you are wearing tonight."

Rebecca assumed this was sarcasm but took it in stride, thanking her while crossing and then uncrossing her legs. She wore a flowing black silk top with a midi skirt completed by black leather running shoes, matching her favorite knee-length soccer referee socks, all black with white stripes around the top. Underneath a plain black linen shirt, she wore a T-shirt from the Buglife charity promoting the preservation of bees and insects.

Petite and perfectly coifed, Farres was dressed in a royal blue business suit with a tailored white blouse and a bold red scarf around her neck; her manicured nails glittered blue. An intoxicating perfume — smelling like fabricated flowers no bee would be attracted to — clogged the air around her.

Rebecca had to restrain herself from gagging.

"Welcome, Ms. Tree." Farres said, initiating the formal part of the program.

"Thank you. I am pleased to be here," Rebecca said, her tone and facial expressions auditioned in front of her bathroom mirror earlier in the day.

"Let's start. Certain media outlets have been relentless, after the second debate, in aggressively attacking you. And some seem very focused on framing you as a spoiled 'trust fund' baby born with a silver spoon in her mouth, out of touch with the problems of average Americans. Can you respond to these attacks?"

"I think we are talking about Wolf Global, which practices an unfortunate brand of journalism based on lying first, lying loudest and not worrying about the truth being revealed down the road."

"Fine, that's a strong editorial, but let's focus on their claim."

"Sure, I wish I was a trust fund baby because that would normally mean that my parents had lived out full lives, but sadly they died at an early age. There was no trust; instead, a term life insurance policy named my sister and me as beneficiaries. The monies from that policy paid primarily for my education and related expenses. I started working part-time at the age of eighteen, and I have worked part or full-time ever since."

"Why do you think Wolf Global has become so nasty about you?"

"Because I knocked out their candidate. Wolf Global has historically influenced legislation, which gave them unwarranted exceptions to long-standing media ownership rules. This speaks to the primary problem the American political system faces. Monied special interests influence and even write legislation in their favor. And ordinary Americans are hurt in the process. Wolf Global has its eye on the next Supreme Court and is worried that in the event there is a vacancy, they might not get a nominee of their liking. Lord Trippington and his editors are the Pinocchios of the news business and the American people are getting bored with their manipulations."

"Okay, your position seems clear. Let's move on. Your grandfather is considered to have been the most powerful senator in America. Can you speak about your relationship with him?"

"Merewether Tree was my legal guardian after my parents died. But, in truth, I saw very little of him growing up or as an adult."

"But going back to Wolf Global, they say, if you are elected, you would be his puppet."

Rebecca laughed, a bit too loudly, as she became increasingly annoyed with Farres. "Let's be clear here. Merewether Tree and I don't see eye to eye. We're hardly buddies and don't share much common ground. He is an old-school oil and gas man; my business career has been devoted to supplanting oil and gas with renewables."

"But you are the nominee of his party, the Millennium Populists."

"Understood. And I agree with some of their positions, but not all. I am my own woman. My grandfather started this journey, by asking me to run, but I will go down a path of my choosing."

"Okay. Turning to the last debate, Governor Withers attacked you about your religion, painting you as the member of an obscure Christian sect."

Rebecca chuckled; she knew she could hit the question out of the ballpark. She straightened her back and crossed her long legs again, knocking one knee under the table.

"Withers seemed to want to say 'cult' in that exchange, but he or his staff should have done some homework. If he is so badly schooled on the facts, he shouldn't be thinking about running a country. I am a Claphamite, with Born Again credentials well established in nineteen-century England. I am proud of my adopted faith with its history as a voice of charity and political action in defense of the powerless and the oppressed. They fought valiantly for issues deeply unpopular in its day."

"So as to it being a sect?"

"Of course, it is a sect. Most churches from the Anglican Church to the Methodist and so on are breakaways from larger groups, and usually, the bigger group had only unkind words to say about the non-conformists who wanted to leave."

"Okay, let's move on."

"Could I say one more thing about Texas Governor Withers?" Rebecca said, a mischievous smile flashing.

"Please."

"I think the governor might have some kind words about the Claphamites as they fought, with others, against debtor prisons. After all, he declared bankruptcy not once but twice over the last fifteen years."

"Touché," Farres said, a look of pleasure crossing her face, as she appeared happy with the ratings that would come with a spunky guest. "Are you a billionaire, Ms. Tree?"

"I've earned a few billion, but I recycle my earnings."

"What does that mean?"

"I tithed my salary in my first full-time job to my church. The standard ten percent."

"And your first job?"

"U.S. Army. Private then lieutenant. As I earned more money, I gave more away, so now I am a reverse tither and I give away ninety percent of my income to a cross-section of charities."

"*Ninety* percent?"

"Yes, but don't feel sorry for me. I have more than ample funds to live on, and I receive an added benefit: the government gets less of my money to misspend and waste."

"Huh," Farres said, looking stumped. "I would like to revisit the first debate," Farres said, appearing to struggle a bit to recover control of the interview.

"There was a lot of back and forth about terrorism, and you tried unsuccessfully to chime in. Can you share some of your unexpressed thoughts? And a couple of post-debate commentators criticized eye rolls on your part and looks of disdain."

"Well, if I had received fair time, I would not have had to resort to non-verbal clues. But I was excluded from a subject that I have some personal knowledge about and the others have none."

"Okay, let's hear what you wanted to say."

"Hot air is not a defense against terrorism. Braggadocio is not a defense. Name-calling other religions plays into our enemies' game plans."

"Sure that's fine. But give us some concrete proposals of how to combat these global threats."

"Well instead of blowing hot air and hate rhetoric everywhere, the Senate could start by ratifying the global Banking Transparency Treaty, which would allow anti-terrorist units to drill down deeply into financial transactions. This would cripple some forms of terrorist organizations' transactional ability. Money, when used as a weapon, must be disarmed."

"But congressional opponents say this treaty threatens our sovereignty."

"This is nonsense. Sovereignty is not absolute. We have treaties for arms control, fishing rights, enslavement of children. Come on. It isn't about sovereignty; it is about added costs which the bankers don't want to pay for compliance."

"And what else would you propose?"

"I would recall all one hundred dollar bills and ask the EU to do the same for the one hundred Euro note."

"What, that's crazy."

"Excuse me. Don't say that's crazy," Rebecca said, her face flushed with anger. A headache hit her temples from a toxic mix of the host's perfume and personality.

"The one hundred dollar bill is the currency of choice for drug traffickers, money launderers, black marketers, and terrorist organizations. I would recall and reissue as well as tax all bills with questionable bona fides."

"Okay. Can we talk a bit about your military career?"

"No. This interview is supposed to concentrate on the issues. I would like to stay there," Rebecca said, as she could hear the producer screaming at Farres through her earpiece. A few words came through . . . *losing control . . . hit harder . . . under her skin.*

"Ms. Tree. Are you a liberal?" Farres asked, sounding rattled, searching.

"Hardly an issue, but you're the interviewer, okaaay . . ." Rebecca said, a sarcastic tone coming into her voice as she began to mimic Farres' nasality. "I don't believe that these political catchalls are either helpful or accurate, and they obscure the real issues. I am an environmentalist, which I see as the purest exercise of conservative principals. I believe in fiscal responsibility and that the government needs to be prudent in how it spends, which might make me a conservative. I believe that women should have control over their destinies, especially when it concerns their health, reproductive issues, and workplace rights. So that might make me a liberal. I am fully committed to equal rights for all Americans, majorities as well as minorities, so that should make me a liberal as well as a conservative."

"So left or right?"

"It's an artificial distinction."

"Ms. Tree, I am asking the questions," Farres said, pushing her finger into her earpiece as more loud but indistinguishable words came out from the control room. "Do you want me to repeat the question?"

Rebecca glared at Farres. She had worn her running shoes; she could make a run for it. Instead she reluctantly anchored her shoes into the carpet. "No. I would prefer a term of my choosing. I would like to be seen as a futurist, looking forward to solutions that will resolve the urgent problems that we face now in the present."

"Sounds like a point of view that is very difficult to implement. We need to go to a break now. We will return to our lightning round with short listener-supplied questions and one-sentence maximum responses from you. Are you up for that?"

"Sure, I will dust off my best run-on sentences," Rebecca said, relieved that at least the Farres questions were over.

* *

"Okay, here we go with the lightning round." Farres had a stack of index cards she rifled through. "Our first question is from John Taranto from your hometown of Boston, who asks, 'Do you think the Boston Red Sox can win the pennant this year?'"

"Yes, if they can find a good left-hander to bolster their pitching staff."

"Okay, good. Next, is from Alyssa Collins of Denver. "Are there any innovations that would improve community-police relationships?"

"Cities should fund police scholarship funds with incentive monies from reductions in lawsuit payouts."

"I'm sorry," Farres said, "but I am going to break my rules here. Can you flesh that idea out a bit?"

"Sure, Boston has a program like this. The city used to average fifty million dollars a year in payouts for legal claims and lawsuits. They have cut this number down by seventy-five percent with one-third of the savings going into a higher education fund for children of police and fire personnel. It is very popular."

"Okay, next question from a law professor, Robert Darbyshire, who asks 'What would you look for in a Supreme Court nominee?' And back to our short responses, please."

"I would look for a person committed to the concept embodied in the statute of the scales of justice, the blindfolded lady, adjudicating without fear or favor, impartial to wealth or power."

"We have another court question, from another law professor, Melissa Beyers, which asks for your list of the worst Supreme Court decisions."

"This might be a long sentence," Rebecca said, momentarily hesitating as she gathered her thoughts, "but we could start with *Dred Scott*, which allowed free slaves to be returned to slavery, then *Plessy v. Ferguson*, which affirmed separate but equal, then *Korematsu*, which endorsed the detention of Japanese-Americans during World War II, and finally *Citizens United*, which helped aggravate the political mess we now find ourselves in."

"This question is from Florence Anderson from Detroit, who says, 'I am thinking about voting for you, but I would like to hear about how you would create jobs.'"

"The federal government, in partnership with state governments and private enterprise, needs to kick-start targeted vertical industries like micro-farming, recycling, home health care and others with a goal of one million new bootstrap jobs per year."

"Your sentences are getting longer."

"Don't you have any more sports questions?" Rebecca said with a grin, her mood brightening.

"I do. This is up your alley. A soccer fan, Beth Calyer, from Austin, Texas asks you to comment on last year's World Cup suspension of star striker Lindsay Carmichael."

"Sports are not meant to be war, so I would describe it as painful and unfortunate, but still a fair call by the referee."

"Okay, two more. Bob Perlman of New York City asks, 'What would you do on your first day after being inaugurated.'"

"Easy, if it isn't too cold, I would take a jog around the National Mall to the Lincoln Monument, quietly ask for a little help from the spirit of Abraham Lincoln, return to the Oval Office and begin to find ways to help Americans have better lives."

"And if it was very cold?" Farres added.

"Run anyway. Just add thermal layers."

"Ok then. The last question in the lightning round comes from Anne Napier of Chicago who asks whether there is a special someone in your life."

Rebecca immediately turned livid, turning to Farres, saying, "We had an agreement that tabloid-style questions are off the table. Why have you done this?"

"I agreed to a restriction on my questions but not the viewers."

"I like to play by the rules, you don't," Rebecca said, wagging her finger at Farres while taking off her microphone. "You can finish the show without me. And I apologize that my last response has to be two sentences."

"And . . . that's a wrap," Farres said, smiling awkwardly at the curved table with the empty guest chair.

Chapter 19

Rebecca's Path to Victory

Women voters, offended by Wolf Global's vicious attacks and taking her side on the walkout from Asra Farres' CNN special now gave Rebecca's campaign some additional traction. They joined the growing number of Hispanic voters who felt they had a candidate they could support. Rebecca's polling numbers rose several more points, now passing the third-ranked contender, closing in on number two.

Six weeks before the election, Rebecca decided to organize a cross-country tour, bicycling by day, taking a hydrogen-fueled bus by night. She would try to reach as many states as possible, pedaling fifty miles each day to three mid-size towns, where she would give a short speech and answer questions. The final stop each night would be in the state's largest city, for a town-hall-style gathering where former President Sanchez-Smith would join her.

Rebecca's campaign found itself scrambling to find larger venues, as Hispanic-Americans overflowed halls to see their beloved Sanchez-Smith. The crowds diversified more each day, as women, college students, trade unionists, and environmentalists joined in on the overnight mass movement. Between each town, the line of local bicyclists joining her grew, now stretching three to four miles. Media outlets dispatched young, fit correspondents to report the tour, conducting energetic interviews with Rebecca along the way. Pundits dubbed her the "Pied Piper" as the snaking line of two-wheelers behind her lengthened.

* *

"We are moving as many lawyers as we can spare into New Hampshire," said Roger Ainsworth, head of voter fraud monitoring for the Tree campaign. "A district judge, in response to our allegations of voter intimidation, has ordered the polls be held open another four hours."

"Good work," Rebecca said, who had taken to chewing on leftover campaign pencils imprinted with *Rebecca Tree: Restore Rationality*. There was a cup of them on each table of the large industrial warehouse building in Brookline just outside of Boston, which they had rented as their headquarters.

"Fatima is getting calls from Sanchez-Smith's people," Rebecca said. "They're very apprehensive about Nevada and Florida."

"Florida isn't going to happen," Ainsworth said. "Our exit polls don't support our fighting it out there but the Justice Department Civil Rights Division is doing a good job documenting flagrant abuses and, I am told, they will act."

"How bad is it in Florida?" Rebecca asked as she cracked her knuckles loudly.

"It looks like a Banana Republic election. Osceola, Seminole, and Polk counties have been flooded by big, beefy men in pickup trucks with Texas plates and shotgun racks riding around slowly in Puerto Rican communities. The residents are terrified."

"And local law enforcement?"

"Conspicuously absent."

"What can we do?" Rebecca asked. She wore blue jeans, brown cowboy boots, and a white tee that said FREE PEOPLE VOTE FREELY.

Fatima rushed in, trailed by three aides all of them carrying sheaves of printouts.

"Nevada and New Hampshire," she yelled out in a half-scream.

"What are you saying?" Rebecca asked, confused.

"Withers will take the entire south, and the Great Plains states and all of the Rocky Mountain States except for New Mexico, which looks pretty good for you. Nevada is in play. You will take the entire Northeast except for New Hampshire, which is in play. And the Pacific States are yours," Fatima said, as she looked at her watch. "Can we turn up the volume on the news? It's the top of the hour."

Ainsworth reached for a television remote.

"Good Evening: This is Amanda Schieffer with a special extended edition of the CBS Evening News."

"Tonight is a special and, I might add, historically unprecedented Election Day all across America. Four months ago American voters had expressed mostly apathy about this election and disdain for most of the candidates. Only John Spencer had attracted a committed following, fueled by his grand plans to deport all undocumented aliens and to institute loyalty tests for Muslim citizens. Rebecca Tree, after dramatically knocking Spencer out of the race by showing the nation, and the world, what his hate really looked like, had begun to put together an insurgent coalition of women, environmentalists, and young people. But she has been bedeviled with accusations, which have not gone away that she is merely a puppet of the Tree family and their money. John Spencer, for his part, is demanding a federal investigation into any role Ms. Tree might have had in the illegal wiretapping and burglaries, which occurred at his home and offices. But the attacks on her faded away with the stunning game-changing endorsement of her by former President Sanchez-Smith.

"Emotions are running high tonight. Sanchez-Smith has energized Hispanic voters who are turning out in large numbers in Florida, California, New Mexico, and Nevada. It is too early to tell whether these voters will make a difference in the results, particularly in the Rocky Mountain States. Americans have belatedly been following and participating in this continuing drama for the last few weeks. Other Americans have publicly and more often privately expressed their dread about the results. Let's go first to CBS's chief pollster, Anthony Winter, who can give us a snapshot of the critical races we need to watch tonight."

"Let's look at Florida—polls taken last week indicated that it's possible that Iris Santana, endorsed by former President Sanchez-Smith, is in a very competitive race for an open U.S. Senate seat—and this could be a big one. The reform candidate is one of the 'Band of Sisters' as they call themselves. Santana, a thirty-eight-year-old Hispanic-American from Orlando, is a decorated war veteran. After leaving the Army, she went to the University of Florida's Law School, and subsequently became Orlando's District Attorney. She amassed a formidable national reputation in fighting corruption."

"We are going live now to Rebecca Tree's headquarters in Miami. We have Aaron Kenyon standing by. Aaron, is the Senate race spilling over to the presidential race?"

"Well, Rebecca Tree is believed to be doing better than anyone would have imagined in Florida, but Texas Governor Ron Withers has built a formidable campaign machine here. Even with Iris Santana's surge in Florida's northern counties, all indicators seem to point to Withers taking Florida with the Senate race being a horse race."

"Hold on, we are going live to Santana headquarters where Martha Boyden is. Martha, can you give us an update."

"Thank you there is a lot of excitement here, but also worrisome concerns as reports have been coming in of anti-immigration activists driving through small towns menacing voters. The Tree campaign has joined the Santana campaign in asking the Justice Department Civil Rights Division to move more observers into the northern Florida counties."

* *

Rebecca turned to Fatima, "Do you have better information than the networks? How do we know that Florida is lost?"

"No, they have the same information. But the new media guidelines that the Federal Election Commission published don't allow them to release any of their exit polling except on the issues; they agreed to a voluntary embargo on calling any contests until the Pacific states' polls close. We have the best mathematicians and pollsters assembled by MIT; they say New Hampshire and Nevada, that we must put all our resources there. The counting of returns could go on all night and maybe into next week if there are recounts."

An aide, with a worried, fearful look came into the room and whispered into Fatima's ear.

"No, they can't do this," Fatima said, slapping her palm on the desktop.

"What is it?" Rebecca asked.

"I am being told that Wolf Global is going to break the embargo, call Florida and New Hampshire for Withers, and to more or less coronate him as the next president. If Wolf Global does that, it will cut into Hispanic voters in Nevada and New Mexico who work all day and can only get to the polls at night."

"A lie travels halfway around the world before truth gets its boots on," Rebecca said paraphrasing the famous quote variously attributed to different historical figures. "What can I do to help? I can get Lord Trippington on the phone and berate him."

"That won't help. We can file complaints with the FCC and FEC commissions but all they will do, at best, is make a few verbal reprimands."

Another aide came to speak with Fatima.

"Hmm, looks like someone is after Wolf Global," Fatima said, a hesitant half-smile coming across her face after consulting with the aide. "Most of the day they have been fighting off denial-of-service attacks on their websites, and now it looks like their network transmission computers have been compromised. Can we switch the channel from CBS to Wolf Global?"

Everyone in the room watched mesmerized as the Wolf Global screen displayed only a typographic message: PLEASE STANDBY, WE ARE HAVING TECHNICAL DIFFICULTIES. The message faded and was replaced with a man's body bobbing wildly, topped with a head like an iguana. The lizard hissed, and a pinwheel kaleidoscope rotated in the background.

A few minutes later, Rebecca received an encrypted text from Beijing on her cellphone from Albert Ling, her old friend, and former primary business partner. She pushed the unencrypt button.

Hi, Becky. Best of luck tonight. Wish I could vote. I was watching the coverage on Wolf Global, but it suddenly went blank. Strange!"

A second message arrived unencrypted from Keith Forsyte, Annie's widower. He had risen from Chancellor of the Exchequer to serve now as Prime Minister of England.

Becky, I couldn't be more excited for you. My sources at the BBC say you are going to take it. Know that your many friends in England and the

European Union are praying for your victory and the hope that sanity might return to the American political system.

* *

Several hours later, Rebecca helped serve a buffet of crab cakes, tuna burgers, salmon, and fish tacos for her exhausted volunteers. She did her best, despite her fatigue, to give them all a needed inspirational speech.

The presidency hung in the balance through the night as lawyers fought in New Hampshire and Nevada over the procedures to be followed, if it became necessary, in the coming days for certifying and counting absentee ballots.

Volunteers brought a cot into her office. An exhausted Rebecca lay down on it, quickly sliding into a dream:

Giant single-digit numbers came towards her before passing off to her sides . . . a swamp unfolded with dozens of bald cypress trees, each tree limb holding baby baskets, each basket filled with crying twins. The spongy, moist ground gave way beneath her, and she began to fall and fall with increasing speed seemingly endlessly into a deeper darkness . . . She moved like a meteor in outer space . . .

Her shoulders shook involuntarily, and she returned to a groggy partial consciousness.

"Becky, wake up," Fatima said shaking Rebecca's shoulders hard. "You're having a nightmare. You were screaming."

"Oh?" Rebecca said, as her eyes finally focused on Fatima.

"Congratulations," Fatima said, displaying a satisfied smile on her face. "New Hampshire just certified you the winner of their state's electoral votes. You received enough votes to clear the mandatory recount number."

"Ohh, that's nice. And Nevada?"

"The same. Becky, you will be the next president of the United States."

Chapter 20

"This is HC-CAD. That's HC for Ecuador, CHARLIE APPLE DARWIN," Janet Scanlon, the senior pilot, said. "That's a confirm Washington control; we'll be holding. Give us a squawk when you want us in."

Rebecca had registered her plane in Ecuador because of her love of the Galapagos Islands. Today, behind schedule with six hundred extra miles logged on a westward arc, the plane finally got a priority clearance for D.C. Metro airspace. The Lear banked sharply; from her seat, Rebecca extended arms and feet to secure herself against anything not bolted down as the plane turned one hundred and eighty degrees at Charlestown, West Virginia, setting its flight path due east for Washington National Airport. A squadron of new generation hydrogen fueled F-59's flying north from Alabama turned with the Lear into an escort formation for the President-elect.

Rebecca had been elected with only twenty-eight percent of the popular vote, nudged into the presidency by an unexpectedly strong turnout of Hispanic voters. Fewer than thirty percent of American's registered voters even bothered going to the polls, but enough Americans were moved by her message to cobble together a narrow electoral victory.

For the more than two-thirds of Americans who didn't bother to vote, Election Day, now a national holiday, seemed like any other day, and they stayed home facing an uncertain future with little to celebrate.

Rebecca's cellphone display lit up, playing the friendly chords of *Take the A-Train*. The display read FM, the acronym for Fatima Massiri.

Fatima tried her best in the beginning to steer clear of the campaign—honoring her family's concerns about the image of a Muslim woman being exploited by the popular press—but as Rebecca's momentum grew, Fatima, although out of the public eye, inevitably lent her support and troubleshooting skills. Now with the election a *fait accompli*, Fatima tried unsuccessfully to slip back into the shadows.

"Rebecca, Gilad is overwhelmed this week, so I promised to give him some backup."

"Oh good. Maybe you can talk to Hess's people for me. I've lost an hour here to weather. I'm supposed to meet with Hess at noon. Does he know I'm running late?"

"They've been calling your campaign office," Fatima said. "Hess's people seem a little terrified of talking to you directly."

"Am I scary?"

"No more than usual."

"We're cheeky today," Rebecca said.

"Gilad's been teasing me lately. He calls me 'Tree's Brain' or being 'Tree-Brained'"

Rebecca chuckled. "Someone said a mysterious advisor to Rebecca Tree with a middle-eastern name is the Rasputin of the administration. Do you think they're talking about you?"

"Of course. I walk the streets of Boston every night looking for hemophiliacs lying in gutters. And then I speak in tongues and their bleeding stops."

"That's the kind of magician I need with me in the new administration."

"Oh, hold it, Rebecca, don't. I suspected this was coming but please don't put me in the position of offering me something that I have no choice but to refuse. Last month, a girl my family knows, wearing her hijab was thrown onto the New York City subway tracks by a group of rowdy high school boys, who screamed racial epithets and spat on her. Fortunately, some other passengers came to her aid. My parents, as you can imagine, are very reluctant for me to work in the White House."

"I understand their concern and your loyalty, but I don't think I could do this without you. Let me see if I can find a way to fix this."

"'Fix?' This isn't something that just gets *fixed*, Rebecca. This is the frightening reality of the country we're in right now. I don't need to be careless, or worse, *cruel* to my loved ones."

"Let me do some research about non-public roles that would protect your anonymity."

"Okay," Fatima said, her voice softening slightly. "I think some Swedish scientists invented an invisibility machine a few years ago. Maybe we could borrow it."

"You're so brilliant. I'll order one for you and one for me."

"In the meantime, I'd like to meet with Caleb, as late as possible, at Washington National aboard Charlie Darwin—this airplane is the only place that gives me privacy."

"I'll call him now. Anything else?"

"See if you can set up a conference call with Professor Boies at Cal Tech, and her colleague, Sukinder Ravi from the Delhi Institute to talk about their bio-diversity food research. I have to go . . . they're flashing the landing lights," Rebecca kept her eye on the screen showing Captain Scanlon's calm face and swallowed. ". . . I'll call you this afternoon."

Thirty minutes later, a heavily guarded motorcade pulled into the driveway of the White House. Rebecca had to admit, having a motorcade was a nice way to avoid the usual DC-Metro traffic.

Hess sat under a portico, wrapped in a blanket.

"My dear Rebecca, let's get out of this sudden Washington chill. I haven't seen you in person since the glorious day of your electoral triumph, and there is much to talk about. Are you alone—no aide-de-camps?"

"I think I can handle you by myself. Let's get down to business." They walked a long corridor to an oak-paneled suite of rooms several steps away from the Oval Office. Inside, on Hess's grandiose desk, piles of papers and folios sat arranged neatly with color-coded tabs.

Hess leaned forward. "We have business to discuss today. But let's talk a little about the campaign. Congratulations are in order, though you disregarded most of my advice."

"Not true, I think I ignored *all* of your advice."

"Look," Hess said. "Now that you've been elected, you can fire me if you'd like. But let's get something straight. I'm a professional, and many would say that I'm the best in the game, and you only hire the best."

Rebecca couldn't have cared less if Hess was the best; she would have fired him on the spot if Fatima hadn't cultivated him as a useful source of valuable information and advised that he remain. It was another of Fatima's not so subtle suggestions which indicated to Rebeca that she wanted to stay onboard for the presidency.

"Let's go over your laundry list."

"Fine," he said. "First, the cabinet. The Big Three — Defense, State, and Treasury — stay, plus the Attorney General."

"Your first wish is granted. See how easy I am to work with? You can keep the entire cabinet."

Advanced Military Strategy was a required course at Army Intelligence School. "Plan A is worthless unless there is, at least, a Plan B," the instructor had emphasized.

Rebecca's Plan A as president was to bring change through reason and quiet persuasion.

Plan B, unfortunately, the more likely scenario, would be to clean house. For now, the physical presence of these cabinet members, and their paper trails, forensics of a possible crime scene that needed to be secured, must remain undisturbed.

". . . except for Agriculture," Rebecca said, in conclusion.

"Why Agriculture? Please keep in mind that agri-business support is consistent with the principles of our party. And," he nervously added, "they've most generously filled our party's campaign coffers with their contributions."

"It's a policy decision. Agri-business needs to focus on growing renewable hybrid energy crops. Don't worry, they'll make more money from this administration than ever before. The food model needs a reboot with consumer health and corporate profits having equal weights. My mind is made up on this."

"Very well. Are there any other appointments on your list?"

"Yes, the Secret Service Director. Does he still plan to retire?"

"The last I heard," Hess said, "he notified Homeland Security that he will be taking full retirement at the end of this year. Do you have a replacement in mind?"

"I have a candidate in mind."

A puzzled Hess said, "Do you mind sharing the name with me?"

"I'll get back to you on that one."

* *

Rebecca and Hess wrapped up the final points on Hess's transition agenda when they heard a light knock on the door. It sounded like code, one tap and then a quick double. Hess looked up from his paperwork, "Oh yes, I forgot to mention that President Bayou would like you to visit him briefly in the Oval Office."

They must be getting ready to send him to a museum. Poor old man, Rebecca thought.

"Of course . . . now? I have to depart D.C. airspace before the night-time flight restrictions lock my plane in."

"I'm sure it won't be a minute. Besides, you are the President-elect. Get used to it. Air traffic control will give you an exemption.

Hess ushered Rebecca into the Oval Office where, looking out on the South Lawn with his back to the door, President George Jenkins Bayou sat in a wheelchair.

His aide, Cynthia Sumners, stiffly greeted Rebecca. A petite forty-year-old with coifed hair and premature crow's feet, she wore a blue pin-striped suit and rocked back and forth on pointy high heels, which grated on Rebecca's nerves. She squinted at Rebecca, giving her a coach class Pan American smile while her eyes remained dark and half-shuttered.

Sumners approached Bayou, stating loudly into his ear, "Mr. President, Rebecca Tree is here to see you." She turned the wheel-chair around and Bayou, his body trembling from Parkinson's, said, "How good of you," his voice breaking up, "to come and see me . . ."

Sumners shouted into his ear, "Ms. Tree . . ."

"Yes, Ms. Tree," Bayou repeated.

The aide put a piece of paper in Bayou's right hand before placing reading glasses over his eyes.

Bayou spoke haltingly. "I must apologize," he paused, "as age and disease have slowed my speech." Another pause. "I have something for you. I wrote you a little poem." The paper shook in his hand, so he handed it to his aide to read.

The frozen-smiled Sumners reddened; her expression pained. She bit her lip, coughed twice, and expeditiously read Bayou's poem.

Politics isn't an easy game.
It's best to have a known name.
God on your side.
Doesn't make a free ride.
Always people knocking on your door.
Never wanting less, always asking for more.
I wish you the best of luck.
And don't forget to duck.

Rebecca smiled with surprise, touched by his kind, quirky sense of humor. At a loss for words, she walked over to Bayou and shook his hand. With eyes watering and spotted hands quivering, he weakly gestured for her to lean closer.

When she did, he whispered into her ear. "My wife, Annabelle . . . beautiful, just like you. She died almost five years ago. I'm going to see her again—quite soon. And, something else." His voice dropped to a whisper and, looking at Sumners, he flipped the back of his hand at her in a dismissive motion. She retreated to the far end of the room.

"Be careful, dear . . . you've already made," he paused, as a rumbling cough rattled through him, ". . . enemies.

"Don't sign the D.C. Relief Act. I won't. Trust no one." His head slumped down. "I'm sorry.

I need to rest now . . . God bless you."

A week after Rebecca's inauguration, Bayou lapsed into a coma. He died three months later.

Chapter 21

Night had fallen by the time Rebecca's entourage pulled into a secured private aviation terminal at Washington National.

Toussaint stood beside the plane. As Rebecca got out of the limo, she extended her hand. "I'm glad you could meet me. Let's go in. I need to talk to you."

Once inside the plane, Toussaint said, "Reverend Turner sends his regards. Although he got some flak from the church elders about your visit, they quieted down when they heard praise from the parishioners."

"Oh, that's good," Rebecca said, clapping her hands together. "Please tell the Reverend how much I enjoyed singing in the choir."

"Actually, he didn't get much feedback on your voice."

She roared with laughter.

"However," he rolled the three syllables with a drumbeat flourish, "many of the old-timers in the Movement called him—they'd love to sit down with you and ask some questions. Would you be interested?"

"I'd be delighted," she said, with a chuckle. "You seem to be taking a bit of a partisan role here. Are you considering a run for office when you retire?"

Toussaint flashed a grin, two hundred and forty pounds of charm muscling his face. "No thanks. Early retirement for me; I'll stick with helping the wife in the garden."

"I don't know. This is America. We're meant to work until we drop," she said with a teasing tone until her face grew serious.

"I have a favor to ask you."

"And what might that be?"

"Could you stay on at Secret Service as Director for a while after Brad Morris retires? I need you."

"Camille was right again. After Fatima had called me about this meeting, I went home for lunch with my wife, and she said you'd ask me to stay on. I don't know."

"And what's her opinion?"

"That's not fair."

"Why?"

"Because you know she'll take your side. She told me to say yes."

"Well, that's the trick to your marriage. Your wife is always right."

"It's two against one," Toussaint said.

"Tough," Rebecca said with a grin.

"I'll think about your offer, but I'd like some *quid pro quo.*"

"Something for something," Rebecca said, a little startled.

A note of bitterness entered Toussaint's voice. "The Secret Service has undercover operations."

"Right, for counterfeiters."

"Yes, for that, but much more. We have a unit that infiltrates groups that may harm the president. We call it Jacob's Unit, and all the agents take it personally."

In her last year of office, President Sanchez-Smith had stopped for a reporter's question on the steps of the Capitol, and a lone gunman raised a 9-millimeter Luger pistol aiming it at her head. A spectator deflected the assailant's arm, as a line-of-fire agent, Jacob Nathans, alerted by movement in the crowd, threw himself in front of the president, catching a bullet fatally in the heart. A Capitol policeman killed the alleged assailant, Hardy Tucker, instantly with one shot to the brain.

"Everyone in the Service is damn angry about Jacob's death and the unexplored gaps in Hardy Tucker's background; Sanchez-Smith did her best, but it seems people in high places would like it to go away. If you want me to continue, I will, but I want full funding for Jacob's Unit. It's getting ugly in the country, and the Secret Service has to be allowed to do its work without political interference."

"And Homeland Security, they're not helpful?"

"Bureaucracy. A problem to them is an event in the past tense. They lack vision."

"What do you need?"

"Four times the money, two times the staff. We need enough money for two hundred more undercover operatives—to recruit, train and support them."

"That sounds like a lot."

"It's a big problem, and it's going to get a lot bigger. We broke up other plots to assassinate Sanchez-Smith."

"By whom?

"Forerunners of what are now much more organized anti-Hispanic groups. Spencer's crowd."

"You'll get whatever resources you need," Rebecca said. "I won't allow vigilantes to operate on my watch. Consider it done. So, do we have a deal?"

"All right. Deal." Toussaint's smile came back slowly. "I just don't want to be away from home too much. It's not like when we were younger, when Camille worked the required long hours at Walter Reed as a pediatric surgeon and I traveled a lot, doing executive protection."

"Okay. I don't want to interfere with your love life. No overseas trips; you can supervise them remotely. I need your help. This 24/7 protection makes me itchy. Sometimes I just can't handle it—I've already had a few run-ins with agents."

"Yes, I've heard. They like you, a lot. They're all veterans, and they respect your military service, but you're a real pain to protect. Unfortunately, contrary to what the world might think, the Secret Service is powerless to tell the president what to do or not do. We can only suggest, cajole or advise."

"Sorry, I've always had an issue with authority."

"Maybe you can be reprogrammed."

"Good luck on that."

"How do you like your code name?"

"Freckles?" she laughed. "It's okay. Better than guys saying into their cuffs, 'Elvis inbound,' 'Keep the crowds back from Elvis.' Thank

God my code name isn't POTUS. That sounds like what mountain goats leave behind."

"Just make sure you do a better job than the last few POTUSes."

"It's not going to be easy." Rebecca looked at her watch. "I'd better get going. They're keeping D.C. airspace open until I take off. Call me later in the week. Give Camille my love and tell her Fatima has her sitting in the front row at the inauguration. You're probably going to have to work that day, but not the night shift. For that, you'll be needed on the dance floor. Ask Camille if I can reserve a waltz with you at the Inauguration Ball."

"Waltz? I heard you've been sneaking over to my house for dance lessons. Camille's still struggling to get you up to speed on the foxtrot."

Rebecca's face reddened with embarrassment.

"Among my many flaws, I cannot dance. "

"Thankfully that will not disqualify you from the position."

Chapter 22

Rebecca Tree's Home
Boston

With her first year-end bonus from trading currencies, Rebecca had hired an architect to design a home in an old two-story commercial building, which she bought from the city of Boston's abandoned property rolls. Built just after the Civil War, it had been a small family-owned canvas shop. The brick façade's faded letters said Samuelson & Sons, Canvas Goods, Est. 1867. When she bought the neglected warehouse, the wide pine floors were rotten from years of water damage, the brickwork had crumbled, and a beard of mold had overtaken the basement. With her second year's bonus check, she undertook a gut renovation. With the third check, she finished restoring the original building, adding one floor of pre-fabricated concrete slabs and glass panels. The original structure fronted on one street, and an eight-foot brick wall surrounded the building and its equally sized yard, which exited onto a second street in the rear. An enclosed alleyway ran along the back of the building, and four other attached buildings provided egresses in case of fire, as well as a common space for storing a dozen well-traveled bicycles.

The buildings comprised a full, albeit small, square block.

A bulldozer had dug out the yard, and a thermal exchange drew from the earth's constant temperature to warm and cool the building. Dual water systems, a gray water recycler, and rain capture units made the structures water independent. The roofs were covered with solar panels, and native New England plants canopied the yard.

A month passed since the election, and Rebecca promised herself a quiet weekend at home. No press, no aides. But that promise had been disrupted by an unexpected phone call.

Arthur Gelbwags had been her grandmother Catherine Tree's personal attorney, and the executor of her estate. Rebecca liked Gelbwags, but she dreaded his calls, as they usually preceded another letter sent metaphorically from the grave. Two days earlier, Gelbwags announced that a courier carrying a sealed envelope from his San Francisco office would arrive at Boston's Logan airport Saturday morning.

The sun had just risen in Boston; Rebecca, dressed in green running shorts and a white T-shirt that said "All Animal Lives Matter," paced nervously around her living room. An early riser, Rebecca bicycled when she had time, usually before dawn. But now exercise required plans, an approved Secret Service route, and agents to escort her. She felt she had already inconvenienced her neighbors enough; the Secret Service and Boston police had both ends of the small commercial street blocked off.

Rebecca wasn't good at waiting. She looked at her thermal driven timepiece, realizing that the courier wasn't due for at least an hour. If it were colder, she might be able to sneak out on a bike in disguise, wearing full winter cycling gear. She knew it would be irresponsible, but she felt tempted.

She walked over to the kitchen, where a row of sticky notes stood arranged on a Euro-slender stainless steel refrigerator. She had a system. She always tried to have a system: yellow indicated overdue tasks, pink highlighted urgency, and blue captured minutiae of random thoughts or projects. A yellow sticky currently instructed her to "Call Dr. Jayshon," her opera-loving dentist who wanted advice on filing a patent for his anti-snoring mouthpiece in the European Union. A pink one said, "Buy Fatima's birthday present," and a second line said, "Something really special." On the far right side, a strip of small blue squares ran the full length of the unit, each one outlining a step for authoring a business method patent for a consumer-based alternative energy market.

A few minutes later she trotted down the steps of the building's internal staircase to a cavernous basement with twelve-foot vaulted ceilings, most of the space dedicated to an environmentally balanced archive room. She went through that room into the smaller part of the basement where, under hanging nano monitors, a stair climber stood in front of a wall of free weights. The other wall racked with DVDs—mostly classics—categorized and labeled by genre: thriller, documentary, comedy, science fiction, and foreign French, foreign German, foreign Swedish. She shook her head as she browsed the arrangement. *Why do I have to order everything?* She kept all of life's apples and oranges separate. Her systematic collection of T-shirts in her closets was ranked by color over six spectrally dedicated shelves—reds, oranges, yellows, greens, and blues.

She honed in on the science fiction section. She owned all the great classics from the 1950s that mirrored the country's paranoia about the Cold War. Her friend Annie, a classic film fan, had gifted her the first dozen titles in the now robust collection. She selected *The Day the Earth Stood Still*, an all-time favorite, putting it into the DVD player, and stepped onto the machine, tucking her locket and chain underneath her fitted shirt. Thirty minutes later, with the stair climber at maximum speed and resistance, she jumped off, drenched in sweat. A punching bag hung in a far corner of the room. She approached it, repeating a line from the end of the film. ". . . forgive me if I speak bluntly. The universe grows smaller every day, and the threat of aggression can no longer be tolerated. There must be security for all, or no one is secure."

She jabbed at the bag as she had been taught in the military. Left . . . left . . . right . . .left . . . right . . .

She punched harder, visualizing an image on the bag, her grand-father's face, his single azure eye taunting.

She imagined his voice: *Hit me, harder. Come on girl, you can do better than that.*

She slammed the bag so hard the chain connecting it to the ceiling began to dislodge, small chips of white plaster falling to the matted floor. A Secret Service agent's voice came over the intercom.

"Ms. Tree, the courier from San Francisco is here."

Chapter 23

Aboard Rebecca's Plane
Westward Bound

The early morning sky, layered with a flaming orange-red at its base, crept into full daylight behind shelving wisps of cloud. Charlie A. Darwin took off from Wayfarer Ketch, heading west with a flight plan to touch down at Malstrom Air Base in Great Falls, Montana. A team of Secret Service agents led by Caleb Toussaint escorted Rebecca.

"Are you okay?" Toussaint said to Rebecca shortly after takeoff from the seat alongside her.

"I'm fine. Just fine," Rebecca said, having failed to discreetly wipe the sweat from her brow. Her stomach felt like an oversized knotted rope sat in it. She started at her reassurance monitors, which showed the faces of the two pilots.

"You look a little pale."

"I'm good. All good."

"If you say so," Toussaint said, with a puzzled look on his face. "Let me get this straight. You got this package from Gelbwags by messenger, and as far as you know it's the last one you'll get from your dead grandmother's attorney?"

"That's what he says," Rebecca said, cocking her head to one side, exhaling the remaining takeoff tension. "This one my grandmother labeled 'at the executor's discretion.' She left a vague note, to be released only on the occasion of a 'monumental event in my life.'"

"You think she meant a terminal illness, perhaps a marriage, or the birth of a child?"

"One second," Rebecca said, pushing her intercom button. "Janet, will we be at cruising altitude soon?"

"A couple of more minutes," the pilot replied.

Rebecca turned back to Toussaint, as more color returned to her face. "Gelbwags is interpreting my election to the Presidency as a monumental event."

"Well, Sherlock Holmes," Toussaint said, "that's a pretty obvious conclusion. Read the letters to me. Read Gelbwags first, then your grandmother's."

Dear Rebecca,

I am sorry to encumber you with another letter, especially after the remarkable achievement of your election. But that event is of such significance, that I believe it triggers the conditions, which my legal obligations as executor of Catherine Tree's estate require of me.

I hope and pray that, whatever its contents, it provides some comfort to you. You certainly deserve it.

Please call me. I will provide you with any additional information not protected by attorney-client privilege.

With my warmest regards,

Arthur Gelbwags

"Nothing to read through the lines there," Toussaint said. "But from what you told me, Gelbwags has always been a straight-shooter. Now your grandmother's letter," Toussaint said, closing his eyes to concentrate.

Dear Rebecca, she read. *I am sorry to have burdened your life with so many messages from the "other side." I don't know when in your life you will receive this letter. If Merewether is still alive, then you must take every precaution that he never finds out anything about its contents.*

Ask the dear Mr. Gelbwags to provide you the file on the Western properties. They are all lovely hunting and fishing lodges bought by my father as an investment during the Great Depression. They were passed to me in his will, on the condition that his law firm holds them in trust. They sit scattered all over Montana, such a beautiful state. Each lodge is buffered by hundreds of acres of protected land. I hope you take the time to visit them all.

In the horribly unlikely event that, God forbid, I'm sorry to even write this, that you pre-decease Merewether, the properties would pass to the Western Land Trust, who'd be required to preserve the lodges and land.

If Merewether pre-deceases you, then you will inherit the properties without restriction.

The Paradise Valley lodge was my favorite; its foundation rests on a sloping hill. The key, which you now possess, opens two double doors at the rear of the house. It leads into a climate-controlled finished basement. In secret, I gathered a collection of family mementos — scrapbooks with photographs of four generations — from my parents to my grandchildren. There are some beautiful love letters there — some between your father and mother, and also from Merewether to me before our relationship went sour. I know he has been cruel to both of us, but he was a different man when I met him.

Rebecca pushed the letter quickly away, afraid that the precious message would bring tears.

"Rebecca," Toussaint said, "It's going to be all right." He put his arm around her and drew her to him protectively.

"I'm sorry," Rebecca said, her body stiffening as she handed him the letter. Inside she felt a deep pain triggered by Toussaint's touch. "Can you finish reading it?"

Why would Grandmother have to hide memories? Rebecca said to herself.

Toussaint put on his eyeglasses and continued the letter.

There are other things in the basement I pray that you will enjoy. I wish I had been stronger in life . . . perhaps God will have mercy on my soul. I know he will look favorably on you and your sister.

My eternal love,

Grandma

Rebecca got out of her seat and looked at Toussaint. Her palms felt sweaty, and her heart raced. She excused herself and sought privacy in the plane's small bedroom.

In front of a wall mirror, she wiped her tearing eyes. She felt rent asunder. Her expectations for this trip seemed as far apart as the poles of the earth. One inner child saw it as Christmas Eve, believing that dawn would bring a tree fully ablaze with ornaments and multi-colored lights, neatly wrapped presents, a home crowded with parents, siblings, uncles, and aunts. The other inner child, more familiar, dreaded the next morning, knowing she would creep down to the stairs to an unadorned room, vacant and joyless.

Chapter 24

Paradise Valley, Montana
North of Yellowstone Park

Only God can make a tree, Rebecca recalled the line of the poet, Joyce Kilmer, as a gentle wind blew across her face.

A convoy of bulletproof, four-wheel drive mountaineering vehicles approached the Paradise Valley lodge from the north, navigating hairpin turns and switchbacks. As they approached a peak, Toussaint, suit cuff to his mouth, received real-time updates from a mobile command center being fed with overhead drone images. He turned to Rebecca, "Let's get out for a minute. I want you to see something."

She followed Toussaint a hundred yards along the road toward a crest. Agents on all-terrain vehicles dressed as hunters buzzed along paths through the woods. Toussaint took her by the elbow and said, "a few more yards to walk to the top."

Rebecca felt a light electrical current pulse through her; her body tingled. The hair on her neck lifted. In her mind, Toussaint's touch became a gesture by proxy, as if Jackson's hand reached from the grave and transmitted his love through his father. Rebecca momentarily shut her eyes, as she felt herself ache for Jackson.

Recovering, she opened her eyes to gasp at the stunning view that stretched in front of her, a foreground of green fir trees shimmered in the sun, as if lit from within. The vistas unfurled like a fantasy of a nineteenth-century landscape painter whose easel was first to discover the West. Four primary visual sight lines made a symmetry of design: the firs in the foreground, with a soft hazy air clouding the tops, a mountain range panorama, centered by a massive white-capped ridge that stood sentry over the valley. The road wound down the hill, revealing the centerpiece, a two-story mansard-roofed, log-cabined lodge, rimmed with a full porch. Over each doorframe hung twelve-point elk antlers.

Wild sweetbrier wafted like a delicate perfume and lingered with the firs' resins, flowing syrupy, sweet and piney. Rebecca inhaled the moist air rising from the forest floor. It smelled like an old wool sweater hung to dry in the afternoon sun.

This is where God's work began.

"We need to hold here for awhile," Toussaint said, before talking command language into his shirt cuff.

"I need the lodge key. They've got a team of bomb-sniffing dogs waiting outside."

"Dogs? Come on," she said.

"I know, but it's the procedure."

Rebecca glimpsed at a shape moving across her periphery, a black body with a white top, high in the sky. "Look, it's an eagle," she said, rotating her body, as the bird glided across their sight line.

Salvation, redemption, and resurrection. For Native Americans, the eagle's feathers promised power and healing. To Rebecca, the bird soared to such heights it could touch the face of God. As a child, she believed eagle wings signified protection, but the adult qualified the belief; the bird's gripping talons symbolized ruin to evildoers.

"How long do we have to wait?" she asked, turning to Toussaint.

"Sit with me in the lead car. We can watch what's happening on the monitor."

They settled in the back seat as Toussaint activated a flat screen. With a remote in hand, he pushed a single button.

"What the devil is all this?"

"Get used to it. It's called protecting the principal. That's you. I can't let you enter an unverified area without fully checking it out."

She slumped in her seat, fingers steepled. She wanted to run into the woods, find a solid, well-limbed tree and climb it.

"Okay, the first camera is feeding a walk-around." She heard static in the car. Toussaint raised his suit cuff. "Roger, we're holding until you're ready for her. Okay, I'll switch." He pushed another button on the remote, which showed a wide shot of the back of the cabin. A dog exercise pen had been set up over a floor of drop cloths with two beagles inside barking raucously. One at a time, the dog-handlers picked up the beagles. They booted their feet, dressed them in cotton leggings and sweaters fastened with Velcro, and finally slipped saliva-catching bibs under their chins.

"What are they doing with those dogs?"

"We're running it using basic crime scene protocol. If we want to dust for prints or look for forensic clues later, we need to keep it sterile."

Rebecca was speechless, but she knew Toussaint was right.

She envied people who can just look at family albums without being surrounded by security teams.

Toussaint talked into his cuff again. "Okay, Roger . . . go ahead . . . but let's not take all day. Freckles is getting restless." He turned to her. "You'll have to be a little patient," he said. "This is what we're going to do. It shouldn't take more than thirty minutes. First they'll drill a hole into the room, and insert a camera probe through it . . ."

"Why?"

"To make sure there are no surprises. Then they'll run the two beagles through."

"Grrrr."

"Hush. Dogs growl. Presidents don't."

Rebecca went to open her mouth but thought better of it.

"Before you go in, a photo team will set up a quadrant camera— it'll image two-foot squares, and a tech in another van will stitch it together digitally. If something gets moved, we can put it back exactly in its place."

Rebecca tried to calm herself by visualizing the bald eagle and writing it a resume: top of the food chain, eats mainly fish from fresh and salt water, has few enemies because of its size, lifting power about four pounds.

"They've taken an inside picture now. Have a look."

Rebecca muttered a nearly inaudible affirmative, then stared at the screen. The wide shot displayed as green, unlit, taken with a night vision lens. It showed a big fireplace, with a couch facing two armchairs. Drop cloths covered the furniture. Bookcases lined the walls, each shelf filled with binders, labeled in neat block letters she couldn't decipher. As the camera panned the walls, her body juddered; a dozen large picture frames displayed each containing a collage of images.

She grabbed Toussaint's arm. "Please . . . ask them to zoom in on those picture frames."

A few seconds later, Rebecca uttered a cry. "Look, I think it's my parents on a beach. Ask them to hurry; I need to see everything."

As the beagles left the room, Rebecca and Toussaint entered wearing face masks, white paper suits, paper shoes, hair covers and cotton gloves. Agents brought in two folding chairs and a card table. Rebecca trembled as she systematically looked at the first album she found marked PARENTS on the left side of the first shelf. She stroked the black leather grain of the volume, and then reverently opened the first page.

"Look, Caleb, these must be my great-grandparents. They look so happy. It must be their wedding day." Surrounded by guests, the couple, with linked arms, each held a bouquet of roses. Rebecca looked at each image like a death row inmate regarding her last supper. Twenty minutes later, she picked up the next volume, labeled MY BABY PICTURES. It was her grandmother.

Toussaint sat, mainly silently, for the next few hours. Rebecca made small noises, some of childish joy, some of pain as the images awakened fragments of memories. She went slowly, one album at a time, studying each image like a vintner inspecting the color of the wine.

Sometimes her cottoned finger would trace over the faces of the dead. She thought about sacred rituals; she imagined a Ghost Dance—fresh soil would be covered with new grass and young trees—buffalo and wild horses would roam. The dead would come back for one day, celebrate a great reunion, a grand picnic on the land of a Paradise Lost before retreating to sleep undisturbed in eternal peace.

Sometimes she smelled a page, as the acid content of the paper released a sour almost nitric odor. As soon as she could, she would send the whole treasure trove to a restorer.

Make it last a million years.

Rebecca turned to Toussaint, who appeared to be staring at the last bound volume on the right side of the shelf. The same bold handwriting on a white label read: THE TWINS VOL. I.

Chapter 25

Return Flight to Boston

During the first part of the returning flight, Rebecca sat quietly, hunched in her seat, studying on her computer hastily assembled digital copies of photos from the two volumes labeled THE TWINS.

Images stirred memories.

The twins sat on a hill overlooking the big house. Their grandmother sat between them; they had small easels and boxes filled with an array of colored chalks. Rebecca scrabbled on all fours to peek at her sister's drawing. Allison sharply pushed Rebecca away.

Her sister's act of sibling rejection still lingered with Rebecca. She fretted at her childhood scar until a sharp pain shot up her left arm.

A picture emerged of her first childhood bedroom with three beds.

Separating the girls was a Hungarian nanny, an old woman, always dressed in black with shoes shaped like boxes. The woman's smell clogged her nose and throat; it was sulfuric, like the first whiff of a decaying mouse under an old pine floorboard.

Toussaint stood in the front of the cabin, speaking softly into his cellphone to his wife.

From the computer's monitor, images of the twins reflected on Rebecca's reading glasses as she slowly paged through the albums. At the end of the second volume, a terrible coldness came over her body, and her feet began to ache. She felt for her pulse, scared when she couldn't find one. Waving her hand, she tried to get Toussaint's attention. Another agent noticed and nudged Toussaint on the shoulder.

"Are you okay?" Toussaint shouted out as he skittered on his lame leg down the aisle.

"Yes, but I'm freezing. My left foot is numb. It's probably my blood pressure."

"And no sleep, and stress." Toussaint reached into a small closet behind her seat, removing two thermal blankets and a blood pressure kit. He covered her as if she had been pulled from frigid waters and rolled up the sleeve of her left arm.

"Let's see how low you've gone."

Toussaint pumped the pressure ball, watched the needle register the systolic. "You're not dead yet, but it's under one hundred," he said before he yelled to another agent. "Tell the pilot to raise the cabin temperature ten degrees. And tell her to descend slowly to ten thousand feet."

"I'm okay. Give me ten minutes under the thermals. It'll be back up over a hundred. I'm feeling better already."

"Be quiet, I need to get the diastolic again." As he stared at the pressure gauge, a bead of sweat broke over Toussaint's mustache. "It's not even seventy. If it doesn't come back up in the next ten minutes, we're going to have to land."

"Please, I'll be okay." Rebecca didn't want the stress of another landing and takeoff.

"Sorry, this one is not your call. Close your eyes. Think of the ocean. I'll be right back."

Toussaint walked to the cockpit. "We have a possible problem," he said to the pilot. "Rebecca's blood pressure is 95 over 60. We might need to make an emergency medical touchdown."

Janet Scanlon glanced at her co-pilot briefly. "It's not unusual. We had this problem last year on a flight in from Tokyo. Did you wrap her with the thermals?"

"Yes, and I'm going to take her pressure again after we talk."

"We've got a medical kit with adrenalin. As a last resort, if it keeps dropping, we could inject her."

"Did that ever happen? It's not on the Secret Service chart," Toussaint's jaw appeared clenched.

"No, never," Deborah Pierce, the co-pilot said tersely.

"In the medical kit, there's a small leather case," Scanlon said, "with a hemodynamic monitor that looks just like an athlete's heart-rate watch. When her pressure is back up to normal, put the bracelet on her, and push the set button."

"How long has she used this monitor?"

"As long as we've known her. She wears it when she plays sports."

"How come I don't know about this?" Toussaint said.

"It's not a big deal. It just warns her that she could faint. If she fell on the soccer field, and if it started beeping, then she would know to get up slowly.

"Look," the pilot said, a tone of irritation coming into her voice "we just fly her around the world. That's our job, but she has a routine for flying, and the Secret Service procedures are upsetting it."

"What the bloody hell are you talking about?"

"She needs a half an hour by herself before we start the engines. Then she will be fine. Otherwise, she gets nervous."

Toussaint's jaw went slack. "And what does she use the half hour for?"

"Yoga, self-hypnosis, relaxation breathing; it is a routine which she might modify from time to time."

"Are we talking a medical condition here? If so, I need to know, right now."

"No, but she doesn't like to talk about it. Aerophobia, fear of flying, mostly the takeoffs rattle her: pretty reasonable I'd say for a girl whose parents died in a plane crash when she was barely out of diapers."

"Where's the nearest Air Force base?" Toussaint said curtly, as he bit down on his lip. Pierce punched into a computer screen. "We're about thirty minutes north of Scott, in southwest Illinois."

"All right, head for Scott. Let me check her blood pressure again. Then we'll decide."

When Toussaint returned to her seat, he found Rebecca shivering, eyes shut. "Rebecca?"

"Oh," her eyes opened wide, before appearing to freeze like an animal suddenly aware of a stalking predator. "You told me to think about the ocean. But the water was ice-cold."

"Think about the desert then. I need to take your blood pressure again."

"I'll be okay. It's going to pass," Rebecca said, sighing deeply. She started to recall a bleached memory of a boarding school-sponsored safari. Dressed in a traditional Arab gown, a white dishdasha, her head wrapped in a Bedouin Keffiyah scarf, she had rolled and jumped with her classmates off towering dunes, tumbling and falling harmlessly in what felt like a gigantic sandbox.

"The sand is so soft . . ." Rebecca mumbled as she remembered her first memory of giggling with friends she finally made.

"Don't talk. Just listen, for once." He rolled up her sleeve, wrapped the cuff, and squeezed. She went to open her mouth, but Toussaint hissed her silent.

"It hasn't come back up enough. We're going in. I want a doctor to look at you." Rebecca tilted her head left, opened her mouth wide, and her brows furrowed. "Don't look at me like that," he said.

Toussaint went back to the pilot's cabin. "Touch the plane down at Scott. We need to speak to NORAD air traffic control."

"Right," Scanlon said. "NORAD CENTRAL, this is HC-CHARLIE APPLE DARWIN, we need to make a level-one emergency landing at Scott Air Base."

"This is air traffic control, Charlie. What can we help you with today?"

Toussaint made a throat-cut hand gesture to Scanlon.

"Hold on," Scanlon hit the mute button on her microphone. "What should I tell them?"

"Tell them you need a mechanic. You don't have a secure communication line so tell them it's an emergency light malfunction."

"Roger. We need a mechanic, a quick oil change, and a new filter. No biggie. Seriously . . . just a warning light on the engine. Better safe than sorry."

"Roger, Charlie. We'll VIP you in. Our radar has you wet-feeting over Lake Superior. You need to hang a full right now if you want to land at Scott, ninety degrees due south.

"Ground controller is expecting you to check-in at 22:00," the air traffic controller advised them. "They're clearing out a full approach corridor for you. Scott's small; it's only one runway. Come in at nine-four hundred. Visibility is three miles under cloud base. Twenty-five percent overcast . . . and the ground temps . . . not to worry."

Toussaint punched into his hand-held an encrypted email to a Secret Service field office. *Need chopper with cleared agency doctor inbound at Scott Air Base. Preventive check of President-elect: issue low blood pressure. Not critical, repeat, not critical. Keep profile low.*

* *

"Do you feel that?"

"Yes."

"How about now?" the doctor said as he brushed a soft nylon fiber, a monofilament on the soles of Rebecca's bare feet.

"Yes."

"And again. Do you feel it?

"No."

The doctor picked up Rebecca's Secret Service medical chart and studied it for a while.

"Everything seems fine. You have very slight peripheral neuropathy on your left side, which most likely is residual nerve damage from the bullet that struck you in the thigh during your army service. No doubt, even though we categorize it as a relatively minor wound, it would have done local damage tearing tendons, muscles, and nerves. No one is better at trauma wounds that the Army field surgeons, and I expect you also had good physical therapy."

"Yes, the best," Rebecca said, feeling relieved that this is all the doctor could find. "At worst, I feel a tinge on that side when I run, and I guess that the left foot gets cold more than I realized."

"I will email Director Toussaint a series of exercises that you should regularly do to stretch the foot and calf muscles. If it gets worse, you can take some anti-inflammatory medicine."

"I'll pass on the pills, but I promise to do the exercises."

"Okay, to be safe, I think you should sleep the night before you fly again. Your pressure is back to normal, for you. You're at 110/70. That seems to track with the chart the Deputy Director handed me."

"Thanks, I'm sorry to create such a fuss. I feel much better now, and

I'd like to get back to Boston. I'll sleep better in my bed."

She looked up at Toussaint; his face wore a stern Secret Service look, but quickly softened.

"Okay," Toussaint said, "why don't we stay on the ground for an hour. The doctor can wait, and if everything remains stable, we'll take off. If not, we'll overnight."

"That's fine," the doctor said. "I have a Cessna I fly on weekends. Maybe the pilots will give me a cockpit tour. Oh, by the way, Ms. Tree, my wife voted for you. She wasn't going to vote, but she got all charged up by your debate performance."

"Really? What did she like about it?"

"She went into Super Bowl mode when you took on Spencer. The whole neighborhood could hear her whooping—war-whooping."

Rebecca smiled, her strength returning. "And who did you vote for?"

"I haven't voted for twenty years. Politics is too depressing for me."

* *

"Can we get going?" Rebecca asked.

"Tell me what happened?" Toussaint said.

"What do you mean? Nothing happened. I caught a chill."

"Something triggered it. I know you."

Rebecca stumbled. She began to stammer. "I . . . I don't know. I was looking . . . at the," she paused, "pictures of Allison and me. When I got to the last page of the second volume, suddenly ice shot through my veins." She paused again. "I got cold . . . I guess . . ."

"You guess what?"

"I . . . I . . . okay . . . the truth?"

"Yes," Toussaint said, "the truth."

"Everything got dark. Part of me is really happy to have these pictures. But," she struggled to understand her thoughts, "these memories feel abducted to me. Kidnapped. Does that seem so crazy?"

"No, but maybe there's a trigger in that photo album that caused your body to shut down."

She turned away from Toussaint's gaze and her body shook. He kneeled down and took her elbow. "Let it out . . . Rebecca, it wouldn't be terrible to let your guard down."

"Can you clear the plane?"

Toussaint moved his hand signaling with his index finger to the other agents. They left, joining their colleagues stationed on the tarmac.

The cabin went quiet. "What is it?"

Rebecca bit hard on her lip and looked like she might cry. She spoke in blurts. "All the pictures . . . it was really hard . . . but I shut down when . . . I realized." Fighting back, she regained her composure enough to look straight into Toussaint's eyes. "The pictures of us together end on our third birthday; the last twin sequence shows a cake with three candles; she died when she was four. But the later pictures, where we were photographed separately—we appear as interchangeable, same freckles, unruly red hair, pale skin, except there's one major distinction: Allison doesn't look at the camera anymore."

"I must be missing something here," Toussaint said. "What does that mean, that she doesn't look at the camera?"

"It's one of several possible early childhood indicators of autism."

Chapter 26

Rebecca Tree's Home
Boston

Camille Toussaint had skin the color of ebony, offset by thick, blood red lips, a straight nose, and high cheekbones. A tightly cropped Afro, more salt than pepper, haloed her small, almond-shaped head. Caleb Toussaint asked his wife to spend a few days with Rebecca in Boston, and now the two women sat in the living room drinking coffee.

Rebecca didn't want to talk about the Montana trip; instead, she begged Camille to tell her again about her mother and Jean-Claude Duvalier, known to the world as Baby Doc.

"He was disgusting, she had told me. *C'etait degoutant.* My grand-father, not a nice man, I'm sad to say, let him take her out as a thirteen-year-old child. An armored column drove them through the hills of Pétionvile overlooking Port-au-Prince as she sat in the backseat of an old Mercedes convertible."

"How did she describe him?"

"He had this horrible, geometrically shaped haircut. Paris fashion enslaved upper-class Haitians. They imported this awful 'Bob' style, and Baby Doc had thick, long, greasy sideburns with the whole coiffeur sprayed into place. It stank. His shirt's buttons popped from the stress of his pig-fat stomach."

"And he tried to touch her?"

"The first two times on these drives, he kept wiggling in his seat. Every time he turned toward her, she moved away."

"Wasn't she scared?"

"Terrified, but she knew if she let him touch her. Well, she didn't know . . . another girl told her they had houses filled with young girls, imprisoned, left there to pleasure the Duvaliers and their cohorts."

"Tell me again how it ended?"

"The third time he told his driver to stop the car. This time, he put his fat arm all the way around her and pulled her to his lips."

"God, how awful."

"She bit him. Then she jumped out of the car. He came after her in a fury. Soldiers with machine guns surrounded her. A soldier pushed her to the ground with the muzzle of his gun. She thought she was dead. Out of one eye, she could see Duvalier standing over her with his mouth foaming. He spit blood from his lip on the ground next to her face, and then he screamed at the soldiers to take her back to her home with a message: 'Tell your father your skin is too black to ever marry a Duvalier.'"

"And then?" Rebecca knew the rest, but she loved hearing it.

"My grandfather had no choice, as he did business with the Duvalier family, but to send his daughter out of Haiti. My mother was exiled to France, straight into a Catholic convent school, *Lycée du Sacré-Cœur*, in Amiens, north of Paris; later she became a well-known pan-Nationalist poet and I, her only child, was born. A love child, out of wedlock."

"Lucky for you and your Mom," Toussaint boomed as he came in at the end.

"No, Caleb," Camille said, as she licked her lips lightly, blew her husband a soft kiss, and winked at Rebecca. "Lucky for you."

* *

Rebecca excused herself saying she wanted to take a short nap. In her bedroom, she took out the messaging device that Oswaldo Lemus had given to her earlier that year when they met on the Charles River.

Please call me as soon as you're free.

A few minutes later Rebecca's cellphone rang.

"Thanks for getting back to me so fast. Can I hire you again?"

"Depends on the job, the last one was a blast."

"I want you to look into what happened to my twin sister."

"Again? We do this fairly regularly with no results."

Rebecca recounted her trip to Montana and the uncovering of

the trove of photo albums. "It's possible that Allison in her last year, between age three and four, showed signs in the photographs we found of being mentally disturbed or autistic. And . . ." Rebecca paused, now having trouble continuing her narrative.

"And what?"

"Okay. Look history is filled with examples of the disappeared children of the rich and powerful."

"Disappeared? What do you mean exactly?"

"European royal families often put their physically or mentally challenged children into asylums where they were never heard from again. And then they just declared them dead. Joseph Kennedy had his eldest daughter lobotomized perhaps to avoid a political embarrassment to the family."

"Your story makes the Spanish Harlem gangbangers I grew up with sound like bleeding hearts."

"Right. No doubt," Rebecca said. "As a child, I thought my sister was still alive. 'Twin vibrations' they call it. It's like amputees trying to scratch missing limbs. I need peace on this. Please Ozzie, can you help me?"

"Becky, I'll do what I can, and because it's you I won't even break any laws, just really bend some rules. But the photographs you brought back from Montana, they need to go through photo analysis. I don't do that kind of work."

"Okay, but I will send you copies of the photos we retrieved."

"And I need birth certificates."

"My grandmother's lawyer has them. I'll ask him to send copies to you."

* *

"What about the other lodges?" Rebecca asked Toussaint later that evening. "Maybe there are some more albums, a picture, a letter?"

"I'll speak to the attorney," Toussaint said. "Let me work with him to get access. I'll have them watched, and we'll search for them as soon as we can do it discreetly."

"That would be great," Rebecca said, as she clenched and unclenched her right fist, trying to release the tension she felt.

"But one thing, let me handle it. You have got a country to run and your well-being to take care. If I have something of significance to report, I'll brief you."

"You mean I can't micro-manage?"

"No. You can't," Toussaint said, putting on his official Secret Service stern look.

"Who's going to analyze the photographs?" Rebecca asked, deciding to leave out activating Lemus for the moment.

"I suggest you outsource the whole job; the Brits have a world-class company, Davis and Parkis. They're alumni of the Scotland Yard. If you agree, I'll send the originals by courier to England."

Rebecca trusted Toussaint's judgment. She would listen to his advice, but she had another problem that needed resolving. She needed Fatima to sign on as her chief of staff or private secretary, any title she wanted, just as long as she was on board.

Chapter 27

Visit with Fatima's Family
Greenpoint, Brooklyn

A few weeks after the election, Rebecca slipped out the back door of New York's Waldorf Astoria hotel and sped over the Queensboro Bridge, heading for the God Bless America Deli on Nassau Avenue in the Greenpoint section of Brooklyn.

Movie trucks, union technicians, and unemployed actors filled the streets that night, all hired for a television series pilot shoot. The script's opening shot depicted limousines and security units whisking an Arab potentate to visit a long-lost cousin, a Brooklyn deli owner.

Rebecca had arranged through a lawyer, at considerable expense, to create this fake movie set to enable her to visit Fatima's family in private.

In the limousine, she put on a full Arabian emir's ceremonial wardrobe: a black linen robe lined with gold, a headdress, and sandals. It wasn't the first time she'd traveled in disguise, and recent Secret Service protocols allowed it. The entourage whisked up the blocked-off street; the film crew, bored, stood about listlessly. The film set must have seemed to them more like a holding pen—not a foot of film had been shot—but at double overtime, no one asked questions.

Rebecca entered the deli and held out her hand to Ahmed and Chaylia Massiri, who sat at a small café table at the back of the store with their children—Fatima, and her brother Hammad.

"I'm Rebecca Tree, and it's a pleasure to meet you finally. I'm sure you're as proud of your daughter as she is of you. After all these years with her at Argyle, I know I couldn't get along without her."

Fatima's father's round face exuded an air of ethereal kindness and warmth that caused her to falter. His brown eyes shone with love and intelligence.

Ahmed wore a white dishdasha robe with blue jean cuffs peeking out the bottom and dark brown tasseled loafers evoking elegance from an American age now long forgotten. Chaylia wore a floor length one-piece black dress with intricate gold embroidery on the chest and sleeve cuffs. The top of her head was covered minimally. Fatima wore a wool two-piece pantsuit with a white silk blouse and a bright red scarf around her neck, which then pulled up to double as a hijab.

Fatima's excited and precocious younger brother, Hammad, who had been adopted by the family as a one-year-old, jumped in to give Rebecca a VIP tour of the God Bless America Deli.

"See, Ms. Tree, half the store has the usual deli items, but now we've expanded, and we're selling more Middle Eastern specialties." Hammad, a tall fifteen-year-old, had a head of thick, wavy hair, black eyes, and olive skin. He wore a blue blazer, blue shirt, red tie, chinos, and tasseled loafers like his father. "And now Mama does all the hummus, labneh, and lentil soup homemade, and guess what?"

"Your same-week sales from last year jumped considerably."

"How did you know?" a beaming Hammad asked. "Pop and I are changing the store name soon to *Massiri New York.*"

"Leave her in peace, little brother," Fatima said, guiding Rebecca by the arm. "We've dinner waiting upstairs where you can try all my mother's specialties. My parents would like to make it their project to fatten you up."

They ascended the stairs to the Massiri's apartment; Rebecca and the men sat on the floor, Arab-style, as Fatima and her mother served a feast. First, they had homemade labneh, a traditional Lebanese yogurt dish, followed by lentil soup. Next came the main course, a baby lamb covered with saffron, currants, and dates. Rebecca's nostrils quivered; the apartment smelled like the spice market in Istanbul. A side plate of roasted eggplant conjured the light-headed perfumes of coriander, warm and nutty, crisscrossed with cumin. A sheet of baklava, stuffed with pistachios, baked in the oven. The smell of honey floated through the room. In the background, the stereo played a classical recording of

Sayed Darwish, considered the father of Egyptian popular music.

"Ms. Tree," Fatima's father began.

"Please, call me Rebecca."

"Ms. . . . sorry . . . Rebecca, did you know that President Garfield could write Greek with one hand and Latin with the other?"

His face radiated like the soft warm light that came with the magic moment just after sunset.

"Daddy, please don't bore Rebecca with presidential trivia," Fatima implored.

"It's fine. I love arcane facts. Mr. Massiri, what do you know about Theodore Roosevelt?"

"He won the Nobel Prize in 1906," Fatima's father quickly answered.

"Correct, and in 1907, he wanted the motto 'In God We Trust' removed from the new twenty-dollar gold coin," Rebecca said. "He thought it blasphemous to use the Lord's name on coins."

"Okay, Daddy, come on, it's your turn," Fatima interjected. The family looked toward their patriarch, smiling. Rebecca waved Fatima and her mother to sit down. "Please sit," she said softly. "Join us."

"Let's see. How about this: Roosevelt kept a parrot in the White House that could whistle 'Yankee Doodle.' Roosevelt started the tune, and then the bird finished it."

Hammad snorted with glee. "Pop, you messed up. That wasn't Roosevelt; it was McKinley."

Now Chaylia interjected, "The Teddy Bear was named after Teddy Roosevelt."

"John Quincy Adams," Hammad said, "kept a pet alligator in the East Room of the White House."

Ahmed, recovering from his earlier error, said, "Martin Van Buren's autobiography never once mentions his wife."

"He also presided over the Senate with loaded pistols," Rebecca added dryly, "a practice I might consider reinstating."

"At his inauguration," Fatima chimed in, "George Washington had only one tooth. His speech, 183 words long, took only a minute and a half to read. It was difficult talking with only one tooth."

Everyone giggled. Rebecca smiled like a chipmunk displaying a full set of teeth.

"Even though you still have all your teeth, you might take a page from his book," Fatima said playfully.

"This is what my father did in our home in Cairo every night with my brothers and sisters," Ahmed said. "We'd play trivia games. It brought us all close, and created a way to teach history to the children."

Fatima knelt behind her father with her hands affectionately wrapped around his shoulders.

Ahmed continued. "Fatima tells me you're a pious Christian. That's good, it's important to have faith. I'm devout, and I've instructed my children, although I don't impose it on them."

"Religion is a wonderful thing," Rebecca said. "Sadly, politics intermingles with religion, and then faith becomes manipulated and polluted."

"Enough said," Ahmed said. "I think the term, in English, is being on the same page. I'm glad to have finally met you after all these years."

Turning to Fatima, his wife, and son, Ahmed said, "Can I borrow Rebecca for a few minutes? I want to show her something in the store downstairs."

Rebecca and Ahmed walked back down the stairs as Ahmed asked Rebecca to sit back down at the café table.

"Look, Rebecca," Ahmed said, as he paced nervously around, reaching occasionally to aimlessly adjust a can of beans or bottle of hot sauce on the store's shelves. "Fatima, of course, wants to continue working with you, and the family would like to support her. But it is a bigger problem."

Rebecca nods, "Fatima told me about the young girl who was thrown onto the train tracks. Hate crimes must be stopped."

"I fought for democracy in Egypt," Ahmed said while nodding his head in agreement with Rebecca. "My wife and I paid a heavy price. We came to the United States with the dream that our family could live freely and in peace. This girl was treated like garbage for rats. That's not the America the world has always admired."

"I will fight for equal protection for all Americans," Rebecca said. "I risked my life for my country and watched American soldiers of all faiths and ethnicities die or get wounded. Hate and discrimination have no place in our society."

"I am torn," Ahmed said, focusing his eyes sharply, "between protecting my family, and putting my daughter in harm's way for a just cause. There are nearly six million Muslims living in America, from dozens of countries. We love America as much as any other group. We have prospered here and we have contributed. Now we no longer feel safe. Yes, a small handful of Muslim, many of them converts, have engaged in terrorist acts, but no more than so-called 'white extremists.' I was adamant about not letting Fatima work for you, but now I wonder if I have a greater obligation to contribute to making America a safe home, once again, for Muslim families."

"I will respect the decision your family makes."

"There is something else we need to discuss. I had an argument with Fatima a few weeks ago about her new job prospect. And I said a few harsh things to her that I regret. I pushed her and she fought back, which she does well if necessary, and then she told me about the role you played in getting me out of jail. In my culture, I have an obligation to you besides just wanting to thank you."

"You owe me nothing. There is no obligation. You were unjustly detained. All I did was point that out to the authorities. Let's not talk about it anymore. It was a long time ago."

"Alright then. But I do owe you the promise that I will give fresh consideration to your offer to Fatima. Now let's go back upstairs and enjoy the rest of this shared special night."

They ascended back to the warm carpeted room just as a platter of baklava was making its appearance. "Dessert!" Ahmed said, nearly breaking into song.

"This is amazing," Rebecca gushed.

"Next time we dine I'll bake my mother's desert, Yemen Honey Pie," Ahmed said.

"He cooks well, for a man," Chaylia said, nudging him as he resumed his position on the carpet.

"And who does the best couscous in this house?" Ahmed said.

No one answered. Hammad covered his mouth with his hand and tugged his sister by her sleeve.

"I guess they didn't hear me. Anyway, I was about to say that America has produced some of the world's greatest leaders," Ahmed said.

"And do you have a favorite?" Rebecca asked.

"Harry Truman."

"Why Truman?"

"Because he said no to the British and French in the Middle East. He felt their colonial interests weren't healthy. And Eisenhower maintained the same position when my country nationalized the Suez Canal. Unfortunately, he had his mind changed later in Iran."

"You know, there might be an opening in the State Department for you, Mr. Massiri," Rebecca said coyly. "This could be a family thing."

"No thanks, I've had my share of politics in Egypt. I'm happy here. But if Fatima does end up working for you, then she must have a very low profile."

"Stop!" Fatima said as she began to lose patience with her father's charming manipulations. "What's this? Daddy knows best."

"I'm just negotiating."

Fatima broke between Arabic and English. "Do you want a *daq raqbatha,* a 'fee for the bride's neck?'"

"Fatima, I'm just trying to do the best for my little girl."

"Save it for when I pick a husband, then show him no mercy," Fatima said, shaking her head.

Rebecca remembered an Arabic expression her army language teacher once used. *Hal bidosh y'ati binto biyaghli mhārha,* she said.

"He who does not want to give his daughter in marriage increases her dowry," Ahmed said, in translation. "Exactly my strategy. My children are priceless, well, perhaps worth an emir's ransom at the least."

"All right, now that your daughter might be on the auction

block, her proposed title would be executive secretary, which would exempt her, by law, from any exposure in the press, but she'd be my *de facto* chief of staff. We can re-visit the title later if you become more comfortable."

Ahmed looked at Fatima, who nodded, and then he stood and extended his hands to Rebecca. She took them, and he pulled her off the floor, looking into her eyes, holding her hands as he spoke.

"May God bless you and protect you. The whole troubled world will be rooting for you. I will have the family's answer no later than your inauguration day." He kissed Rebecca on both cheeks. Rebecca tried to hold back the tears, but one escaped down her cheek.

"I wish I could stay longer," she said, wistfully. "You're going to come to the inauguration, I hope? Please come. I'll have front row seats for you."

Ahmed smiled. "We'll come. But seats toward the back — remember — *low profile.*

Chapter 28

Inauguration Day
Washington, D.C.
Dawn

The residents of Washington, D.C. always complained that their January weather was the nastiest in the country, and a presidential inauguration only seemed to aggravate nature. Howling winds and a furious blizzard had greeted Sam Tree's swearing-in. Two weeks before Rebecca's inauguration, a foot of snow had buried D.C., and the weather forecasters predicted wind chills of twenty below. Then, three days before the event, an unexpected warm front moved across the mid-Atlantic, and athletic-minded Washingtonians responded by jogging in their shorts.

Dawn broke over the capitol, and the sun winked out from the east. At the Washington Monument's base, nearly one hundred protesters in blankets huddled together to ward off the early morning chill. The police department had greeters out; young, personable officers mingled with the crowd, answering questions and tamping down hostility levels. Undercover 'eagles,' mixed among the greeters, scanned the demonstrators to spot trouble: the over-or under-medicated, flunk outs from anger management therapy, would-be or real terrorists and, most dangerous of all, agent provocateurs. Community affair officers handed out hot coffee, fresh donuts, and free tickets to inaugural events: concerts, films, poetry readings, even an opera.

Toussaint coordinated the strategy with the District Police Chief, Jonathon Watson, with whom he stayed in continuous radio contact.

At seven a.m., while walking around the monument area, Toussaint's cellphone rang.

"Rebecca," Toussaint said, "if you still have this foolish idea of taking an early morning run on the Mall," he said, "then you better wait an hour if you need anyone to cheer or jeer you. The place is nearly empty."

"I guess I'm not as interesting as President Nixon. Call me if the Grannies for Peace show up," Rebecca said, speaking from the presidential suite at the Hay-Adams Hotel.

Forty-five minutes later, two prom-length white limousines pulled up three blocks from the Washington Monument. Out of the first, twelve well-tailored octogenarian ladies delicately disembarked, waiting patiently while the driver unloaded their Grannies for Peace placards from the limousine's trunk. From the second vehicle, another seven elderly women emerged, craning their necks like baby robins in a nest. The driver and a male nurse took a wheelchair out of the trunk, unfolded it, and helped the group's longtime leader, Emma Belsky, into the chair.

Murray Belsky, a wealthy Wall Street hedge fund manager who adored his grandmother—although he vehemently disagreed with her politics, had paid for these limousines. On the first of every month, she visited him in his office like a landlord collecting rent. To his continuing chagrin, he would always write at least a ten thousand dollar check for baby seals or a death row inmate's legal defense fund.

Within a few minutes, the platoon of gray-haired ladies assembled with signs around their leader before marching in a formation toward the Washington Monument.

Rebecca's cellphone rang.

"Your friends just arrived. Guess what?" Toussaint said.

"Let's see. They're carrying signs that say IMPEACH REBECCA," Rebecca said, as she regarded a tray of Italian specialty cheeses and olives sent by her old friend Bruno Settepani, the owner of Salumeria Settepani, her favored Boston-based grocery.

"You're so impatient; give them a bit more time."

"Thanks," Rebecca said, as she spread raspberry jam on a crisp croissant.

"You're welcome. They came in two stretch limos, and they're marching in step."

"In step?" Rebecca got up and looked out the suite's master bedroom onto a panoramic view of the White House, hoping to catch a glimpse of the procession.

"Sort of, they're around a sharply-dressed granny in a wheelchair."

"I'm on my way. I deserve to have fun on my inauguration day before I get thrown to the lions."

Rebecca picked up her birding binoculars and looked out of her suite's window, her eyes first focusing on the heavily armed snipers perched on the White House roof. She picked up her day calendar and wrote a note: *Install migratory bird listening station? Who controls W.H. roof?*

She dropped her sightline to Lafayette Park, where a small band of protestors gathered. A thickly bearded man had mounted on his bicycle's handlebars a large stuffed frog, an American flag panel, and a sign, which read, GOD BLESS AMERICA written in black letters, with red letters asking underneath, WHO'S GOD?

When Rebecca stepped out the door of the Hay-Adams Hotel's presidential suite, the Secret Service inner defense snapped to attention. With her hair in a ponytail, she wore shorts, an oversized cap, blue-tinted running sunglasses, and her favorite pair of sneakers, which she had carefully cleaned the previous night.

The lead agent, Lynette Fenton, asked, "Madam President how can we help you?"

Rebecca glanced at her watch. "You can't call me Madam President yet. Maybe in a couple of hours."

Fenton's face flushed. "Beg your pardon. Sorry about that, Ma'am."

"I'd like to go for a run."

"Where to?" Fenton asked.

"Oh, a little run around the Washington Monument."

"Ma'am that'd be quite difficult. They're expecting thousands of protesters. We can't provide security for that on such short notice."

"It'll be a short jog. I'll be quick and discrete, and I have the director's reluctant agreement. Anyway, I'm going; if you want to come, you're welcome, but please don't crowd me too much."

Agents began to scramble while frantically talking into their suit cuffs. Fenton argued with Toussaint on a cellphone while Rebecca went down the hotel's back stairs and out a backdoor. Secret Service agents jumped into their SUVs, and a scrum of muscular, agitated agents now surrounded her.

"Look," Rebecca said, addressing Fenton as she stopped. "If you want to send agents a block or two ahead of me, that might work, and then four of you could run with me, casually."

"Ma'am, begging your pardon," Fenton said. "We've got our procedures."

"Yes, but I have my sneakers on, and I run pretty fast, besides I will soon be the commander-in-chief and, the bottom line, is that, with all due respect, I make the decisions, as to where I want to go . . . and when."

"Yes Ma'am," Fenton said, unhappily. "Let me speak to the director again."

Ten minutes later Rebecca trotted across the National Mall. Toussaint put six undercover Secret Service agents around her. When she found the Grannies, encamped a few hundred yards south of the Washington Monument, she stopped and removed her sunglasses.

"Good morning," she said, to a woman wearing a Granny pin. "Welcome to our nation's capital. My name is Rebecca Tree."

The woman gave her a dazed look. A second woman put her hand over her mouth, looking like she'd seen an apparition. A third woman, wearing a multi-carat diamond ring on her finger, didn't seem phased in the slightest.

"Why, Ms. Tree, this is most unusual. My name is Linda Wolfstein. My late husband Herman worked as Publisher of the Wolfstein Press until a provision of the Garcia-Winthrop Sedition Act landed him in prison."

Rebecca was momentarily nonplussed. Recovering after a pause, she said, "Nice to meet you." Reaching out her hand, Rebecca said, "I'm truly sorry about the loss of your husband."

"Thank you. I appreciate that."

"I know your husband's press. I collected their Nobel Laureates' biology series."

Wolfstein smiled skeptically, narrowing her eyes as if trying to measure her.

"The legal system cannot be used to abuse the rights of our citizens," Rebecca said. "I give you my word that, before the month's out, I will personally review your husband's case."

"I intend to hold you to your word," Mrs. Wolfstein said. "I've heard some good things about you. I'm a skeptical woman, and I'm unhappy about the last few decades of American history, but I still try to keep an open-mind."

"The country needs to chart a new future," Rebecca said. "But it's not going to be easy, given the intransigence of our legislators. I'll need the people's help."

"Let me introduce you to our senior member. She's in a wheelchair, but her mind is sharp." Wolfstein guided Rebecca over to the group's leader. "Emma, this is Ms. Tree, our next president. She's come to the Mall to welcome us. I think that's most gracious of her."

Belsky directed an intense gaze at Rebecca as the two women clasped hands. "My dear, I woke up this morning and thanked God that I have a clear mind," Belsky said. "But as I look at you, I'm a bit worried now that dementia is setting in."

Deeply chiseled lines marked Belsky's face in contrast to a surprisingly long graceful neck like a woman in a Modigliani painting. A small goiter type growth and a patch of ingrown hair marked her triangular shaped forehead.

"You seem of sound mind," Rebecca said, mesmerized by Belsky's steel gray eyes.

"Then what the hell are you doing at the Washington Monument at eight in the morning, wearing those ridiculous shorts on your inauguration day?"

"Well, Mrs. Belsky . . ."

"Please, call me Emma. I insist."

"Emma it is. The day ahead is going to be long and maybe a little boring. I thought I'd start it by getting some exercise and meeting people expressing divergent opinions."

"You found the right lady," Belsky said. "I'm one life-long divergent opinion. And I had a great mentor."

"Who was your mentor?"

"My grandmother. She was Eleanor Roosevelt's private secretary, her confidante, and possibly one of her lovers. My grandmother, when I was a child, told me great stories about going to Mrs. Roosevelt's home, Val-Kil. They had grand picnics, on the grounds, attended by America's brightest intellectuals and artists."

"It sounds so special," Rebecca said.

"It was. America had such hope then, such promise."

"Pretty remarkable woman, Mrs. Roosevelt," Rebecca said.

"No greater woman ever lived. Do you know, my dear, that she had a terribly difficult childhood?"

"Yes, I know. Her mother didn't accept her," she said, recalling Randall Wilson's biography, *The Roosevelt Dynasty*. "Her father was a terrible alcoholic. She was sent away to live with her grandmother, who often locked her in her room."

"Terrible. Why would anyone treat a child like that?"

Rebecca nodded as a slow wave of misery washed over her.

"Locked in her room," Belsky painfully intoned. "And look what she became, the world's first lady. Go figure that."

Out of the corner of her eye, Rebecca saw Toussaint approaching, wearing his sternest Secret Service expression. Upon reaching her, he whispered in her ear.

"Rebecca, we've been monitoring the television news frequencies. They just got word that you're here. If we don't get you back right away, there'll be a full-scale press riot."

"Okay, one minute." Rebecca took out the small pad and pen she always kept in her pockets, wrote quickly and ripped off the top piece. "Emma, here's my private cellphone number. Why don't you have lunch with me at the White House, and we can have a long talk. Will you come?"

"Of course. I'd be delighted. But don't expect me to hold my tongue."

"If you hold your tongue, then you won't be invited back," Rebecca said, with a laugh. Toussaint jerked his head in the direction of a waiting limousine. "I guess I have to go." Rebecca gave Belsky a big smile and a wink. As she left, she looked back at the Grannies for Peace, most of whom still looked stunned, except Belsky, who energetically waved good-bye like a parent at a train station sending her child off to a sleep-away camp for the first time.

Chapter 29

Inauguration Day
Washington, D.C.
Late Morning

"I spoke to President-elect Tree at eight a.m. this morning," Belsky said, appearing on television monitors, seemingly pleased at the prospect of having reporters from all three networks surrounding her. "My group and I had prepared for the day's demonstration, but we hadn't expected to meet the new president. Many of us here have marched for well over half a century. When Martin Luther King gave his 'I Have a Dream' speech in front of the Lincoln Memorial, my mother Frieda sat on the podium."

"How did your mother first meet Dr. King?" a reporter asked.

"Dr. King? She always called him Martin. In jail, where else? Albany, Georgia. Lousy food, and no hot water, Mama always said."

"How many times have you been arrested, Mrs. Belsky?" asked a sandy-haired reporter.

"Oh, just a few. But I'm still young," Belsky paused, like a stand-up comic waiting for the audience to laugh. "My mother, may she rest in peace—well, there's a story—she spent many a night in jail for having fought for the right to organize. She, along with her mother, my Granny Esther, stood on those same steps arm-in-arm with Eleanor Roosevelt, as seventy-five thousand Americans protested segregation and listened to Marian Anderson sing. The year? 1939. And on Easter Sunday."

"Young lady, stop pushing that microphone so close to me. Control yourself. Oh yes, it was Toscanini, who told her she had a voice 'heard once in a hundred years.' Who? Are you dense? I'm talking about

Marian Anderson—look her up on one of those Internet machines they have in your office. And the Daughters of the American Revolution refused her permission to sing in Constitution Hall. Can you imagine?

"You want to know my opinion of Rebecca Tree? I'd describe her as friendly and gracious. I don't think we've much in common politically, but I'm not too old to be surprised. She seems intelligent enough. Who knows, maybe she will be this century's Roosevelt. God knows, we need another Roosevelt.

"No, silly. I mean Eleanor, not Franklin."

* *

At ten a.m., Wolf Global International's weekly political roundtable show, *Inside Washington* began. The host, Bob Daad, set the scene. "Today the country inaugurates a new president. Many look to this day with fresh hope, while others are filled with skepticism. The nation has elected Rebecca Tree, who at age thirty-seven becomes the youngest American president ever. She takes office with the smallest plurality in this country's history. At no time since the Civil War of the nineteenth-century has the country been so bitterly divided and deeply disillusioned. Many say this new administration, lacking any popular vote mandate, begins on shaky ground. Let's go to today's panelists. Marla, could you start off?"

"Thank you, Bob," said *The Washington Post's* Marla Pazer. "Well, I felt skeptical at the beginning of this campaign. Ms. Tree ran a highly irregular campaign. Right out of the starting gate, she shocked older Evangelicals with her blunt talk about ending the 'culture wars' and making near heretical comments for some about the 'reprieve.' With the unexpected endorsement of ex-President Sanchez-Smith came a wave of Hispanic-American voters, and that, in the end, made all the difference."

"But Marla," Theodore 'Tug' Cabrera from CNN interjected, "I found her hypocritical, a view shared by many of the two-thirds of Americans who didn't vote for her. What is she? A born-again Christian? A Darwinist? I think she slid through a minefield of issues. She certainly was clever enough."

"Let me finish," Pazer broke back in. "In the first debate, where she performed so poorly, her four opponents—all male, I might add—ignored her. Women voters didn't like that; they felt it was patronizing, and some sympathies swung in her direction. Her second debate performance was explosive. I mean, what drama: she pretty much challenged John Spencer to go out in the alley with her. But the last debate was awesome. The three men left standing attacked her in a cowardly fashion. And she kept her cool. The awkward smile of the earlier debates became an animated grin. And she gave an excellent rendition of the core issues facing the country. She's one smart lady if you ask me."

"There you go again," Cabrera said. "I don't buy it. My old friend, from the *Post* and her comrades-in-arms, wants to turn every issue into a man-woman issue. I think she sandbagged her opponents; she cleverly set a trap, and they stepped right into it. I think this woman is highly manipulative. Our country is facing serious problems. The Congress is deadlocked, war continues to flare up in the Middle East, and Pakistan remains in a tailspin. If this four-party system continues, the country is going to collapse. All she's offering is more chaos. We need reason in the White . . ."

"Wake up," Pazer interrupted. "The country is already in free-fall. Rebecca Tree wasn't on anyone's radar at the time of her brother's death, at least not in politics. She's highly regarded in the business world, with a reputation as an excellent manager, and she's known for her innovative approach to problem-solving. Maybe I stand alone, but I see a ray of hope for a troubled country."

"Excuse me," Daad said, "we need to switch to a breaking news story out of New York City. One of their seawalls breached about an hour ago, and their waterworks department is scrambling to repair it before downtown Manhattan goes underwater."

* *

At 10:30 a.m. two hikers, a young male and female in their twenties, passed through MPDC's main inauguration spectator checkpoint at Fourteenth Street, just past the Jefferson Memorial. The officer, who questioned them—stationed here since before dawn and desperate for a distraction — appeared to take a particular interest in the girl. Her male companion, who had already passed through the checkpoint, waited impatiently.

"Brother and sister. Well, you certainly look alike. Been to Washington before?" the officer asked, adjusting his badge which he noticed was askew.

"No officer, we're so excited. And we hope to see the new president," she said. "I hear she's real pretty."

The officer glanced ahead to see the girl's companion checking his phone; he squinted to zero in on her face, the details of which were hard to make out under her floppy hat. "Not my type. I prefer blondes."

The girl stroked a panel of her yellow super-straight bob.

"Why don't you show me the pretty eyes under those sunglasses of yours?"

"Why officer, I can't take them off. Blondes with fair skin, like me, are very light-sensitive."

"I'm sure," the officer said, starting to pull back with the sense that he was being put on. "If you're lucky someone will give you a ticket to one of the inauguration events."

"Wouldn't that be far out? Maybe I could get into the ball, and then I could dance with the new president."

"I don't think she dances with girls," he said as he saw his supervisor heading in his direction. "All right, you've been cleared, young lady. Keep moving."

"Oh, that's not what I heard. She'd dance with me, if she met me," the girl said as she walked through the barriers to meet up with her companion, who grabbed her sharply by the arm.

"Damn you, why do you pull shit like that? That dumb cop is going to remember you. Keep pulling stuff like this and you're going to be out of this operation."

"Yeah, what are you going to do, kill me?"

"That might be a good idea."

"Maybe I'll kill you first."

* *

Reverend Spurgeon lowered his boombox voice as he leaned into Fatima's father, sitting next to him in the Old Supreme Court Chamber on the first floor of the Capitol, where a group of Rebecca's friends enjoyed a pre-inauguration brunch.

The new White House Chef, Gudrun Ødegaard, had prepared an elaborate meal: a tomato and leek frittata, gruyere popover sandwiches with fried eggs and creamed spinach, lemon poppy-seed pancakes with Greek yogurt and jam, and a Julia Child berry flan. Ødegaard had proposed starting with a Hangtown Fry featuring oysters, a recipe made famous during California gold rush days. Upon hearing the menu described, the departing White House chef had turned ashen, reminding Ødegaard that Sam Tree's last meal had started with oysters. Unsympathetic pundits at the time had made unflattering comments about Sam Tree's gluttony and his 'death by oysters.' Ødegaard revised the menu.

Rebecca, like a bride on her wedding day, remained hidden out of sight in a holding room before the ceremony.

"I'm just getting to know Fatima," Spurgeon said. She's so bright; a pleasure to be with. She and her brother are delightful."

"Thank you. We cherish them," Ahmed said. "Tell me about your family. Do you have children?"

Spurgeon's eyes misted. "My son Stephen is an agronomist for the United Nations, devoting his life to God's work — well, he'd say science. He helps our brothers and sisters in less fortunate countries. I'm quite proud of him."

"Is he married?" Ahmed said.

"When he was young, I imagined — well I hoped, to be honest — he'd end up with Rebecca. They're childhood friends."

"Matchmaking's not easy," Ahmed said. "My wife's parents tried to arrange her marriage, but luckily she, I should say we, fell in love first. Love starts with chemistry, but shared values are important."

"Yes, Stephen and Rebecca kept up their friendship all these years. And they had something in common: older boys bullied them."

"Bullies are awful. My kids suffered their share for having skin a bit darker than most Americans."

"It affects them. Rebecca fought back; by the time she reached seven, she turned into a pretty ferocious little scrapper. And she stuck up for Stephen as well."

"And why did your matchmaking fail?"

"To be honest with you, as the years passed, Rebecca didn't seem terribly interested in boys, and Stephen ended up being interested only in boys."

"Hmm," said Ahmed, pausing to form his words carefully, "well, we're all God's children."

"It was hard for me at first," Spurgeon said, stabbing his fork at a piece of endive. "I guess I suspected it, but Stephen told my wife and me ten years ago. I kept preaching against the sins of homosexuality, but a year later, I cried in Stephen's arms, begging him for his forgiveness. He just kissed me and said he loved me no matter what I preached."

* *

Rebecca kneeled beside a chair and crossed herself, a habit ingrained from her childhood attendance at the Catholic church of her mother's faith.

She had deliberated earlier over many variations, but had finally landed on her inauguration wardrobe: a magenta wool crepe blazer on top of a black merino wool turtleneck with a matching pencil skirt draped over custom-made knee-high black leather boots. Keith Forsyte had sent her the boots as a present from Anello and Davide, England's most famous shoemaker, where Rebecca's foot measurements were on file. They did seem to hold some magic; her confidence on this day felt like it grew from the boots up. She said a short prayer while pulling at the chain around her neck; her lips brushed the locket. She vividly recalled the day she received it, as an unescorted eight-year-old, taken by a chauffeur to Denver International Airport and deposited on a plane bound for New York.

Rebecca had arrived at John F. Kennedy six hours later, tearful and terrified. An airplane employee escorted her to a waiting lounge, gave her a snack of a granola bar, an apple, and slices of cheese and told her to get comfortable: there would be a five-hour delay for the connecting flight to Switzerland.

Rebecca found an airline magazine in the lounge, which had a centerfold route map traversing five continents. She slowly ran her fingers across the pages recreating the fantasy trips of great adventure she had taken with her twin sister, distracting herself by softly spinning an out loud narration away from the ears of other passengers. She became sad as she imagined where on the world route map her parents had disappeared from her life forever. Finally, she fell asleep under a red Swissair blanket.

Two hours later, a steward shook her shoulder softly.

"Ms. Tree, a courier from Denver just dropped off this package for you."

"What is it?" she asked groggily, struggling to awake.

"I don't know. I'm told your grandmother sent it on a later plane, and we're supposed to let you know that she's sorry."

Rebecca's mouth opened wide; she averted her eyes, caught between fear, hope, and embarrassment. She hesitatingly accepted the small padded envelope with her name on it, and the steward went back to his desk to attend to the demands of newly arrived first-class passengers. Rebecca looked around and saw a partition; she needed to find a temporary hiding place like the one she had in the woods at the edge of her grandparents' mansion.

When she found a seat behind a pillar and felt safe from prying eyes, she slowly pulled the tab on the envelope, and peeled the tape from a small bubble-wrapped wad. At first, she felt dazzled by the bejeweled gold heart-shaped double-chambered locket she found inside, and then when she finally worked the clasp to open it, her body went limp.

A miniature photo rested in the first chamber, which must be her father and mother since they held before them, two identical infants.

Rebecca bit her lip, trying to fight back tears as she strained her eyes to discern the details of the faded gray-scale picture within. She had never seen a picture of her family together like this; never even her parents apart. The second half of the heart was empty, leaving a space about as big as her fingertip that felt massive. She felt alone and frightened fearing her grandparents were sending her to a prison, not a school. At the same time, she felt guided by this gift, the gesture of her grandmother sending her this secreted treasure and the kind of quiet promise it offered.

She would have to be brave; she had a plane ride ahead to Switzerland, and hopefully a path to a happier life. She would try to make the best of it, be loyal to the image enshrined, and someday find a picture to fill the chamber's other half.

* *

Five minutes before noon, Rebecca was in the holding room on a phone call with the mayor of New York when William Tree, his face flushed, came in noisily, uninvited. Rebecca suspected he started his morning with scrambled eggs sautéed with scotch.

She raised her index finger to Tree indicating that he had to wait.

"Do you need additional aid?" she said into the phone. "I will have the power to declare a state of emergency as soon as I'm sworn in. Ok, if you change your mind then call me right away. Yes, and we will be working on 'wet state' relief proposals."

"Rebecca, what's going on around here?" Tree half-screamed as Rebecca finished her phone call. "What's this stunt you pulled this morning? The news cycle is supposed to be dominated by another Millennium Populist president, another Tree, ascending to the highest office in the land. But the networks led their coverage all morning with some syrupy tale of an old woman in a wheelchair who thinks you're the second coming of Eleanor Roosevelt."

Rebecca's face tightened as she spoke with a false sincerity reserved exclusively for her great-uncle and her grandfather. "Why, Uncle William, you and I might disagree on Eleanor Roosevelt's politics, but surely we'd agree on her stature as a singular historical figure."

"Mrs. Roosevelt! God-forsaken communist, and worse. My father knew the Roosevelt family well. Nothing there but drunks, lesbos, commies, and moochers."

Rebecca looked at her watch. Sub-clocks of Beijing, Sharjah, London, Boston, and Chicago circled a centered time display set to Greenwich Mean Time.

Would the whole world be watching this day?

"It's time to make this official. Wish me luck, Uncle William."
William Tree strode off to his appointed seat.

* *

"I do solemnly swear that I'll faithfully execute the Office of President of the United States, and will, to the best of my ability, preserve, protect and defend the Constitution of the United States."

Rebecca finished reciting the oath of office to the Chief Justice of the Supreme Court without the optional final phrase "so help me God." He looked at her expectantly, but Rebecca, ignoring him, nodded to the Protocol Chief, who gave the hand signal to the band, which played "Four Ruffles and Flourishes," and then "The Star Spangled Banner," after which came a twenty-one gun salute.

Rebecca noticed Fatima and her family sitting more than a dozen rows away. Much to her relief, Ahmed had called her a week ago to give the family's permission for Fatima to work in the White House.

He and his son wore conservative three-piece black business suits. Rebecca had sent them colorful ties as presents from the Audubon Society catalog. Ahmed had received a Mallard Duck tie and Hammad a Ivory-Billed Woodpecker tie. Fatima and her mother also wore black suits with modified hijabs.

She could hear the murmurs behind her of dignitaries shocked that she had omitted the phrase sacrosanct to the Millennium Populist's Born Again constituency. She turned slightly to see a red-faced William Tree, so lost in fury that he didn't realize he was kicking the leg of the chair in front of him, a chair occupied by former President Maria Sanchez-Smith, who, in turn, did her best to ignore the commotion. Senator Saunders Albright, the Nobel laureate retired senator from Mississippi, and a leading global voice for ecumenism gave a big thumbs-up. After the gun salute, the Ebenezer Baptist Church Choir, under the direction of Horton Johns, prepared to perform a gospel selection starting with "Amazing Grace."

As the choir stood, an empty place emerged in the mezzo section. To her surprise, a grinning Johns waved to Rebecca and pointed to a seat. With solemn dignity, she joined the choir.

After the choir had finished, Rebecca returned to the podium. She opened her personal Bible, a facsimile of the 1560 Geneva Bible famed for being quoted by Shakespeare and brought to America on the Mayflower, and commenced with a reading from the book of Micah.

He hath showed thee, O man, what is good; and what doth the Lord require of thee, but to do justly, and to love mercy, and to walk humbly with thy God.

She turned and looked at Senator Albright, who used this biblical quote in his Nobel Peace Prize acceptance speech. Rebecca paused, then acknowledged and welcomed the various dignitaries.

She turned, looking briefly at the last five seats on the third row to her right. Rebecca told the Secret Service ed signs on them and allow no one under any circumstances to take the seats. Rebecca blinked her eyes hard and visualized her parents and sister spiritually emerging from those vacant spots. Her father, Nathaniel, sat erect with bright white hair and wire-rimmed glasses framing sparkling, soft gray eyes. One petite hand neatly manicured rested tenderly on his wife Caitlín's shoulder—her reddish hair now graying, freckles fading, free arm wrapped tightly around their other daughter, identical to Rebecca. Doctor Allison Tree. Professor Allison Tree. Ambassador Allison Tree.

Surely they would have been proud and happy this day.

Next to them, she imagined Jackson, her lost love, and Annie, her best friend, as if they too aged in stride with Rebecca. She noted a few laugh lines around Annie's mouth when she smiled; Jackson's face had rounded slightly with time, but he remained robust with eyes that still sparkled. For Rebecca, he remained the bright star in the night sky.

They deserved a full life. They were so special.

Rebecca turned back and continued. "I'm honored to be inaugurated today as the president of the United States. So help me God." Behind her, Rebecca could hear the relieved applause as she had finally uttered the words that custom, not law, demanded.

She began her speech, speaking slowly.

"The winds of history swirl around our great land.

"Over five hundred years ago, monarchs of England and Spain

financed explorers, conquerors, and missionaries to seek new worlds. The winds favored them, and they planted their flags across the Americas. Colonists followed in ships, carrying bags of seed, hoes, and spades as their currency. They prayed to God for a good harvest, and for their children to survive the hardships they knew would come. Native Americans regarded them as illegals, but lacking muskets, and cannons they succumbed to their firepower or alien diseases. A new nation emerged and prospered, and prevailing winds blew pioneers and settlers ever westward, seeking fertile land, opportunity, or the lure of gold in the hills of the Dakotas and California.

"Nearly two hundred years ago, the skies went dark from the smoke of gunpowder, as a nation split into Blues and Grays, and, on now hallowed land, not far from where we stand today, over fifty thousand died at Gettysburg over just three July days—one of many bloodlettings, scarring a nation's heart.

"A little more than a hundred years after the guns of battle lay silent, a minister named King came here, to Washington, to redeem Lincoln's promise. The preacher's words still resonate with us today. 'Now is the time to make real the promises of democracy.' However, not since Lincoln have we faced such a bitterly divided nation. Surely the Emancipator's heart would fill with sadness if he could see the divisions breaking out anew throughout our land. The winds of history have becalmed our great nation. Our ship seeks fresh breezes; our sails need to fill up anew.

"Our democracy has an extraordinary history. As a nation of immigrants, our country has soared to unimaginable heights. We have built great industries and fine universities. Our scientists have led the world in their searches of discovery. Our citizens hold more patents than all the other nations of the earth combined. We have conquered outer space, and unraveled the mysteries of the brain. In medicine, we have blazed new frontiers joining scientists worldwide in the use of stem cells to regenerate the organs of our sick or wounded.

"But our work has just begun, as we also live in a world troubled by war, famine, and despair. Environmental catastrophes have severely impacted our nation. Only this morning, New York City narrowly averted a serious breach of its seawalls. These ongoing crises, which divided our country into red states and blue states, have split us further into four bitterly partisan interests, with two more unfortunate distinctions: wet and dry. Congress must address these issues, urgently. Inaction can no longer be tolerated. Our military remains mighty, but force is rarely a good option, and must always be reserved as a last resort. As I speak, young boys and girls are leaving their loved ones and preparing to stand watch in desert lands, to finish battles their parents, even their grandparents, already shed blood for. We must find new solutions to old problems."

Rebecca looked at the folder holding the rest of the speech that she had pondered over for weeks, and had finally written out two nights ago, in long hand.

She put it aside, extemporizing. "As I stand in this hallowed place, I feel humbled. Great leaders took the oath of office that I take this day—Washington, Jefferson, Lincoln, and Roosevelt to name a few. They were sometimes men of action, sometimes men of words, and more often they are remembered as both. So today I have decided to keep my words short, and pledge myself to devote my presidency to action. Thank you. I look forward to serving as your president."

Rebecca's inaugural address became the second shortest in history. When asked later, she said she had been inspired by the example of George Washington.

She turned and shook hands with the dignitaries in attendance. From the corner of her eye, she spied her uncle, looking like a poker player with a long face after being dealt an unpromising hand.

What did he expect?

He left the podium with an entourage of associates.

Washington that day became uncharacteristically awash in a rare moment of reverie, as a procession of ceremonial military regiments, citizens' groups, marching bands and floats led by a coterie of politicians paraded slowly up Constitution Avenue. To the chagrin of the Secret Service, Rebecca left the armored presidential limousine and joined the Ebenezer Baptist Choir as they performed a hit parade of gospel's greatest songs. When Rebecca passed the button-plastered contingent from

Grannies for Peace, applause broke out from the octogenarians before they proudly hoisted all their signs of protest.

* *

The two hikers walked parallel to the parade route.

"Look, I can see her," the girl said, nesting her sunglasses in her wig. Her hat kept flopping over her face, so she had thrown it in her backpack. "Oh, she looks delicious."

"Shut up. Just observe her habits."

"Habits? Okay. She's got long legs. She's tall, sometimes taller than the agents who surround her."

The boy looked back at a tree line. "If we had a kill contract, I could hang upside down by my legs in that tree," he said and pointed in the distance. "And I'd get her, one shot, right through her eye, left or right. I could pick either one."

"You're full of hot air. Hang, right, like a monkey. They've got all those tree lines shut down like submarine hatches."

"How would you get her?"

"Hey bro, killing is the ultimate sport. Any 'wus' can kill with a sniper scope. I'd trap her and gut her with a knife." Then she clasped her hand over her mouth and widened her eyes mockingly. "Monkey boy, he hangs from trees."

The boy grabbed the girl and pushed her hard. "You've got a pin for a brain."

She put her hands on her hips, twisting her head. "Jonnie, little Jonnie, Daddy is calling you. He needs you to go out in the shed with him. He did me earlier; now he wants to do you."

"Shut up, you bitch," he cried out in agony, as his palms squeezed over his ears. "I'm getting a migraine. You have my pills. I need one of each—the yellow one and the blue one. Hurry."

* *

Rebecca turned to give a final wave to Emma Belsky and the Grannies for Peace. Fifty yards over their shoulders, her far-sighted eyes locked into a young couple walking parallel to the parade route. The boy had

191

strangely straight and vivid yellow hair reaching down his cheeks from under a baseball cap. She blinked; he held a long lens camera and wore shorts exposing well-muscled legs. A flash of déjà vu briefly unsettled her.

Quickly engulfing the couple, demonstrators dressed like fish marched in a chorus line fashion, high-stepping as they went.

Chapter 30

January 20
The Inauguration Ball

Rebecca had released the complex bun arrangement constructed by a fussy hairdresser and changed into a black silk dress, its top shirred, her shoulders bared and adorned with a pearl necklace. The dress stopped just above her knees, and her legs sky-scrapered off the ballroom floor, which made her self-conscious, as there was no way of hiding her clumsy dance moves.

Rebecca had been appalled when the incoming White House staff began to plan a series of inaugural balls. Lacking a first husband, and feeling still very awkward about her reluctance of being thrust into the world's spotlight, Rebecca insisted that there should be only one ball. She banned spotlight dances with fancy lighting designs projecting the Presidential Seal. In the end she relented somewhat; it was too difficult creating a plain vanilla version of the ball, but she made substantial modifications.

On the inaugural ballroom stage, twelve servicemen stood formally while in front of them one wheelchair-bound wounded veteran represented each service sat in full dress as well.

The Homeless Musician Outreach Program, led by six singers rescued from the streets and restored back into society, performed.

A local gourmet soup kitchen catered the event. A wealthy supporter donated one thousand, ten dollar farmers' market coupons, which were converted to meals for the inauguration guests.

Rebecca first danced with the head of the Army, General Peter Grace, who, fortunately, wasn't much of a dancer either; she had no problem following his militarized steps.

Grace, with a thinning head of nearly pure white hair framing his light blue-gray eyes, stood two inches taller than Rebecca.

"The food's great," Grace said. "I loved the tomato dish."

"Yum, an heirloom tomato no less, with melting chunks of goat cheese. Listen," Rebecca said, knowing she couldn't postpone addressing Grace's recent loss, "I was so sorry to hear about your wife."

"Thank you. It was sudden." Grace paused, his eyes moistening. "Far too sudden. Our family appreciated the lovely letter you sent."

"How are your children doing?" Rebecca asked as they moved in a mechanical synch through the crowded floor.

"My oldest, Kelly, is having the most trouble adjusting," Grace said. "She misses her Mom . . . we all do. We're a pretty tight-knit family."

"And your son?"

"Jack's a soldier. He's like his father. We keep walking in our boots." Grace managed a wistful smile. "Actually, he keeps his flippers on. He's a Navy Seal."

"Does he want to be a lifer, like his old man?" she said, with a nervous laugh.

"Ah, to tell you the truth, he's not happy in the Navy. He wants out."

"Why?"

"It's your inaugural ball," Grace said. "You should enjoy it. There'll be plenty of time to talk business."

"Tell me."

Before responding, Grace surprised her with a twirl. They now faced Caleb and Camille Toussaint dancing cheek to cheek. Their faces radiated a happiness that Rebecca couldn't help but envy.

Camille glanced at Rebecca's feet appearing startled as she noted the plain ballet flats. Rebecca had been afraid to wear heels, as most of the men she might have to dance with would be shorter than her. Worse than that she knew the heels would increase the chances she might stumble or fall on the dance floor.

Finally, Camille pursed her lips and nodded her head up and down supportively. Then she momentarily took her right hand off her husband's shoulder and gave Rebecca a thumbs up.

Both couples stopped. "General Grace," Rebecca said, "I believe you know Director Toussaint. Have you ever met Camille?"

"No," Grace said, directing his gaze at the Toussaints. "I've never had the pleasure." Camille wore a black chiffon full-length gown with a crepe backed satin bodice and plunging V-neck that shimmered against the fabric of her husband's tuxedo. Around her neck dangled a silver necklace with garnet, amethyst, and blue topaz stones.

Toussaint whispered into his wife's ear.

"General, would you dance with me?" Camille asked.

Toussaint held out his hand to Rebecca, completing the exchange. The orchestra played *The Blue Danube Waltz* at full speed. He swirled her around the ballroom; she struggled to follow his steps as he executed a series of complex moves, two Viennese turns and then a reverse fleckerl. Hoping not to stumble, Rebecca tried to turn off her mind and enjoy surrendering to his lead. They passed Fatima's young brother, Hammad, in a tuxedo, proudly dancing with his mother. Rebecca laughed harder and harder as they continued to whirl. Out of the corner of her eye, she noticed three additional teams of Secret Service agents taking up positions at the ballroom entrances.

On the sidelines, the young British king plied the Brazilian ambassador's daughter with flutes of champagne as he stuffed cornbread tartlets with ricotta and green zebra tomatoes into his mouth.

Only nineteen, the king stood over six-feet and had broad, muscular shoulders. The First Playboy of Europe, he traversed through Monte Carlo, Cannes, St. Moritz in the old world and St. Barts in the new. A full head of sandy-blonde hair framed a set of sparkling blue eyes. His teeth glistened a polished pearly white. A British pundit had famously described him, "as long of hair, and of teeth. He has pretty ears, and a full royal 'em dash' in between." Rebecca would do her best to avoid him.

A moment later an agent interrupted their dance and requested a private moment with the director. Before departing, Toussaint twirled her back to General Grace and whispered quickly into his wife's ear.

"What's going on?" Rebecca asked, continuing the waltz with General Grace.

"I don't have a clue. They look like they're running a threat assessment. But it can't be imminent, else they'd have done the Secret Service hustle with you."

"Hustle? Not in my limited dance repertoire. Finish your story, Peter," Rebecca said. "Why's your son unhappy with the Navy?"

"I'm finishing a report, for your eyes only. It'll be on your desk by the end of the week."

"Preview it. I'm your boss now — please."

"If you insist," he paused. "All the branches, except maybe the Air Force, face a similar problem. We're being infiltrated by subversives." Grace's face reddened, his eyes pulsed with anger. "Who'd love to destroy our democracy."

Rebecca's brow furrowed. "Who? Which groups? America-Firsters?"

"Yes," Grace said. "They've been infiltrating the services for more than a decade now. They try to get into elite units — Delta or Zebra — but they favor the Navy Seals. They seek to learn skill sets, which they can take back to their vigilante groups. And they've been successful, particularly with their cross-border raids into Mexico."

"It has to be fixed," Rebecca said, remembering Fatima's offense at her use of the word 'fix' once when she vowed to convince her parents to let her take a job in the White House. But fixing such matters, or giving her all in the attempt, was why she was here. Her eyes burned as she pictured night riders in white robes terrorizing Mississippi and Louisiana, and the man who might have stopped them — Abraham Lincoln — had he not been assassinated.

"They're not going to operate on my watch."

"I hoped you'd say that," Grace said. "Whatever you decide to do, you need to circle your wagons. The government you just inherited doesn't have many reliable players."

She ticked off a list of names. Grace shook his head negatively on many of them.

A few seconds later, Toussaint tapped Grace on the shoulder, "General, I need to borrow Rebecca for a few minutes. Would you mind if I cut in on you?"

"Something happened. Spill, what's up?" Rebecca asked, as she clumsily stepped on Toussaint's foot.

"It's nothing, not yet," Toussaint said.

"Tell me, or I'll step on your foot again."

"We've been flooded with threats."

"Isn't that usual?"

"Yes, but they're usually unfocused, coming in wholesale, if you like, against the executive branch, Supreme Court judges, Little League coaches, the guy who does the weather . . .

"And now?"

"We call them boutique threats, and we take them much more seriously. We've gotten a lot on the Mexican embassy, the Venezuelan Embassy, Hispanic talk-show hosts, Latin movie stars. It's all too cohesive, and the Internet chatter keeps ramping up, getting more ugly and more virulent. Our analysts are worried that something is imminent.

"Before I changed clothes for the ball ..."

"Oh, your dress looks great," Toussaint said. "You look beautiful. Camille and I were just talking about it."

"No, I wanted to tell you that I signed the executive order that you asked for—my first act as president. Jacob's Unit will have the funding and resources you requested, and I'll get you more, if necessary."

"That's good news. Thank you, my agents will appreciate that, a great deal. I'm just concerned, though," Toussaint sighed. "I didn't want to say it before, on your inauguration night, but we're getting more threats than usual that we're tracing back to the border states, Arizona, and New Mexico. America-Firsters."

"Threats against whom?"

"You."

Part Two

Chapter 31

Three large moving trucks had arrived, at the White House, several days before John F. Kennedy's first term. Ronald Reagan left the White House with sixty moving trucks carrying presidential papers and personal possessions.

For Rebecca: a single van with Massachusetts plates arrived bearing a painted slogan, BACK BAY EXPRESS, ALWAYS ON TIME, NEVER OVER PRICE. Moving men unloaded five suitcases of clothing, twelve boxes of books, two cartons of photo albums, and one frayed wood and leather steamer trunk. Later, a larger truck pulled up to deliver her personal desk, a Tesla VII, manufactured by Electric Office.

Rebecca's desk had a mechanical bureau panel that held her main computer and an array of embedded remotes, which controlled a network of wireless monitors, telephones, and intercoms that she had installed in the Oval Office.

She knew an office covered in sticky notes wouldn't do, so she created a new system using 3x5 index cards of assorted colors. She slid each full card into a dedicated scanner slot on the lower right-hand corner of her desk. The scanner sent it to her computer, which recognized her handwriting and analyzed the content, noted header and date, and filed the contents while cross-referencing and indexing all the data and the card color. After scanning, the cards passed through a ultra-violet eraser that blanked them, thus recycling them for additional uses. The system worked as a seamless extension of her mind.

After the moving vans unloaded, the Chief Usher, Sylvester Sutton, a portly man with a ruddy face and a bulbous nose, arrived to give Rebecca a tour of the White House. His left eye twitched and blinked repetitively, and he jokingly referred to himself as the last Protestant to serve in the White House. When Rebecca asked a question, he would squint and wrinkle his nose. The edges of his mouth sometimes trembled.

"If you need a light bulb, or if a toilet leaks or the King of England can't find his coat, I'm your man," Sutton said, clearing his throat.

"Can we walk around the grounds?" Rebecca asked.

The White House struck Rebecca as a drafty, archaic structure that consumed energy needlessly. If she had her way she'd tear it down and start over, installing thermal pumps, gray water recycling systems, and worm composting bins. She wasn't sure she could sleep in a building made of materials that off-gassed twenty-four hours a day. Maybe she should have packed a tent and a hammock.

"Whatever you like. I'm at your disposal. I work days, nights and weekends," Sutton said, leading her down a corridor to a door that exited onto the South Lawn. "I like to dazzle new occupants with facts about the White House."

"Please do. I love facts."

"Good, well the White House has 132 rooms, 32 bathrooms . . ."

"Thirty-two? You must waste a lot of water."

"Well, yes," Sutton paused, and seemed to wait for his eye to stop fluttering, "there are 412 doors, 147 windows, and 28 fireplaces."

Rebecca made a face. "Fireplaces, they've got to go."

"*Go?*" Sutton said, his mouth now in full twitch. "Impossible, you'd have to tear the building down."

"No, not go, but I won't allow wood to be burned. I intend to cut the White House's carbon footprint by at least half. Tell me, Mr. Sutton, do you have the stats on water and fertilizer usage for the lawns?"

"No, maybe I should get the groundskeeper over."

Rebecca kneeled down, pushing her finger into the turf. It felt spongy to her. She looked up at Sutton, "Didn't Woodrow Wilson graze sheep on the South Lawn?"

* *

A flustered Sutton directed Rebecca back inside.

"Whenever you wish, I can arrange for the groundskeeper to answer the questions I couldn't. Perhaps tomorrow? I'm sure he's already left for the day."

"That would be fine. Remind him to bring a list of native plants as lawn substitutes."

Sutton wiped his quivering lip with a handkerchief from his waist pocket, and he appeared to be swallowing grunts. "Yes, of course. We've moved your suitcases to the President's Bedroom."

"Didn't you get my email? I want to sleep in the Lincoln Bedroom."

"But Madam President, we're not set up for that. It lacks command communication capability."

"You have electricians; they can re-wire the Lincoln Bedroom."

"Madam President."

"Just get it done, Mr. Sutton." Rebecca took off her glasses and glared at the Chief Usher. She would sleep with Teddy Roosevelt's ghost, even Calvin Coolidge's, and the spirits left by Abraham Lincoln. But not with Sam Tree's ghost. Never.

Chapter 32

Pentagon Situation Room

In the Pentagon situation room, lights flickered momentarily before going dark as Admiral Messerole, chairman of the Joint Chiefs of Staff, finished his presentation.

Rebecca, surrounded by briefing books, sat at the far end of the conference table. She came to the meeting supplied with yellow erasable legal pads, a deck of multi-colored index cards, and green, red, and yellow highlighters. She had already filled one pad and a dozen index cards with block letter titles and notes, all in her distinctive cursive with its left-handed slant.

"Give us a minute, Madam President," said Messerole, "my aide is checking whether we have a full blackout."

Rebecca rifled through the soft orange leather messenger bag that accompanied her on most occasions with its invaluable cubby of inner compartments. She'd been lugging it around with her since Annie gifted it to her at Oxford. It had scuffs, tears, even a patch but it had served her well. Digging into it she found in a side-pocket the shape she was looking for: a thin LED flashlight with a recessed crank. She gave it a few turns and pushed down two flaps on its chassis, creating a three-pronged wand of light. She placed it on the table, minimally lighting the room. "There we go, gentlemen. Perhaps we can get Congress to appropriate monies for a few of these for our military."

A ripple of laughter went through the room, and it appeared that General Grace couldn't resist playing Rebecca's straight man. "What else do you have in there?" he asked.

"Let's see," Rebecca said, doing her best to work the moment, like a magician pulling scarves out of a top hat. "One miniaturized crank radio, iodine pills in case a power plant goes amok, water purification tablets, a compass, a pen that writes upside down, dental floss and . . . well, you know, lip gloss."

Washington's infrastructure, like the rest of the country's, had deteriorated. The Pentagon's basement flooded a dozen times a year; sump pumps worked around the clock and employees complained of mold. Construction of another story on top of the existing structure remained three years behind schedule and four billion dollars over budget.

The room lights flickered back to half power. A naval officer said into Halsey's ear, "My aide says it's a rolling blackout through D.C. and Northern Virginia. We're on generators now. Hopefully, we'll get full power shortly."

Rebecca stood up. "This power failure has conveniently highlighted one of my primary concerns."

"Yes, Madam President, please — the floor is all yours," Messerole said.

"First let me compliment you and your staffs," she said, extinguishing the flashlight and throwing it back into her bag. "The briefing books you prepared for me are excellent — perhaps not the cheeriest of reading, but that's not their purpose. Let's see if we're on the same page. Why don't we open this discussion with each of you picking a single threat you feel is facing us this decade? Maybe we could begin with the Air Force?"

"I see Russia's re-militarization as the primary threat," General DeSeco said. "They're well-supplied with long-range bombers, intercontinental missiles, and nuclear weapons."

"China continues to gain an upper hand over us in technology," Halsey, the Navy man, said. "Their Mao drones, which can carry 50.2 kilograms, have enough lift to carry mini battle tanks which can be dropped behind enemy lines. Outfitted with ultralight ion lithium batteries, each of these armored vehicles can engage in conventional warfare for up to five hours."

Halsey continued with his detailed list, pulling Rebecca toward sleep. She managed to stifle a yawn before anyone noticed. Looking down at her messenger device, she read an incoming request from Jock Bollinger, the head of Davis and Parkis.

Madam President, we are making good progress analyzing the family albums provided by Director Toussaint. We would like you to send to us by courier some samples of your hair and saliva swabs to do DNA testing.

Why? Rebecca texted back.

Just to create a baseline for any DNA profiling we might look at in the future.

The request unsettled Rebecca, as she often thought there must be some generational poison in her genes that she was better off not passing along. But if her DNA could possibly unlock any clues about Allison, well then, so be it.

"State sponsors of terror," said Owens, from the Marines.

Rebecca's head snapped up at this.

"Iran continues to strengthen. Iraq is now their ally, and their new Prime Minister, Tariq al-Dhouri, could re-emerge as a strong man. Iraqis are already fearfully calling him 'Little Hussein.' Add to the mix Pakistan, which has more nuclear weapons than ever, and half the country under resurgent Taliban control. It's a poisonous brew."

"I've become increasingly concerned," General Grace of the Army jumped in next, "about being able to maintain stable military forces. The military mirrors the civilian world and domestic instability is spilling over into the service branches."

"All right, let's put the overviews on a short pause, " Rebecca said. "I've spoken to the British, French, and German governments in the last few days. We all agreed that we need to develop a unified strategy of de-escalation, leading to a global treaty on reduced defense spending."

"With all due respect," DeSeco, the Air Force general, spoke out, "I don't think the Russians can be talked into de-escalation."

"Not talked," Rebecca said, "but they have an Achilles' heel."

"Which is?"

"Their economy has been propped up for the last two decades by the astronomical price of oil. When oil hit three hundred dollars a barrel, they spent without limit. At two hundred dollars today and falling, they're feeling stretched."

"But Madam President, this is not a military question."

"Of course it is. Our forces uses seven hundred million barrels of oil a year. We have to take a leadership position on conservation; cutting consumption is a strategic military decision that will further squeeze the Russians."

"Yes, that's true, and no doubt, we in the military could do better, but it's still a drop in the bucket."

"Not so fast," Rebecca said. "The American military is the single-largest purchaser and consumer of oil in the world. I want all four services to soul-search this issue. At any rate, let's move on, as this session is meant to look at the big picture. Let's talk about technology for the moment. I'll be looking for more initiatives. We can't allow the Chinese to widen a technology gap between us; it'll cause irreparable damage."

The Air Force chief of staff smiled at Rebecca for the first time in the meeting.

Turning to Admiral Halsey, Rebecca said, "Am I correct that we have three carrier groups currently stationed in the Persian Gulf?"

"Yes, the Eisenhower, Kennedy, and Roosevelt have been stationed there since last year's air attacks on Iran."

"Draw down one," Rebecca said.

Admiral Halsey bolted upright in his seat. Suddenly his monotone voice disappeared. "That could be a rash move. May I ask why?"

"Three is overkill. We need to make a gesture of good intentions in the region, particularly to the Iranians. Their new president, while no friend of the West, is more moderate than his bombastic predecessor. The French are convinced that they could re-start the stalled tripartite talks. Talk is cheap — we've got nothing to lose by pulling back a bit."

"As you wish, Madam President. I'll bring the Eisenhower Group south to the Gulf of Oman."

"How about a little farther," Rebecca said with a smile, "how about the Gulf of Aden?"

"I could live with that. It's only one additional day's sail."

"Good, let's turn to . . ." a humming sound came into the room, as power was fully restored to the Pentagon, and the noise of air ventilators softly filled the background. "…General Grace's concern about a reliable military. Peter, you wanted to make a background presentation on subversion within the armed forces?"

Grace stood up, holding a pointer, waiting until an aide finished placing some charts on the wall.

"Let's start with Buford Brown," Grace said.

"He was a former Army Ranger from Taos, New Mexico, who is credited with founding Native Force a decade earlier and recruiting members out of the ranks of Army Special Forces and Navy Seals. The election of the first Hispanic president, Maria Sanchez-Smith, charged the growth of the movement, and circumstantial evidence linked them to failed assassination attempts on her."

Grace looked around the room briefly, before continuing.

"Alcohol, Tobacco and Firearms agents, tipped off to a military arsenal of machine guns, explosives, and bazookas killed Brown in a shootout, but not before he had built a network of cells that shared a common ideology, engaging in random acts of violence against Hispanics and federal government property."

"Have you improved screening techniques for your recruits?" Rebecca asked.

"Yes," Grace replied, "but the conditions that spawn these malcontents keep broadening."

"Like?"

"High unemployment and hardening racial attitudes cause them to re-wire their social connections. They're birds of a feather; they flock to each other."

"Great," Rebecca said with a look of disgust, as her fingers drummed the table, "so they're viral."

"I'm afraid so," Grace said, before continuing his narrative.

After the raid on Brown, Grace explained, the ATF agents found paperwork including a list of a dozen cells identified, each with a coded commander and drawn in a tree structure. There was an empty space in the first spot in the chart; Commander Beta stood in the second, and then Commander Gamma, and Commander Delta. The uncovered information cache included target lists, mainly federal buildings and immigrant rights centers in the Southwest.

Rebecca sprang from her seat and began to pace. "We need more resources on this," she said, interrupting Grace. Her throat tightened, she swallowed hard as she tapped the void on the chart. *Circle your wagons*, Grace had told her at the ball. "Who's Alpha? There must be a Commander Alpha? Have we identified any of the named commanders?" she said with urgency.

"No," Grace said, "but we think Buford's code-named his first lieutenant Cobra, and groomed him to take his place and be the Commander Alpha if Buford died."

"Why?"

"The ATF agents found three sheets of paper, not in Buford's handwriting or his style, written in block letters, with a 'literary' description of a gruesome killing."

"*Literary?*" Rebecca asked.

"Well, an amateur attempt at being very graphic," Grace said. "There's a copy in your supplementary folder, and at the bottom, Buford scrawled, 'Cobra, great page-turner. Make it all happen. You're the man.'"

Rebecca stood behind her seat; she put her reading glasses on and picked up the top two sheets out of a folder marked TOP SECRET. The first page proclaimed universal copyright under the common laws of the sovereign citizen nations and the second page proclaimed the title, *Part Two: Murder Across America.*

Chapter 33

Oval Office

Old habits die hard, Rebecca thought. She sat, before dawn, behind her desk in the Oval Office, watching the BBC twenty-four hour financial news, the same station she followed weekday mornings for years to help assess fluctuations of global currencies. The markets had not opened in New York and Chicago, but the dollar continued to fall in Frankfurt. The *Financial Times* correspondent explained, in an on-the-air commentary, that smart money short-sellers, betting heavily, believed the new American president lacked the strength to assert fiscal restraint over a divided Congress.

Little Tree and Baby Tree had llar. When Little Tree, her great-uncle William, became Secretary of the Treasury, one dollar and a half bought one Euro. By the time her brother Sam, Baby Tree, had died, it took three dollars to buy a Euro. With an enormous currency exchange discount, Arabs, Asians, and Europeans arrived in hoards to visit America, essentially a fifty-state outlet mall. Shoes, hats, brownstones in Manhattan, urban shipping ports in Baltimore or Seattle, vast farmlands and factories in the Midwest — they bought it all with glee.

At seven a.m. Rebecca heard a knock on the Oval Office door.

"Come in."

"Good morning," Fatima said. "What are you doing here so early?"

"Me? What about you? Come over here and watch this with me."

Fatima pulled up a chair and looked at the screens.

"What do you think?" Rebecca said.

"The dollar lost two percent against the Euro in the last two weeks. Sorry, but that's huge. My textbook says global financial markets aren't very impressed with you."

"Exactly," Rebecca said, switching to Wolf Global's morning talk show.

". . . the country needs more than a few good church sermons," said the commentator, "before our inexperienced new president can move the country in the right direction, and, as we can see this morning, the global financial markets opened jitterily."

Rebecca slammed down the remote, shutting off the television. "Is the Congressional delegation on time for their breakfast meeting?"

"Yes, Gilad gave me a heads up. They'll be here at eight-thirty," Fatima said.

"Good, are you joining us?"

"No, I'm invisible, I hope you remember."

"Yes. The 'invisible machine' is still being shipped from Sweden," Rebecca said. "It will arrive any day."

"Anyway, I've got videoconferences backed up all morning, with task forces presenting more recommendations for executive initiatives or proposed legislation. I'll re-cap it for you at the end of the day."

* *

Seven men and one woman sat at a round dining table, tenuously attempting a genteel political discussion with the new president. A four-party system, now a political reality in America, brought the legislative agenda, except for spending bills, to a complete halt.

"Gentlemen and Lady," Rebecca said, making her first Plan A stab at persuading legislators, "you have no choice but to put aside your partisan differences and legislate. The country is facing several critical emergencies that have to be dealt with."

"Madam President," said House Speaker John Mauro, "with all due respect, my friends from the wet states are demanding too much. The nation can no longer afford to repair the damages done by forces of nature."

With the meeting almost in its second hour, Rebecca's patience was worn thin. *Not this 'act of God' bunkum again. Only God acted while men stood still?* Voice rising, she stood up from her chair. "In a few days,

I intend to send to Congress emergency legislation for coastal infra-structure relief."

No one spoke; then the Millennium Populists' senior senator from Colorado, Brody Kemper, emitted a low growl. "Madam President, before you send us legislation, perhaps you might re-think signing the D.C. Relief Act," he said.

The act, which had sat on Sam Tree's desk, awaiting his expected signature when he died, proposed moving the waterlogged seat of government from Washington D.C. to a western state not at sea level—with Colorado, Utah, or Idaho the prime candidates for the new location. A provision of the act compensated all elected represen-tatives for real estate losses on homes they had purchased in the last twenty years. Pundits called it the Congressional Real Estate Relief Act and applauded the caretaker president, George Jenkins Bayou, who, to the shock of his fellow Millennium Populists, refused to sign it after Sam Tree's death.

"The D.C. Relief Act is unconscionable," Rebecca said, enraged. "The Army Corps of Engineers spent twenty billion dollars on the Potomac Basin seawalls, and they leak like seventeenth-century Dutch dikes. Congress has failed to take any responsibility for the environ-ment for decades. And now you want reimbursement for your real estate losses from global rising seawaters?"

An angry murmur rippled the room. Rebecca knew she had no friends in this group. "I'll look at an amended D.C. Relief Act only when the Congress comes to the aid of the coastal states. If I can't make my case with you, I'll make it with the American people."

Rebecca heard a muttered comment passed from Mauro to his col-league from Michigan, "Seventy percent of Americans didn't even vote for her. She's got nowhere to go."

Rebecca knew that no one in Washington would be willing to give her even the shortest of honeymoons. Disgusted, Rebecca gathered her papers and started to leave the room.

At the door, she gathered herself and turned back reluctantly to address the group. "Thank you for spending your valuable time with me this morning. The country is looking forward to your leadership. Good day, I'm due at another meeting."

* *

Toussaint waited for Rebecca in a conference room down the hall from the Oval Office.

"Good morning, Madam President."

"Stop calling me that. It sounds like you're mocking me."

"Are you enjoying governance?"

"It's awful. I never knew the world had so many idiots, and that the majority of them live and work in Washington D.C."

"Trust me, it will get worse."

"Thanks for the consolation. You wanted to show me something?"

Toussaint picked up a remote and a screen dropped from the ceiling while a video projector ascended from a slot in the desk.

"This footage is from the Secret Service archives — the visuals and audio come from drones, fixed surveillance cameras and buttonhole cameras worn by agents involved in this incident."

"Why do you want me to see this?" Rebecca said, taking a seat.

"The Secret Service archivist recently reported some missing files. One of them is the cover folder that the senior agent on this incident filed. So we pulled all the associated material."

"Caleb, where is this going? You still haven't answered why you want me to look at this."

"Perhaps for your amusement. Also, I'd like your comments."

"Somehow I think this is for your amusement, not mine. It better be more entertaining than my breakfast meeting."

"It will be; trust me."

The opening shot, a fixed camera, showed a tree line of mature aspens. A solitary figure, a tall young girl, emerged from the woods burdened with a heavy rucksack. She had jet-black hair and a face that appeared ghostly white.

"Recognize the hiker?"

"Don't think so."

"You sure?"

"No comment."

213

Rebecca slipped back into a scene she had, until now, long forgotten. Seventeen years ago, she emerged from these woods, looking down into the valley where Merewether Tree's sprawling mansion, dubbed the White House of the West, reposed. A thick mask of white foundation covered her freckles, and she was in a phase of dyeing her hair from a box from the pharmacy.

Her heart had pounded that day as her eyes surveyed land she had last seen as a child. Several rock formations lay ahead, and she had to gamble on moving quickly for cover before anyone could spot her. Deciding to run for the first outcrop, she was halfway there when a man exited a small shed near the main house, holding a rifle with a sniper scope. Rebecca burst the last few yards and dived behind the formation as three rapidly fired bullets pinged the rocks over her head.

Rebecca's mouth had gone dry, and her legs felt mushy. She hadn't bargained for this; at worst she thought she might be charged with trespassing. Being shot at with a sniper scope wasn't on her agenda. She would have to try to handle it; she had reached into her rucksack and took out her only weapon, a boomerang. If the marksman got close enough, she planned to distract him with an errant rock, rise quickly and, with luck, kneecap him. *Terrible odds*, she had thought. She would wait to see if he would come to her.

Several minutes had passed until she heard a whirring sound. A CH99 ultralight helicopter with the Secret Service logo emblazoned on it dropped down over her.

A loudspeaker barked out commands: "Attention: this is the United States Secret Service. You are trespassing on protected private property. Come away from the rocks and stand with your arms over your head and your palms extended forward."

Two agents holding sub-machine guns soon surrounded Rebecca.

"Who are you? And what are you doing here?" the shorter of two agents asked. His voice bleated out stridently, like the ring of a vintage telephone.

"I'm on a hiking vacation," Rebecca had said, her voice trembling, as she tried to get her bad leg to stop shaking. "I'm a birder. A black-throated gray warbler was spotted in this area two months ago.

I'm hoping to spot it and photograph it."

"What is your name?"

"Sandra Kingsland," Rebecca had replied as naturally as she could.

"Where do you live?"

"Do you think you could use a more pleasant tone?"

The older of the agents, tall and gray-haired, who had been observing the encounter, stepped forward. "Alright Ms., I'm in charge at this location. You can talk to me. May I ask where you live?"

"Kuwait. Why did your agents shoot at me?"

"We didn't shoot. A private guard did. He has been temporarily disarmed. He says he put out warning shots. Why Kuwait?"

"I'm on vacation. I have six months left of active duty. That's where I am stationed."

"Can I see your I.D.?"

Rebecca had handed the man her Sandra Kingsland identity provided to her by the Army. The older agent passed it to the younger, unpleasant agent, and told him to run it through their wireless computer.

"It matches, but the record is photo-restricted," he said, passing the screen to the lead agent, who stared at it for a minute. "We should take her photograph and fingerprints before . . . if we let her go."

"Look, last time I checked, trespassing is a misdemeanor," Rebecca said. "I've answered your questions, and you've checked me out. I'm not submitting to anything else. If you want to call the local police and arrest me, go ahead, but I'll hire a lawyer, and you can explain in court when I sue the Secret Service why you've arrested an active duty soldier on a bird-watching vacation."

"We should arrest her now," the young agent said.

"Stand down. It's my decision to make, not yours." Turning to Rebecca, the older man said, "We would like to test and search your rucksack. If there are no weapons, we'll drive you back to Hillock and let you go."

"Go through the rucksack if you like, but I'd rather walk back to wherever the national park begins."

"Okay," the polite agent said, who then had given a hand signal to the two other agents standing by the second ATV. They took the ruck-sack, ran a wand over it for explosives and gunmetal, and then went through the contents, finally signaling back to the lead agent.

"I am going to walk with you. You need to retrace the last two hun-dred yards from where you came out of the woods and then you're back in God's jurisdiction."

"Thanks," Rebecca said. "And thanks for being polite to me."

"You're operational in Kuwait?"

"I can't answer that."

"I was operational ten years ago. Your ID has one additional digit and your photo restriction pretty much answers my question. It's a bit unusual to see a solo hiker out in this terrain."

"I had planned to come with a friend, but, unfortunately, he couldn't make it." Rebecca moved a piece of jewelry up and down a chain around her neck.

In the conference room, Rebecca and Toussaint looked at each other. Rebecca thought about asking to pause the tape but feared she would fail whatever test she was being subjected to.

He knows, he must know, she thought. *Is this why he's showing me this?* Rebecca replayed the scene of Jackson's death, as she often had.

His final words had come in fits and stutters, blood bubbles form-ing on his lips. Rebecca had struggled to hear his choked whisper, lean-ing in closer as he died, afraid she might miss a word that she'd never get back. He told her to wait; he promised to get better, or was he asking her to promise to wait for him?

There would be no 'better.' To this day, Rebecca still honored his dying wish through her silence.

She vividly remembered how she felt at that moment the agent had commented on her being a solo hiker; she began to quake with that old feeling that her chances for a normal happy future died with Jackson. They had planned the vacation for over a year: hiking, bird watching, and, as a grand finale of the trip, sneaking into the woods of her grand-father's estate to show him where she played as a child.

"You're limping," the older agent said. "Were you wounded?"

"It's nothing, a bit of shrapnel."

The footage showed them hiking the last one hundred yards in silence.

"Okay, Ms. Kingsland. You're now back in public land. I hope you find your warbler."

"Thanks. Can I ask you a question?"

"You can try."

"When does deer hunting season begin around here?"

"In two weeks."

From her pocket Rebecca took out a small-caliber bullet.

"Last night, about a half a mile up the ridge and five or six miles inside the forest, I buried a deer, shot with this bullet, which couldn't have weighed forty pounds. It's not right."

The agent took the bullet from Rebecca, turned it around several times in his hand as he examined it, before staring at Rebecca.

"Do me a favor. Don't come back this way."

Rebecca had silently departed from the agent, heading into the woods before turning back to the agent on hearing his voice shouted out.

"You know I don't believe your story."

"I know."

Rebecca watched the end of the archived clip, recalling what she had said to herself that day:

I'll be back some day. Next time I'll be better prepared.

The screen went dark. Toussaint said, "Whoever our mystery hiker is, she was lucky I wasn't the senior agent that day."

"Why?"

"Oh, I would have arrested her," Toussaint said, a small impish smile crossing his face. "Kept her in lock-up overnight, sweated the truth and hair dye out of her."

"You're so right," Rebecca said with a grin. "I would have at least waterboarded her."

Chapter 34

Oval Office

"Madam President, I understand your ideas," Walley Walters, the White House's head groundskeeper said, "but that budget is controlled by the Parks Department."

Rebecca tried to be diplomatic in her early encounters with governmental bureaucracy. Getting up from her desk, she walked over to a sideboard piled with stacks of papers sectioned off with paperclips; on top of each group stood a subject tag. She reached for the pile labeled "energy," and began thumbing through a dated chronology.

"Here it is. The Energy Security Act of 1980. There's an addendum, which updated the law in 1981, and I also have President Carter's signing statement. It clearly entitles the president to initiate reasonable non-structural modifications to the White House and its grounds to improve energy-efficiency and highlight sustainability."

Rebecca reached for a set of blueprints, rolling them onto the floor. "I've had a mark-up done. I want to break ground as soon as possible, to create a quarter-acre vegetable and herb garden on the South Lawn. And I want another quarter-acre restored with native plants to replicate the land of a particular year, let's say 1492."

"I'm sympathetic, Madam President, but this could cause an uproar. Vegetable gardens, okay. We've done that in previous administrations. But touching the lawns will be trouble. Vast expanses of manicured lawns are a symbol of American power and wealth."

"Exactly my point. Great empires fell because they never understood the unintended consequences of their successes."

Back behind her desk, she drummed her fingers on its surface.

"Check with the White House legal counsel office, and ask them their opinion," Rebecca said. "You have an excellent record as the executive groundskeeper, and I want you to be comfortable, but I do intend to undertake these projects," Rebecca said.

Rebecca's intercom panel flashed. "Excuse me a second. Yes, Gilad, what is it?"

"Sorry to interrupt, but Fatima asked me to tell you that the hearings on Dr. Waziri's nomination are getting ugly. She thought you should see it on C-Span."

"All right. Tell her to give me five minutes, and ask her to join me. Thank you."

Turning back to Walters, Rebecca said, "We'll have to finish our conversation another time."

Rebecca walked Walters out of the office. "Write me a note by the end of the week as to your thoughts on the matter. And don't forget the environmental impact statement for the White House lawn, with a side-by-side comparison of the benefits of native plantings in replacement."

"I'll get on it right away. You have some good points. And thanks for inviting me to talk; you're the fourth president I've served, but this is the first time I've been in the Oval Office."

Fatima looked furious, as she scurried into the Oval Office, carrying files under her arm. Rebecca hadn't seen her this angry since the day they met.

"These senators are outrageous." Fatima grabbed a remote control clicker off the Oval Office desk. "Watch this."

C-Span filled the screen. It showed a room half-filled for a hearing being held by the Senate Agriculture Committee. The tension appeared to be mounting as more senators, their aides, journalists, and spectators starting filling empty seats. Several women with infants playing around their feet held signs that read OUR CHILDREN DEMAND HEALTHY FOOD and BILLIONS FOR WAR, NO DIMES FOR NUTRITION.

"As I already explained to you, Senator Stanhope," Dr. Waziri said. "Palestinian families tend to be large and extended. The last wedding

I went to, my cousin Abdullah's son, had five hundred guests, all family members."

"I have a list here, provided by a foreign intelligence service, which identifies five of your cousins as Hamas supporters," Senator Stanhope said.

"Which ones?" Dr. Waziri said.

Waziri lifted a pen, looking as if he wanted to take notes.

"It's classified. I can't share it with you," Senator Stanhope said.

"What?" Rebecca, from behind her desk, shouted at Stanhope's image. "You're a demented idiot."

She pushed the intercom button. "Gilad, can you connect me to the Israeli ambassador? Tell him it's about the Stanhope hearings."

Turning to Fatima, she said, "Alert our congressional liaison. I want to sit at Dr. Waziri's side. This is intolerable. No, on second thought, better I go unannounced. Tell the Secret Service I want to move in the next few minutes."

"I don't know if that's a good idea," Fatima said. "The press spins everything you do to sell more single copies or get a better audience share. *The Late Show* has even started a new feature . . ."

"I've seen it. 'Ten Dumbest things President Tree did today.' It's a hoot. I try to watch it every night."

Rebecca's intercom rang.

"I have the Israeli ambassador on the line," Levine said.

"Dov," Rebecca said. "Thanks for getting right back to me. On C-Span, a few minutes ago—Oh, you already know about it. Good. It's not your list he's waving around. I didn't think so. You're preparing a press statement now? That's great. Thanks for your help. Yes, I have an hour scheduled for you next week. I look forward to seeing you."

Rebecca reached into a large glass jar sitting on the top of her desk embossed with the presidential seal. She regarded the red, white and blue Tofutti jellybeans inside and seemed indecisive; finally, she popped a blue one into her mouth.

As she swept out of the Oval Office with Fatima by her side, Rebecca said to Levine, "I'll be back in an hour."

"Where are you two going?"

"Capitol Hill."

Fatima shook her head negatively. "I'll run ground support," she said into Rebecca's ear.

"Okay, I'm going alone."

"What'll you be doing there?" Levine asked.

"Breaking legs."

Chapter 35

En route to Capitol

"This is George Edgardo for ABC News. We're cutting into our daytime programming to follow an unusual developing drama in Washington, D.C. between the White House and Congress. The Senate Agriculture Committee, chaired by Senator Stanhope of Nebraska, is holding hearings on President Tree's first cabinet appointee, Dr. Farid Waziri, nominee for Secretary of Agriculture. A naturalized American citizen born in Palestine, Waziri is a co-recipient of a Nobel Peace Prize for his work on bio-diversity. Senator Stanhope is now pursuing a pointed line of questioning concerning his background. We're waiting to pick up a feed from C-Span."

Six modified electric carts stood in the White House driveway. Rebecca insisted that, whenever practical, the president should be moved without leaving a carbon footprint. The Secret Service cooperated reluctantly, citing security concerns, to which Rebecca counter-argued that spontaneous movement maximized protection.

She had also declared that she would not be using the gas-guzzling Air Force One except for emergency or high-security situations. Two weeks ago, Rebecca attended a United Nations environmental conference; unannounced she had boarded at five a.m., on the Potomac River, a high-speed hydrogen-fueled hovercraft arriving in New York's East River two hours later. To her surprise, the New York press corps applauded her initiative of finding a carbon-free route to New York, which more importantly did not tie up midtown traffic.

Edgardo from ABC updated viewers. "While we're waiting for the C-Span patch, we're going to cut to a live feed from our White

House correspondent, Jack Smathers. "Jack, can you give us an update? I understand the president is in motion."

"Yes, this is unprecedented," Smathers said. "I'm sitting as pool correspondent, on an electric cart, which is part of a small caravan shuttling over to Capitol Hill. We've just started off in the direction of the Washington Monument. Our camerawoman has a live shot of President Tree. Take a look."

In her cart, Rebecca sat wearing a black business suit and overcoat. Her red mane began the day as a ponytail, but before leaving for Capital Hill, Rebecca had pulled it into a knot, held together by a long leather lace. A hairdresser in Boston taught her the style, calling the result "Bun of Steel." The carts, painted green with white letters reading ECO CART, had been purchased by the Secret Service and modified with lightweight armor plating. A wireless monitor attached to a swivel bracket displayed real-time footage of the committee hearings, which Rebecca watched, frowning, while furiously taking notes on a yellow legal pad.

"The president doesn't look too happy," Edgardo said. "Did she make any comments before embarking on this journey?"

"Yes, she answered some questions, but she nearly bit the Wolf Global's correspondent's head off when he asked her whether she felt Senator Stanhope's line of questioning seemed fair," Smathers said. "She said, and I quote, 'I don't like bullies, Mr. Daad.'"

"Well, given Wolf Global's coverage of her, I think that comment might have a double meaning," Edgardo said. "Let's look at the wide shot of this unusual entourage. It's quite the image: six armored golf carts moving at about five miles an hour; still, it should take them about ten minutes to get to the Capitol which might be faster than assembling the customary fleet. Two dozen Secret Service agents are jogging in a solid line next to the carts, so that's a lot of footprints, though none of them carbon."

Chapter 36

Rebecca sat at the witness table of the Senate room. She whispered into Dr. Waziri's ear. He wore a bemused smile and shook his head, apparently in agreement. Senator Stanhope banged his gavel, trying to restore order after the commotion caused by Rebecca's unscheduled appearance.

"Welcome, Madam President," Stanhope said. "This is most unusual, but we are always honored when a president comes to visit us humble legislators. I am told you would like to make a statement."

"Yes, I'll be brief," Rebecca said.

"Good," Stanhope stated in a tone as flat as an all-night talk show host.

"Senator, I must say that you've opened a Pandora's box," Rebecca said. "You're here to advise and consent."

"Or not consent, if we wish," Stanhope banged his gavel again, "with the concurrence of the rest of the committee members."

"You've tried to bully this witness, a globally-acclaimed expert on agriculture," Rebecca said. "You've not questioned him on the merits, and you've waved a piece of paper which is nothing but a fabrication."

"Madam President, are you accusing me of being a liar?" Stanhope said.

"Not yet. But the paper you brandished about today is false. Now maybe someone duped you into presenting it. Perhaps it was an innocent mistake on your part."

Sebastian Derry, the senior senator from Maine, tried to get the chair to yield the floor to him.

"Mr. Chairman," Derry said. "I would like to question the nominee on the merits. These innuendoes are not proper, and belittle the dignity of the Senate."

"I'm the chairman of my committee," Stanhope said. "I have a sworn duty to the American people to investigate the backgrounds of cabinet nominees relevant to my committee's mandate. I'll run this hearing as I see fit."

An argument broke out between the two senators, which soon became a dispute on the rules and procedures of the committee.

Stanhope is an old gasbag, Rebecca thought.

Tedium momentarily overtook the hearing, and Rebecca began to sketch a caricature of Stanhope on a pad she carried. She drew a head shaped like a watermelon, propped on top of a ninety-seven-pound weakling's body. She fashioned his nose into a carrot, and his eyes stared like a near-sighted owl, ears pointy like elf shoes.

As an anxious aide briefed him, Stanhope angrily eyed Rebecca, who flipped the drawing to the underside of her pad. One of Fatima's aides entered the hearing room and brought Rebecca two sheets of paper, which she quickly skimmed, before passing it to a soon-smiling Dr. Waziri.

"Mr. Chairman, if I may," Rebecca said. "I have just been handed a document from the Israeli ambassador to the United States, restating the congratulations of his government to Dr. Waziri and referencing his work and his character at the time he won the Nobel Prize. Also, the Israeli government categorically denies it is the source of any list banded about in this hearing room."

Stanhope, in response, appeared groggy, listless. His mouth hung open like a late round boxer with only defeat to grasp, eyes blood-speckled, shoulders hanging like he had been shot hard in the ribs.

"Mr. Chairman," Senator Derry said. "I think it's time we send this nomination to the Senate floor. Our country and the world are suffering from unprecedented disruptions of the global food chain. Every hour children die of malnutrition in sub-Saharan Africa. Childhood diseases, from meager food and water sources, have spread through North and South America. Dr. Waziri has the expertise to address these problems. Continuing these hearings serves no purpose."

An aide approached the dais and spoke into Stanhope's ear. At first, the senator's head bobbed up and down. The faces of the press corps betrayed a disappointment, perhaps fearing that the hearing might fizzle out faster than a wet firecracker. Stanhope shook his head side to side, almost violently, like he might come off the ropes. He ungraciously pushed his aide aside and gaveled his desk so hard that a photographer's tripod quivered.

"Order, Order — we can't tolerate these interruptions," Stanhope growled. "If the room doesn't calm down, I'll consider issuing contempt citations."

"Mr. Chairman, will you yield?" Derry said.

"No, I'll not yield!" Stanhope said. "Order, Order! I'm suspending these hearings until further notice."

The room broke into chaos as the senators argued. The press shouted out questions at Rebecca, but she didn't respond. As she made her way to the exit, the Wolf Global White House correspondent said to her, in a near-whisper, "Not very presidential. A bit unhinged of you, if I might say so."

A smile crossed Rebecca's lips as she stumbled on a step, nearly falling as she managed to drive her knee simultaneously into the correspondent's groin. A secret service agent on her left flank cleared a path for the president, completing the takedown, blocking the entire incident from the cameras. Then Rebecca swept out of the room.

A moment later, Edgardo of ABC News came back on the screen.

"President Tree stormed out of the hearing room in response to Senator Stanhope suspending her nominee's hearing. Led by a flying wedge of Secret Service agents, a bit of a melee ensued with her exit leaving the Wolf Global correspondent, Bob Daad, on the ground. She appeared to be quite angry.

"Daad responded to other correspondents questions with a terse 'no comment.'"

Chapter 37

Oval Office

"I never felt so frustrated in my life," Rebecca said, turning to Fatima in the Oval Office after clicking off another network news panel of experts hammering away at Rebecca's policy initiatives.

"You've become so impatient," Fatima said. "You never behaved this way at Argyle."

"Yes, but I . . . we . . . were in control. We worked with competent, intelligent people who got things done. The government is filled with idiots—morons and imbeciles." Rebecca twisted a thick wad of shredded paper in her hands. "If the Senate can't confirm a Nobel Laureate then nothing will work," she said, grabbing a cluster of six paper clips, methodically unbending them, one at a time.

Fatima had project-managed more than a dozen academic task forces from Harvard, Chicago, Berkeley, and the Universities of Texas, Virginia, and Alabama. They compiled plain English studies with legislative recommendations on a broad range of topics: the environment, conservation, job-creation, micro-finance, tax reform, and fair trade. They prepared a bill for Congress, requesting fifty billion dollars for a government-guaranteed micro-finance bank, projected, after three years of implementation, to create 250,000 new jobs per year and generate ten billion dollars of annual new tax revenues. On tax reform, they focused on one proposal: to eliminate the cap on social security withholding that would keep the retirement system solvent for an additional thirty years. A few media outlets gave good reviews, but most labeled the proposals as grandiose, preposterous, delusional, or worse.

"Everything is 'dead on arrival'. This idea of going over Congress's head and appealing to the American people—now I see that's naïve," Rebecca said, assembling shredded paper and paper clips into a human-like figure on her desk.

The intercom panel embedded in Rebecca's desk glowed, as a color thermometer indicator climbed from green to red, like a car with a busted radiator hose on a hot summer day.

"Yes, Gilad, what is it?"

"I'm told to give you a heads up. A series of dams collapsed in West Virginia. We don't have a damage assessment yet."

"All right, thank you." Turning to Fatima, Rebecca said, "Could you check this out for me, and let me know how serious it is?"

After Fatima had left, Rebecca took another paperclip, unbent it slowly, and stabbed her paper doll.

Chapter 38

Schell, West Virginia

Sitting on cots set up on the high school's gymnasium's floor, dazed survivors of flash floods that ravaged Kentucky and West Virginia did not appear to notice a tall young woman surrounded by men in suits standing underneath the basketball hoop.

Rebecca pushed her way out of the circle of suits and moved toward one woman in particular whose head hung limply over her lap. She was looking at a wrinkled picture of a boy, a posed school portrait with a peacock blue background that matched his eyes.

"We're doing everything we can to find your child, ma'am."

The woman looked up, slowly, as if being awoken. "Are you? His troop was camping somewhere below the dam; they had been working so hard toward their wilderness survival badges. No one's heard from them. Will you tell someone to look for my boy? His name is Dane Buchman. He's only nine. Please, ma'am, no one's telling me anything," as she reached for Rebecca's hand.

"Do you want me to pray with you?" Rebecca asked, squeezing her hand.

"Please . . . anything. I just want Dane to be safe."

Rebecca got on her knees next to the woman's cot. "Dear Lord," she said, in a quiet voice, "hear me in my plea. I ask You, if it be Your Will, for the quick and safe return of Dane and the rest of his troop to their loved ones." The woman put her hand on Rebecca's wrists, her eyes leaking tears as she joined in saying her own prayer.

As Rebecca rose, the woman looked up at her quizzically. "Are you from the Red Cross?" she said.

"No, I came from Washington to do what I could to help out."

"God Bless You," the woman said as Rebecca moved back to the suits.

"It's no excuse that your governor is in the middle of the Caribbean on a cruise boat," she said to Governor Shondell's aide.

"West Virginia is doing everything we can to rescue the missing," he said.

"I'm sorry, it's not enough. Your answer is unacceptable. I have responsibilities that exceed the concerns of individual states. Look around you."

Sitting listlessly, survivors sat sporadically nibbling at Red Cross meals. They hugged family members who had lived through the ordeal; the faces of the less lucky swelled with grief. The Saint Ignatius Elementary school, now serving as an emergency shelter, stood on high ground four miles away from the rampaging waters of the Stony River.

Marine One had bucked rough weather flying through a pause in the storm to land at the schoolyard outside of Schell, West Virginia. A wall of water ten feet high had swept down a twenty-mile valley, obliterating everything in its path.

Rebecca learned that the first of the dams broke sometime after midnight. The Boy Scout troop leader's last GPS had them camped a half-mile below the main dam at Stony Bottom.

"We can't get our rescue choppers up until this new storm front breaks, and the river has caved in all the roads," said Shondell's aide. "We have rescue units trying to move on foot along the banks; they hope to get to the dam area by dawn tomorrow."

"That's not good enough," Rebecca said. "We have Special Operation commandos at Fort Bragg. Their all-weather rescue choppers are state-of-the-art, and they can drop mountain-ready teams. If anyone can find survivors out there, they will."

"I'm sorry, Madam President, our governor is adamant that this is a matter for the State of West Virginia."

According to the information Fatima prepped her with before this trip, the governor of West Virginia, Bobby Shondell, led a group of state executives who militantly opposed any federal influence in their states' affairs. They adamantly refused government funds allocated for health care, housing, and education and clogged the court systems with law-suits challenging any imposition of federal mandates.

"Hold on, please. I'm getting an incoming call from our state's attorney general."

Rebecca looked at her watch and began tapping her foot, trying not to explode, as she digested her first taste of local states' rights politics in action.

"Madam President, I just spoke to our attorney general who con-tacted the governor. I'm told that the Colorado National Guard is send-ing all-weather helicopters with mountain rescue teams. They'll be here in ten to twelve hours."

"That could be too late," Rebecca said. "I'm calling in airborne res-cue from Fort Bragg."

"Madam President, this lacks legal precedent."

"There's no more time to waste," Rebecca said, brushing a strand of hair away from her eye as her mouth set tight. "I'm overruling your Governor in the name of a nine-year-old boy scout, a legal resident of your state."

"Who? I'm told you can't do that. It violates the Posse Comitatus Act. We take states' rights seriously in West Virginia."

"Good for you. I take human rights seriously," Rebecca said, turn-ing to the Justice Department lawyer who had accompanied her. "Would you give this gentleman a copy of the Defense Act of 2007, which vests the executive branch with full authority to deploy federal troops for a natural disaster? Now tell your governor and attorney gen-eral that I would appreciate their cooperation in this matter; I would like to avoid any finding that West Virginia authorities appear negligent in saving their constituents' lives."

"I need a written order then," said the aide.

The Justice Department lawyer handed Rebecca a one-page autho-rization letter citing the congressional law and its relevant sub-section. She scanned it quickly and signed the bottom. The lawyer used an embossed stamp to certify the signature and signed as a witness.

Rebecca handed the letter to the aide. "The Federal Government is taking charge of this operation until the situation on the ground stabilizes. Choose a classroom; if we could assemble a representative from the sheriff's department, the state police, Homeland Security, and the governor's office there, in say fifteen minutes, we could run a coordination meeting."

Rebecca speed dialed General Grace from her security phone.

"I'm on the ground in West Virginia. How many mountain rescue teams are ready to deploy?" Rebecca listened for a minute. "Two? See if you could get two more up? No, I insist. I don't care what you have to do. Just do it. Now. That should work. I'll get you the scoutmaster's last GPS coordinate. Two hours flying time? Every minute might count. Some of those kids might be clinging to tree branches. I'll get back to you on that."

Chapter 39

South Lawn of White House

"Welcome back," Fatima shouted over the roar of Marine One's helicopter blades. "Good job with the rescue operation, but your trip is getting a lot of flak."

When the whoosh and whir of the helicopter blades quieted, Rebecca said, "Thanks. Wait a second before you splash cold water on my face, okay."

"You're not a one-woman show running a private company. Everything you do now comes under intense scrutiny," Fatima said as they walked to White House.

"A desperate mother asked to me to help save her son."

"Well, that's good. But the press had a field day mocking and criticizing your actions."

"All right, let's go into the Oval Office. Then you can scold me privately."

Rebecca hardly had her coat off when Fatima threw on her desk a sheaf of newspapers, many with harsh headlines. PRESIDENT ABUSES EXECUTIVE AUTHORITY screamed the *Washington Times*. ON QUESTIONABLE MISSION spoke New York's *Post*. The discovery of the entire Boy Scout troop got a scant mention, as they had fortunately diverted themselves nearly half an hour before the dams burst in an attempt to rescue an injured baby deer.

The New York Times took a more neutral position, with an article entitled, MANY IN CONGRESS CRITICAL OF PRESIDENT'S ACTIONS. The *Times* article declared that despite what might have been the best of intentions, many considered the president's actions precipitous, lacking the measured calm required of a chief executive. Congressional sources questioned whether President Tree demonstrated a temperament appropriate to a leader, characterizing her behavior at the Senate Agriculture Committee hearings as angry and erratic.

States' rights advocates pulled no punches, with quotes describing the president's actions as "irresponsible, unconstitutional, and dictatorial." The Governor of New Mexico asserted, "Our great state will never allow our citizens and their rights to be trampled on by the federal government."

"What else?"

"The FBI Director and his team are waiting in the Situation Room."

"Who scheduled a meeting with them?" Rebecca said.

"I did," Fatima looked at her watch, "in half-an-hour."

"What's the meeting about?"

"A couple of unpleasant murders which they think have ominous overtones."

"This doesn't sound like it belongs on my desk."

"I think it does. They previewed the files for me."

Rebecca began to turn back to her desk but stopped. "Fatima?"

"Yes?"

"Let's get something straight: *I'm* the president."

Fatima, only a twitch at the side of mouth hinting at a break in her composure, left the room without a word.

Chapter 40

FBI Director Teddy Moscovi
Oval Office

"Conspiracy," said FBI Director, Teddy Moscovi, his fist slamming into an opened palm making a loud slap that echoed across the room. "Two ugly murders two hundred miles apart, and it looks like the same killer or killers."

Moscovi stood in front of a map of the United States, his face flushed beet-red. A sharp dresser who favored tailored suits, cashmere scarves, and custom-made Rocket Buster cowboy boots, he had the physique of a half-grown brown bear. He financed his luxury tastes by writing a best-selling book, *A Cop's Life.*

"This was a well-orchestrated hit with an ugly *modus operandi,*" Moscovi said, continuing his presentation. "New Hampshire State Police found the first body two nights ago, and the coroner believes the killing happened between sixty and seventy-two hours prior. The victim was Jack Switzer, a Pulitzer Prize reporter whose investigative pieces ran in *The New Yorker* magazine.

"The preliminary autopsy reports that the victim had been ice-picked to death," Moscovi looked to Rebecca, who was biting her lip, "with body parts dismembered."

Rebecca felt her stomach roil. "What about the second murder?"

"Early this morning, NYPD, at an abandoned construction site in East New York, Brooklyn, found a decomposing body, a girl in a dumpster. The coroner says this one died, at least, a week ago, killed with a stiletto, but the dismemberment has the same signature."

Lynching images came to Rebecca's mind, in which the murderers took sadistic pleasure in severing body parts. People got killed every day in America, but chopped up bodies were rare, and now there were already two in the first months of her presidency.

"The killers, if they're plural, looked like they trained together," Moscovi said. "The damage done by the weapon thrusts is nearly identical in pattern."

"Trained?" Alarm bells shrieked in Rebecca's mind. "Why do you think the killer or killers were trained?"

"Most indications point to a professional but, other aspects seem to be the work of a psychotic."

"Explain please," Rebecca said, exhaling the tension building in her body. She had always seen herself as tough, if required, but now she doubted that she was strong enough.

"We can start with no fingerprints in the cabin, except the victim's, but . . ." Moscovi paused, "are you sure you want to hear all this?"

"Yes," Rebecca said. *No*, she thought, *I don't want to hear any of this.*

"The killer left a clue," Moscovi said, "meant to taunt. Switzer had an ugly bite mark on his penis, as well as multiple lacerations."

"What about saliva left by the bite?" Rebecca asked, feeling her eyeballs bulging against her sockets as she struggled to maintain a professional demeanor.

"No DNA. The forensic dentist retrieved a partial impression, and it shows the biter has a snaggletooth; it could be a partly broken tooth or a deformity, but the perpetrator wore a latex bite and mouth guard, which is an Internet or drug store item. Given the size of the impressions left, the crime lab believes with a high degree of certainty that the biter is female."

Rebecca's brain felt like melting butter. Trying to shift gears away from the gory details, she asked, "Do we have any information about the story Switzer was working on?"

"No. Not yet. His editor told us he treated his work, the subject, and the details, as top secret. *The New Yorker* never knew what he was up to until he sent in a final draft. Every other week for ten years they sent him a check; they might get back five stories one year and then not even hear from him for the next two. His laptop is gone, and it looks like a cleanup squad sanitized a writer's customary tools — paper files, notes, and appointment books."

"Back-up files?" Rebecca asked.

"Nothing yet; he used a continuous hard drive, but that's gone as well. We're trying to determine if he had an online backup account or a confidante to whom he emailed drafts."

"What kind of dragnet do we have?"

"New Hampshire troopers set up roadblocks in coordination with neighboring states. But the killer or killers most likely escaped before the authorities secured the area. These killers are adept, and they've crossed state lines. The only lead we have suggests a pair."

"What's the lead?" Rebecca asked.

"A couple of day hikers who had come through a police roadblock fifty miles north in Maine told an officer that they had passed, the previous week, two other hikers — a white male and white female, moving south on the Appalachian Trail. They didn't think anything of it at the time, but they appeared loaded heavy with gear, a little too heavy for the Appalachian Trail, and . . ."

"And, what?"

"A mountaineering ice pick stuck out of each pack."

Rebecca paced the room, and her voice rose. "ID's? Is *anything* coming up from any law enforcement databases?"

"No — race, size, and sex are all we have to feed into the computer. The dental impressions are a long shot, but we're working it. The hikers spotted stood about two hundred yards away from our eyewitnesses, and both of the suspects wore floppy hats and climber's goggles."

"Hair color?"

"FBI sketch artists worked all morning with the witnesses. The way the drawings are coming out, it's possible both suspects wore wigs."

"Wigs, in the woods? That's insane."

"Maybe not. When they composited a drawing of the rucksacks, the eyewitnesses realized they had both seen two small antennas on the packs. One of our analysts theorized that they had portable ground radar units, not much bigger than a cellphone. Perhaps they saw the hikers coming, moved as far away as they could, and beefed up their disguises."

"Why do you think they didn't kill the hikers?"

"Day-hikers. If they killed them, a search party would have been out looking soon after nightfall. It must not have worked with the killers' timetable."

"And what about the girl in New York?" Rebecca asked. "What do we know about her?"

"Erin Rodriquez, nineteen years old, unemployed, no known family. Her girlfriend, who she lived with, put in a missing person report ten days ago. The friend said they went to a cowgirl club, and a girl, with a baby doll voice, wearing a red wig with a face made up like a clown picked Erin up. A lot of transsexuals go there for a weekly costume night. Our suspect threw some hundred-dollar bills around. Erin went off with her and that's the last time she was seen."

"Any other physical clues?"

"Yes, CSI in the dumpster found some strands of red wig hair; NYPD is out checking every dollar store in the city. And again no fingerprints; the bartender said that the suspect wore long white ladies gloves like you might find in a thrift shop."

"Bite marks?"

"No, but we haven't found all the body parts, but there was a swastika carved recently, on her breast."

Moscovi's last comment triggered a surge of nausea. Rebecca stood up too quickly from her chair, trying to suppress the gagging as she made a stop-sign gesture with her hand. The room began to spin and tilt; she steadied her arm against a chair, waiting until her blood pressure came back up.

"I can't go here. This isn't my job," Rebecca said, swallowing a salty taste she realized must be her own blood; she had bitten the inside of her cheek.

"This is a matter for the FBI, not the president's office.

"You should not have brought this to my attention. It's inappropriate." She turned on her heel and stormed out of the room, angry with herself, as well as Moscovi.

Chapter 41

Lincoln Bedroom

PRESIDENT AIRS HER DIRTY LINENS, screamed one tabloid's headline, while another proclaimed, CLUCKER IN CHIEF?

Among her first acts as president, Rebecca instituted an exemplary White House ban on the use of clothing dryers for non-personal items. White House table linen and bed sheets hung daily on clotheslines for the entire world to see. Rebecca unwittingly served the perfect pitch to eager pundits who started a not-too-subtle campaign, hinting that Rebecca was neurotic and delusional. The correspondents and commentators of media mogul Lord Trippington's Wolf Global empire shock-trooped themselves as first responders, sharpening their blades to lead the battle.

Then Rebecca caused a public outcry when she sent to Congress a proposal to tear up a half-acre of White House lawn to install a chicken coop pilot program as well as a vegetable garden, with local churches sharecropping with her. White House chefs received strict instructions to buy produce from area farmers, and to grow herbs and salad greens rather than flowers in the greenhouse.

Time magazine published a satirical cover spoofing her environmental initiatives. They depicted Rebecca, in illustration, dressed in farmer's overalls, with a collarless shirt and black suit jacket, holding a pitchfork handle, three prongs up. She stood in front of the White House, rendered architecturally as a farmhouse, with a red weathered barn visible in the background and a scrawny rooster on her shoulder. Newspaper cartoonists piled on next, portraying her as a broomstick-riding red-headed witch, a thin bony finger pointing, as she proclaimed, LAWNS

ARE EVIL. REPENT. The image of Rebecca hovering over the White House, twirling a wand, native flora and fauna replacing solid American turf, became so iconic that it went into mass production for T-shirts and posters. When Rebecca formally announced the White House carbon footprint reduction plan, the late-night talk show hosts responded with spirited delight.

* *

In the Lincoln Bedroom, with position papers strewn about her, Rebecca, wearing a flannel nightshirt embroidered with nocturnal birds of New Zealand—a Kiwi, a Weka, a Morepork and Kakapo—watched the CBS *Late Show*, hosted by Monty Mingo.

"Good evening, Ladies and Gentlemen," Mingo said. "It's been quite a day over at the White House. President Tree formally announced her carbon-cutting initiatives, and, I must say, we're quite impressed over here at the *Late Show*. We've been honored with exclusive footage. First we'll go to our aviation consultants the Wrong Brothers, Wilville and Orbur. Hi boys, I understand you've got a *Late Show* poop . . . sorry . . . a little scoop for us."

"Yes, we're aboard the old Air Force One," Wilville said, "which just got decommissioned earlier today."

"What's all that noise in the background?"

"Great question, Monty, glad you mentioned the poop first," Orbur said. "Let's ask the cameraperson to pull the lens for a wide shot. Wonderful program the president started. It's awesome. Air Force One is going to a new greater glory, to be used to raise goats, the first twenty arrived about two hours ago, and, as you can see, they're busy at work recycling the seats."

"Pretty expensive goat farm?"

"Perhaps, but the good news is that within a week, we've been assured, this old antique flying hulk will supply enough goat's milk and yogurt to keep the White House fully self-sufficient in the dairy department."

"Thank you, Wilville and Orbur. Today is truly a great day for environmentalists. And before you viewers send us your usual vitriolic, ugly, demented outraged emails, the answer is yes: the White House swore to us that all Air Force One dairy products are certified Kosher and fully organic.

"And now we have a special exclusive report from our sports correspondent. As you might have heard our new president will travel to England tomorrow. No, she's not visiting the Queen — or is it the King now? — Or selling back the colonies to the British. She's going to play a bit of soccer — you heard me correctly, *soccer*. We'll see how she fares in dear old England, arriving already with two yellow penalty cards, one from the Congress, and one from the press, the question hanging over soccer fans everywhere is:

"Madam President. Will you be getting the red card in England?"

Chapter 42

Oxford, England

"It is an honor and a pleasure for me to introduce a distinguished Oxford alumna tonight," said Prime Minister Keith Forsyte.

Forsyte, England's youngest prime minister in the past two hundred years, stood barely more than medium height; he was built stocky, with a rough-hewn face.

Rebecca thought that it was exciting to be at an age in which her peers from the different phases of her life, were coming into their own; it was even more thrilling that she numbered Britain's elected leader among her few special friends. She fondly recalled his trademark long straight student-era hair, now cropped close. He still wore a dramatic pencil mustache with a fashionable beard stubble.

If only Annie had lived to see this day. It would have been a bloody marvelous day for her.

"Our guest arrived at Oxford at the tender age of seventeen; her passport certified her as an American, but her French and Italian were easier to understand than her English."

The Prime Minister seemed to swell with pride as he continued his introduction. Rebecca's face warmed from the attention.

"I was an upperclassman at the time tonight's honoree arrived at Balliol College, so her arrival made little impression on me—not immediately, although apparently some of our football lads like Lord Arlington, who I see sitting just over there, and his teammates, did take notice." The Prime Minister gave a short wave to a hulking figure at one of the banquet tables, now slumping in his chair.

"In any event, our plucky new student, in response to her welcome from fellow Oxonians, quickly learned to speak our language, poorly,

I might add. Her first words of note on English soil later quoted as, 'Go banger your pong.'"

Lord Arlington raised the edge of the tablecloth, pretending to disappear underneath as the crowd roared. Rebecca, laughing, lifted her shoulders and smoothed the front of her blouse with moist palms.

"So just for the historical record, a 'banger' is a sausage, not often eaten by peers in the realm like Lord Arlington and his mates. And pong originated as a nineteenth-century Royal Navy jibe at the Army, derived from 'where the Army goes, there the pong goes.' And I won't embarrass our guest, as to what 'pong' really means, but let's say it lacks the refined cologne smell so smartly found on our Royal Navy sailors . . . when they arrive for shore leave.

"Now, if I may, a serious word. I'd like to welcome Rebecca Tree, currently employed as president of the United States. Before this weekend is out, the college will present to her an honorary degree as a Doctor of Science in recognition for technical advancements, which she, and teams she led, made for solar glass technology. I give you, my dear old friend and colleague, Rebecca Tree."

The crowd, now on its feet, gave Rebecca a boisterous reception. Two tables of hulking men, most with substantial bellies, struck their drinking glasses with spoons. Rebecca noticed that the whole rugby team turned out. This had a bittersweet undertone, to be welcomed here like a conquering heroine, while in her birth land an intransigent Congress and a hostile popular press took seemingly great pleasure in marginalizing her presidency, her ideas, and her personality.

Rebecca took the podium. The crowd remained standing, and it took several minutes of repeated thanks to get the audience back in their seats.

"Thank you, England. Thank you, Mr. Prime Minister. Being back here is great. Thank you, Balliol College and a special thank you to the distinguished gentlemen of the Oxford rugby team. For them, I'll say that I'm chuffed to bits to be here today."

Lord Arlington and his teammates, wearing school jackets and team sweaters, stood as one clapping wildly.

"And I'll do my best to give my speech today," Rebecca said, beckoning for the audience to be seated, "in proper English.

"Before I left Washington," Rebecca continued, "I wrote a speech for this occasion, but on the plane over here, I became engrossed in a biography of Winston Churchill. By the time Land's End came into view I threw away my speech, so I beg your indulgence as I extemporize a bit.

"History would be hard-pressed to find a more intrepid wartime leader than Churchill. He understood the danger that faced England and the world perilously encamped a few short miles from Dover's cliffs.

"Standing with Churchill, the English people showed extraordinary courage, perseverance, and ingenuity in executing modern history's greatest mobilization. From every nook and cranny of England, from every social class and strata, from factory floors to boardrooms, England stood united, rooted in a great heritage, to survive a devastating war and defeat an unimaginably evil foe.

"Churchill entered the House of Commons in 1940, and on being asked his plans to form a new government, he uttered the words which will survive the ages. 'You ask, what is our policy? I say it is to wage war by land, sea, and air. War with all our might and with all the strength God has given us, and to wage war against a monstrous tyranny never surpassed in the dark and lamentable catalogue of human crime. That is our policy.'"

The crowd broke into sustained applause; some of the older members of the audience reached for their handkerchiefs.

"The world again," Rebecca continued, "is facing an unimaginable crisis, a tyranny, though, sadly, mostly of our own making. Yes, we remain challenged by external forces; fundamentalists have furthered their causes in other continents while here in Europe ominous nativist groups have made inroads into parts of Italy and Spain. In my country, hate crimes are on the rise, and citizens and visitors, mostly of Hispanic descent, have been unjustly attacked.

"We live, as we've long known, in a world of growing populations competing for finite resources. History had a traditional option for this dire situation; they called it war—war for the homeland, war for the Nation, or war for the Church. We are civilized nations, and these are not acceptable choices. Just as Churchill organized every Briton to defend against fascism, it falls on us to mobilize an entire world to conserve and protect our shrinking resources.

"The battle we fight needs to be waged not on the traditional battle-field of opposing armed forces, but on multiple fronts united. Our scientists have made extraordinary strides, which might someday reverse global warning. But like an old science fiction movie, we might be held in bone-tingling suspense waiting for a redemptive denouement. We can pray for science to carry us through our dark hour, but first we must exhaust every means and method to save ourselves and thus, preserve our planet."

Rebecca had to raise her hand to quiet down a rolling thunder of applause. "The forces of reaction arrayed against these efforts are not insignificant. There are still sadly a few, a powerful few, in industry, in government, and in the media, still looking to make a quick killing—a final extra dollar, Euro, or ruble out of chaos. Profiteers pre-date the Bible, and those who seek such gain must be driven out of humanity's temples.

"I'm proud to pledge on this day that my government will stand with England, the European Union, and governments and people around the world of good will to fight for a common good.

"I would like to close my remarks with Churchill's words. 'The day will come when the joy bells will ring again throughout Europe, and when victorious nations, masters not only of their foes but of themselves, will plan and build in justice, in tradition, and in freedom a house of many mansions where there will be room for all.'"

Chapter 43

The following day
Ten Downing Street

A team of investigators from the firm of Davis and Parkis set up in the Cabinet Room at 10 Downing Street, which Prime Minister Forsyte had lent for this private matter. A fifty-inch nano screen dominated one side of the room, paired with a projector feeding images. The treasure trove of albums collected by Rebecca's grandmother and retrieved from the Montana lodge arrayed on a sideboard.

Jock Bollinger, head of Davis and Parkis, introduced the team and summarized their mission. "I'm sorry that our research took longer than we originally estimated, but we kept, as you requested, to strict archival standards. Some of the photographs had been glued into the albums, causing us to use more time-consuming methods. We methodically removed each image, analyzed its chemical contents, and dated each as closely as we could. We then copy printed, digitally scanned, chemically re-balanced and finally re-mounted them in their original albums. Also, we duplicated the sets, so you can take one with you today. We'd like to hold onto the originals until we've finished all our investigations."

"That's fine," Rebecca said. "You asked me for my DNA. Did it tell you anything?" She gulped, expecting the verdict at last: *yes, you are damaged goods.*

"Yes, good news. You have no unusual disease markers, at least not for dementia or Parkinson's."

"Tell that to the Washington press corps. I am sure they would happily disagree on dementia."

The room exploded with laughter.

Rebecca had dreaded this meeting, and she tried to distract herself by asking questions.

"How long will the original photographs last?"

"Probably five hundred years or more."

"That's a relief," Rebecca said though she couldn't imagine who at that point would care.

"Let me start a slideshow," Bollinger said, "with minimal comment on our part, and then we'll offer some observations."

"Please," Rebecca said, "we're under no time constraints. I have only one other appointment scheduled today." Later she was to meet with Forsyte's closest friend, the BBC's top investigative reporter, who claimed he had confidential information on Merewether and William Tree's role in the recent election.

"All right, first let me show you some sequences which I believe will bring you some pleasure."

The first slides showed her parents holding their daughters; she and Allison must have been less than two years old. The background, wooded and hilly on one side, had a blank horizon line on the other.

"Do you know where this is?" she asked.

"Yes, a geolocation satellite matched the terrain in the photo. It's twenty miles inland from the French coast, close to Nice, outside a village called Saint-Pancrace."

"Why there?"

"We're still looking, but we think your mother, or perhaps her family, had some friends there."

"There must be a house still standing where they stayed." Rebecca's lips clamped.

"We're on that. Our agents are looking for houses that match the terrain."

"Everyone looks so happy," Rebecca said.

A different image made everyone laugh. The twins were indistinguishable: each dressed in red nearly knee-length shorts, with sneakers and white socks sliding down, and long T-shirts illustrated with inchworms. The girls' backs were dramatically bowed out.

BUG PATROL MEMBER read the shirts, which featured two large, sad brown eyes perched on worm bodies precariously balanced on four pairs of shoes. One twin wore a duck-billed cap backward, and the other a blue plaid golf cap. They sat together on an old wooden park bench, side by side with their mother, who wore a billowing linen dress. Their father, in a collarless shirt, baggy hiking trousers, and suspenders posed theatrically on one knee, making a courting gesture to his three females.

"What a lovely scene," Rebecca longingly blurted out before her throat locked.

"Yes, we're going to quickly run a batch of these pictures for you, and Ms. Addington, who's a behavioral psychologist sitting to your right, will comment on them."

"Please go ahead." Rebecca watched as dozens of photographs flashed by. So normal in appearance: two children, a mother, and father enjoying family time on a holiday. Rebecca wondered why her brother Sam never appeared in the pictures.

Addington rose from her seat, carrying a thick folder.

"I can arrive at academic-sounding conclusions and deductions from looking at the pictures," Addington said, "or I could run other photographs of other mothers, particularly with twins at that age, but I think, in this case, the conclusions are simple. Your parents and I'm focused on the visual clues I'm reading off your mother's face, seem enthralled with their young children."

"But how can you be sure from these photographs?" Rebecca asked. "People always smile for the camera."

"I have looked at enhanced blow-ups of just your mother's eyes. We've run facial expression recognition algorithms—it's hardly an exact science, but it shows that both you and your sister elicited joyful feelings from your parents, and you looked well nurtured, physically and emotionally."

Perhaps for most people, it would seem like a little thing, some happy family snapshots, but Rebecca took it all in as an affirmation of parental love. Her heart lightened, cheered by the proof that her history had happy days.

"I'm thrilled you're able to say that. Can you learn anything, from these pictures, about the relationship between my sister and me?"

"I'm not sure," Addington said. "Nothing conclusive. But there are some hints."

"Like what?"

"Ethan," Addington said, to her assistant, "could you put up slide . . ." as she looked down at her notes, "number six, hold it and then show slide nine and then fourteen."

The first slide had one twin's arm entwined around the other. "Whoa, do you know who's who in this picture?" Rebecca asked.

"Yes, in the scans, we determined that the density of your freckles is higher than Allison's. Also, your hair color is a bit different."

"I thought identical meant identical—end of story." Rebecca felt disturbed by these hints of other options, besides identical twins.

"Yes, but there can be other factors," Addington continued, "environmental for example. Without both sets of DNA, and we don't have a DNA sample from your sister, I'd just be speculating. Another observation from the photographs is that you display protectiveness toward your sister."

"At the age of two?" Rebecca asked, flabbergasted.

"Yes, there's a school of thought among animal behaviorists that kin recognition works in pack animals, with the first born in the litter instinctually defending the younger members of the litter."

"Nice theory," Rebecca said wistfully.

"Twin studies reinforce this theory—the older twin, no matter by how few minutes, seems motivated to protect the younger one. If there are twin fantasies, which there almost always are, the older one often stages the younger one as the star, the elder preferring to play a supporting role."

"Yes, I've read that." Rebecca knew all too well about twin fantasies; she probably could write a definitive book on the subject. In her vivid dream world, Allison always appeared as the star, more beautiful, more personable, more charming. Perhaps also in her actual life, Allison would have played as the better president. "I appreciate your insights," Rebecca said cautiously, "your analysis of the family photographs puts my history in a better context. What about the pictures of Allison's last year? Something seemed off when I looked at them."

"Right," Bollinger interjected. "Our findings here might disturb you."

"I suspected that. I'm prepared, best as I can be."

"All right then. Let me turn this part over to Doctor Baker; her specialty is body mass, and she worked closely on this study, with John Greenfield-Saunders, who's our visualization expert.

"Doctor Baker?"

"Thank you, what we tried to establish is a reverse chronology of the most recent pictures available of Allison before she died, going back to pictures taken on her second birthday. We estimated from tables, her appropriate weight, we used digital calipers much like mechanical ones, to prod her skin, and construct body fat estimates and then we ran the same method against pictures of you."

"Why?" Rebecca said. Her calf muscles in one leg felt like a horse kicked her as her toes tingled. She quietly stomped her foot to wake it up.

"A couple of things didn't add up. Allison appeared to get bigger in the photographs, but it's not showing up as body mass. Not in her face, not in her arms, not in her legs when she's wearing shorts. She took on a larger appearance."

"I don't get it."

"Look at these superimpositions; we deconstructed the pictures and placed you on top of Allison. John, using Photoshop, moved your body parts, so everything was identical. We'll run them in chronology. John, could you start?"

Rebecca strained her eyes, but it was unpleasant to watch the reconstructed body parts overlaid like doll cutouts. The room got quiet and tense, and when they projected the sixth sequence, sweat broke out on Rebecca's brow, her hand shot across her mouth. "Oh my God, is she swaddled?" she said. "Is that what these composites show?"

Rebecca's felt her insides shift like tectonic plates in play, engaging and grinding. She steeled herself against her inner turmoil.

"We knew something looked wrong, but we weren't sure," Dr. Baker said. "First, we thought she got out of diapers later, which is probably the case, but as you can see, especially in the overlays, you fit inside of her. We think that she was wrapped in protective layers."

"Not to injure herself." Rebecca wanted to cry, but it wouldn't help.

Chapter 44

After the meeting had ended, Keith Forsyte came into the conference room. He leaned his hand on the table and twisted his body awkwardly.

"How did it go?" Forsyte said as he tried to straighten the snarled knot of his tie.

"More information. Only more disturbing. Their findings seem to indicate that something was wrong with Allison, or maybe not, perhaps she was mistreated, even physically abused."

"I wish I could help," Forsyte said. "I know this isn't easy for you."

"You're a good friend, Keith. Knowing that is help enough."

Looking nervously at his watch, Forsyte said, "I'm afraid I have to run to the airport now to see off the prime minister of Japan."

"Will you be around later?"

"Back in two hours. Are you ready for my BBC friend, Allan McNally? He has an American investigator with him, Oswaldo Lemus, a rather frightening looking chap."

"I know Lemus. He told me a couple of weeks ago that he has been working with McNally and that he might be here today, but that's all I know. We served together. He has done some work for me. I need to talk to him about another matter first before I meet the reporter.

"Can we have dinner together tonight? I haven't had a moment to thank you for those beautiful boots," Rebecca said.

"My pleasure. I so enjoyed, when I couldn't be there in person, seeing footage of you wearing them at your inauguration. Where would you like to go?"

"Go? Where would a prime minister and a president dine without the world's weight shifting from everyone running to see? I'll cook for us at my hotel. I brought you a present, and I have New Zealand mussels that came this morning by diplomatic pouch. I'll make a super pasta with them. Say, nine p.m.?"

"Great. I'll get white wine."

"Organic?"

"Of course."

"It's a date then. Why don't you send Lemus in?"

* *

"Why were you born in Boston?" Lemus, seemingly agitated, asked Rebecca. "We pulled the long form birth certificates."

"I don't know. I never wanted to look at the certificates," Rebecca confessed. "It made me too upset, thinking how come I lived and my sister died. My copies are in a sealed envelope in a safe deposit box."

"But your parents lived in New Haven, two hours away from Boston."

"What are you getting at? Why does it matter where we were born."

"I'm not sure there is anything wrong with the birth certificate, but the doctor, Liam Ryan, who signed it disappeared without a trace."

"I thought he had died after retiring in Florida."

"A doctor of the same name retired, but not the doctor who delivered you and your sister."

"What is going on?"

"The only person we have found who seems to know about the doctor is a woman who, by her own account, raised his child as a single parent. She thinks he probably disappeared back to Ireland to avoid child support."

"That sounds extreme."

"That's what we thought. We've looking for more information on the doctor in Belfast."

"And?"

"This Doctor Ryan appears to have been certified in multiple specialties."

"What does that mean?"

"Well it is pretty rare to be certified in unrelated fields, but he had been certified as an obstetrician and a plastic surgeon."

"What, that seems crazy."

"Sure, but the Irish, always desperate for doctors during their times of trouble, often bent the rules on certification."

"So what's going on here?"

"Listen to me, Becky. Ireland has a dark and tortured history, and very few of the Irish in the north escaped the turmoil. What happened, happened, and a long time ago."

"Ozzie, give it up. You're not being straight with me. You think my mother or her family had a connection to the IRA?"

"I wouldn't be surprised. Boston, at the time of your birth, acted as a sanctuary city for the IRA."

After the original Good Friday accords had shattered, Protestants and Catholics fought a bitter ten-year second round, Lemus explained. "Fugitives hunted by British intelligence often looked to Boston as a safe harbor. Men, guns and money flowed from the north of Ireland back and forth through Boston."

"I had that suspicion about my mother and her family in the past and asked that it be looked at. My sources told me that all the British intelligence records remained sealed as part of the revised peace treaty. Do you want me to ask the Prime Minister?"

"Maybe, but don't push him on it. See if you can just plant the seed and then save that contact for when, and if, we're only missing one or two pieces of the puzzle."

* *

Allan McNally, the BBC reporter, was unexceptional looking, Rebecca thought. He was short and wiry with sandy hair and a pasty complexion.

"We've been able to track money movement," McNally said, "involving a dozen elected officials, some of it going into John Spencer's accounts, some of it going to county supervisors in Colorado, Utah, and Idaho."

"What does this have to do with Merewether Tree?" Rebecca asked.

"We haven't found Merewether Tree's fingerprints on any of this yet, but we think we have found William Tree's."

"Merewether's errand boy. That makes sense."

"Can I speak off the record, Madam President?" McNally asked.

"You can if you reveal things obtained legally."

"All right, let's just say that I've seen bank records and copies of wire transfers. A lot of undeclared money began flying around the country right after Spencer entered the race."

"And what is your theory about all this?"

"I've looked at all the polling data at the beginning of the race. It's not hard to conclude that you might have been put into the race to draw votes away from the other candidates, so as to tip the race to John Spencer."

Rebecca laughed heartily. "It certainly made no sense at the time that my grandfather would want me as president. But why would he want Spencer?"

"I think a few more weeks of research and I will have my story complete. But it appears to be an old-fashioned corrupt land deal. County supervisors have been paid off to sell public land cheaply to a consortium, which would then bid to be the contractors if they can get a president to sign the D.C. Relief Act and move the nation's capital to Colorado, Utah, or Idaho. We're talking about billions upon billions of dollars at stake."

"Well, I look forward to seeing your story in print, and you can rest assured, that I will never sign the D.C. Relief Act."

"Yes," McNally said, "but the next thing they'll try is to impeach you."

"Let them. I will welcome that fight. Thank you for previewing your work."

"One request, Madam President," McNally asked.

"Of course, if I can."

"When I break this story, will you give me an exclusive first interview?"

"Absolutely."

Chapter 45

Rebecca picked the Brown's Hotel for her overnight in London. Built in 1837, the hotel was a favorite for Winston Churchill, as well as Rudyard Kipling, who had written his classic tale *The Jungle Book* while a guest. Composed of eleven Georgian townhouses, Rebecca had two top floors for her privacy. Secret Service and Specialist Protection Branch (SO1) personnel had secured the roofs and surrounding streets.

"Tell me about the gentleman with the dramatic scars," Keith Forsyte said.

"We served together. He was in a jeep at the end of the convoy the terrible day we came under attack. He saved a bunch of lives that day, including mine."

"What did he do?"

"I don't want to get into it. It's too hard for me to relive that day."

"I'm sorry."

"He runs an investigative agency. He found the evidence on John Spencer."

"Good for him. So we owe your election to him."

"More or less. He interfaces with the American intelligence agencies. His network is a major asset to us."

"Can I thank him for his good work if I meet him again?"

"No, leave him be. He is an American asset. Listen, Keith, I had a question for you."

"Sure."

"Have you ever read the Northern Ireland intelligence files?"

"No, they are sealed for another eighty years."

"So I couldn't take a peek at them?"

"Absolutely not."

"Has anyone read them?"

"Of course, but those who have read them are obligated to take the secrets to the grave. I know what you're looking for. I wish I could help you but . . . "

"But what . . ."

"I was told that you had been digging into this five or six years ago and . . ."

"And what?"

"Off the record. This would be a serious violation of British law, but I do know that your mother never showed on the 'short list.'"

"What is the short list?"

"A list of IRA operatives or Irish nationals living in the U.K. or abroad wanted for major crimes. Look, I've already gone too far. If I say another word, I could be in violation of the Official Secrets Act," Forsyte said, discomfort seeming to fill his voice.

"Maybe it's best we table this," Rebecca said, forcing herself to smile.

"If I can find a way to get you more information I will. You have my word on that."

"Okay, let's drop it. I don't want the evening spoiled," Rebecca said gamely trying not to lose her forced smile. "I am starved. Are you ready to help me cook?"

* *

"This is quite a treat to have a real home-cooked meal," Forsyte said at the table-for-two they shared in her hotel room. "I would not have taken you for someone interested in the culinary arts — no offense, you just seem, well, a little preoccupied with other matters."

"I love to cook. I learned at Oxford. Some of the meals at the White House I make myself. Tastes better that way."

"I should try that, but I'm sure my staff wouldn't let me. My cooking might burn down 10 Downing Street.

"By the way, the king is very upset with you, and me as well."

"The King? That oversexed royal brat?"

"You refused his invitation to stay at Buckingham Palace. He is in a total twit about it."

"The boy-king. He has a potty mouth, and he is hornier than a cane toad. I'm not sure I brought enough Secret Service agents to protect me from him.

"He's shameless," Rebecca said. "Did I ever tell you our conversation when he cornered me toward the end of my inauguration ball."

"No, tell me."

"'Europe is quite charmed by you,' the boy-king said to me. 'And, indeed, we are smitten with you.' Are you referring to England," I asked "or are you actually using the Royal We? The boy-king, either confused or crestfallen, didn't say anything, and I'm afraid I had one too many champagne toasts by then. So I got cheekier: I said something about how interesting it was that the word for referring to oneself as a 'we' is called 'nosism,' which sounds so eerily like 'narcissism.'"

Rebecca and Forsyte laughed and sighed at the same time. "Thank you for the wine; it's perfect," she said, savoring a sip.

"You're most welcome," said Forsyte, raising his glass as sadness shadowed his eyes.

"I brought you something," Rebecca said, getting up to retrieve it from her luggage. "It's a photo album from our undergraduate days at Oxford. We went on a picnic, do you remember?"

"How could I forget. We did a little performance of *As You Like It*. I played the impoverished Orlando, and Annie, starred as Rosalind, the love of my life. You played her loyal cousin."

"Sit over here on the couch," Rebecca said, "so we can look together."

"Such memories, such happy days," Forsyte said, turning each album page slowly. "She's been gone so many years now, but not a day passes when I don't think of her, and even, in private, I confess, I still talk to her."

Forsyte started his career as an economist recently elected to parliament at the time, who some claimed was destined to be a future Chancellor of the Exchequer. His wife of only a few months had just begun teaching botany at University College, University of London. After giving a lecture on an extinct Hawksweed plant of Wales destroyed by global warming induced shorter winters, she had the misfortune of sitting next to a suicide bomber on her way home in the London underground.

She was buried as a collection of remains.

"Our losses never leave us," Rebecca said, vaguely. "I lost my love seventeen years ago and, I've never recovered."

"But, all this time, there must have been others?"

"Not really. Sometimes I'd like to try for a new relationship, but men, most of them seem terrified of me, or else they have this macho disease where they start conversations by offending me. I haven't been on a date in five years."

"Really? Me neither."

Rebecca laughed. "Here we are, two of the world's most powerful people and we can't even get . . ." Rebecca stopped herself and clamped a hand over her mouth.

"A date?"

"Yes, that's a nicer way of putting it," Rebecca said, as her face turned crimson.

"I have a confession to make," Forsyte said. "I hope you don't think me strange."

"Well, I'd hope you don't find me 'plain vanilla' normal."

"For the last three years, every time you left me a voice message on my phone, I saved it until the phone's voicemail filled to its limit with your voice."

"Then what did you do?"

"Being a bit technically challenged, and not wanting anyone to do it for me, I just bought another phone.

"To throw my hat in with the boy-king, I suppose—darn him— I can say, truthfully, that even the Prime Minister is smitten with you."

Rebecca put her hand on Keith's knee with an ease she hadn't felt in a long time. She knew now where this would lead, and she nervously welcomed it.

"Keith, do you want to kiss me?" Rebecca asked as she licked her lips.

"I kept replaying your voice," Forsyte said so softly that Rebecca could barely hear his words.

Chapter 46

Heathrow Airport

As the pre-dawn light swelled, a diplomatic protection unit from the London Metropolitan Police formed a perimeter around the two world leaders facing each other on a tarmac at Heathrow. A decade earlier, the King of Saudi Arabia's private jet had been blown up just before take-off with the king and his immediate family aboard. In response, the English government built a remote runway for heads of state inaccessible to both the public and the press. Four Typhoon VII jets sat parked around a hydrogen fueled Learjet, recently purchased by the Defense Department and commandeered by Rebecca to fly as Air Force One.

"When can I see you again?" Forsyte said, his voice trembling as his hand fretted nervously on his stubble. "Last night meant so much to me. I can't get a read on what it means to you."

"Darling. I don't do one-night stands," Rebecca said, as she leaned in to straighten his ruffled collar. "Check your schedule. We could spend a weekend at Camp David."

"That would be wonderful. It's a shame your visit is so short."

"Too many problems in the colonies, but I'll be back as soon as I can."

"You're always welcome here, especially by the Prime Minister."

"That's sweet," Rebecca said, wincing at the trite word choice the moment it came out of her mouth; speeches were easier. "Maybe next time I'll be seeking political asylum."

"I'll look into preparing one of the Channel Islands for you."

"Perhaps a little cottage overlooking the sea," Rebecca said, grinning as she looked over Forsyte's shoulder. The sky blackened as the first drops of a rain fell. "I better get going. My pilots are worried about a storm coming in from the north."

She gave Forsyte a long hug, forgoing a public kiss, and began walking up the steps of her plane. Rebecca felt heavier, more melancholic with each tread of her foot as she shuttled toward the entry door. She felt like she carried Allison's swaddled weight over her.

As she turned around for a final wave, a staff car pulled up short on the tarmac. An aide emerged, rushed over to the Prime Minister, and handed him a newspaper. Forsyte glanced at it, broke into a smile and shaped his hands into a megaphone, shouting toward Rebecca. She couldn't hear him over the deafening noises created by the Typhoons revving their engines.

"What?" Rebecca mouthed, cupping her ear.

As the jet engines quieted, she heard him the second time, as he put more force into his words, adding an exuberant thumb up.

"Great picture of the goal you scored." He held up a newspaper, the *Daily Mail*. The Typhoon's jet blew the paper out of his hand just as Rebecca managed to read the headline:

OXFORD TOPS CAMBRIDGE AS PREZ TREE SCORES.

Rebecca grinned, and her mood brightened slightly.

Not too bad for a girl closing in fast on forty years old, she told herself.

* *

The pilot's voice came over the intercom. "Madam President, we're ready for takeoff, but Heathrow ground control is suggesting we might consider a delay."

"The weather?"

"Yes, Secret Service is okay with a lift-off if we go right now, but the first twenty minutes will be a bit rough."

"How long of a delay if we wait it out?"

"At least two hours. The commercial flights are being held, including British Airways #12, the hydrogen liner, with the White House press pool."

"So it's not a safety issue, strictly a comfort issue, and the press pool won't get off in any event for a few hours."

"Yes, that's correct."

"And there is no way we could wait another thirty minutes?"

"No, it's either now or two hours."

Rebecca was torn. She feared going into the flight without time for a preparation routine, but staying on the ground meant—she looked out her window at the back of Forsyte's coat as he returned to his car. She supposed it meant a new sort of life, a life she may not be ready for. She reluctantly turned away from the window.

"*Let's go,*" she said. Terror filled her gut.

The Lear thundered down the runway, followed by two of the Typhoon VII's. Rebecca began her countdown; often on takeoff, she slowly counted to thirty, feeling relieved when she hit the number, and the plane still ascended. The sky blackened as the morning light fled in front of the storm, and Rebecca's plane began bucking almost immediately; a few minutes later, it felt like rockets slamming into its sides. She was still counting, one thousand and twelve, one thousand and fifteen.

She lost count. She tried to write in her diary, but the pen jumped out of her hand, nearly piercing her eye. She gave up.

"Are you hanging in there, Madam President?" asked the pilot over the intercom. "It should smooth out in another fifteen or twenty minutes."

"I'm fine," she said, trying to keep her voice from quivering. "Just keep your door open so I can still see that I have pilots." She hadn't had the time to fiddle with the controls and get her screen feed going.

An airsick Secret Service agent rushed passed her for the toilets.

The retching noise echoing from the chamber threw Rebecca over the edge.

"We need to return to Heathrow." Rebecca said over her intercom to the pilot, in a poorly restrained shout. "I'm sorry. Can't do this. Please, can we return to the airport?" Rebecca said, trying to keep her voice from exploding.

"Roger. We'll be back on the ground in three or four minutes," the pilot said.

Rebecca spoke into her phone. "Convert to text. Message to Keith.

Are you still at the airport? We're turning around. I need to talk to you."

A few minutes after landing, Forsyte and Rebecca huddled in her private cabin as he toweled the sweat off her forehead and her arms, and waved a magazine as a fan in front of her.

"The White House doctor wants to look at you again," he said.

"Bullocks. I'm all right now. It's more important that we talk. We can thank my problem with planes for . . . well reminding me to stay grounded."

"*Problem with planes*?" He laughed, amazed, "the woman who has to fly probably more than anyone, what torture. Well, if it helps any, I appreciate that you are so complicated."

"Ha, that's just an inch of the iceberg. Okay, since we're talking complications. Don't you think this —," she motions her arm in the space from his chest to hers and back, "is a little awkward, or *wrong*, when we both loved Annie so much?"

"She brought us together; we can thank her for that. Don't you think from what we know of her that she'd want her two favorite people to find happiness? And finding happiness together. Even better."

Rebecca teared up picturing Annie. They had bonded from that first day they met, laughing as they drove blithely across Oxford's bike paths, two seemingly carefree, shimmering young women with worlds ahead to conquer. One day, a serious-looking student, his head buried in a book, accidentally stepped into the bike path in front of them. Both women slammed on their brakes, but Annie's bike knocked over the young man who, after brushing himself off, and apologizing for not looking introduced himself as Keith Forsyte, a third-year student reading economics.

"Do you remember what Annie said when she ran you over?" Rebecca asked now.

"Of course. Annie . . . the ever-salty Annie said: 'You must be one daft idiot. Not only you don't look where your walking but you're reading the dullest textbook ever published — Schumpeter, not exactly worth getting run over for."

"*Social Classes in an Ethnically Homogeneous Environment*," Forsyte said. "No wonder it took me three months to get up enough courage to ask her to come out and have a coffee with me."

"Annie kept saying to me. 'You think that Schumpeter guy is brave enough to ask me out.'"

"And I told her. You're the fearless modern woman. Why don't you ask him out?"

Forsyte's face glowed momentarily but then quickly darkened as his voice took on an imploring tone. "Becky. It helps me so much to talk about her. It only honors her. Tell me about your lost love."

"Annie knew." Rebecca felt her feelings were like a dam, leaking slowly for a long time until finally bursting from accumulated pressure. "Only Annie knew the whole story, and I swore her to secrecy. His name is . . . was Jackson Toussaint and his last wish was that I'd wait and let him tell his mom about us when he got better. There was also the Army's new anti-fraternization policy that kept us secretive. Because of that, I was worried that Jackson wouldn't then get the posthumous decorations he deserved. So, I guess you can say, I've been a little stuck, since he died in my arms."

"Toussaint? Related to the Secret Service director?"

"Yes. His son, his only child."

"But Becky, who would possibly object now? You need to speak to his parents."

"I know. I'm waiting for the right moment."

I've been waiting for years. This isn't right. I have to let go, of all the secrets.

Rebecca breathed deeply as Forsyte held her hands in a tight but comforting grip. "I met Jackson the first week in the Army intelligence school. He had quite a smile." She paused for a moment and touched her locket. "I kept thinking about him and that smile. All the time. Then he came up to me on the campus when I was lying on the grass reading a book. He sat, and we started talking; six hours later we realized we should get something to eat. He was that kid who everyone picked first to play on their team. I was flattered this time he seemed to pick me."

"As much as I mourn Annie," Forsyte said. "I thank God for the time we had. Try and think of Jackson that way, what gifts he gave you."

"I do. I hope I do. At first I was very bitter about his death, slumping around with dyed black hair and hiding from my feelings, but eventually I took myself to task. I decided I had to carry on and accomplish things in honor of those I had lost—my parents, my sister, Jackson, then Annie."

"And look at us now, how far we've come and in other ways, not at all," Forsyte said, wiping his eyes, and their heads momentarily leaned together, hands still clenched. "Power and fame can't shield us from being wet, teary messes."

The pilot's voice came over the intercom. "Madam President, we have a break in the weather. Ground control is recommending we consider taking off in ten minutes. And Director Toussaint just called in from Washington. He would like you off the ground. They have a threat assessment issue."

"Ha," she laughed through her tears. "Nothing like a threat assessment to get me revving to go home. You've calmed me, though."

"Wait, I want to say . . ."

"There's plenty more to say next time," Rebecca said, putting her fingers to Forsyte's lips and walked him to the plane's exit. The Secret Service agents moved away from the open exit door as the couple clung in a long embrace.

* *

The turbulence finally lessened. "We're at forty thousand feet now," the pilot said, "and it might be a bit choppy, but the worst seems behind us. It's quite a storm in the North Atlantic. The Brits are about to peel off. Do you want to say goodbye?"

"Sure, put them on the speaker."

"We'll be dropping off now, Air Force One," said the lead Typhoon pilot. "It looks like better skies ahead. Come again, anytime. You're always welcome in England."

"Thanks for babysitting us up," Rebecca said. "Godspeed."

"Roger, Madam President—oh, I thought you might not mind me saying. My family watched the soccer game on the 'telly.' Lovely goal you scored."

"Thank you," Rebecca said, and her cellphone began to ring. The caller I.D. told her it was Fatima.

"Hi, no, takeoff was a bit rough. It's okay now. I've got time to talk. Let me put you on speakerphone. "How's Washington?" Rebecca said.

"Lousy. What a miserable town," Fatima said. "I've never seen so many men with faces that look like flat tires."

Rebecca laughed nervously at Fatima's comment before asking, "Any progress?"

"No progress in Congress."

Rebecca's heart sank; she wished she could have stayed in England, bought a fishing pole and headed for an imagined cottage in the Channel Islands, hung out with the ghost of Victor Hugo, perhaps become his adopted daughter.

Léopoldine Hugo, Adèle Hugo . . . Rebecca Hugo.

"Rebecca? Are you there?"

"Sorry." She paused. "We'll just have to do more."

"I know," Fatima said.

"What else?"

"A couple of blowhards went on the Sunday morning talk shows and started making veiled threats about impeachment."

"Which ones?"

"Mainly John Mauro. He's the worst, but you're getting some good press out of your trip to England."

"That's nice. I'm glad someone finally liked one of my speeches."

"I didn't hear too much about your speech," Fatima said, with a mischievous tone. "But the English papers splashed their front pages with action shots from the Oxford-Cambridge soccer game."

"Can you email some of them to me?"

"Hold on. I've already got them queued for you. There they go. You've got mail."

Rebecca hit the preview button, and the images popped onto her screen. "Ooh, not bad. I like the first one."

"Have you read the caption?" Fatima asked.

It read, "President Tree connects with a diving header, and passes to midfielder, Jamati Williams, for Oxford's first score." The final picture captured Rebecca high off the ground, hair flying, face lit up, eyes ablaze with focus; two other players in the frame looked up at her as her left foot connected to the corner of the ball. The caption read: "'Red Striker' Tree outruns Cambridge sweeper and executes Oxford's Winning Goal."

"And where does Red Striker come from?" Fatima asked.

"Well, I guess it was my *nom de sport,* back, in my heyday," Rebecca said wistfully.

"You want to talk about it?" Fatima said, her antennae apparently picking up Rebecca's tone.

"What, about my future as a soccer player?"

"No, I can tell you're emotional about something. Might this have some connection to the donor of a certain prized pair of boots?"

"Perhaps."

"Okay, we'll leave it at that for now. The bad news is that your grandfather's bugged us all day calling the White House. He's chomping at the bit to talk to you."

Rebecca felt she had no longer scored goals at the Oxford-Cambridge game. The fun of the moment, seeing people in England dear to her, the respect she received from her speech, the glowing sentiments expressed to her at dinners, the eager faces of questioning students, the comradely interplay from the British Typhoon pilots, and the hours with Keith all slid away at the mention of Merewether Tree.

How powerful this old man could be.

"Tell him to call me on my private cell, in the next fifteen minutes if he wants to schedule a video conference. After that, I'm turning off the phone and going to sleep."

Rebecca hung up. Trembling, she reached for a blanket.

* *

Rebecca's plane started its descent into Washington's airspace by the time Merewether's video conference call came in.

"Grandfather, how nice to see you again." *Rattlesnake,* she thought, as she looked at the outfit he wore.

Dressed in a sleeping robe of cashmere with leather elbow patches,

Tree lay on an adjustable bed that had been tilted into a reading position. Underneath the gown, he wore red silk pajamas with pantaloons and shearling-tasseled slippers adorning his feet. On his nightstand stood a bottle of uncorked wine.

"How are you feeling?"

"Never felt better in my life," Tree answered. "I don't have to worry about a thing."

"Why that's lovely. I'm so pleased that you don't have a care."

Tree reached for a glass and the bottle. "Do you mind if I have a glass of *Languedoc-La Clape*?"

She put on her glasses, glaring at his dominating video image, which transmitted at a larger-than-life magnification.

"Care for a cigar?" Tree said. "Straight from the finest tobacconist in Havana. I could ship some to you at the White House. A gentleman caller might enjoy it."

Gentleman caller? Did he know about Keith — what in the world was he hinting at?

"No. Looking at it makes me sick. I hate smoke. What do you want, Grandfather? I'm tired and jetlagged and not in the mood for you."

"Tired, you say. Exactly what I wished for us to discuss. Perhaps you might think about stepping down."

"Resigning?" Rebecca didn't know whether to laugh or scream. "I don't quit. You started me on this mission, so I'll finish it. Is this plan C?"

"Plan C? What the devil are you talking about?" Tree went to light his cigar.

"I just met in London with an investigative journalist, a well-regarded one," Rebecca said. "He's working on a piece that points to you as a silent supporter of John Spencer in the last election. That was your Plan A."

"Are you insane? You stood as my party's nominee."

"Stood or stooged?" Rebecca said. "A dupe in your game. Was that the grand plan? A pawn meant to draw votes from other candidates, to favor yours?"

"Why no, not correct. Why would I do such a thing? This is slander."

"It's true all right, and you know it. How could you do such at thing to your grandchild? And now that I've won, all you can do is ask me to step down, because you never intended me to be here in the first place."

"I did no such thing. Perhaps you might have noticed that I afforded you much liberty during the campaign, and then after your win to make your own messes. And sister, have you ever. Installing chicken coops? Saving Boy Scouts that didn't need saving? This isn't a merit badge contest; you're a laughing stock. Every time you open your mouth, my phone rings off the hook from the same Millennium Populists who went out on a limb to support you."

"You don't seem to understand. You're not in a good position." Rebecca reached into her orange bag, pulling out a duplicate of one of the photo volumes she had retrieved from the Montana lodge, THE TWINS VOL. I, and held it up so he could see it clearly.

Merewether recoiled as he peered at the image, regarding it as a bomb ready to detonate.

"What do you have there?"

"Pictures of my sister, in an album, from the last year of her life. They're quite revealing. "

"Where did you get these?" Tree looked alarmed.

"It doesn't matter. I had the photographs analyzed. The analysts believe she wore padded clothing."

"I don't understand what the devil you're talking about."

"Was something wrong with her? Was she disturbed? Was she autistic? I want to know."

"I can't help you. I don't know," Tree said, reaching for his cigar, as his voice turned brittle with an insistent tone. "Where did you get these?" Tree asked again.

"From Grandmother Tree, your wife, who also wrote me a series of letters at a point when she was lucid. Her lawyer, who handles her estate, released them over the years, on a schedule. They make chilling reading, and they don't paint you in the best light. Each one is a cliff-hanger."

Tree glared at Rebecca. "And what're you trying to do, blackmail me?"

"No." Rebecca wanted to make one last attempt to reach him. As much as she despised him, and all he stood for, he was, for better or worse, her only family. "Grandfather, some people yearn for money, some for fame, or power. I have those things. I yearn for my history. I want the narrative of my father, mother, and sister. Is that so much of an inheritance to ask?"

"I can't help you. I won't. Leave the dead in peace."

"You know more than you'll tell. You're a liar. Was my sister abused? Who else did you abuse? Your wife—I know you did because I have her letters. Did you abuse your son, Nathaniel, my father?"

At the mention of his son's name, Tree slammed his hands so hard over his ears that his brain must have shook.

"Go away. I wanted to make peace, and then you attack me with accusations and lies. Don't talk about my son, my boy. You wish to go to war with me—good—I'll destroy you. I'll crush you, little girl."

Rebecca silently got up to terminate the video transmission but paused for a final face off.

"Grandfather!"

"How dare you scream at me?"

Rebecca took a deep breath, exhaling slowly. "You're going to die alone in your house, with a few paid employees at your side." Rebecca paused. "Or maybe you'll die in a jail cell. Put there by your grand-daughter, your beloved son's child. Don't call me again unless you have something to share. Do you understand? I'll call you if I want to."

Chapter 47

Lincoln Bedroom
The White House

The bedside security phone began to trill in the middle of the night, waking a still jet-lagged Rebecca. She moaned in distress.

"Madam President. This is Winston Hollander. I'm tonight's National Security Emergency Officer. I'm sorry to have awakened you, but Homeland Security just issued an internal code red."

"What's the threat?" Rebecca said, slurring her words.

"I have the Secret Service Director on the line. He wants to brief you."

"What's going on?" Rebecca groggily asked as Toussaint's voice came on over the phone.

"Murder, a hideous massacre, happened a few hours ago," Toussaint said.

"Where?" Rebecca felt her blood rush. She sat up.

"Just outside Las Cruces, New Mexico, a few miles from the Mexican border."

"Who was killed?" Her voice tightened.

"An extended family of Mexicans executed and butchered. The killers left signatures similar to the Switzer and Rodriquez murders."

"Oh my God," she said. The FBI director had warned her about this, and she had reacted badly. Was it just that she was squeamish or too overwhelmed to bear any more bad news? The room gyrated, and her chest felt like a boa had clamped onto it.

"Our head agent at our field office in Albuquerque got a call from an old Army pal in the New Mexico State Police. He told him to chopper into the crime scene right away."

"And?"

"The crime scene has the blood prints of Native Force vigilantes all over it. They wrote their call letters, NF, everywhere and used the victims' blood to write a threat. I want your authority for the Secret Service to intervene in this."

"Intervene? On what grounds?" She had been so publicly trounced for daring to activate assistance in West Virginia. "What was the threat?"

"Freckles is next."

* *

"Didn't they have cellphones?" Rebecca asked as she sat behind her desk in the Oval Office while Toussaint and Grace briefed her on the murders of three generations of the family of a one-time illegal immigrant-turned-citizen who had served his country in battle—Augusto Diaz. She kept nervously licking her lips, dehydrated.

The first set of stored satellite images of the crime scene showed three separate pairs of all-terrain vehicle tracks converging on the compound where the Diaz patriarch had built a main house and two smaller houses for his grown children. Two miles from the homestead the main incoming phone line had been cut, and an electrical feeder line was severed, cutting off all power to the Diazes and their neighbors.

"Investigators picked up four cellphones at the crime scene," Toussaint said. "They all belonged to the family. It looked like each one tried to place outgoing calls, to 911 and some neighbors, both during a two-minute period. But none of the calls went through."

Rebecca looked sharply at Grace.

"Two years ago, the Navy Seals lost, among other things, portable all-frequency cellular jammers," Grace said.

She clenched her right hand so tightly that the veins on her arm popped out. "What else did they lose?"

"I'm not sure you want to know," Grace said.

Rebecca's hands formed fists. She pressed against the desk and rose from her chair. She pushed her eyeglasses down, her eyes blazing out over the frames. "Stop pulling your punches, Peter. I'm not a Girl Scout. I want it all, now."

"Enough weaponry and related equipment are missing to stock half-dozen field units. My aide just shook this information out of the Navy."

She turned and looked out the Oval Office window into the Washington night. The last flights had landed hours earlier at Washington National, and the sky, in a moment of clarity, shimmered with stars. Rebecca thought about the coming day: dawn breaks, alarms sound, coffeemakers percolate, showers run, commuters begin their journeys, but for Rebecca time had stopped. She could tolerate attacks on herself, being the butt of an endless loop of late-night show gags, but she couldn't let innocent people be murdered.

"Madam President?" Grace finally said. "What do you want to do?"

Her mind raced as she spun around.

"First, Caleb," she paused briefly, "your people need to take charge and secure the crime scene. Fly in a full Secret Service lab. If it's the work of Native Force vigilantes, get me the hard evidence. And get it soon."

Rebecca paused to digest the gravity of words before she spoke. "If the facts support it, I'll declare it a terrorist act and use the full powers of the presidency to bring these barbarians to justice."

Chapter 48

Zebra Force Situational Room
Northern Virginia

Photographs covered one wall showing blood everywhere, broken windows, strewn furniture, necks slashed. The adults had been dismembered; the children shot with single bullets to the head, all but one chopped into pieces. No one spoke as the images from the crime scene silently sunk in. The bloody assassins had swept away a legacy, a lifetime of labor, three generations of Diazes brutalized in their modest and tidy compound.

Rebecca's body ached from stress and sleeplessness. She sat at the head of a conference table during the security briefing at Zebra Force command and control center, fifty miles outside Washington. Sipping a cup of black coffee that tasted like burnt mushrooms, she listened as General Grace spoke at the other end of the room. Grace, a hand on a remote, projected an infrared satellite map of Las Cruces, which identified human heat sources triangulating the Diaz compound.

"Most likely, we're looking at three human execution teams, with four persons in each team. Let's look at the conventional satellite map. By chance, it captured an image probably a few hours before the attack took place." Grace flicked a control, and a new picture came up.

Rebecca rubbed her eyes. It looked like a made-for-TV action show. The new map showed three Navy Seal squad tents, a four-passenger, fat-tired ATV vehicle beside each tent.

Rebecca rose out of her chair nearly knocking over her half-filled cup of coffee. "Let's pause here," Rebecca said, attempting to restrain her rage. "I want Director Toussaint to update us on the ground situation. Caleb?"

"Secret Service has secured the crime scene. The New Mexico state police and the Doña Ana County Sheriff are unhappy, and a bit of an in-the-face occurred between the Service's lead agent for the region and Sheriff Sherwood. I have fifty agents on the ground now; another one hundred are inbound in the next few hours."

"Do you have a trail yet?" Major Sandback asked.

"We've got trackers on the ground, on ATVs and horseback," Toussaint said. "We've got three teams of bloodhounds out of their kennels, and another four teams flying in from Guam. We're running choppers around the clock."

"Do you have everything you need?" asked Grace.

"No," Toussaint said, "but I hope this meeting will release more assets. Madam President has already seen . . ."

"I've seen enough," Rebecca interrupted, her brain stamped with those gruesome images. "The clock is ticking. The photographs and the satellite images speak for themselves. This is the worst terrorist act on our soil in a long time. The attackers are armed, organized vigilantes, killing citizens for political motives, threatening me and taunting the country to wage war on them.

"Peter," she said, as her gaze flew to the general, "are you ready to put Zebra J-2 teams on the ground to do advance work?"

"Ready, willing, and able, Madam President."

"Deploy self-contained J-2 teams into the mountains of New Mexico immediately," Rebecca said, "followed by more units dropped into Arizona, Utah, and Idaho. We'll spare no resource to bring these butchers and their associates to the ground. I want the agencies to pull out all the stops. Tap into discretionary budgets if you need to, use all your undercover agents and informants, and . . ." Rebecca paused, directing her gaze at Toussaint, "use every special unit at your disposal. As for the chain of command — the FBI deals with the crime, the Secret Service deals with the threat to the president and takes the lead on tracking. Zebra J-2 teams are reconnaissance only. Their mission is to identify cells and support groups, mark them, implant surveillance devices if feasible, prepare all the necessary groundwork for a full combat operation. All agencies will report to General Grace, and he'll report to me directly. Understood?"

"I've been waiting for six years for a president to say that." Grace's body stretched well past his armchair. His eyes keenly narrowed. "My soldiers are ready to . . . and the orders? What is the ultimate disposition? Dead or alive?"

"Alive. We'll use the Army's live capture technology. I'll sign an executive order authorizing it domestically."

"Wait," Toussaint said, "have you cleared this with the White House counsel?"

Rebecca slammed her fist on the table, and her face turned crimson. "If it doesn't cut constitutional muster, then it's on me. I'll face impeachment if needed. I wish these barbarians a long, unhappy life in a Federal prison. I don't want them martyred to their fanatic followers; let the world watch them rot.

"Questions?" Rebecca said, to the silent room. "Before I leave you to finalize the logistics." Half the men around the table now had ashen color faces.

"What about the border with Mexico?" asked Colonel Andreas Paz.

"I discussed this scenario earlier with General Grace. I'll authorize moving five thousand regular Army troops to the border section near Las Cruces."

Another hand shot up. "We've got issues with the New Mexico National Guard. They have to be . . ." a young black woman Lieutenant-General, Yvonne Gubb, who was speaking paused ". . . segregated from the regulars. There might be problems. Their ranks are infiltrated."

"I'll be calling the Governor of New Mexico," Rebecca said, "and I'll order him to confine all his guard troops to their barracks."

"And if he disobeys?" asked the same officer. "He's believed to be a fellow traveler to the Firsters."

"If he refuses," Rebecca said. "I'll issue orders to the Secret Service to arrest him."

Around the table, jaws dropped at the president's last directive, but many faces in the room suppressed smiles of satisfaction. Colonel Paz, sitting at the far end of the conference table, had been decorated three times for bravery on Zebra combat missions. Last year, near the Mexican border, vigilantes murdered his second cousin, dragging his body with a pickup truck for five miles. Rebecca watched as Paz's face swelled with pride; his fist curled and rose under his chin, his neck flexed. It appeared to her that his training intervened at the last moment and constrained him from expressing a full Mandela thrust of solidarity.

"Let's be clear," Rebecca said. "The decisions I take are fully invested in the powers of the presidency, as defined in the Constitution. I believe if Lincoln, Eisenhower, Truman or Roosevelt sat today in my chair, they would take similar action. As to the nuances of these actions, they're enabled by four different Patriot Acts as well as the Garcia-Winthrop Sedition Act."

Most of the men and women in the room now wore full, broad smiles; a few still looked deeply uneasy.

"Ladies and Gentlemen," Rebecca said, "I intend to pray tonight for the souls of the Diaz family and for our soldiers who face danger in the coming days. Before we conclude this meeting, we need to talk about the funeral, which will be held the day after tomorrow.

"I will be joining the mourners."

Chapter 49

The Country Prepares for Diaz Funeral

Citizens grew nervous as fear of insurrection spread. Customers formed long lines outside gun stores particularly in the border states. Some businesses closed early, restaurants reported a surge in cancelled reservations, and audience numbers for network news shows soared as many Americans stayed home, looking to their televisions for answers. Ministers scheduled special services and photographers recorded small groups conducting prayer vigils in town squares. A NATION ON EDGE read one headline, above a feature article that depicted farmers sitting in pickup trucks, listening to the radio.

The murders had taken place on a Friday. On Saturday, Secret Service agents swarmed southern New Mexico. By mid-afternoon support teams landed in airports at Boise, Twin Falls, Provo, Flagstaff, Reno, and Las Vegas. History would record it as the largest operation every launched by the Secret Service.

By sunset Saturday, two-person Zebra Force expeditionary teams had begun parachuting into the western mountain ranges stretching from Silver City, New Mexico to Boise, Idaho. From the air, drones continuously fed information on the terrain in front of them, and monitored each unit as they moved silently through rugged, remote land. More teams would be deployed by nightfall Sunday.

Sunday afternoon, a chartered Aero México jet dropped down between the Sandia and Manzano mountains, landing at New Mexico's Kirtland Air Force Base. It carried Augusto Diaz's younger brother, Eduardo, and Diaz family nieces and nephews from the Mexican village of San Jose del Penasco.

Rebecca had issued compassionate visas for the family.

All day Sunday buses filled with Mexican-Americans, and their sympathizers convoyed from the west coast across Nevada, Utah, and Colorado before turning south at Durango toward Albuquerque. They avoided Arizona. From cities across the mid-west — Chicago, Detroit, St. Paul — more buses headed toward Colorado, turning south at Fort Collins. At the Colorado-New Mexico state line and patrolling Interstate 25 and old Route 550, five thousand federal marshals staged to protect the mourners and their buses. An executive order federalized the New Mexico, Colorado, and Arizona state police for seventy-two hours, putting them under the direct control of the marshals.

Every commercial flight into Albuquerque was booked within hours of the announcement of the Diaz funeral. Within twenty-four hours, civil rights groups and religious organizations chartered four 797 super liners, each holding more than a thousand passengers.

Air Force One took off from Andrews at five a.m. Monday morning. For security reasons the flight path took an unconventional arc north from Washington, out into the Atlantic and turning westward over Block Island. The rising sun brought a cloudless day; as the plane turned slightly southwest, crossing the Long Island Sound, it passed over the remains of the south fork of eastern Long Island. Rebecca looked out the window; sadness flooded her eyes as the plane flew over an archipelago, of once proud, valued solid paths of land. Four feet of rising seawaters had made Montauk, Easthampton and Bridgehampton isolated islands of high ground only accessible by boat or seaplane. The land once belonged to the Secatogue, the Shinnecocks, and the Montauks. Their common language of Algonquin was overtaken first by Dutch and then English. Smallpox, even deadlier than the colonialists' muskets, ravished the tribes, and the land passed to Woodhulls, Giggs, Satterlys, and Jenners. Now the rising ocean abrogated all treaties, all wars of conquest; nature, with an indisputable finality, exercised eminent domain, nullifying all land deeds. Salt water leached into the ground water and destroyed vineyards and four-hundred-year-old farmlands, which had once dotted eastern Long Island. Climatologists, in bitter debates with "reprievers," predicted another four feet of ascending oceans before the century ended.

Homeowners abandoned unsustainable coastal areas; thousand of "wet" refugees, sometimes with their possessions on their backs migrated westward towards the dry states. The "dry" states argued that they could not absorb all the "wets" and some states attempted to close their borders.

Three hours later, Rebecca looked out over a landscape dismally dry; large patches of once fertile farmland now appeared parched as farmers desperately competed for shrinking supplies of water.

The trip to New Mexico represented a major logistical undertaking, and Rebecca agreed to fly on the plane historically used by the president, a gas-guzzling Boeing 797. She had requested that Congress appropriate monies for a hydrogen liner, but as with nearly all of her requests, Congress refused to act. The funeral was scheduled for two p.m., Rocky Mountain Time.

Rebecca was in such fury that she felt no panic when Air Force One had lifted off.

* *

Rebecca and Toussaint stood alone in the executive cabin, continuing an ongoing argument that had been raging between them for the last twenty-four hours.

"You're taking unprecedented risks," Toussaint said. "I can't guarantee your safety."

"You're right. I wouldn't ask you to make such a guarantee," Rebecca said. "Can't you see that I have no choice?"

"God might be on your side," Toussaint said, "but the Kevlar protecting your body won't protect your face. These guys are lunatics; the Navy trained some of them as Seals. They love knives; they know explosives."

Rebecca shuddered. Knives made her queasy; conceptually she'd much prefer getting shot, or even exploded, but there was a horrible intimacy of getting stabbed, the comparative slowness and closeness. She wasn't afraid really of dying, but of how. More so, she feared failing, not finishing her mission, not doing her duty to God, country, her loved ones. She faced a shrewd enemy, sick and deranged, and she knew another part of their profile all too well: smart, twisted overachievers who had too much to prove and lacked emotional outlets.

"No one is expecting me. Your agents woke up the press pool, escorted them to Air Force One and required them to surrender their cellphones."

Toussaint slammed his fist against the cabin wall. A vein popped on the surface of his face. She had never seen him like this.

"You're giving me a load of crap. I'm sorry but they painted a personal invitation to you, in blood to the Diaz funeral. They're expecting you to attend."

Freckles is next. One of her twin fantasy adventures played out at fast time in her mind, girl pirates on the high sea. *"Batten down the hatches!" Allison barks out orders as thunderclouds blacken the sky. The schooner crew scurries to secure anything not tied down; Rebecca nearly knocked over by the giant boom. The ship points straight toward the blinking, flashing eye of it; there's no other course with this enemy vessel on their tail and out for their gold, or blood.*

"Rebecca," Toussaint's voice shattered the daydream. "Damn it. This is personal to me," he said, as he reached and touched her arm with a firm grip. "I'd be, and I wouldn't be the only one if something happened to you."

"I'll listen to my brain, and I'll listen to my heart," she said, as she fortified herself with her sense of duty. "General Grace is waiting for you in the administrative cabin. He wants to review the aerial technology they'll deploy for the funeral."

Chapter 50

Little Black Mountain
Outside of Las Cruces, New Mexico

The night before the funeral, helicopter traffic intensified over Las Cruces, as Red Hawk Heavy Lifters landed at a hastily assembled off-road base in a hidden canyon just west of Little Black Mountain. The first six Red Hawks carried armored Saber wagons, built by Rover in England to withstand high-impact explosions. With ninety-millimeter auto tracking machine guns embedded inside their front and rear head-lights, the state-of-the-art vehicle also deployed flak throwers to confuse incoming missiles' guidance systems.

Throughout the night, the helicopters made dozens of round-trips from Fort Sam Houston in San Antonio and Fort Bliss in El Paso. They came back to Little Black Mountain with more combined firepower than Eisenhower's troops had when they hit Omaha Beach.

* *

An hour before the funeral, a fleet of Secret Service helicopters flew Rebecca, Toussaint, and two squads of line-of-fire agents from Kirtland Air Force Base to Little Black Mountain. She watched at the scene unfolding on the roads below: in her heart, she felt she had done the right thing. For as far as she could see, chartered buses, carrying a coalition of Americans wanting to pay their last respects to the Diaz family, filled the roads converging on Las Cruces. She could read some of the signs hanging out the windows or taped to the top of the buses.

VIVA LA CAUSA! VENCEREMOS! NO VIOLENCA EN LAS CRUCES.

* *

Early nineteenth-century Mexican settlers built the Church of Santa Maria de Pueblo a few miles southwest of Las Cruces. It had fallen into ruins until the Diaz family and their neighbors raised enough funds to buy the land and restore the church. The refinished sanctuary had exterior walls of fresh white adobe, and three small wood shuttered windows displayed on each long side. A small cross peaked the front of the clay-tiled roof. A pigeon perched on the church's steeple could enjoy a panoramic view of Mexico. A white picket fence guarded the church, and a stone well stood near the front door, offering water to baptize parishioners as well as quench their thirst.

Hours earlier nearly a hundred of the Diaz family's neighbors assembled, quietly sitting in the church's simple wooden benches as another thirty people stood in the back. The front rows on either side of the aisle were reserved for the family and their guests. The archbishop of Denver and a parish priest prepared for Requiem Mass in a side room. At the foot of the altar lay ten closed coffins of varying lengths.

Outside the church, in a field at the base of the Santa Tomas Mountains, a temporary assembly area with a stage and broadcast loudspeakers stood for the mourner overflow. Over twenty thousand had already gathered, with another ten thousand expected to arrive over the next few hours. Buses backed up for twenty miles on New Mexico county roads.

At two p.m. Toussaint told Rebecca the funeral would be beginning as scheduled. He was unyielding that she had to lift off from New Mexico before darkness fell. The family of Augusto Diaz had just been seated in the front pew. Twenty minutes later, the armored Sabers pulled up in front of the church, and Rebecca entered from a side door, escorted by Secret Service agents. The White House press pool recorded a photograph of her on church grounds wearing a black suit, a pillbox hat, and veil; inside all press was banned. Murmurs of astonishment swept the rows as she entered. At the end of the family aisle sat ex-President Sanchez-Smith, who had escorted the Diaz relatives to New Mexico. As she hugged Rebecca, she said, "Thank you. You did a good thing today."

Rebecca spoke in Spanish to each member of the family. Eduardo

Diaz, the youngest brother of the deceased, insisted that she sit with them; two teenaged nieces gladly accepted the hug she had offered before they sat with linked arms.

The service opened with the parish priest reading from Revelations:

And I heard a voice from heaven saying unto me, blessed are the dead which die in the Lord from henceforth: Yea, saith the Spirit, that they may rest from their labours; and their works do follow them.

Rebecca felt the body warmth of the two nieces on either side of her. They looked confused as they stared at the ten coffins of relatives they had never met. From the vantage point of the primitive country shack they lived in, the stories they had been told of their uncle, Augusto Diaz, who had gone to America and prospered, probably seemed more fairytale than reality.

The Archbishop of Denver started to sprinkle holy water on the coffins. The parish priest lit incense, as a pungent smoke floated through the chapel. He read:

> *May the choirs of angels come to greet you.*
> *May they speed you to Paradise.*
> *May the Lord enfold you in His mercy.*
> *May you find eternal life.*

The archbishop, with a small wave of his hand, indicated that the mourners could approach the coffins. Adult relatives knelt, crossed themselves, and wept. Once a month, Rebecca had been told, Eduardo Diaz and his family gathered for a Sunday dinner after church in the town of San Jose del Penasco. Nearly every month they read a letter from their El Norte relatives. Each letter contained a money order sent by Augusto Diaz for a hundred dollars, often more, which paid for their health care, and ensured that the children received an education.

Rebecca knelt before the coffins and crossed herself. She felt like she had aged a decade. *Dear God*, she prayed. *Let these souls rest in Peace, may they sit as your children on your side.*

She imagined herself drawing a sword; she knew metaphorically, or perhaps literally, that soon a bloody battle would be fought. *Dear*

God, I beg your forgiveness. I've always believed in your enduring love, but I promise, this day, to avenge these deaths.

An honor guard of Army officers from the regiment Augusto Diaz had served with in his adopted country, ceremoniously placed the coffins on donkey-drawn carts for the family's journey to their final resting place. Rebecca and Sanchez-Smith, along with the two clergymen, and the Diaz family surrounded by Secret Service agents, gathered up behind the procession. The carts wound their way down a dirt road south of the Church of Santa Maria de Pueblo. Vehicles manned by Secret Service agents and federal marshals lined the road. Six armored Sabers and four Army ambulances drove a few hundred feet in front of the coffins in a V-shaped protective wedge.

Rebecca walked arm-in-arm in one row with the mourning family. Under her funeral attire, she wore an earpiece and a Secret Service transmitter on her chest; its microphone cord snaked down her arm and stopped short just at the end of her cuff.

The church's graveyard sat at the end of the dirt road. It had been two-thirds full. Now the Diaz family would fill the site. Ten freshly dug graves awaited the pine coffins, which, one at a time, took positions beside their final resting place. The archbishop consecrated the graves. As two Secret Service agents flanked each mourner, Blackhawk VIIs circled the periphery overhead, door gunners clamped to the skids.

* *

Seven miles south in Command Trailer B, two climatologists sat hunched over a computer screen.

"Run this by me again," said the senior scientist.

"Winds are sequencing, they may converge in the valley outside Las Cruces."

"Can you be more specific?"

"I'm showing a local cold front coming down over the Baldys and the Tortuga Mountains. And we're getting hot air coming up from Mexico. That front just passed Guzman Lookout Mountain."

"Damn, are you talking tornado?"

"No, I doubt that. It's a tornado scenario. But these winds aren't cyclonic."

"I need something definitive for command."

"Let me finish the modeling; worse case scenario is wind gusts, maybe up to thirty or forty miles an hour." The junior officer, with a line of sweat showing on his brow, looked up at his superior. "But I don't think they can execute a presidential liftoff by chopper from the cemetery. Not according to the flying restrictions I've read in the Secret Service manual. She'll have to come back to base by ground."

"All right, keep watching it. I need to run this information over to General Grace."

* *

The archbishop read from the Book of John:

In my Father's house are many mansions: if it were not so, I would have told you.

The archbishop's words wriggled through her brain. "God has a big house with many rooms."

Rebecca's loved ones had already checked in — her father Nathaniel, her mother Caitlín, Jackson, Annie, and Allison . . . perhaps.

* *

In the command trailer, General Grace showed Toussaint the climatologist wind-sequence modeling.

"We can't pull her out on a chopper now. The wind is gusting at over thirty miles an hour," Grace said.

"Damn," Toussaint said, "that nice quiet dirt road we ran her up on earlier is lined now with America-Firsters in their pickup trucks, holding ugly signs."

"Can't we push them out?" Grace said.

"Nope, Service Legal won't go for it. The Colorado State Police we commandeered are manning all the ingresses and egresses. They've searched them all for weapons, and a bunch of them had to leave their shotguns at the checkpoint. It would take too long to put up barricades. Let's re-position some of those troopers to run a linked-armed barricade.

It could get nasty, running the gauntlet with this crowd."

* *

The winds continued to pick up, scrambling sagebrush across the fields that bordered the cemetery. Farther out, tumbleweed blew into a cattle fence, catching itself on barbs. The sky darkened, and on the horizon lightning bolts illuminated Goat Mountain.

From the Little Black Mountain command center, Toussaint transmitted into her ear. "Rebecca, you need to move out now. The Sabers will convoy you back, and six helicopter gunships will be on your bumpers."

"Give me five minutes." The gravediggers finished shoveling clay-colored New Mexico soil on top of the caskets. "I want to say my good-byes to the mourners and the priests."

"Be quick," Toussaint said. "I want you out of New Mexico."

The last hand she shook belonged to the Archbishop of Denver. He clasped Rebecca's wrists. "My prayers will be with you every night," he said.

"Thank you, you've been most kind. I'm sorry we met at such a tragic event."

"Go with God, my child." The archbishop hesitated. "You were once a Catholic?"

"Yes, I took the sacraments as a child. My mother was a Catholic."

"I know your godfather, Reverend Spurgeon. We meet every year at an ecumenical conference, and he has spoken to me about your childhood, your parents, and grandparents. Reverend Spurgeon is very proud of you and your accomplishments."

Before she could respond Rebecca's earpiece came alive. "Now! We have to get you out of here now," Toussaint's voice rippled with urgency.

* *

Secret Service agents shouted orders as they escorted Rebecca into her vehicle. The armored Sabers roared to life, activating their retracted electrically charged rods, and formed themselves into a battle formation. The roadbed underneath shook as they began the five-mile drive to base camp at Little Black Mountain. The scene seemed cinematic to

Rebecca, like an armored train wintering through the Ural Mountains as Mother Russia shattered into revolution.

As the convoy moved back toward their base, the America First cadre lined the road. Their faces silently expressed hate. The sunken eyes of the women appeared to Rebecca as battered.

"Devil woman! Go home! Satanist!" voices from the crowd began to shout.

Rebecca's eyes narrowed as her car slowly passed the onlookers.

These were the fellow travelers. Dupes of other players, trained to hate.

The assassins had long fled, leaving the hollowed frames and minds of their supporters as the entrails of their beliefs.

Parched desert dust blew across the clenched faces. Some hats went flying, but like sentinels at their posts, the America-Firsters held their positions.

A mile down the road, the caravan came to a sudden halt. Rebecca could hear an agent transmitting through her earpiece. "Two women and a child are lying on the road in front of the lead Saber. Please advise, Command Central, do you read me?"

"You've got twenty agents on foot outside the caravan," Toussaint said urgently. "Move the protestors. Arrest them if you have to, but try not to incite the crowd."

"Hold off a few minutes. We're moving in more firepower," Grace said, "I've got six APC's coming to you. They have sniper teams. If we have to, as a last resort, we'll use tranquilizer darts. They'll be there in a few minutes."

Stopped in her car, Rebecca's eyes honed in on a woman, in her mid-forties, wearing farmer's overalls, a weathered denim jacket, and steel-toed barnyard boots. Shag-short gray hair framed a tattoo, LIVE FREE OR DIE, etched on her forehead. She held a sign that said, GOD MADE YOU BARREN, BITCH. Rebecca bit her lip and felt as if a barbed sting had pierced her heart. To the woman's left, a legless Army veteran sat in a wheelchair with his head slumped, his thinning hair tied in a ponytail. His face was pulpy, and it looked like he might have a glass eye. He wore a Purple Heart next to a button, which read, I ALREADY DIED FOR AMERICA. Two boys wearing Boy Scout uniforms rested their hands on each side of the wheelchair, looking embarrassed as they held SEND THEM BACK TO MEXICO signs.

Rebecca took a deep breath before speaking into her transmitter. "I'm getting out."

"You can't do that," Toussaint said. "I can't protect you—Rebecca, listen to me." Her ear rocked from the higher decibel.

"I know what I have to do," she calmly responded, as she pushed the emergency override button next to her, which unlocked the passenger compartment doors.

"No way," Toussaint said, his voice pitching up toward a scream. "You can't do this."

General Grace interrupted him and began speaking into her earpiece. "Rebecca, this isn't a smart move. We need to keep you covered."

"Do you have any reason to believe there are guns in the crowd?"

"No," Grace said. "They've all been searched. And our drones are continuously reading the metal content. But these people would kill you with their bare hands if they could, and vulture your remains. Don't do it."

"Akashat Twelve," she said, as she hit the mute button on her receiver. The last line of ex-President Samuel Jenkins Bayou's poem slid by her: *Don't forget to duck.*

In the command center, Grace turned to Toussaint. "You can't stop her. We need to make the best of it if we can."

Toussaint wasted no time to bark out commands. "Urgent, Convoy Charlie, listen up. Red Striker is in motion." The Secret Service had re-coded her, following the procedure when a subject's code name became public. "She's wild-carding. Don't squeeze her, but put a V-shape of agents in front of her, with titanium shields ready. Expect rocks to be thrown. Don't react without my orders. The choppers are going to close in overhead, doors open with snipers readied." Toussaint paused and looked at General Grace, who nodded affirmatively while relaying commands to Zebra forces.

"If any metal is flashed, grab her and throw her back in the car. End of story. Understood?" Grace said.

When she stepped out of the back seat of the Saber, the slogan-shouting crowd grew eerily silent. Fixing her gaze on the woman wearing the farmer's overalls, she walked directly toward her inside the cocoon of the Secret Service agents who left a sightline open at the front of their V formation.

Rebecca stopped five feet before the woman and coldly eyed her. The woman raised her middle finger and mouthed what seemed to be an obscene expression. Rebecca smiled while further focusing her gaze on the woman, taking two steps closer. The mob rabbled, like a dead-end bar's patrons itching for a back alley fight. Rebecca took another step closer to the woman; she could see her eyes twitching nervously. The boys she assumed to be her children tugged confusedly at her sleeves. The veteran in the wheelchair didn't look up.

She held out her hand to the woman. "My name is Rebecca Tree, but I guess you know that. What's yours?"

The woman started to work her tongue and jaws as if trying to create spit, but her mouth must have been too dry. Rebecca ignored her now and leaned over to the veteran, speaking into his ear. "There's too much suffering in this world. It's not God's way. You gave up your legs for your country," she said, as she looked down at his stumps. "We need to help each other."

The man still didn't look up. The woman, enraged, took the back of his wheelchair and flipped it over. The man fell out of the chair and lay helplessly sprawled, and stunned, on the ground. The crowd, some assuming Rebecca had pushed the man, grew in agitation, screaming insults at her: TRAITOR, HANG HER, TYRANT.

Rebecca ignored the shouts while directing two Secret Service agents to help the man off the ground and right the wheelchair after the woman fled back into the crowd, leaving her terrified children. Rebecca approached the two boys as her mind searched for some long-stored information.

Finding the thought, she asked, "Do you know the Boy Scout Code?" One of the boys turned and fled into the crowd when Rebecca spoke. The remaining child, looking frightened, seemed adrift. His mother, who most likely told him what to do, had disappeared. The man who seemed to be his father didn't speak, so he probably couldn't look to him for cues.

"When I was your age," Rebecca continued, addressing the child, who looked wide-eyed like a deer caught in headlights, "someone told me to be kind like a Boy Scout. I was told that a Scout understands there is strength in being gentle. He treats others as he wants to be treated. He doesn't hurt or kill harmless things without reason."

Out of her pocket, she took out two gold–plated ballpoint pens engraved with the words "Rebecca Tree, President of the United States," and handed them to the boy. "One's for you. Give the other to your brother."

A tentative smile replaced the fear, as he muttered softly, "Thank you," and a second later, he added, "Ma'am." He stuffed the pens in his pocket, and then looked nervously around to see who might be watching.

"You're a brave boy, a very brave boy," Rebecca said, as the terror of second thoughts appeared to flash across his face.

As she backed off toward her waiting car, Rebecca stopped and stared intently at the faces of the crowd. A minute later, a few people started throwing small rocks. Secret Service agents snapped open their shields.

Toussaint screamed into the transmitter, "Get her out now."

"Let it play for a few more seconds; I know what I'm doing," she said into her transmitter as her voice filled with grim determination. "And don't let the agents touch me." A dozen more rocks clambered harmlessly against the titanium shields. "Okay, it's finished," Rebecca said.

There's no place like home, she thought, eager now to go.

Chapter 51

Rebecca, wearing a khaki-colored flight suit embroidered with her sig-nature on the pocket, was wrapped in two thermal blankets drinking hot black tea as Toussaint berated her. She picked at a plate of scallops, green beans, and home fried potatoes. Her legs felt like pudding.

"You can't do this kind of stuff."

"I did what had to be done," she said. "I won't stand by while inno-cent people like the Diazes are butchered."

General Grace knocked on the partly opened door and came into the plane's airborne executive office. Overhearing the last exchange, he said, "Caleb, could I talk to you alone for a few minutes? Do you mind, Madam President?"

She looked at them like two boys conspiring in a locker room. "Sure, go ahead. Have a man-to-man chat." A weak but mischievous grin danced across her face. "Do some male bonding, see if I care."

The two men left, and a wave of loneliness passed over Rebecca. She had lived now too many years without an intimate human companion.

To be held, hugged, and have a partner to lick her wounds — was that so much to ask, she thought.

Looking for comfort, she turned her inner thoughts to a Biblical passage: *Seek justice. Defend the orphan.*

* *

"Peter, I'm sorry . . . but I've got to think about resigning," Toussaint said. "As much as I think the world of Rebecca, I can't be in charge of protecting a president with so little regard for her own life. It's too much responsibility."

"She went operational on you," Grace said quietly. "That's what she was trained for years ago in Zebra Force."

Grace and Toussaint stood in a corridor in the middle of the plane. The White House press pool was sequestered in a cramped forward cabin while the Secret Service filled the rear cabin.

Toussaint slammed his fist into his palm. "Operational," his voice ratcheted up. "She's the president, not some damn secret agent. And what the hell does Akashat Twelve mean?"

"Let's not get excited; come, let's sit down," Grace escorted Toussaint into an unused office. "Rebecca trusts you and depends on you. But there are some things you don't know about her."

"Like what?"

"Her record with Zebra Force."

"I'm not sure I care at the moment."

"She did fifteen operational missions, including five as an operational unit commander before being re-assigned to Zebra's command center."

"So it's the Army's fault that she has a thrill-seeker's personality."

"In the Army, we called them Type T's."

"Exactly."

"No, we tried to drum out Type T's. Rebecca evaluated as being methodical and cautious," Grace said. "She always brought back all her soldiers from the operations she commanded. But . . ."

"But what?"

"There was one operation in which she disobeyed command orders."

"Like how she behaved today?"

"Yes, she put herself in personal danger, much more than today, but it ended with twelve hostage orphans set free without a shot exchanged."

"So twelve," Toussaint said, "referred to the children, and I assume Akashat denotes the place where this little caper happened."

"Correct, Akashat in al-Anbar province."

"You should've kept her in the Army," Toussaint said, his voice seeming to calm.

"Well," Grace replied, smiling conspiratorially, "I wish I could have."

"So what's the moral of this story? Spies, spooks, and secret agents now run what little is left of our great democracy?'

"No," Grace said, breaking out into a full belly laugh. "Seriously, I doubt she'll do again what she just did at Las Cruces. It was high noon today for the Firsters' supporters. It might take weeks or years to round up the hard-core, but their B teams are demoralized now. And Caleb, what happened to the two women and the child lying on the road in front of the lead Saber?"

Toussaint glared at Grace before grudgingly saying, "Okay. Well taken. They got up to see all the excitement when Rebecca got out of her car. Still, I don't know," Toussaint said. "If she pulls this sort of stunt again, I'll stay home with my wife and collect retirement pay."

Chapter 52

Her eyes moved rapidly under her lids, and her major voluntarily muscle groups, chin, and neck, stiffened. She was in a REM sleep cycle replaying a dream set in the Civil War. Her father, Colonel Nathaniel Tree, already known as a Union hero from the Battle of Spotsylvania Court House, led his cavalry as they charged through a dense stand of woods. Stray Confederate troops huddled behind pine trees and boulders, trying to get one last shot at the Yankees before they went inevitably to meet their God. At his side, rode his twin daughters in blue uniforms, who, like other children in 1865, had begun to reinforce Union troops. Then the scene switched, as quickly as a silent movie projectionist changing reels, to a ballroom in the White House with women in hooped dresses, ribbons tied in their hair.

A bedside security phone began to ring while hooped dresses swung back and forth like bells as the women scurried around the dance floor.

"Rebecca, are you awake?" Toussaint said.

"Yes," Rebecca said, disorientated. "There's a grand ball at the White House with Abraham Lincoln. I danced with one of his sons and my sis . . . " Rebecca finally realized what she was saying. "Sorry, I was in a dream. What time is it?"

"It's almost five in the morning. I've got something you need to see. Can you come down to the Secret Service conference room? Are you up for it? You didn't seem all there during the after-action briefing in the Situation Room."

"Thanks, I'm better. I went to sleep after lunch, and I slept for over ten hours. I was exhausted."

Twenty minutes later, Toussaint pushed a memory chip into a projector.

"What's this?"

"A videotape sent to the FBI field office in Phoenix. This copy came by courier last night to the White House. I called you as soon as I looked at it."

The tape opened in deadly monotony, with windshield wipers moving methodically against a hard-driving rain as a country road unfolded. The view shifted slightly to the driver's profile. He wore black plastic glass frames, and a few wispy hairs crowned his head. Under a work coat, a collar of a flannel shirt poked out, and his head darted back and forth like a baby bird in a nest watching a predator circling. Sweat dripped from his forehead, and he lifted his hand from the steering wheel to wipe his brow with his coat cuff. The camera drew back more, and Rebecca gasped as the enlarged frame showed a hand, with a small tattoo, reaching from the backseat, holding a knife at the side of the driver's neck.

"Is he Native Force?" Rebecca asked.

"Maybe. We don't know yet. Let me fast forward," Toussaint said, pushing on a remote. "We've bookmarked scenes."

Rebecca watched the frames catapult forward at 32x until a sensed bookmark slowed the tape down to standard speed. "There's dialogue here."

A woman's voice could be heard whining in a contrived baby-dollish way. "Thought you might get some action tonight, huh, Gramps? Picking up a stray hitchhiking girl, hungry and desperate."

"Please," the driver said. "I thought you needed help. Don't hurt me. Take the car. We can stop at an ATM. I have two," he stammered, "maybe three hundred dollars in the bank."

"We'll see. Maybe you could drive us somewhere."

"Where do you want to go?"

"The west coast would be nice. San Francisco."

"Anywhere you want. Just please don't hurt me."

"What do you do Gramps?"

"What do you mean?"

"For a living."

"I inspect meat."

"Far out, my friend in the back seat with me is a famous writer."

"Shut up," said a male voice.

"Yeah, he's modest. He's written two books, but I think his first one, *Murder Across America,* looks like a best-seller."

Rebecca grabbed the remote out of Toussaint's hand, hit the stop button, and then rewound the last few seconds.

"...his first one, *Murder Across America*."

Rebecca hit the pause button, as she paced around the room. "That's the title ATF agents found after the shoot-out with Buford Brown, the founder of Native Force. The voice from the backseat must be the first lieutenant that Brown trained, Cobra, Commander Alpha. And the girl could be the 'Unidentified Female, the Psycho Biter.'"

"We're running voice analysis recognition software on a copy of the tape now," Toussaint said.

"This whole thing is getting worse every day," Rebecca said. "I'm going to have to look at stronger actions," she said, hitting the remote as they continued to listen to the tape.

"Damn it, shut your slut mouth," said the male voice from the backseat.

"Please, I have two children and a grandchild on the way. They need me."

"Don't worry," the woman's voice whined. "I wouldn't hurt you. But sometimes my friend in the back seat, he gets these terrible migraines. And the only way he gets relief is by using his knife. Something about blood spurting out of arteries seems to steady him."

The driver began shaking uncontrollably, and the car swerved erratically.

"Hey, watch your driving." The camera jiggled, catching a hand slashing a knife lightly on the skin behind the man's ear before blood trickled out. "Slow down. Pull over there." The car veered sharply and came to a skidding stop, tilting down, which suggested it was now off the road.

"I think I'm getting a migraine," said the voice in the backseat.

Chapter 53

One week later
Oval Office

Rebecca took a phone call from the publisher of *The New York Times*, Amanda Whitney-Sulzberger.

"A team of our reporters in collaboration with a BBC investigative unit has pieced together the story that Jack Switzer, the murdered *New Yorker* writer, had been developing. We're a few days away from publishing our findings, which will reveal that four wet state senators are involved in land deals with six of their dry state colleagues. Together they form a secret gang of ten, which has blocked infrastructure relief for the wet states. And off the record, we have additional information, not yet fully developed, that your great-uncle William Tree has a hand in this."

"And Merewether Tree?"

"We're still looking into that."

The reality of its imminent publication shook Rebecca. She looked at her watch and then looked at her calendar. A congressional recess started in three days. The *Times* told her that they hoped to publish in two days; Rebecca implored them to wait.

"I'm not asking you not to publish; I'm only asking you to wait four or five days."

"Madam President," Whitney-Sulzberger said, "I'm willing to listen, but I need a reason."

"I'm not going to give you an explanation today," Rebecca said, testily.

"Is it a national security issue?"

"No, but I could twist it that way if I have to. I don't want to go in that direction; I'm just asking for a few days. I have no intention to stop you from publishing. In fact, I applaud your work and welcome seeing your story. But the timing is a serious issue. Do you want me to say, please?" Rebecca said. "Okay, I'm begging you. The president of the United States is pleading to sit on your story for a couple of extra days for the sake of the country.

"Your BBC collaborators are led by Allan McNally?"

"Yes, how did you know?"

"I know stuff. Give me two additional days, and McNally can have an exclusive interview with me to get my reaction to the story."

"We'll think about it and get back to you in a couple of hours."

* *

Rebecca gazed out of her window toward the Washington Monument. A month ago, she gave the groundskeeper a list of a dozen bird feeders and specified locations for their placement on the South Lawn. The House Government Operations Sub-Committee on the White House turned down the request, citing it as inappropriate. Rebecca, in an unpresidential fit of rage, flipped backward photographs of ex-presidents hanging on West Wing walls. In the middle of the night, the White House staff turned them back.

The next day, Rebecca ordered thirty bird feeders, solar birdbaths, suet holders, and woodpecker logs. In the *Congressional Record*, a Congresswoman from Ohio cited Rebecca's actions as illegal. Then a tabloid notched up the story with a headline BIRD WOMAN OF PENNSYLVANIA AVENUE.

Rebecca increased her purchases, buying custom designed nesting boxes for nearly extinct birds. As her battle with Congress and the press intensified, she staked more birdhouses into the White House lawn for kestrels, warblers, wrens, and woodpeckers. She bought a ladybug house, recalling the last ladybug she'd seen, some fifteen years back, a vibrant red bug with black spots crawling on the leaf of a plant in her Boston garden.

Ladybird, ladybird, fly away home. Your house is on fire, your children alone.

The local Washington D.C. beautification committee complained to the White House that the South Lawn looked like Appalachia and the public agreed that they had a fair point.

In her final act of defiance, which violated local ordinances and federal laws, she purchased bat houses in the hopes that the flying mammals might take up residence on the White House grounds and eat virulent mosquitoes. In recent years, as global warming lengthened insect breeding seasons, the mosquitoes had taken a deadly toll on elderly Washingtonians with West Nile virus and St. Louis encephalitis.

Rebecca was still at the window when she heard the Oval Office door open, and Fatima entered.

"Come over here. I want to show you something," Rebecca said, passing Fatima a pair of birding binoculars. "You might need these."

"Oh, look how active it has become," Fatima said. "I see tons of sparrows and finches. Look, a bluebird, it's so beautiful."

"Pan your binoculars to the right, slowly, a bit more. We have some new guests."

"You got your wish," Fatima said, lowering the binoculars and happily clapping her hands together. "I've never seen cardinals. Only pictures. They're gorgeous. Which one is the female?" she asked after raising back the binoculars.

"The dull one, of course. The bright one is male."

"Why?"

"According to Charles Darwin, the females are drawn to the male's bright colors."

"A bit sexist?" Fatima said.

"Perhaps, but there are other theories. For example, the incubating female being less apparent to predators is another. Interestingly, if a bird species nests in tree hollows, then the female is often the same brightness as the male. Also, the conspicuousness of the male's colors warns predators that the area is occupied and that the male bird is in good condition and prepared to fight.

"Look," Rebecca shouted out, "another cardinal, a female, just landed."

"How can you see that far? You're an eagle."

"Yeah, I know. My eyes became the body part that first interested the Army after I finished basic training."

"Your eyes?"

"They wanted to train me to be a sniper."

"And did they?"

"No, I refused."

Fatima began to ask another question but Rebecca quickly changed the subject. "In my closet, I have a bright red business suit. I bought it when I graduated Harvard, but I never wore it. I intend to wear it this week. Within a few days, we'll be going to war."

Rebecca recounted her conversation with *The New York Times* publisher outlining a political conspiracy in the Senate, along with growing evidence from the intelligence agencies that domestic Native Force insurgents flying a banner of hate, had laid the groundwork for an inter-racial civil war in the border states. She thought of Lincoln holding the fate of the nation in his hands while he agonized each night over reports arriving from Union spies of death and destruction.

Rebecca's mission had become all too clear. She needed to subdue a whole cast of characters, bad performers in a tragic play — rogue actors whose future would be soon predicated by legal briefs. They represented corrupt interlocking interests — from Congress to boardrooms to pressrooms. If she failed, the body of the nation would rip apart.

Rebecca outlined to Fatima the specifics of an immediate plan of action, the Plan B that had been percolating in her for some time.

"Call it 'women's work,' if you will —we're going to do some housecleaning."

A shocked Fatima responded, "No, they're going to call it emergency powers, abuse of executive power, and they'll try to impeach you."

"Yes, but I have no more options. If it's too difficult for you, I'll understand if you want to leave."

Fatima said nothing for a moment.

"I'm tough, too," Fatima said, after a pause, her brown eyes seemed to narrow with intensity as she handed the binoculars back to Rebecca. "I better get to work. There'll be a lot to prepare."

Chapter 54

Congress had just gone into recess, and her first appointment for the day, Attorney General Gregory Markey, had just arrived. Markey, at first glance, appeared to be wider than he was tall with a build like a keg of beer. Rebecca wanted to kick him and see how far he might roll.

Neither seemed to be in a mood for formalities. Markey nodded to the president as he sat down, opening the conversation with, "I assume, Madam President, as you hinted at the last cabinet meeting, that you wish my resignation letter. I've brought it dated today, and I could begin clearing my office first thing in the morning." He opened his thick leather briefcase and extracted an envelope and handed it to her.

"Mr. Markey," Rebecca said, "I appreciate your coming to see me and bringing me your resignation letter. Pursuant to Article 7, Section 8 of the United States criminal code, I'm ordering your office sealed."

Markey swallowed hard, and the folds on his neck flared blood red.

"As we speak," Rebecca continued, "a letter is being hand-delivered from my office demanding the immediate resignation of the Justice Department Inspector General, and he'll be replaced by a new I.G., appointed under recess powers."

"This is unheard of," Markey spluttered.

Rebecca stop-signed him with her hand. "You're accused of no wrongdoing, not yet. But you have failed in your duties."

"Which duties?"

"Your job was to undertake legitimate investigations, to find and bring to justice people who constituted serious threats to the safety of the United States and its citizens."

"I did my job."

"Your department turned into one big pork barrel with contracts to cronies."

"Untrue."

"No? I've also seen convincing evidence that you failed to take action against terrorist cells working throughout the border states."

"That's not an easy problem."

"For six years now," Rebecca said, "America-Firsters have attacked Hispanic-Americans. I intend to stop them and find a committed attorney general who'll end this lawlessness. I've nothing more to discuss with you."

Markey rose slowly from his chair, his eyes burning. For a brief moment, Rebecca wondered if he might attack her. Then a wordless Markey abruptly turned and stormed out of the Oval Office slamming the door behind him, which drew to his flanks several Secret Service agents.

Later in the day, one of the agent escorts described Markey's departure to Rebecca.

When he exited the White House, he stopped for a second, spun around, and stuck up his middle finger. He stamped his foot twice and then heaved himself into the government limousine for his last ride at the taxpayers' expense.

Chapter 55

Coup d'état?

The battle was on.

Before the sun set over the Potomac on the first day of congressional recess, Rebecca appointed new Secretaries of Treasury, State, and Defense. The following day she filled out the rest of the cabinet, except for the attorney general, with more recess appointments.

On the third day, she dropped the bombshell, which the press characterized as the "nuclear" option. She named as attorney general, Harriet Ogden, Harvard's Miles Rose Professor of Constitutional Law, whom she had met nine months earlier at Emily O'Brian and Lucretia Fironznia's house, but instead of a recess appointment, she used emergency executive powers enumerated under the Garcia-Winthrop Sedition Act.

By the next morning, the country had gone ballistic. The popular press screamed, TYRANNY. ABUSE OF POWER. TREE DYNASTY GOES MONARCHIC. Over seventy percent opposed her actions in the first opinion polls, believing Rebecca should resign or face impeachment. Forty percent of those polled echoed the message pushed by the tabloid publications that the country's president appeared unstable.

Wolf Global resurrected legacy smear campaigns across their empire's media platforms. Their tabloids ran stories claiming she had been violent as a child, while their websites besmirched her military career with stories of her inappropriate behavior with an unnamed fellow soldier, dropping innuendoes that she had been court-martialed. An Italian newspaper published a "tell-all" from a countess, whom Rebecca never heard of.

REBECCA TREE'S BOARDING SCHOOL LOVER BARES ALL screamed their headline.

Chapter 56

Workout Room
White House Basement

Agent Fenton's foot slammed into Rebecca's padded midsection. Sweat poured down Rebecca's forehead as she tried to keep balance and maintain a defensive posture, but she couldn't concentrate. The two women worked out once a week in the White House gym.

Rebecca kept missing and Fenton, short but torpedo quick, tapped light kicks in rapid succession into Rebecca's mid-section. Rebecca's knees buckled slightly, and she found herself caught off-balance as she backed up to avoid another score. Fenton spun, aimed another kick at the torso, but accidentally hit Rebecca above the target zone, glancing her neck.

That was the last thing Rebecca remembered of the sparring, as images of twisted bodies and exploding vehicles replaced them. Al Duwadimi, on that awful day: one Humvee was already shredded from the first IED, as Lieutenant Tree forced a jammed door open with her rifle. Jackson sat slumped forward over the steering wheel, blood streaming out from under his vest. It seemed silent for a moment, like the silence of deafness, but then it was broken by the ping-ping sounds of incoming fire, as she wrenched Jackson free of the wreckage. Rebecca pulled his body another twenty feet before an RPG struck his Humvee, blowing it up and incinerating the two other men trapped inside and already killed by the first explosion. She lay on top of him, trying to shield his body from the incoming fire as she whispered desperately in his ear. "Don't go. Please, don't go. It's not your time."

"Madam President, Madam President." Voices broke though, and she felt strong arms lifting her to a bench. Fenton lay, gasping for breath, her face red as a beet, coughing and clenching her throat. Two Secret Service medics attended to her on the floor.

The room swirled like an out-of-control carousel.

"Madam President, can you hear me? Do you hear me?" an agent said.

Medics slapped blood pressure cuffs on each arm. The room slowed down, but it seemed six times its normal size. She drew quick, short rabbit breaths from her nostrils. Another agent lifted Fenton off the ground, and, Rebecca returning to the present, tried to piece together the scene.

Fenton tried to stand, but the agents still held her. "Lynette, are you all right?" Rebecca said, "God, I'm sorry. I must have lost it."

Fenton gestured to the other agents to put her down on the bench. She sagged toward Rebecca. "I'm okay." The words came out low and gravelly. "But maybe no more sparring for a while."

Rebecca managed a weak smile. She felt like her legs had been cut off above the knees. An agent spoke slowly into her ear. She shook her head with resignation. "All right. Give me some time, and I'll want to change. I won't go to Walter Reed, not in an ambulance. Let the White House doctor look at me first."

Chapter 57

The hairs on her neck prickled and the scar tissue below her shoulder blade throbbed. Rebecca, unable to sleep, got out of bed and took a hot shower. After her meltdown at her sparring session, she had refused the White House physician's prescription for a mild sleeping potion but agreed to a thrice daily fortified protein shake as well as a tranquil sleep machine with water sounds placed on her nightstand. As she toweled down, Rebecca looked in the mirror at the worry lines surrounding her eyes. She pulled at her hair seeing, for the first time, gray roots now sprouting. Her rib cage looked like it poked out. She stood on the scale and to her horror, realized she lost five pounds since inauguration day, to add to the five she had already lost campaigning. In the background, she could hear her security phone ringing.

"Yes, what is it?" Rebecca said as she answered, her voice nearly cracking.

"Something ugly happened," Toussaint said. "I need you in the Oval Office."

"What?" Rebecca nearly snapped. "What happened now?" She didn't think she could take any more pressure.

"I'll tell you when you come downstairs. Brace yourself."

A few minutes later Rebecca slid into her office chair. Toussaint looked terrible like he had just fallen off a cliff.

"What happened?"

"Sometime last night, someone tried to deface your sister's gravesite."

Rebecca felt daggered. Her stomach churned and her legs numbed as her ribs dug into her chest. "Details." Rebecca's voice approached a screaming pitch. "Tell me the details," she said, cracking a ballpoint pen in half with her hands.

"We got an alert from the Barnstable police. As part of executive protection, we ask local law enforcement to keep an eye on the gravesites of family members. Someone spray-painted some ugly words on your sister's tombstone and got as far as chiseling off the first two letters of her name."

Rebecca, her face drained of color and her fingers clenched in a viselike grip, took a deep breath. Frozen for a few minutes, she finally sighed, unclenched her fingers and took out a blank pad. "Tell me what they wrote?"

"Satan's Sister and Rest in Hell," she copied the words to a notepad as her fingers trembled, her normally neat letters looked jagged.

"Does the press know about this?"

"No, the police chief is buttoned down. Only he and the two officers in the patrol car know about it. And he assured me that nothing went out that could be picked up by a scanner. There are some houses near the graveyard; he thinks it's only a matter of time before the news leaks. They're going to keep watch all night until we tell them what to do."

A wave of hopelessness swept over Rebecca.

"Rebecca, I'm sorry. If I caught whoever did this, I might kill them. What do you want to do?"

Rebecca looked at her watch, making some quick mental calculations.

"I'm going to move her to a safe place."

Chapter 58

Allison Tree's gravesite
Barnstable, Massachusetts

A tent covered the gravesite.

At the edge of the cemetery, partially obscured under a line of trees, a black hearse waited alongside a convoy of armored vehicles, the president's ambulance, and a telecommunications mini-van linked globally to America's military forces. Trying to minimize their presence, they decided not to use earth-moving equipment and opted for a slower hand dig. Secret Service agents began digging at nine in the morning.

A federal district judge had been woken at dawn. Two legal teams, from private practice and the government, argued Rebecca's case. The private lawyers cited a recent case in Maine where a sister won the legal right over the objections of the parents to move her brother's grave, which was endangered by rising seawaters. The Secret Service lawyers argued a threat against the presidency could be physical or emotional.

A Secret Service agent came into the judge's office and handed Rebecca a printout showing the results of ground-penetrating radar probes just completed of the gravesite. A sheet of metal, perhaps lead, obscured the casket and prevented a x-ray result. Disturbed by it, the judge signed the order.

* *

Rebecca paced the perimeter of the gravesite, her legs cramping. She felt as though steel rods threaded her veins.

The front of the graveyard was toothed with crooked old tombstones. The grave of her sister stood in the middle of the last row against a high brick fence. Strangers surrounded her.

She knelt at the edge of Allison's grave and made the sign of the cross. "Ally, hi. It's Becky."

Her fingers slowly and lovingly traced each of the letters chiseled, the damaged A and L, scars, leading to the clearer carving of "L I S O N" into the monument's faceplate, her only tangible connection to her sister.

The undefiled inscription had read:

Allison Tree. So small, so sweet, so soon.

Toussaint walked toward her and took her aside. "I just got word that your grandfather is trying to get a cease-and-desist order from a Supreme Court justice. I'm pretty sure it's Justice Coyne."

"How did he find out?" Rebecca asked.

"Someone leaked it."

"I'm not going to stop. I intend to move her someplace where no one can disturb her. She's entitled to rest in peace."

"I understand. But are you willing to defy a Supreme Court justice?"

"I don't intend to obey it," Rebecca said, her voice torn between defiance and anguish.

For the next hour, the agents continue to dig.

Rebecca's legs felt rubbery, her breathing sped up, and her heart raced; in the background, she heard Toussaint talking on his command phone.

A helicopter appeared hovering over one end of the graveyard; it carried the markings of a CBS affiliate television station out of Boston.

Toussaint rushed over to where Rebecca was pacing.

"You have to go into the command trailer now. You can watch everything on the video monitors there and communicate with me through your radio earpiece."

"Why?"

"If that chopper gets an image of you, then the whole security situation changes. You cannot be exposed. Absolutely not."

"I'm staying out here."

"You can stay if you like, but then my resignation letter will be on your desk first thing in the morning."

Rebecca shut her eyes hard. Wordlessly she turned on her heels and headed for the command trailer, which had full video and audio of the events unfolding at the gravesite.

The sheriff's department and Secret Service agents put up more roadblocks as word spread to the wire services and local papers. A rabble of reporters started to congregate on the roads leading into the graveyard.

The overhead helicopter shot, which showed a tent constructed around the gravesite, quickly morphed into a news bulletin flashing on television screens across the country: SECRET SERVICE EXHUMING PRESIDENT'S SISTER'S GRAVE.

Rebecca listened through the monitors as Toussaint communicated with the other agents. "Confirm on that, how far away? Yes, if the courier is carrying a court order then you have to let him through. But, listen, the paperwork must be correct, and read it carefully. Yes, read it twice, and then read it twice again."

"How much time do we have?" Rebecca asked Toussaint through her headset. Her throat burned as if she had swallowed a hot ember.

"Ten, maybe fifteen minutes," Toussaint said, as he shouted to his men to dig faster.

Rebecca could now hear the shovels clanging against metal.

"We've hit the metal shield," one of the agents yelled out.

"It looks like a flat piece," said another.

"Can you rope it?" Toussaint said.

"Roger, we need to clear more dirt on the sides now."

"Where's the court courier?" Rebecca asked.

Toussaint's walkie-talkie was pinned to his ear. "Two state trooper patrol cars are escorting the courier. Our chopper spotted them five minutes from our first roadblock. So we've got less than ten minutes."

Two agents on the ground assembled a winch, while, in the gravesite, the others wrapped a rope around the shield. "Hoist away," came a cry from the pit.

Halfway up the rope suddenly slipped, the winch sending the heavy plate back into the gravesite. An agent below screamed out in pain. "It landed on my leg. I'm pinned."

"The top of the casket has split partially open," Rebecca shouted into her microphone from the command trailer, her eyes glued to the video monitors.

"Hold on," Toussaint said, as agents scrambled to improvise a new winch and lift the metal plate off the agent. This time, they rigged the rope to the bumper of an SUV. Toussaint stood on the edge of the grave talking to the pinned agent. "We'll have the plate off you in a minute, and we've got a medical chopper coming in."

Agents shimmed two-by-fours under the plate as they pulled it now smoothly up and clear of the gravesite.

As the injured agent was pulled out of the pit, Rebecca heard the sirens of the state troopers escorting the court's courier. Looking at her watch, she sank deeper into despair.

Please God, give me more time.

The three agents left in the gravesite frantically tried to remove the rest of the dirt that sealed the casket into the earth. Out of the corner of her eye, Rebecca saw a man carrying papers un-flap the entrance to the tent and head toward Toussaint.

Now she watched another monitor as Toussaint read out loud the court order handed to him.

"The Secret Service must cease all operations currently being undertaken at the gravesite of Allison Tree in Barnstable, Massachusetts."

Rebecca's heart beat against her ribs. The acute angle of one of the video cameras revealed to her more than the agents in the pit could see: the inside of the small coffin came into view. Horrified by what she thought she saw, she went flying out of the command center. She ran for the gravesite as the remaining three secret service agents in compliance with the court order climbed out.

Toussaint was late to see her, and his attempt to block her failed.

As she flew past him, she shouted, "The court order doesn't cover me."

Rebecca picked up a crowbar and jumped into the now empty grave pit.

She pried what remained of the top of the casket as sweat dripped off her face. In the background, she could hear men's voices arguing. The rest of the lid began to give way on one side; more helicopters whirred overhead, and then the lid cracked fully open, as the sound of the approaching police sirens on the ground intensified. Rebecca kept prying, leveraging her body, until the final board of the coffin lid flew off, sending her, at the same time, backward against the far wall of the grave.

She was lying flat on the back wall of the excavated gravesite. She shut her eyes; the dirt smelled earthy and sweet. Small bits of rock dug into her back; loose dirt fell under the collar of her shirt, tearing at her skin. Opening her eyes, tears streaming, she pushed off the wall, reaching into the casket, her hands shaking. To the waiting Toussaint, it must have seemed like an eternity until Rebecca, seconds later, climbed out of the grave. She walked toward the tent flap carrying a shroud she had pulled out of the casket. It hardly weighed twenty pounds.

Toussaint stood at the flap. Shock filled his face, and his jaw appeared caved in.

"This is my sister, Allison Tree, who died at the age of four," Rebecca said, dropping a half-filled sandbag at his feet.

Chapter 59

Two days later

Rebecca hadn't eaten, slept, or spoke in the last thirty-six hours. They opened the bogus grave on a Friday morning. Toussaint took one look at her haunted, hollowed eyes and decided to take her out of the public eye to Camp David. By Sunday morning, she began to speak again.

"How do you feel?" Toussaint said, entering the sunroom where Rebecca sat staring out the window.

"I've been better," Rebecca said, turning away, holding in her hands pieces of graph paper taped together.

"It's not your fault."

She put the graph down on the writing table. Fault was exactly what Rebecca felt. A tape played in her head, looping and re-looping. She should have known; she should have found out. She had failed in her duty to protect her sister. And she had failed Jackson as well. The multiple burdens were more than she could bear.

Toussaint picked up the graph paper and stared at it as he walked around the room. At the bottom, were numbers from one to thirty-seven. The vector angled up, fell precipitously at two, before struggling upwards, until crashing again at four. It resumed a slow zigzag trend upwards, until it reached twenty-one, where the line fell again, and then, like a turtle climbing a mountain, it slowly moved upwards. The last segment moved upward thirty-seven, when another line plunged straight down, surpassing the depths of the previous plunges.

Toussaint went over to where Rebecca sat and spoke softly. "Can you explain this chart to me?"

"Yes, maybe I should," Rebecca said, looking up at Toussaint, her voice sounding lifeless. "It concerns you. It's a chart of my life. I don't know why I do them, but every time something awful happens, I make one."

"How does it concern me?"

"This is my age across the bottom. The plunge, at twenty-one, marks the year Jackson died."

The moment arrived to share the truth of Jackson, a truth she wanted to express so many times before, but being afraid of hurting him and his wife, and bound by her promises she had made to Jackson, had stopped her in the past, or at least, excused her. But there was an additional burden that she could no longer bear alone: she blamed herself for Jackson's death.

Rebecca searched for the clasp behind her neck and unhooked the locket, tearing a few entwined strands of her hair. She held the jewelry in her hands and opened the casing for Toussaint to see. On one side, her barely identifiable family. On the other, the beaming, close-cropped image of Jackson's face at his graduation, cut just above his bowtie to fit in the small frame. Jackson had once given her, from a stack of notebooks alongside his Army cot, a postage-size copy of the very same photograph she saw showcased in his father's office.

Toussaint's teeth ground as he clamped down on his mouth. His face looked pained. "You've worn this around your neck all these years?" he asked.

"Caleb, I loved your son."

The room was silent. Finally, he said, "I guess I always knew that, but if Camille did, she didn't want to hear about it. She wouldn't have accepted an interracial relationship for her only child."

"I understand," Rebecca said, nonetheless feeling a fresh sting of rejection.

"She came to adore you eventually, but she had some hard-core beliefs about race then. All the first years of our marriage, we struggled, even argued bitterly, over our differences. My family followed Dr. King's teachings like scripture. Camille had her background: from a family of despotic Haitian aristocrats who sent her mother away to boarding school in France and later disowned her. The mother embraced pan-Africanism and followed Dr. Nkrumah of Ghana, instilling her belief system in her daughter—until the day Camille put aside her political feelings when she threw the final handful of dirt on Jackson's grave."

Rebecca talked slowly, her voice releasing long bottled up pain. "We wanted to get married; but we weren't going to consider ourselves engaged until he got a ring and asked for your blessing, which he obviously didn't get to do." Rebecca watched the tension rise visibly and go into his body, like a soldier preparing for battle facing an uncertain tomorrow.

"But there's more to why I couldn't share this with you until now," Rebecca blurted out a full confession, which she had repressed for all these years. "You see, I was in charge of the explosive spotter cameras that day; I was the one operating the new system, where you had to toggle between the visible and the infrared and adjust for time of day. I hadn't detected anything on the ground and then it blew. I must have calibrated it wrong."

Toussaint stared at Rebecca as if he had never seen her before. There was a long stunned pause. "*You're an idiot*," he finally said, resting his head in his hand. "Excuse my word choice, but you don't know what you're talking about. I wish had I known you believed that all these years.

"Behind the scenes I had a bitter battle with the Army. Finally, when I became Deputy Director and had the highest security clearances, they showed me the classified after-action reports following Jackson's death. It wasn't an IED they ran into, Becky. It was a friendly-fire incident. An RPG fired supposedly by accident that day by our Saudi allies. It came in so low that it skimmed the ground, tunneling the last fifty feet, so it would have been hard to tell from a buried explosive. It was deemed too sensitive ever to release. Another thing I never told Camille. You should have come to me."

Tears came to Rebecca's eyes as she surged with a mix of shock, regret, and relief. A weight had been lifted that, as it turned out, she never needed to be carrying. "I'm sorry," she said.

Maybe she had wanted that weight. Until now. She continued, "At the funeral, I only told you the first part of his dying words. 'Tell my

Mom and Dad not to worry. I love them both so much.' His last words to me as he died in my arms were, 'Becky, I'll get better, and then I'll talk to my mom about us, but wait for me to get better. Promise,' then he died." Rebecca's eyes flooded with tears. "He thought he could win her over eventually," Rebecca said.

"He would have."

Toussaint went silent and looked away from Rebecca. She could see how difficult it was for him to process so much.

"The mystery hiker on the edge of Merewether Tree's estate," Toussaint said as he turned back to face Rebecca. "That was you? Right?"

"Yes."

"And the friend who couldn't join you on the hike . . . Jackson?"

"Yes, he died earlier that year. I didn't want to continue without him. There were moments earlier that day when I climbed a rock face and thought it would be better just to slip, or let the sniper I encountered later just shoot me." She paused to catch her breath. "It was his death that seemed to trigger in me a fear of flying—probably setting a flame under some uncooked stew about my parents' death. But my fear of flying has had nothing to do with a fear of dying. I've wanted so many times just to join Jackson."

Toussaint turned fully away, his back now to Rebecca, his fists anchored to his sides, his shoulders shaking. Rebecca rose out of her chair, the locket moist in her fist as she walked over and wrapped her arms around him from behind. Trained not to cry, Toussaint's body now quaked and shuddered like a tree buffeted by a hurricane, its roots digging into the earth trying to hold its ground as its leaves blew off.

Rebecca let go of him and spun him around. "Tell me what to do? I need someone to tell me, please," she said, her voice imploring.

"You have to fight back, Rebecca—for all of us, for your sister, for my son. Just fight back."

"I've fought my whole life since I was six years old. I don't know if I've anything left to fight with."

"You've got no choice," Toussaint said.

"I'm afraid."

"Becky, that's the bravest thing I ever heard you say."

Part Three

Chapter 60

Merewether Tree's Mansion
Poplar, Colorado

On the bank of a small pond, a family of loons huddled as the morning mists rose. The sky, in pre-dawn light, blazed a fierce mango color. Venus, forty million miles away, regarded earth aloofly. Four Secret Service commando teams, in camouflage, faces painted olive and tan, trotted out of the woods. A western screech owl sounded first alert; the loons took flight, rabbits headed for holes, squirrels clambered up nearby trees. Within minutes, the front and rear guard posts of Merewether Tree's mansion had been secured without resistance. A trio of Blackhawk VII helicopters, flying low in tight formation from the west, burst through a pink plank of clouds and began to circle the mansion. Toussaint oversaw the operation from the command helicopter. As the sun began its ascent, armored SUVs approached at high speed. Another dozen commandos came out of the woods, completing the perimeter's closure. Federal agents, carrying documents, pounded their fists on the steel-plated front door. The voice of Albert French, Tree's elderly security director, trembled through the intercom's speaker.

"You have no legal right to enter these premises."

"We have warrants, signed by the attorney general, which must be personally served on Merewether Tree," the lead agent shouted out. "You have thirty seconds to open up. If you don't comply, we'll blow out the door."

A demolitions specialist carrying a magnetic satchel charge took up position. The lead agent looked at his watch. "Ten more seconds," he shouted through the intercom.

Motor whirring, the heavy door creaked opened slowly like a drawbridge. Two agents entered holding sub-machine guns. French raised his hands; they frisked him and removed a small antique pistol. Four more agents swept in and checked the main floor.

In the distance, a second wave of armored SUVs, the rising sun behind them, neared the mansion. They wound around Colorado mountain roads, crossed the Little Snake River, cut through Lost Valley and Granny's Gulch, and finally climbed a hairpinned road to Pyramid's Peak. Rebecca wore a headset communicating from her SUV with Toussaint on his command helicopter.

"Two problems," Toussaint said.

"Which are?"

"We still haven't broken the encryption on his phone system. Merewether's got military hardware, which Sam Tree must have provided."

"We'll deal with that later," Rebecca said. "What else?"

"We've got six nano drones sitting in trees surrounding the property, but not one has been able to penetrate the house. Everything is sealed."

"Is there a way I can carry one in?"

"No, they would have to be off then, and we wouldn't be able to activate it. If you get into Merewether's bedroom, try and open the window facing the lawn. It doesn't have a screen on it."

A fly on the wall, the greatest of the Army's secret technology, Rebecca thought, as a wave of apprehension crashed across her, brought on by the impending confrontation with her grandfather.

As they turned a final bend, she could see the Tree mansion hovering over a defoliated landscape like a vulture sitting in imperial repose in wait of its prey. The mansion remained a work-in-progress, its current incarnation forty years in the making. Merewether's grandfather bought it during a nineteenth-century financial panic. Tree's father, a local judge, used his influence, after his father died, to save the property from being taken by a bankruptcy court. Originally built by a railroad baron, the property once boasted fifteen thousand acres of pristine forests. A spur train line from Denver had carried freight cars filled with marble from Italy, freshly cut redwood, and quarter-sawn oak from England for furniture. The mansion sat two thousand feet below a mountain's peak and the original cleared estate land sprawled from the lodge to the peak at an equidistance south, east, and west.

When Tree departed the Senate, he sought refuge in the mansion. At great government expense, through bills with earmarks, elaborate security had been installed. He insisted to colleagues that one day they would come for him—swarthy, mustached assassins bearing greetings from the grave of a deposed dictator. First he demanded that all the land be bulldozed so that no one could pass undetected, destroying five thousand acres of timber in the process. Guard posts were added, and the Secret Service, through a special legal dispensation protected him for ten years after he left office, protesting privately that this was more than enough. Each year Tree became more persistent, and, in response, the two current sitting senators from Colorado created additional earmarks to gratify the state's omnipotent senator emeritus. One year, he requested that electronic sensors be implanted in the razed fields; the next year, he wanted a moat and a solid fourteen-foot fence, and then a steel front door reinforced with bank vault closing mechanisms.

A final round of government money fortified the interior bedroom walls, replacing the plaster and lathe with bolted four-by-eight sheets of steel. The bank vault front door was duplicated for two of the bedrooms, one in the east wing and one in the west. When Tree went to bed at night, a remote controller moved a half-ton of solid steel across the entry door. Still he slept with a pistol on his nightstand. The Secret Service code-named the mansion Xanadu, the lonely imagined fortress of Orson Welles' *Citizen Kane*.

Tree called it home.

Rebecca entered behind a wave of securing agents. A foyer led to the main staircase of the mansion's residential wings and ultimately, up to her grandfather's bedroom. The staircase had been shipped from a French château more than a hundred years ago. The main chandelier hung over the midpoint of the eighteen-foot red-carpeted expanse, its gas lamp fixtures flickering on carved posts. Rebecca remembered how the staircase contained a small broom closet at its base, a convenient hiding place for a six-year-old evading a nanny.

The agents mounted the stairs. "No," Rebecca said. "I'd like to see him alone."

"Madam President, we can't allow that. We've got to pre-clear the space."

"He's my grandfather."

"We need to check with the director."

A few moments later, Toussaint, circling the mansion in the command helicopter, spoke on the headsets to Rebecca. "You can't go into an un-cleared space."

"Yes, I can. Read your manual. Exceptions on pre-clearance are granted for immediate family members and their residences."

Toussaint hesitated. "I don't like it."

"You told me to fight back; I have to confront him on my terms."

"Do it your way, but the agents need to be right behind you." His tone suggested he knew he couldn't win this one. She was the commander-in-chief; custom dictated that she acquiesced to Secret Service directions, but no law demanded it.

Rebecca, followed closely by six agents, swept up the stairs. An intercom was mounted to the side of the vaulted doorframe of Tree's bedroom. Rebecca pushed the button.

"Yes."

"It's Rebecca, open up the door."

"And if I don't are you going to huff and puff and . . ."

"We can explode it open; it'll take only a minute." No response came from the intercom. Rebecca looked at the agents behind her. Two held sub-machine guns, two holstered pistols, and another two, demolition specialists, carried equipment to blow the door.

"Grandfather?"

A few seconds later, a whirring noise came from the bank-vault door as it opened narrowly. An agent grasped at Rebecca's elbow; she pushed the hand away and slipped through the thin opening. The other agents tried to follow, but the space was too narrow. The door whirred once more and closed, leaving her inside Tree's bedroom. His long, bony hand pushed shut the nightstand drawer.

Tree sat on his bed reading a two-day-old copy of the *Wall Street*

Journal. An unlit cigar dangled from his mouth, and his two dogs, a pair of King Charles Spaniels reposed in curlicues around his feet. He pointed a double-action six-shot revolver at Rebecca.

"Ah, Rebecca, good of you to stop by. Come and sit by me. May I offer you a glass of port?"

The dogs growled lowly in Rebecca's direction. "Sugar! Lonigan! Hush now," Tree said. "My beloved granddaughter has come to visit. She's family." The dogs went silent, their eyes intent as Rebecca sat down. "I was just reading in the *Journal* about this fund. I might put some money in it. 'Twenty-Second Century Growth.' Ever hear of it?"

"No, I haven't."

Tree reached for the volume control on the intercom next to his bed. "Best we have some privacy for our family chat."

"Maybe you could stop pointing that pistol at me?" Rebecca said, nearly in a whisper, not wanting to agitate the Secret Service.

"And why should I? Ever hear of the Second Amendment of our great Constitution? I have rights. You've invaded my house with your armed thugs. You've disarmed my guards. I have a right to protect myself."

"My sister's grave. It was empty. What did you do to her?"

"Yes, I read about that. Strange, isn't it? Like I told you in our last chat, your grandmother took charge of you twins. Anyway, that still gives you no right. My lawyer is on his way. He'll be here shortly."

Rebecca took out a sheaf of papers from a briefcase she carried, waving them in Tree's direction. "Here are warrants and subpoenas with your name on them. I haven't signed them all, but I've signed enough to enable this visit."

"Hogwash. You're continuing to make a fool of yourself, girl."

"Am I? The Justice Department has recently come into possession of transcripts of taped conversations between you, William Tree, and your candidate for president, John Spencer. They're being reviewed for potential conspiracy charges against you."

"What do they think you're going to do . . . arrest me for some phone chats? I talk to lots of people. Many good citizens seek out my advice and counsel."

"The attorney general is close to seeking indictments against ten sitting United States senators, all pals of yours. And I'm told your lawyer was advised a few hours ago that you're a person of interest."

"Yes, I've gotten some calls. Some of the boys got caught with their hands in the cookie jar. Wouldn't surprise me. Person of interest, you say?" Tree continued. "My feelings would be hurt if I wasn't a person of interest. My *pals*, you say? I'll be straight with you since you're related to me. I've got no pals. Never did. Never will."

"Grandfather, I don't need an attorney general or a grand jury. I can arrest you myself if I want. You should know that. Didn't you ever read any of the Patriot Acts you co-sponsored?"

Tree's neck shook. He didn't seem to know which way he wanted to direct his gaze. For a moment, his head bobbed like a toy figure on a spring. Then his neck stretched until it made an audible crack.

He began to cough, his body convulsing. His eyelids clenched tight over blood-shot eyes. He dropped the pistol as his hands reached down, clutching his right side. Rebecca grabbed for the fallen weapon, snatching it just before the one of the spaniels reached her with a snap.

When Tree opened his eyes, Rebecca pointed the pistol at him. "Good, shoot me," he said, his voice filled with pain. "You'd be doing me a favor."

"A favor?"

"Never mind. Damn it girl; get me my pills, they're on the shelf over my bathroom sink."

Rebecca got up, still holding the pistol. On the nightstand stood a water glass and pitcher.

"Take some water," Rebecca said, her voice polite. *Choke on it,* she said to herself.

She noticed some phlegm, which had dribbled out of his mouth and hung momentarily suspended on his cracked lower lip. She reached for a tissue box on his nightstand. "Let me tidy you up a bit."

Rebecca cleaned his mouth with the tissue. Her mind raced back to her Montana trip, and that ghost dance she had imagined there. The dead returned for their grand reunion, and her grandfather, redeemed from his worldly sins, would, in this version, sit at the head of the table surrounded by the ones he should have loved. Tree, for his part, seemed terrified by her gesture of kindness.

She went into the bathroom, placing the pistol in the palm of her right hand. She pushed the cylinder open. She shook her head; the chambers were empty. His pill bottles stood in front of the mirror: "Plavix 3x," "Ursodiol 2x," and "Nexavar, with meals." She washed her hands slowly and persistently, shaking them off to air dry before returning to his bedside. His face seemed deflated.

"Here's your medicine," she said, handing the bottles to him and putting the pistol on the far edge of his bedside table, positioning herself blocking his sightline while she turned back up the volume control on Tree's intercom.

"What's wrong with you?"

"Nothing. Don't get your hopes up."

Rebecca looked at his nightstand. There were six plastic-wrapped packs of tissues strewn about. *Apples and oranges,* Rebecca thought as she regarded his disorder. She reflexively picked up the extras and started to open up the nightstand drawer.

"Don't go in there. Leave my things alone," Tree screamed, throwing his arm out. One of the spaniels lunged at Rebecca, ripping the cuff of her suit, just missing her hand, before making a hasty retreat. She opened the drawer, and Tree, although coughing heavily, tried to slam it. It caught the tip of her nail just after she pulled out a black booklet stamped with the distinctive seal of the coat of arms of the United States, a bald eagle with its wings outstretched. She bit her lip to stop herself from crying out from the sharp pain.

The lead Secret Service agent's voice came over the intercom. "Madam President? Do you require assistance?"

Glaring at her grandfather and his hysterical dogs, she said, "No, it's fine. We're just having an animated family discussion."

"Give me my passport back," Tree demanded, as his dogs began yapping louder.

"Get your dogs under control." Blood dripped from under her fingernail, as she looked at the passport title page. It was a special diplomatic passport with an issue date the previous year. All its pages were blank.

"How did you get this?" Rebecca said. "You're not supposed to have this. You're not a diplomat."

"Greatest diplomat this country ever had," Tree said, trying to regain his bravado. "I have privileges. Give it back to me. I have immunity."

"Immunity? You're insane. This is illegal. Stand in line and get a blue passport like every other citizen. I'll hold on to this," she said, slipping the passport into her pocket.

"Don't do that," he howled. "You've gone too far. You can't take my passport." Tree's face went milk-white. "I need it."

"Why would you need it?"

"It's none of your damn business."

"Are you planning a trip? Do you intend to flee the country?" Rebecca got up from her seat. "I think I'll take a walk around the old house. Maybe I'll be back in an hour or so. Perhaps by then you'll remember what happened to my sister."

"Wait. You're cruel."

"Cruel. That's interesting. Good that I have become cruel. I'm related to a grandmaster. Let's start over again. What happened to my sister?"

"I don't know. I was hardly here. Your grandmother and I weren't exactly on speaking terms, but she did say that Allison got violent and tried to attack you."

"Attack me? How?"

"I don't know the details. Your grandmother took her to see some doctor."

"And then what happened to her?"

"I don't know. Just give me my passport."

"No. If you refuse to tell me the truth about Allison, then what about my parents?"

"What do you mean?"

"I told you what I wanted from you the last time we spoke. Tell me my family history."

"Your family history?" Merewether said, cracking his neck and adjusting himself against the headboard pillows. He wore red silk pajamas and a black robe embroidered with depictions of white geese.

"That's quite a story." He closed his eyes momentarily and upon reopening them a look of malicious pleasure now flooded across his face. "I'll give you some news. Perhaps you might even like it."

"Which is?"

"Sam wasn't your fully blooded brother. Your father was married to another woman when he had Sam."

Rebecca felt her insides shift.

"So he divorced and married my mom?" She braced herself.

"No," Tree said. "Your father only married once," he smirked, his face re-coloring as if his heart could pump fresh predatory blood. "You and your," Tree paused, and then coughed as he tried to force the next word out, ". . . sister . . . were," he paused again, seeming to look for an exact phrasing, "no, you're illegitimate children." A small noise emanated from Tree's chest. No doubt he felt he had landed a smashing blow.

The first waves of shock roiled Rebecca, but something brought her back into balance. She had another confirmation, like the pictures found in the Montana lodge, that she and Allison were children born of love and passion. Her grandfather had unintentionally blessed her.

Tree's face contorted, one side looked horribly pained; the other seemed all pleasure. The battle was not over; he prepared to lance her soul, but, this time, she stood on high alert.

"Do you want to know about your mother?"

"Yes," her body tautened like a spring.

Tree hissed like a serpent. His face empurpled, and he wagged a bony finger violently in her direction. "Your mother—damn her to hell. She killed my boy."

Rebecca sprung forward so quickly that Tree's body jerked. Sugar and Lonigan, abandoning all correct canine instinct, jumped off the bed and retreated with whimpers to safety under the bedsprings. Rebecca grabbed Tree's ear and began twisting it. "Dishonor my mother and I'll throw your rotting body into jail. Do you understand me?"

Shock filled his face.

Rebecca let go; she could feel short breaths pulsing out of her. Years of anger emitted through her nostrils.

Tree finally seemed to grasp the gravity of the situation. Face to face with his rebellious granddaughter, it seemed like his ammunition might not last through the fight.

"All right. I've got feelings too. I loved that boy so much. You have no idea. I had great plans for him. And he listened to me, but then he met . . ."

"The facts—how did they meet?" Rebecca said, trying to deflect his new attack.

"Yale. Nathaniel was a first-year in the law school. Your mother was an undergrad. Then I don't know what happened. They started an affair; she became pregnant. They left the country before your first birthday."

"Why?"

"Why? Are you insane? I tried to save his career, but I couldn't save him from her."

"From her? What did she do?"

"She was a subversive."

"What are you saying?"

"A communist . . . a terrorist."

"A terrorist. You're delusional. In New Haven, Connecticut? You're lying."

"Don't call me a liar. Do you want proof?"

"Yes."

"Fine," Tree pointed to a chest of drawers. "Open the top drawer, there's a file in it. I thought you might drop in on me unannounced sometime—perhaps not so dramatically—so I prepared a bit."

Rebecca opened the chest's top drawer. Perched atop silk folded handkerchiefs, ties, and some suspender cases sat a leather file, its cover cracked and brittle. While Tree spoke, Rebecca moved to the window facing the front lawn and opened it a few inches. Tree didn't seem to notice her movement.

"Good," Tree continued. "You have one of the files. The one in your hand is the FBI file on her grandfather, Colin McCauley. He raised money and smuggled guns to the IRA and his brother died in a hunger strike in a British prison."

"Fellow travelers, like the Kennedys and most of their friends,"

Rebecca retorted. "Half the Irish in America sent money to the IRA."

"But it didn't stop with his Irish ancestors."

She glared at him silently.

"Then," Tree said, "Mr. McCauley started messing around in Africa and your mother . . ."

"My mother, did what?"

"Colin McCauley, her grandfather; Dillon McCauley, her father; Caitlín McCauley, your mother; they formed three generations of Irish revolutionaries.

"She continued the family's illegal activities, running money and guns, from France and Spain to so-called liberation movements in Africa. Nathaniel didn't know. No, he wouldn't know."

"And do you have a file on that?" Rebecca asked.

"Yes, in my vault. A sovereign government declared her grandfather a terrorist and years later she still carried on his work."

"Which government?"

"The Union of South Africa."

"South Africa? You mean he *aided* the terrorist Nelson Mandela and his comrades."

"The law is the law. South Africa was a post-war ally of the United States."

"Good for him. And I am sure, whatever her political leanings, that she acted courageously and idealistically. No wonder my father loved her."

Tree looked scandalized by her calm response.

"Tell me how they died."

"It was a plane crash, as you know, and there's not much more to it than that. An excursion in a two-passenger Cessna, luckily not enough space that day for you and your sister. A pilot . . . a friend lacking experience. They hit some bad weather and crashed in the Pyrenees."

"Where's the official report?"

"That's the official report." The look in Tree's eyes became furtive. "Speak to the Spanish government. They wouldn't release it."

"You were among the most powerful men in America," Rebecca's voice rose. "What do you mean, they wouldn't release it? It was your son, my parents . . . You're a coward and a worm. Why didn't you protect them, if not in life, then at least in death? You're not a man."

The last comment seemed to finally shake Tree. His neck waffled, and his brown eye misted over. "I did my best," Tree nervously sibilated. "I went to Spain. They showed me the records privately. I saw no evidence of foul play . . ."

"God isn't going to look kindly at you." Rebecca shook her finger at him. "My grandmother told me she wished she could have protected Allison and me. Protected us from what? You?"

"Your grandmother wasn't well." His tongue started to dart out between his front teeth, like an iguana looking for a leaf.

"What happened to my sister?"

"All I know is what I was told. She was sick. Taken to a hospital. And then she was gone. I was in Europe." Tree's face showed signs of leakage. Sweat dripped from his brow.

"And you didn't come home to bury her? You didn't because there was no one to bury. What did you do with her, with your beloved son's daughter?"

"Whatever happened to Allison wasn't my doing. I had other obligations—to protect and preserve a free world —build democracy."

"Grandfather," Rebecca said. Reason now charged her rage. "Let's start all over again. You didn't answer my question. You said she was gone. That's not an answer. Did she die? Where's her death certificate? I've seen only a fuzzy copy and the expert who analyzed it failed to verify its authenticity. Why did she have a phony grave? I think you disappeared her. Did she have a mental problem? Was she a potential embarrassment to your career or your ambitions?"

Tree pushed up off his pillows; a line of sweat collected on his upper lip. He swung his leg onto the floor and tried to get up but his knee buckled, and he pitched back onto the mattress. His gaze locked onto Rebecca and his breathing became labored. Gasping for breath, Tree said, "My chest. I need a doctor."

"I'll go and get the Secret Service doctor," Rebecca said. As she left his room, she glanced up at a fly attached to the wall over his bedroom window.

Chapter 61

Merewether Tree's Mansion

Rebecca descended the winding staircase of the mansion. Three Secret Service agents escorted her, as another agent alerted her traveling physician that Merewether needed attending.

Out of the corner of her eye, a door leading to what Rebecca had remembered as the old kitchen opened up.

"Miss Becky, do you remember me?" asked a tall, stout black woman, polishing a fluted glass.

Rebecca looked puzzled; something rang familiar.

"I bet you remember my pecan pie?"

"Lu," Rebecca said. "What a wonderful surprise." Rebecca unfolded herself like an old dog caught up in a reverie of puppyhood into Lu's welcoming arms.

"Madam President," interjected the estate's head of security, as he rushed to try and stop the conversation. "Lu is an employee of Senator Tree. Your warrants don't cover questioning his employees, and they have all signed confidentiality agreements as a condition of employment."

Lu took up a protective position in front of Rebecca, facing off Albert French.

"Mr. French, you can take your agreement and stuff it where the sun doesn't shine. If Rebecca wishes, she can visit with me at my house and talk to me as much as she wants. It is my property, deeded to me twenty years ago by the Senator."

French glowered at Lu.

"I would love to visit with you," Rebecca said, "but I don't want you to get into trouble with my grandfather or this Mr. French here."

"Becky, Merewether and I go way back. There is no way I'll get into trouble with him. And Mr. French can blow hot air all day through the gap in his mouth. He has no say over me.

"Come, child," Lu said beckoning with her hand, "let's go down to my house and we can sit as long as you like."

Surrounded by Secret Service agents, Rebecca and Lu walked three hundred yards down a slate path toward a modest white frame house. Tree's rattled security director raised objections to the lead agent along the way.

Built as a guest house in the style of an eighteenth-century Georgian Colonial, the property had a distinctive boxy rectangular shape with two brick chimneys paired on the roof. A white picket fence guarded the front of the house; budding rose bushes, hyacinths, and daffodils burst out the front garden, all fighting for prime sunlight exposure.

"Please come in, I was just about to brew some fresh tea. And I do just happen to have a pecan pie. You're welcome to stay as long as you like."

"I'd love to," said Rebecca. "My grandfather is complaining of chest pains, so my traveling physician is examining him now."

"Chest pains? That old bird has a ticker stronger than a twenty-year-old. I know all his tricks. He complains of chest pains when he doesn't want to talk anymore."

Rebecca was stupefied. "The house looks lovely," she said, changing the subject.

Lu served the tea in her sunroom, and then sat down on a nineteenth-century Mission-style couch next to Rebecca, the room still warm from the morning sun. A well-worn Bible lay open next to a freshly fluffed-up throw at the end of the couch.

"Lu, I used to send you a Christmas card and letter every year from Switzerland. But you never answered."

Lu took Rebecca's hand and disappeared it into hers as if in an over-sized children's mitten. "Child, I'm sure you did. But no one ever gave me a piece of mail from you."

"My grandfather?"

"No," Lu said, "all the mail went first to your grandmother. I think there is a lot you don't understand. I can tell you some of it, what I know."

Lu spoke for nearly an hour. Most of what she said shocked Rebecca.

In Georgia, Lu's family had been separated by bad times. She had made her way to Denver, where an employment agency sent her to the Tree estate as a cook's helper. She rarely ever saw the senator or his wife, although she sometimes heard bitter fragments of arguments at night. The staff numbered over a dozen, and they all tiptoed around their employers.

Lu described the night that the news of Rebecca's parents' deaths reached the Hillock-Hill Ranch. A blizzard had moved in across the Rockies; the phone lines had been erratic if not down most of the day. Around midnight, a county sheriff's car with chains on its wheels pulled up at the front door, its flashing lights painting patches of red inside the mansion. A loud knocking on the front door startled Lu, who had been sleeping in the servant's wings. A few minutes later, she heard Mrs. Tree screaming. She put her clothes on; when she reached the front hallway she saw Senator Tree carrying an unconscious Mrs. Tree up to her bedroom.

At the top of the stairs, Tree stopped and bellowed out. "My boy is dead . . . he's dead."

An hour later, an ambulance plowed its way through the snowstorm and took Mrs. Tree to a hospital.

The house quieted down for awhile, and Lu cried and prayed for Nathaniel and his wife. At dawn, she fell into a fitful sleep until howling cries woke her. A gray light washed the snow-covered fields surrounding the mansion as the storm quieted down. From her window, Lu could see Senator Tree, half crumbled in the snow, shaking his fist angrily at the sky and wailing like a mortally wounded animal. Lu got dressed, put on as much heavy overclothes as she could find, gathered up some blankets, and went after him.

Tree was incoherent with grief; Lu wrapped him with blankets and tried to talk to him, but he didn't seem to be aware of her presence. Soon some of the ranch hands billeted further away from the main house came through snowdrifts and joined her. They carried his body, stiffened by the cold, back to the house. He stayed in bed for a week and neither spoke nor ate. Then one day he just got up and left, driven to Denver's International Airport by his chauffeur. Later they learned he went to his office in Washington. He never spoke Nathaniel's name to the staff again, except to Lu.

Mrs. Tree returned from the hospital a few weeks later, about the same time the grandchildren arrived, by ship and then overland by train, from Europe. Mostly Mrs. Tree stayed in her bed, refusing to leave her room. She ordered the staff to remove any framed photos in the house with her son in them; it was too painful to see him. She had all the photo albums of her entire family, once filling several shelves in the library, shipped to a post office box in Montana according to the servant who took them to a freight company. She remained mostly in bed throughout the winter, as a team of Hungarian nannies chaperoned the twins.

"Cold as a Rocky Mountain ice storm," Lu proclaimed, contemptuously describing the nannies.

The next spring, Mrs. Tree's spirits recovered momentarily, and she spent time with the orphaned girls, letting them run in wildflower fields as she painted landscapes of the mountains overlooking the Tree mansion. Senator Tree returned only a few times a year, staying primarily in Washington or traveling on business around the world. Mainly indifferent to the twins, he sometimes made an effort on Christmas Day to fulfill his grandfatherly duties.

Rebecca listened spellbound. Lu was dynamic, a living oral historian who could give testament.

"What can you tell me about Allison?"

"I wish I could tell you more, but I was the cook, first the assistant cook, and my job kept me mostly in the kitchen. The nannies, who in truth I despised, took full charge of the children. But I can tell you about that awful day, the last time I saw Allison . . ."

The tone was so foreboding. "The last time?" Rebecca said, now startled.

Rebecca and Lu sat side by side on the sunroom couch, Lu to Rebecca's right, her arm physically wrapping the couch while her warmth migrated into Rebecca.

"Oh, you poor baby," Lu said, with a shocked look of recognition. "Do you still have a scar underneath your shoulder blade?" Rebecca's eyes widened; she drew Lu's hand to the scar tissue just below her neckline.

"Did Allison do this?" Rebecca's voice trembled. "Tell me what happened."

Lu sighed, "I warned Mrs. Tree, but she never listened. I tried to warn the Senator, but, back then, he still regarded me as help, although I must say at least he treated me with some semblance of respect. Maybe that's why I stayed on. Mrs. Tree was another case. These nannies, I don't know where they found them, but they were not kind. Toddlers, and then twins at that, it's a lot of work, but it'd be better if you at least like kids."

"You were there?" Rebecca asked. It was an imprinted smell that came back strongest: a roasting stench of fat dripping off sizzling pork.

"I was working in the garden," Lu continued, "picking a salad for dinner, and I heard some noise coming from the kitchen. I thought I had better check, as I had left a fire in the fireplace; I had started a pig roasting on a spit, when I came in, carrying a basket of vegetables and some garden tools. You must have freed her . . ."

"Oh, my God, was Allison tied to a chair?" Rebecca asked, reaching back to an image which had plagued her entire life in a recurrent nightmare. She felt the heat of the flames.

"Yes. In the last few months, Allison had become more and more difficult. The nannies must have tied her. Before I could even put my stuff down and get between you, she had plunged a carving knife a couple of inches into you, just where you have the scar."

Rebecca's shoulder blade ached as if it were a fresh wound. She touched it again to make sure it wasn't moist with blood before going limp on the couch.

Chapter 62

Lu brought Rebecca some chamomile tea and a slice of pecan pie.

"You girls brought light into this house, and it hasn't been the same since," Lu said. "It's wonderful to have you here now. Sit here and rest as long as you like."

"I'm okay," Rebecca said, trying to ignore short sharp pains in her head, like barbed wire poking around her brain. "And you didn't finish. What happened to Allison after?"

"She was gone," Lu said.

"Gone?"

Lu explained that a few months later the chief steward informed the servants of Allison's death, reminded them of their confidentially agreements, and distributed a one-time special cash bonus to all the employees."

"A one-time cash bonus . . ." Rebecca repeated in shock; she needed to change the subject. The information Lu provided was too difficult to process.

"I'm waiting for the attorney general to arrive. If I have to go, will you visit me in Washington? Please, you can stay in the White House. Let someone else cook for you for once."

"Oh but cooking at the White House would be the honor of a lifetime, wouldn't it? I would love to come, and I'd like you to meet my son."

"Your son? How old is he?" Rebecca asked, the sharp pains now in retreat.

"He will be thirty next year. He's a lawyer in San Francisco."

"I bet you're proud of him. What's his name?"

"His name. Oh, that's another long story. It's the reason I own this house. He's named Nathaniel, after your father. Merewether begged me to name him that. At the time, I faced a very uncertain future. My fiancée, Mr. Carter, had run off when I told him I was pregnant, and I had already given notice here. Being out of wedlock was too hard for me to admit, so I prepared to go home and live with an aunt until Merewether intervened. In exchange for I guess what you'd call "naming rights," he provided my son a trust fund and paid for his education. He went to private school in the East, then Princeton, then the University of Chicago law school."

Rebecca shook her head in disbelief. "Does Merewether have a generous side?"

"Merewether, generous? I guess I'd have to answer yes and no. He was certainly generous to my son and me. But truth be told, he had his motives. He wanted a namesake, and I guess he wanted to honor your father. But I speak my mind to him, and I've chewed him out many times on how he didn't show the same generosity of spirit to his grandchildren. He could have spent time with them."

"And what did he say to that?"

"Usually nothing. Once he got mad at me. He said, 'No one would understand, but I took some extreme measures to protect them.'"

"What did he mean by that?"

"I have no idea. I pushed him hard when he said that, but he did one of those clutch-his-chest routines. He is a bit childish. Quite childish actually. So I guess you must have given him a good tongue-lashing upstairs."

Rebecca managed a laugh. "If only walls could talk."

A knock came on Lu's door, and Caleb Toussaint entered. After Rebecca had introduced them, Toussaint said, "Merewether seems to be okay. And the attorney general is waiting for you in the library room."

Rebecca gave Lu a huge long hug.

"Here is my personal cellphone number. You will call me and let me know when you and your son will visit?"

"We'll come if they let me into the kitchen for a few hours. I'll bake you the best pecan pie."

As Toussaint and Rebecca walked back together to the main house, Rebecca quizzed him about Merewether.

"His electrocardiogram looks normal, and the preliminary examination looks okay," Toussaint said. "Your traveling physician thinks you got him too excited. What did you do to him?"

"Probably not enough," Rebecca said.

"Denver General's imaging machine just arrived by helicopter. They'll have a picture of your grandfather's heart shortly."

"It won't be much to look at," Rebecca said. "I don't need a machine to tell me that."

Chapter 63

Merewether Tree's Library

Newly minted Attorney General Harriet Ogden was waiting for Rebecca in the library on the main floor. Toussaint left them together to check with his agents stationed around the property.

After Rebecca had updated her on her conversation with Merewether Tree, Ogden said, "I spoke to your grandfather's lawyer this morning. He's prepared to help if he can. He left Denver this morning. He's due here shortly."

"Who's his lawyer?"

"His name is Algis Taub. I've known him for a long time. He's a good man. Do you want to hear an incredible story?"

"I need one," Rebecca said. She felt like a snowman facing an early spring.

Rebecca tried to focus on the story of Tree's lawyer. The man's name sounded familiar. As the details unfolded, she grew more interested. Algis' father, Horatio Taub was born into a family of prairie socialists. A lawyer as well, he represented workers, farmers, and miners against wealthy and powerful interests, which normally crushed them. One client, a hardscrabble miner, came into ownership of what became valuable mineral rights. Merewether Tree headed a politically well-connected consortium that held a dubious land option and wished to force the miner to sell his rights for a pittance. The legal battle raged for nearly a decade with the miner's lawyer losing again, and again, all the way through the Colorado Supreme Court. Then a federal district court agreed to hear the case, and the decisions began to fall in the miner's favor. Six years later, the United States Supreme

Court, in *Atkins vs. Tree et al.* ruled against the consortium. The outcome of the case enraged Tree, but the legal skills and the courtroom charisma of the plaintiff's lawyer dazzled him. For the next ten years, he dangled offer after offer to the lawyer, asking him to be his personal attorney. Year after year the lawyer refused, until the retirement of the original client ended the conflict of interest and the lawyer became Tree's counsel.

"I'm sorry," Rebecca said. "Tell me the name of the lawyer's son again?"

"Algis Taub," Ogden said. "Does it ring a bell?"

"I think so . . ."

"When his father died," Ogden continued, "Algis took over his practice and inherited all his clients, including Merewether. Now Algis heads the biggest corporate law firm in the Rocky Mountains. But it's his *pro bono* work, which he's well known for, at least in legal circles. He appeals death penalty cases, mainly to the Supreme Court. It's difficult, emotionally draining work, and all pretty much out of the public eye."

The name finally registered to Rebecca, who had contributed to many death row inmates' appeals over the years. Like most of her other charitable gifts, she donated anonymously.

"And what case is he best known for?"

"The appeal filed for Pixie Jean Lee," Ogden said, "went to the Supreme Court argued as *Lee versus Tree*—Sam Tree."

Rebecca was familiar with the details of the case. Pixie Lee stood accused of murdering her husband while he shaved and then killing her two sleeping infants. The state's case rested on circumstantial evidence and Lee's court-appointed lawyer, later disbarred for incompetence, failed to follow up on exculpatory leads. The woman's case clearly cried out for a new and fair trial.

After all appeals had been denied, her brother Sam, then the Governor of Colorado and an active advocate for the death penalty, turned a deaf ear to an international outcry to stay the woman's execution. Rebecca personally pleaded with her brother on the night Lee awaited her fatal injection. Sam mocked both her and Pixie Lee over the phone until Rebecca hung up. She never spoke to Sam again.

Three years after the execution, incontrovertible facts emerged proving the innocence of the woman. Sam, then president, refused to acknowledge the legitimacy of the new evidence. Nor would he apologize.

* *

"Harriet, there is a problem with Merewether's lawyer seeing him," Rebecca said.

"Which is?"

"This is classified and on a need-to-know only. The Army has a secret weapon: nano drones, the size of those large pesky houseflies. It's the military's most closely guarded secret. They have used them with great success, flying them into suspected insurgent areas, watching and recording unseen."

"Sounds pretty spooky."

"Maybe, but a lot of lives get saved. Some of the drones are equipped to shoot a tiny barb of anesthesia, usually Propofol, which will put most targets to sleep within twenty seconds. When I was operational in Army intelligence, relying on nano drones, we did dozens of live captures of high-value insurgents with no collateral damage or loss of life to our soldiers. I've signed executive orders to allow these drones to be used domestically. The Army J-2 teams that are hunting down Native Force cells in the mountains of New Mexico and Idaho are deploying hundreds of the drones, which will enable us to capture many of the Native Force cells alive."

"That's great, but what does this have to do with Merewether and his lawyer?"

"I was able to place an operational fly on the wall in my grandfather's room when I visited with him before you arrived."

"So you're asking me about the legal implication?"

"Yes, I wasn't expecting an attorney-client conversation to be captured."

"Well, and I'm sure the Secret Service lawyer has told you this. It's legal. But I don't like it. I had planned to file an *amicus curiae,* a friend-of-the-court brief in the American Bar Association's appeal of a lawyer's case representing a terrorist eavesdropped on in New York some years ago."

"Secret Service legal mentioned the case to me. Do you think it will be overturned on appeal?"

"Maybe, but then it will go to the Supreme Court and those sons-of . . . will uphold the lower court."

Chapter 64

Algis Taub
Merewether Tree's Personal Attorney

Algis Taub had a full mop of wavy hair that perched atop bushy eyebrows and light brown eyes surrounded by delicate rings of pink. His chin gently double-folded, and his skin blotched slightly red, the result of inherited rosacea. Dressed informally in a charcoal gray wool sweater, pleated chinos, and a pair of rubber hunting shoes, he hugged the attorney general upon entering the study.

"Thank you so much taking the time to join us," said Ogden, turning to Rebecca. "Madam President, Algis Taub, your grandfather's personal attorney."

Rebecca begrudgingly shook his hand.

"Ironic, isn't it?" Taub said.

Rebecca smiled warily.

"I spoke to Merewether from my car just before I arrived; he told me they finished imaging his heart, and he's okay," Taub said. "He seems more concerned about his passport than his heart."

"The passport he carries, a diplomatic one, is not legal," Rebecca said. "It's both a fineable offense and a felony punishable by up to ten years in jail. Tell him that, for me, Mr. Taub."

"I will. He wants me to speak to him, and he understands that he is a person of interest."

"And his reaction?" Ogden said. "Are you able to share that with us?"

"You know Merewether, or at least you do, Madam President. He's already bunkered in, but I suspect he's shaken up. Let me talk to him a bit. Maybe there's a way to mediate; it might be productive to all parties, and good for the country."

Rebecca looked at the attorney general who nodded after looking at her watch. "We'll give you an hour with him," Ogden said.

* *

Rebecca paced across the floor of Merewether Tree's study, trying to listen to the attorney general.

"I know this has all been a nightmare, but we'll find the truth of your sister."

"What if she's out there somewhere," Rebecca said. "All this time."

"That would be wonderful," Ogden said.

"Harriet, I spoke to Toussaint about the nano drones and the attorney-client issue. We decided to leave the recording on, but the operator has been instructed not to listen, and the tape will be held in a vault. If you win your court case, we will destroy it. If not, then we'll have the option to listen later if we deem it necessary."

"So, do you still want me to file my *amicus curiae*, my friend-of-the-court brief?"

"Absolutely," Rebecca said. "You need to do what you think is the right thing. I would do the same in your position."

"What do you want to do about your grandfather? Are you prepared to notch up to the next step after naming him a person of interest."

Rebecca didn't answer. She was staring at a bookshelf filled with leather slipcased volumes stacked flat. A few days shy of her eighth birthday, she had waited fearfully in this same study for her grandfather's response to her act of self-defense against her brother Sam. She had discovered then a set of oversized volumes over two feet high and perhaps three feet wide, on a shelf out of reach. Her curiosity temporarily overcame her fear, and she climbed to reach the mysterious volumes until a noise outside the study door stopped her. Heavy footsteps approached. That was almost thirty years ago; now the binders rested at eye level. Transfixed, she removed one case, placing it delicately on a sideboard.

"Oh, my God. Look at this," Rebecca said, as she cautiously opened the bottom case.

"What is it?" Ogden said.

"I believe it could be a complete original edition of Audubon's *Birds of America*. I think only two other hand bound intact sets exist; most of them had been broken apart with the folios sold separately."

Rebecca, sensitive to the historical value of the material and familiar with the standards set for handling archival art, asked a Secret Service agent for evidence gloves. Welcoming the distraction, she slowly turned the pages. Her eyes feasted on the first lithograph she opened, entitled "Carolina Parrot." The bird, now extinct, displayed a lime green body color coordinated with a lemon yellow head and a soft red mask. Three of the species sat on a cocklebur plant, munching contently on the seeds. Rebecca slowly and gently turned the page to an illustration of a male passenger pigeon feeding its mate when a small faded color photograph slid out from between the plates.

Rebecca grabbed it. She held it close to her naked eyes and squinted as her heart pounded so hard she thought it might escape her chest. A quiet sob leaped from her lips, and her hand trembled as she looked at the picture. Allison Tree, looking not much older than six or seven years, still fleshy like a toddler, sat on a man's lap, who was dressed in a Santa Claus suit, in a gunmetal gray room filled with metal furniture, as in the Army, or an institution. A window could be seen in the background of the photograph; it had bars on it. Christmas decorations filled the background.

He was dressed all in fur, from his head to his foot. His eyes—how they twinkled! His dimples how merry! His cheeks were like roses, his nose like a cherry! . . . And the beard of his chin was as white as the snow; He wore a red suit that was trimmed with white fur and wearing black boots.

A signature face popped back out of the fading photograph of the man in the Santa Claus costume. With one blue eye and one brown eye, it was unmistakably the face of her grandfather, Merewether Tree.

* *

Rebecca watched, in shock, as Taub descended the staircase, his face filled with pain. He looked like he had been tortured.

"I'm sorry. He'll admit to no knowledge of Allison after his wife told him she died."

"He's lying," Rebecca said, handing Taub the photograph of Tree with Allison. "She's older in this, and she's with him. Tell him if I don't get the truth, he'll be indicted for making a false statement to a federal officer and obstruction of justice."

Taub retreated to Tree's room. Rebecca heard raised voices from the upstairs of the mansion. He returned a few minutes later.

"Batesville, Arkansas," Taub said, his face lined with exhaustion. "That's where he flew. Then he says he was driven a few hours, but claims he doesn't know the name of the place. He says she was six, and it was Christmas, and he went there without telling his wife."

"He claims no knowledge of Allison, after that Christmas?"

"He must know more," Ogden said.

"Let me keep working on him," Taub said. "He likes to point his finger at the dead. He claims that one of his cohorts, Tom Rainey, took care of everything. But Rainey suffered a fatal heart attack over ten years ago. I think Merewether is finally starting to understand how serious the situation is."

* *

A few moments later, the attorney general picked up her cellphone and speed-dialed her first assistant.

"Jack, yes, we're leaving in a couple of hours. I'll be back in D.C. late tonight. I need some urgent business taken care of. There's a file in my top drawer, marked CONFIDENTIAL, ALLISON TREE, with a chronology and a dateline in it. Right, I'll wait."

"Rebecca," she said, cupping the phone. "We'll spare no resources on this."

Rebecca stood silently.

"Good, you got it," Ogden said, speaking to her assistant. "I want two top-priority task forces out of the Bureau; one is to set up in Denver and the other in Little Rock. I'm emailing you a scanned photograph, taken over thirty years ago, probably in a children's home . . ." Ogden paused and looked at Rebecca, who had averted her eyes. She said quietly, "or a mental institution." She continued, "then, draw a radius circle of one hundred miles around Batesville and Denver, and check all the county courthouse records . . . for," she looked at Rebecca again, standing stiff as a flagpole looking out into the bare landscape which had briefly been the woods of her childhood, "commitment papers. And Jack, anything you find, share it immediately with the Secret Service Director."

Ogden hung up her phone and walked over to Rebecca. "Madam President." Rebecca didn't respond. "Madam President," Ogden said again.

"I'm sorry. What is it?"

"There's not much more we can do here today. I'm going to have Algis served with subpoenas for all of Merewether's legal records. He's already carrying more subpoenas for all his financial records. I'm going to prepare a motion for discovery to present to a grand jury."

"That sounds fine. What can I do?"

"Go back to Washington. You're the Commander-in-Chief. You're going to have to steady your hand. The winds of history are about to intensify."

"All right. I want to go upstairs and say goodbye to my grandfather."

"Are you sure you want to do that?" Ogden said.

"Yes, I'm sure. It's not for me to . . ." she paused. "God will have to make the final judgment."

No longer in his bed, Merewether sat in a wing-back chair, wrapped in blankets, sipping hot tea, staring out the window overlooking the front entrance of the house.

"I'm leaving now, Grandfather."

Tree turned his head slightly; his silent gaze seemed to land beyond her shoulder.

"Thank you for visiting Allison that Christmas. I'm sure it meant a lot to her."

Chapter 65

Rebecca was longing to go home to her familiar hideaway in Boston. Exhausted, she craved a long weekend with her friends, her books, and her diaries. She signed an executive order cutting off all press access for the next three days and left Washington on a private plane. At his insistence, Toussaint sent a minimum Secret Service protective detail with her but compensated by reinforcing the Boston office with extra undercover agents.

Within hours of her arrival, the first disruption began with a call to her encrypted video terminal:

"Where are you transmitting from?" Rebecca asked Oswaldo Lemus.

"I am in a secure transmitting room at a federal prison: FMC Devens. Would you consider granting a pardon to a dying federal prisoner?"

"Why? Who is he? What is this about?"

"His name is Éamonn O'Connell. He is terminally ill with stage IV lung cancer. The doctors say he has three months, at most, to live."

"I have not given any pardons to date. What does this have to do with me?"

"He says he knows what happened to Liam Ryan, the doctor who signed the birth certificates for you and your sister."

"What led you to him?" Rebecca asked, as her body tightened.

"I kept puzzling about this Dr. Ryan fellow, missing with no trail and trained in Ireland as a plastic surgeon. I had the theory that the only explanation pointed to Ryan being an IRA surgeon placed in Boston to alter the identities of high-value Irish operatives."

"Great theory," Rebecca said with a very nervous laugh. "But how did you find him?"

"Criminal informants in different jails and then we poured through a lot of cold cases in the Boston police department files. He won't tell me much, but he wants to talk directly to you."

"That sounds like a bad idea."

"Maybe. You don't have to promise him anything, but I think you could draw him out."

"I don't know."

"Look, you gave me some discretion to be more flexible to try and find the truth. I am getting closer. I need to find a way to get fully inside his brain."

"All right patch him in then."

O'Connell was a tiny man; he looked like he barely weighed one hundred pounds. His shriveled skin appeared as jaundiced; he looked near death.

"Mr. O'Connell. This is Rebecca Tree. Mr. Lemus says you might have information you are willing to share."

"Mrs. Tree."

"No, it is Ms. Tree."

"The doctors here tell me I have a few weeks to live; a couple of months if I am lucky."

"I hope you are not suffering needlessly. I don't know how I can be of any help to you."

"Mrs., sorry, *Ms.* Tree. I want to die at home, in my bed, with my wife, children, and grandchildren beside me. I have only three years left in my federal prison sentence. I am a soldier. I fought for my homeland and the liberation of Ireland. Soldiers aren't meant to be kept this long after the cessation of hostilities."

"What do you know about Dr. Liam Ryan?"

"I heard he died young."

"How?"

"I only heard some rumors."

"Which were?"

"I heard that he might have been killed and dumped into Boston Harbor."

"Killed?" Rebecca said, hearing alarm bells go off inside her. "Did you kill him?"

"No."

"But maybe you know who did?" She tried hard despite the alarms sounding to maintain a calm, measured tone.

"What about a pardon?"

"I might be willing to look into that. I would have to consult with other interested parties."

"You mean the British government. I've paid for my sins. They haven't faced their judgment yet."

"Mr. O'Connell, if you're looking for a pardon, you might consider being more diplomatic. I'll ignore your last comment, for the moment. Let's get back to Dr. Ryan. Why would he have been killed?"

"I heard . . ."

"You hear a lot, Mr. O'Connell."

"If I had a pardon then I might know some things for certain."

"So Dr. Ryan, you heard?"

"I heard he was sent here to do plastic surgery on an important Irishman."

"Did he mess up the surgery?"

"No, but I heard the patient wasn't comfortable about Dr. Ryan being able to identify his new face."

"Do you know the identity of the patient?"

"I have no idea."

"So the surgery was successful, and the doctor needed to be forever silent."

"Yes, that was what I heard."

"Was Dr. Ryan sent here to deliver babies as well?"

O'Connell looked away from the camera and began to cough spasmodically. After sipping some water, the coughing subsided, and he blurted out, "I don't know anything about delivering babies. I thought he was a plastic surgeon working undercover at St. Frances Hospital."

"Did you know Caitlín McCauley?

"Maybe."

"Damn you, O'Connell. Stop playing me. I'm the only chance you have to die at home with your family."

"I knew of Caitlín. Maybe I saw her a couple of times. She's your mother."

Rebecca sat upright in her chair as she began to nervously rub her chin. "What do you know?"

"I saw her twice at a couple of fundraising events. She was a classical Irish beauty with cascading red hair and lovely freckles. All the lads lined up to dance with her."

Rebecca was mesmerized.

"I would have loved to ask her to dance, but, the few public events that I could attend, I had to stay in the shadows, so to speak."

"Can you name any of the other people at the dance who you saw talking to her?"

Lemus spoke to Rebecca through her earphone. "Becky, stop. He is starting to play with you. He is luring you in with details about your mother as his best path to a pardon. Stay tough with him."

"I am not good with names," O'Connell said.

Lemus advised Rebecca again. "See if he'll give you more specifics on his role. He must have been pretty high up with the Provisionals. I am sending you some questions in real-time overlaying the bottom of your screen."

"Okay. Mr. O'Connell, I have a few more questions."

"Then we can talk pardon," O'Connell said.

"We'll see. Depends on the quality of your information. You worked underground in Boston as an active member of the Provisionals?"

"That's a fair assumption."

"So you held an important position in the organization."

"I wasn't a general if that is what you mean. I ranked as a major. I took orders from my superiors and passed them on."

"And you were convicted of multiple counts in state and federal courts for bank robbing and gun running."

"All public record."

"And murders?"

"No."

"Did you know Dillon McCauley?"

"Doesn't ring a bell," O'Connell said, as Rebecca noted his eyes shifting momentarily downwards.

"He was Caitlín McCauley's father. You sure you never heard of him?"

"No."

Lemus spoke again to Rebecca again through her earphone. "I am disconnecting you from O'Connell for the moment. Don't go anywhere. I need to go one on one with him."

A few minutes later Lemus came back to Rebecca.

"He gave me more. He says Dr. Ryan washed up in Boston Harbor, a single bullet lodged in the back of his skull. Acid had erased his fingertips."

"Didn't the Boston police investigate the floater?"

"The police never made a positive identification nor did it appear that they had looked very hard. The murder became just another cold case."

Chapter 66

Assassins Lie in Wait
Salumeria Settepani, Boston Massachusetts

The following evening, Rebecca walked two doors down her enclosed back alley to her neighbors, Alejandro and Nessia Rivera, Spanish architects whose avant-garde work she admired. Dinner with them momentarily lifted her burden and lent a temporary, illusory feeling of freedom.

Before she left, Rebecca asked Nessia if she could borrow her mountain bike early the next morning. Parked unlocked in the alley, the bicycle stood next to a shelf stocked with riding gear for all seasons. Rebecca let herself back into her house just before midnight. As she climbed the stairs, she noticed a fax on her personal line with the letterhead, "Salumeria Settepani, Twelve Hodges Lane, Boston, Mass. Tel: 617-456-8945 Fax: 617-456-8946."

Below was a hand-written message: "Becky, I got your fax. If you can get here before seven a.m., that would be great. You can shop in peace for an hour. Looking forward to seeing you. Best regards, Bruno."

Rebecca woke before dawn. The video conversation with Éamonn O'Connell from prison had left her deeply disturbed. Did the murder of the doctor somehow connect to the history of her mother's family? She knew the only antidote would be exercise and some short moments of normalcy. The image of a caged bird from the famous Maya Angelou poem flashed across her brain. She had to find a way to be the free bird leaping "on the back of the wind" . . . and "dare to claim the sky." She showered, made a cup of coffee, and dressed. First she put on a chamois-lined skin suit and added a black thermal long sleeved jersey to ward off the early morning cold. She slipped on bright red performance socks and a pair of hot-pink cleated road shoes.

She fastened her hair and slipped a light wool balaclava over her head, leaving only her eyes visible. She took a Secret Service emergency GPS mini-beeper leaving it in its off position and put it in the back pocket of her jersey. Finally, she put on her blood pressure bracelet and pushed the start button. It produced her current pressure: a perfect 110 over seventy-five. The monitor would beep softly if the systolic got near ninety, increase in volume toward eighty, and become noisy as an activated smoke detector if the number moved any lower. As she left, a quick look in the mirror made her feel safe in her anonymity. She went into the alleyway, picked up Nessia's mountain bike, and put on gloves, helmet, wrap-around eye goggles, and a biking jacket. Over her right shoulder—her scar smarted too much in cold weather when she wore the bag on the left side—she draped her messenger bag strap.

She lifted the bike over her shoulder and unlocked the alleyway door that led to the street. A Boston Police Department car stood fifteen feet away tasked to secure the exit. Rebecca got on the bike, locked cleats to the pedals, and headed straight in the direction of the patrol car. As she neared it, the officer lowered his window and Rebecca said, talking through the balaclava, which covered her mouth, "Buenos días, señor."

"Oh, good morning, Mrs. Rivera. Enjoy your ride."

Within minutes, Rebecca flew across one of Boston's many well-developed bike paths, legs pumping the pedals, blood racing as the icy wind cut through the small exposed patch of her face. She entered Kingsley Park with enough time to do two quick laps before arriving at Bruno's.

On the first go around she noticed a few fully-geared cycle devotees lapping the bike path. She passed two cyclists with a short wave of her hand and exchanged muffled good mornings through her protective gear. She finished one more lap, breaking into a light sweat, relishing the exhilaration.

She arrived at Salumeria Settepani a few minutes past seven a.m. Bruno Settepani represented the third generation of his family to run this renowned Boston-based Sicilian food specialty store occupying one floor of a stand-alone converted warehouse building. The staff would arrive at eight a.m.

She knocked on the glass door. A shade went up, and Settepani greeted her as he nervously looked around. "Becky, where's the Secret Service? I thought you'd be here with your entourage."

"No, I'm playing hooky. Can I bring my bike inside?"

"Sure, let me lock up, and then you can shop in peace. I've already put together some of the items on your list—prosciutto, calamari, olives, sun-dried tomatoes."

* *

In the basement the assassin waited, 140 buffed pounds, five-foot-seven-inches tall, wearing a gray T-shirt with United States Navy stenciled on its front. Strapped on each arm, just below the cuffs of the shirt, were two daggers. She had tested them during the night, throwing a total of eight times, leaving the corpses of eight Albino Norwegian rats scattered around the basement, each rat's brain punctured precisely through its distinctive pink eye. After each kill, she re-sharpened each dagger with a small whetstone.

As designated killer, she coded as Raven One. The entire execution squad used avian names for their operatives. Below her tee, she wore a pair of skintight Lycra swim trunks, stamped with a small circular SEALS logo. Two more daggers were strapped to her thighs. Black body paint covered every inch of skin, save for the bottoms of her bare feet.

She had entered the store around two a.m. after the Native Force master hacker had intercepted the fax sent to Rebecca from Salumeria Settepani. She had converted an old storage closet in the basement into an ad hoc command and control center. At 6:30 a.m., a Native Force support cell on bicycles in a nearby park had spotted the termination target, Freckles, blithely riding alone. A risk-taker, just as they thought when they first observed her walking down Pennsylvania Avenue in her inauguration parade. She must have slipped her Secret Service guards. Raven One wiggled her toes, groaning with pleasure as the muscles on her legs rippled up her body in response.

* *

"How's your daughter doing?" Rebecca asked.

"Terrific. It looks like she'll be bringing home a Phi Beta Kappa key."

"Oh, that's super. Has she decided about graduate school?"

"Look at these tomatoes. They're hothouse organic. Done right here in Boston."

"Yum . . . do you have any Portobello mushrooms?"

"Sure. I think she wants to go to law school."

"Yellow peppers? I'll be glad to write her a reference. Last time I saw her, she was a ten-year-old performing in her school play."

"My little girl. She played Emily in *Our Town*. Oh, I've got these wild orange peppers. She'd be tickled pink if you wrote her a reference."

* *

Raven One dropped her shorts and pushed a handful of putty-like C-4 explosives into a condom, which she inserted as far as she could inside her vaginal cavity. She ran her tongue across her lips as she savored the pain of the insertion. A detonation string traveled between her thighs; she threaded the long fuse under her shorts as she pulled them back up over her hips, continuing a path across her washboard abs. She stopped and pinched her nipples with hard twists.

The thrill of the kill brought her to a summit of sexual excitement. She knew she didn't have time, but it was too late now. She licked her lips again and reached between her legs where the C-4 had been inserted. It took only a few minutes; the mingling of the kill-to-be with sex overwhelmed her quivering body as she exploded silently. A musky smell floated up from between her legs and her whole body felt afire. She was ready; she activated her ACR locator beacon to alert brother Jonnie, who by now should be positioned close to the kill site. Together they had gutted out the innards of the Diaz family and bathed each other in the aliens' blood. Now it would be the day of their ultimate glory.

* *

"I can have all this delivered by noon."

"That'd be perfect."

"You're not going to ride back on your bike. Shouldn't you call the Secret Service?"

"Yeah, I'll call them in a few minutes. I don't think they know I'm gone yet."

"Okay, what else do you need?"

"I'll just go down aisle two, and pick up some olive oil."

"You know," Bruno said, "you'd be the best stock boy."

"Try, stock girl."

"Okay. Stock girl. You know every aisle, exactly where everything is. Where would I ever find someone as organized as you?"

"Perfect job for me." Rebecca headed for aisle two.

* *

Raven One's disposable cellphone vibrated discreetly with the text message, ABORT. ABORT NOW. DELAYED.

She quickly texted back: LOSER. I NEVER QUIT. With the distinctive click-clack of the biking cleats snapping on the linoleum floor above her head, she began to move. As she glided up the stairs, she undid two wire nuts. One cut off the outgoing phone lines, the other wires she had spliced to re-direct the incoming lines to a voice responder. A pre-recorded voice with a slight Italian accent said, "Welcome to Salumeria Settepani, Gourmet Italian Food Specialties. We're open nine-to-five Monday to Fridays, ten-to-six on Saturdays and Sundays. Come by and see us."

Raven One had spent an hour the night before repairing the back steps leading to the store's basement. Three risers had squeaked. She cut wood blocks using power tools she found and nailed them in from below until the stairs became silent. She flossed the detonation string between two molars, wrapped it tightly, and knotted it. She calculated that it would take a sharp snap back with her neck to blow the C-4 if need be.

She held one dagger in her mouth. As she crept up the stairs, she passed a mirror, looking with pleasure at her reflection. She could be a pin-up poster for righteous boys and girls. They would admire her awesome body, her tight braless nipples pushing out the fabric of her Navy T-shirt, her thighs as powerful as an anaconda. Too bad she couldn't have more time with Madam President.

* *

"Sir, this is agent Atwood out of Detroit. You wanted reports of anything unusual."

Groggily, Toussaint picked up his priority phone a few minutes before seven a.m. at his home in Alexandria, Virginia.

"Yes, what is it?"

"Outside Elba, Michigan, a railroad watchman went missing. It was reported four days ago. The sheriff found his body about an hour ago. He called me right away, and I've just choppered onto the scene."

"What're you looking at?"

"A knife thrower killed the victim with a fatal puncture to the carotid artery. The coroner is looking at him now. Given the shape of the entry wound, he believes the knife was thrown from at least ten feet away with great velocity and unbelievable accuracy."

"Does he have a time of death?"

"Hold on. He's saying seventy-two to ninety-six hours."

"Damn, what about the trains?"

"I'm talking to the regional head of police for Northern Pacific Railway. He says the victim checked trains at Elba. It's a routine inspection stop."

"Can they pinpoint the train?"

"Yes, they found paperwork on his body. He had checked trains up until a scheduled potato express coming out once a month from Boise, Idaho."

Toussaint felt his stomach head south. "Destination?"

"They're saying Boston."

Toussaint jumped out of his bed. He pushed a command console on his nightstand. His wife woke up; a shocked look crossed her face as she grasped it was a crisis.

"Command Center. This is Toussaint. I'm calling a Code Platinum

Alert. Break down Red Striker's door if you have to. She needs a full-body surround. Get ready to pull her out of Boston. I want her taken to Camp David."

Toussaint looked at his watch. It read 7:10 a.m.

* *

Raven One reached the top of the stairs. From where she now stood, she could see the back of President Tree's head midway down aisle two. A sign on top of the shelf said, EXTRA VIRGIN COLD PRESSED. She crouched nearly to the floor and crab-walked in the direction of her prey.

* *

"I don't know what's wrong with these phones," Bruno said, standing behind the register at the front entrance of the store. "I need to fax Ristorante Terremia; they wanted me to confirm an order. Now the line seems dead. Ten minutes ago, it was fine."

"Oh, it's just Boston infrastructure. Give it another five minutes. This Frantoio looks great." Rebecca held a half-liter bottle. She felt the air move slightly around her neck, and a spark like pain flared off the scar tissue under her shoulder blade. Her finely tuned body became alert. She adjusted the strap on her bag, rotating the bag zipper, so it was under her arm, as if out of instinct from living in cities with the risk of pickpockets.

"The Frantoio is from Tuscany. It's popular. And what a great fragrance."

She read the label on another bottle, squatter in shape and more convex. "How's this Biancolilla?"

"Oh, *mama mia*. It's from Sicily. The chef at Assaggio swears by it."

"Do you have any more of these? I'd like to give a couple to friends."

"I think I have a few more in the stock room. I'll be right back."

She took the Biancolilla off the shelf, which had a thin mirror reflecting back on the premium bottles to entice visually the customer. Rebecca now saw, in mirror image, a shape crouched low to the floor, turning from aisle three into two. She held her breath and felt her heart crawl into her throat. "I think I'll probably take the Biancolilla." Rebecca said, not sure if Bruno was still within hearing distance. She paused, breathing deeper, preparing herself, "and I'd like the Frantoio as well but I don't want to take the last one." Now she had both bottles off the shelf, uncovering more of the mirror.

She steeled herself waiting for the inevitable.

As she held the bottles, the mirror revealed a throwing knife held between the assailant's teeth and a string snaking down from her mouth. *What the devil was that?* Rebecca's heart stopped as her eyes focused on the crooked tooth clamped on the knife. She felt sick. The creature coming toward her had a snaggletooth—Psycho Biter—the killer of Erin Rodriquez, Jack Switzer, and the Diaz family.

She tried to list mentally the contents of her bag—had she brought her Mace spray?—But there was no time. Rebecca calculated she had only a few seconds.

* *

Toussaint screamed into his command phone.

"What do you mean, she's not responding? Break in now. You've got the master key. Didn't she have dinner with her neighbors last night? Pound on their door! I'll hold."

Toussaint juggled a phone, looked at his watch, and tried to throw on a shirt.

"Director Toussaint," said a Boston-based agent. "Mrs. Rivera told us that the President asked to borrow her bike out of the alleyway this morning. She assumed it meant the Secret Service went with her."

Toussaint looked at his watch again. "She's either pedaling away like a blissful idiot in a nearby park or . . . Damn, listen. Put all your choppers up. Boston PD has undercover bicyclists. Get them into the parks. Get an accurate description of the bike."

* *

"I changed my mind. I'll just take the Frantoio," Rebecca said out loud, putting the other bottle down as her eyes stayed focused on the mirror. "I'll bring it up front." The shape rose out of its crouch as Rebecca watched. The woman's muscles rippled like stones skipping in a pond as she reached for the knife between her teeth.

Timing is everything, Rebecca thought to herself, as she felt her heart racing. *Perfect timing lives, imperfect timing dies.* Rebecca turned, still holding one bottle and pretending to read its label. Now with her hand behind her, she angled her head toward her opponent, knowing that she retained a split-second advantage. The assailant had yet to realize that she was spotted. The bottle, with its Sicilian pedigree, neared a launchable angle. Rebecca flung the bottle at the assassin and ducked a split second before a knife was hurled. Both the bottle and the knife missed their marks.

"Bitch," snarled Raven One. "Lucky this morning, but your luck won't last."

"Rebecca?" Bruno, back from the stockroom, cried out, "Did you drop a bottle? I heard glass."

"Stay where you are. Don't move," Rebecca said as calmly as she could.

Raven One slid her hand down her thigh. Her eyes glistened with excitement. She spoke in a near-whisper. "I'm going to gut your belly, bitch. Turn you into a fish fillet."

The attacker had the hilt of the second knife in her hand when Rebecca moved, coiling her leg as she spun and then throwing full out. She hit the killer with a rising kick, starting low, and cracking against her mouth high and hard. The reinforced toes of the cleated biking shoes added force to the impact. Two teeth went flying out, and the strange string dislodged and fell out of her mouth, but the attacker held on to her knife.

The woman spat blood and cackled, seemingly taken pleasure in the blow she had received. "Nice kick. Warming up a bit today?"

With the knife raised to attack level, she dove at Rebecca, and the two women fought in close, neutralizing Rebecca's height advantage. The assailant lunged once with the knife, but Rebecca parried the first blow with an elbow into her opponent's wrist. Not enough to dislodge the knife. Bruno yelled out in the background.

"Stay where you are," Rebecca screamed back, momentarily losing her focus. In that instant, the knife's second thrust ripped through her bag strap, releasing it to the ground like a deflated basketball, tore into the long sleeve shirt, until finally cut through the chamois of the skin suit. Rebecca felt her flesh tear. How deep, it was too soon to know.

"You're bleeding bitch, but not nearly enough." The assassin deliberately dropped the second knife and made a theatrical flourish with palms extended. "You ready to be finished off?"

Rebecca was light-headed as she staggered through the aisle, pawing the shelves for support and finding purchase only in jars and bottles. Bright white spots blotted the vision of her left eye as her wrist monitor began to beep slowly and then quickly increasing in volume. Rolling momentarily in her sockets, the assassin's eyes sizzled like red-hot cinders dropped in cold water. Her fingers danced with a taunting motion as she moved them down toward a third knife sheathed to her other thigh.

Rebecca's pupils dilated, fresh oxygen pumped, the wrist monitor quieted down, and the hairs on her arm stood on end. She knew exactly where the store fixture ended, and the next one began. Finding the spot, she summoned up her strength and tipped the modular section four feet wide and five feet high in the killer's direction. She caught the attacker by surprise, and a cascade of olive oil and pickle bottles showered the attacker's feet. Some of them broke, and the assassin now had to move across a floor of oil-basted tiles.

Still standing on dry ground, Rebecca stepped back as her opponent grabbed the hilt of the third sheathed knife, but the attacker couldn't get her footing. Rebecca measured the distance and swirled to land a solid foot of metal cleats angled into the assailant's jaw. Rebecca reversed quickly and eddied another foot straight again into the killer's jaw. This time she thought she heard a crack; hopefully, she had broken it. The woman's eyes glazed over, but she kept her grip on the third of her knives, throwing it before dropping to her knees. The blade plunged into Rebecca's thigh. Rebecca groaned and fell to her knees. Her opponent looked she was shaking off the pain of a broken jaw. The women now faced each other, as Rebecca swung first with her fist, landing a good shot to the killer's eye. The woman started a lunge forward toward Rebecca's heart.

Dear father in heaven.

The woman's head wavered, and then swayed, twisting upward like a Cobra head, her hand holding another dagger; her head kept rising higher as she hissed a noise of ominous pleasure. Rebecca thought that the end had come, but then she heard a sudden cracking noise as loud as a thunderclap.

The assassin's dagger wavered, and she fell head first toward Rebecca.

Settepani, wearing a white butcher's apron with red lettering saying "Salumeri Settepani—Family Owned" stood over the assailant with a baseball bat tipped with blood. The creature was out cold on the floor. The fourth knife's handle vibrated, the blade stuck between two floorboards.

With her last minute reprieve from what seemed to be certain death, fresh adrenaline surged back into Rebecca. With Settepani's help, she flipped the assailant over, looking at the string tied to a broken off tooth. Rebecca traced the string as it went under the assassin's shirt and then down her stomach and into her pants.

"Is your phone working?"

"No, I'll go for help."

"No, not yet. Get some rope. Whatever you do, don't open the door until the Secret Service gets here. I'm sure this one isn't alone. There could be an execution squad within sniper range of the building."

"Oh my God, you've lost a lot of blood," Settepani said.

Rebecca's eyes wavered, and her blood pressure monitor began to beep again, growing steadily in volume.

"Don't talk. Just listen. Reach into the back of my bike jersey, in the big pocket. There is a little beeper. Got it? . . . hit the green button. It alarms to the Secret . . . need four pieces of rope," Rebecca said, her speech becoming intermittent, as Bruno ran off avoiding bottles and oil.

* *

"Her beeper just activated." Agent Rolands in Secret Service Command shouted out over the Secret Service communications line. "We're triangulating her location on GPS. Roger, yes that's a confirm. 12 Hodges

Lane, it's listed as a gourmet Italian grocery. Yes, we're sending choppers, four armored cars and an armored ambulance as well."

* *

"Tie her up across the aisle so she can't move."

The killer groaned, moving her head slightly. Rebecca smashed her elbow with all the force she could muster into the woman's neck. The sight of the assassin's snaggletooth had filled Rebecca with hatred, which probably saved her life, and kept her going a few more precious moments. *God was on my side today*, Rebecca thought. She could hear tires screeching at the front and rear of the building.

"Bruno, we've got to get out of here."

She grabbed her thigh as she got up; the pain shot through her. Blood soaked her clothes and ran down one leg, pooling on the floor. In a half-limp, holding onto Bruno's shoulder, she got to the store entrance. Fists pounded on the door. "This is the Secret Service, open up."

Rebecca, feeling like the wind was knocked out of her, mustered enough strength to shout out weakly, "Agent, I.D. yourself and your code name."

"Agent Collins. Coded as Red Cardinal."

Rebecca motioned to Settepani to open the door as she tried to hold herself up at the checkout counter's edge. "Listen, Collins." Rebecca felt the pain surging. "We've got one assassin tied up, unconscious on the floor," she paused, feeling dizzy, "but there must be others around to back her up."

"Ma'am, you're bleeding. We need to get you to a hospital."

"Damn it," she said. "Shut up and listen. The one on the floor is a Native Force killer. She might be booby-trapped with explosives." The room started to spin. Holding onto the agent, she continued, "And another execution squad maybe," Rebecca's words slurred. "Maybe with sniper sights is out there . . ." she groaned as shooting tingles spread through her body.

"We've to get you to an emergency room, now."

She was fading now. "You need a bomb squad . . ."

"Madam President. You're losing too much blood." The two agents holding Rebecca became drenched in her blood, and her pressure monitor screamed like a desperate smoke detector begging for fire engines.

Her adrenalin finally overcome, she felt light-headed, and the room filled with a bright white light.

"All right . . ." her voice left her, and then the room went black. Agents tented her with bulletproof shields and carried her into the armored presidential ambulance.

Chapter 67

72 Hours later
Camp David

When she awoke, Toussaint's broad shoulders hovered over her like an incoming airplane. At first, she thought it was Jackson, and that she must be dead, but then she realized it was Caleb. She was alive.

She groaned as she felt the pain coursing through her leg. "Where am I?"

"You're at Camp David. The surgeons at Mass General sewed you up, transfused you, and then dumped you back on the street. So we took pity on you and medevacked you."

"What happened? I think I remember how it began but how it did end?"

Toussaint gave her the details. The first knife thrust had wounded her superficially, and for that, she was bandaged. The second came perilously close to severing the iliac artery, but a team of surgeons and transfusions of her stored blood, the rare AB negative, stabilized her. She got treated just in time; five minutes later the chief trauma surgeon had said, and she would have lost too much blood to be saved.

"This sad sack, however, could not be saved," Toussaint showed her the remains of her beloved orange bag, now sliced and stained with patches of oil and blood.

"Ouch."

Because she was fully sedated, the attorney general had requested that the vice president convene an emergency cabinet meeting, which was done, and the twenty-fifth amendment was invoked, placing Aldo Peña as the acting-president.

"What about Bruno? Is he okay? He saved my life."

"He'll be fine. He's quite shaken for the moment."

"Does he have protection?" Rebecca said, fighting to keep her eyes open.

"Twenty-four-seven on his family and his store."

"And Snaggletooth? Who is she?" Her eyelids fluttered; her brain remained partially awake, but her body kept sliding toward sleep.

"Her name is Rachel Reichle, hometown Bozeman, Montana, age twenty-seven, education reform school, a.k.a. Snaggletooth, a.k.a. Psycho Biter. Her tooth, one of the ones you knocked out of her mouth, matches the one left by the killer of Jack Switzer, Erin Rodriquez, and one of the Diaz girls. She was arrested once when she was thirteen years old for nearly killing another girl, and . . ." Toussaint paused, "lacerating her thighs with bite marks. She did five years as a juvenile; when she got out, she worked in a pancake house nearly six years until her brother, Jonnie Reichle, a former Navy Seal, took her to Alaska, where they disappeared."

"Where's she now?" Rebecca asked, looking up at the IV, which had just dripped, probably a drop of painkiller.

"She's at Mass General. In the critical care unit."

"And her brother? Has he been captured?"

"Not yet. A few minutes before the attack, there was a collision between two bicyclists in a park near the store. One party was an undercover police officer on patrol who then was knifed by the other cyclist, whom we believe to be Jonnie Reichle and most likely Commander Alpha."

"Is the officer alive?"

"Yes. Luckily, a road bike club came on the scene momentarily, but the assailant had a mountain bike and was able to flee off road. A massive manhunt is underway."

"Do you have any pictures of them?" Rebecca said, her voice barely audible.

Toussaint picked up a nearby folder and took out a frontal photograph of Jonnie Reichle from when he was a Navy Seal and his sister Rachel taken just before she was released from jail.

Rebecca squinted at the images for a long time and weakly said,

"Pull the security footage from the Ministry of Lord Church, and then the inauguration parade. They must have been stalking me all along. Tell me the rest."

Toussaint continued with more details telling Rebecca that the bomb squad tried to de-activate the C-4 but only partly succeeded. A small part of it blew, the blast staying inside Reichle's body. A team of trauma surgeons, operating around the clock, first amputated her legs just above her knees. Then they will be, over the next days, replacing and rebuilding her stomach, her intestines, her colon, and her urethra. In the last few hours, they stabilized her to a point where they had upped her odds of survival to fifty-fifty.

A fresh wave of nausea surged through Rebecca triggered by an image of her attacker, now having dismembered herself. *Do unto others,* she thought.

"I'll pray for her survival," Rebecca said.

"Why? Are you crazy?"

"I want to see her face-to-face at her trial. I want to look her in the eyes when I testify."

Rebecca's eyes glazed over, and she fell back asleep.

* *

She awoke, six hours later, and Fatima, sitting in a chair at the edge of the bed, jumped up when Rebecca stirred.

"Oh, hi . . ." Rebecca said, shaking her right hand, and making a gesture like waving off a paparazzo. "Don't ask, just tell." She bit on her lip, warding off a wave of pain. "Update? Please."

"Okay, Aldo Peña is now the president."

"I heard. I'm okay with that . . . maybe . . . no, I'm not."

"I have the re-transfer papers under the Twenty-Fifth Amendment, which you can sign when you feel that you're no longer incapacitated."

Rebecca loosely closed her left hand, tapping her forefinger on her thumb.

"Give me a pen."

After she shakily signed three copies, she said, "Okay, I'm not in the best mood. So I'll ask again, what's happening?"

"Sure, boss. Three days ago you nearly died. The global markets, the ones open at the time, plunged wildly. By midnight, your Press Secretary announced that the doctors had declared you stable and in transit to a field hospital set up at Camp David to recuperate."

"Why was I moved so quickly?"

"Toussaint didn't feel confident about securing Mass General."

"So, did the markets keep plunging," she groaned again, as a fresh pain surge hit her, "when they heard I might live?"

"Very funny, Madam President. In fact, they rallied all day and soared when we announced that we expected you to resume your constitutional responsibilities soon. Even the dollar rallied."

"That's so nice . . . of the dollar," Rebecca said. "Oh, I've some unfinished business. On my desk in Boston, there is a file."

"On Éamonn O'Connell? The Secret Service retrieved it."

"Yes. I want him put into witness protection, sent to the prison hospice in Fort Worth, and monies released to bring his family to him."

"Done. Also, Keith Forsyte has been calling me every hour. He wants to see you."

"I'll take care of it." Rebecca didn't want him to see her like this, not just yet.

"He's a good man."

"I'm well-aware."

"You're the boss. Still. Thank God."

Rebecca battled to keep her eyes open. "Where's the doctor. I want this IV off me."

Fatima pushed a buzzer aside the bed and the White House physician, Dr. Erika Burns, came into the room.

"What are you dripping into me?"

"Antibiotics and pain-killers."

"Damn it," Rebecca said, her voice filling with agitation. "No pain-killers."

"We'll start cutting the dose, as soon as it's advisable."

The doctor turned to Fatima. "Could you excuse us for a few moments. I need to examine the president."

"How do you feel?" Burns asked after Fatima left, as she tapped on

Rebecca's neck, and pointed a small flashlight at her pupils.

"Like I got hit by a train. Besides that, just peachy," Rebecca said as the doctor placed a stethoscope on Rebecca's heart, her stomach, and her kidneys.

"Everything sounds good, especially given the scrape you got yourself in. You're lucky to be alive. You lost about thirty percent of your blood. Another five percent and you would have been gone. I'll be back in a bit. I am due on a conference call with the Mass General staff to give them an update."

"Okay. Please thank them for me for everything they have done. And tell them I'm sorry for being such a reckless idiot."

As the doctor left, Rebecca picked up her cellphone to call Keith Forsyte. He picked up before the first ring had completed. Trying to maintain a normal voice, Rebecca said, "Mr. Prime Minister, this is President Tree. I need to discuss your latest proposal on the arms control treaty. I'm very dissatisfied with it."

"Oh Becky, I'm so happy to hear your voice. I've been worried sick. I haven't slept since I heard the news. Can I see you?"

"Not yet. Give me a few days. Then we can arrange a visit. I'm falling off to sleep again."

"I love you."

"Thanks. I'm sorry. I'm fading."

"I want to . . ."

Rebecca only heard the first three words. The effort exhausted her, and she had drifted back to sleep.

Chapter 68

Three weeks later
Camp David

Dogwoods bloomed around the lodges of Camp David. A pair of blue-birds, the female suited with a vest of blazing orange, and a male displaying a more demure solid color, perched on a high branch and ate berries. Oak, maple, larch and birch trees dotted the landscape. Fields of daffodils— whites and yellows— mingled with hyacinths, palmed hands outstretched.

Rebecca sat on a painter's stool. She faced a longer recovery than previously anticipated, as the knife Rachel Reichle had plunged into her thigh had been tipped with rat poison, causing local nerve damage and muscle trauma. She scrutinized a half-finished canvas propped on an easel labeled "property of U.S. National Park's Department." She regarded the landscape before her, painting more flowers into the foreground.

A camera mounted on a tripod sat next to the easel, its long lens focused on a pond a few hundred yards away. Rebecca carried a foldout chart entitled "Migratory Birds of the Boreal Forest." The chart had little peel-off stickers, each one a picture of a species not yet extinct. As she sat, she heard squawking overhead, and then, as she watched, a solitary duck dropped over the horizon, flew straight down and splashed into the pond. She craned into her lens, considering the specimen.

She picked up her edition of Peterson Field Guides, *Advanced Birding.* Flipping the pages, she identified the species—*Aythya Americana,* English common name, Redhead—a gray male with brick-red hair and black breast. Within seconds a duller female landed, brown with a light area around the base of her bill. Most likely, the pair would overnight in

Camp David's pond before continuing north. The three billion birds of her mid-twenties had diminished now to less than a billion.

In the background, she heard a girl's voice shout, "Aunt Becky, Aunt Becky."

Her niece Sarah Tree swept down the hill, arriving with arms outstretched, and Rebecca, bracing her injured leg, lifted her with a hug.

"I'm so glad you came," Rebecca said, struggling not to grimace as a sharp pain shot up her leg.

"I've never been to Camp David. Daddy wouldn't take us."

"Well, you're here now. Where's your brother?" she said as she tenderly brushed some wisps of hair, which smelled like fresh squeezed limes, off her niece's eyes, and lowered her back down.

"Patrick's bothering one of your security guys. He'll come if someone says there's food being served."

Sarah wore overall blue jeans, a sad-eyed panda T-shirt, pink rubber soled Trekkers shoes, a backward baseball cap, and a Barbour jacket with a Tattersall lining. Her thick wavy blond hair fell to her shoulders. She stared at the half-finished canvas that sat on the easel.

"I didn't know you could paint. That's so neat."

"I'm not much of an artist. Do you paint?" Rebecca imagined that her twin sister would have been the artist.

"No, I play the violin."

"That's great; when I was your age, I played the flute."

Uphill near the main lodge, Ashley Tree waved, signaling to her daughter.

Sarah waved back at her mother, and then, tapping her left index finger and thumb with her right hand, she flashed her hands three times. "I'm learning sign language at school. It's my 'fav' subject."

"What did you just say?"

"Mom says I can spend a half-hour with you, and then I'm supposed to take a nap since we've been traveling all day, and then she'd like some time with you. Is that okay?"

"She said all that? Terrific," Rebecca roared. "I'd be delighted to follow someone else's schedule. So the next thirty minutes are yours. Make a wish?"

"For what?"

"For what you'd like us to do, silly."

Sarah shut her eyes tight and then opened them with a smile. "I wish my Aunt Becky would give me a painting lesson."

"Your wish is my command."

Rebecca beckoned a Secret Service agent and asked him to fetch another painter's easel, painting smocks, charcoals, and two blank canvases from the shed.

"Can I feed the ducks?"

"Not that wish. Feeding animals is unhealthy for them."

"Why?"

"Because if they become used to being fed, then they forget to find food."

"I never thought of that."

"Also, there are geese overhead. They'll probably land here in large numbers today or tomorrow."

"Are they pretty?"

"They're beautiful, but you can't go near them." She pinched Sarah's cheeks. "They can bite; they especially like pretty young girls with long, tasty goose-food ringlets of blonde hair."

Sarah giggled, and Rebecca tickled her until she burst out laughing. Two Secret Service agents arrived with supplies. She tied a painting smock around Sarah, and placed her on a painter's stool. Now sitting side-by-side, they looked to the Catoctin Mountains in the background. The foreground was filled with the duck pond and fields of blooming flowers.

Rebecca looked into a paint-box with "Ike" embossed on its lid, once the property of President Eisenhower, which held empty four-by-five slide transparencies holders. "Okay, what do you think we do first?"

"I don't know. Draw a line?"

"Not yet. First we think." Rebecca used her index finger to mimic a sculpted Grecian thinking pose. Sarah nearly burst with laughter. "Then, after thinking, we look." Rebecca lifted a finger and pointed it at her chest.

"What's that, silly?" Sarah said as she slapped the air near Rebecca's cuff.

"It's the sign for 'I,' just like," she pointed toward her own eye, "eye."

"You're funny."

"Good. I'm glad someone finally thinks so. Now look at the pond, and create boundaries, with your eyes, like a picture frame, around it."

"Ooh, that's not easy."

Rebecca came around to Sarah, holding the empty slide mount. "Close your left eye. And now look through this."

"Neat. Now it looks more like a picture."

"Okay, close both your eyes." She moved the frame, tilting it upward. With two cardboard framing L's, she shrunk the picture. "Open just your left eye again."

"Wow, now I can see a different picture, same pond. This is neat. You're a better teacher than Mrs. Mucci."

Rebecca moved the frame several times, creating a choice of landscapes. Then she showed Sarah how to create a dominant line, a foreground point of focus, and two subservient lines that, when put together, created an architecture for the painting.

Ashley called to Sarah from the top of the hill. Sarah picked up the slide mount and framed her mother, blonde hair glowing with the sun behind it. "I have to go in now," Sarah said, handing the frame to Rebecca to look through. "But we were just getting started. Right?"

Rebecca noted even from this distance that Ashley had slimmed down, and cut her hair short. Her skin was radiant. "Here," she put the items back in the 'Ike' box, latched it, and handed it to Sarah. "To be continued."

"Wow, cool!" Sarah excitedly scampered off to show her mom.

Rebecca scrutinized her half-finished painting, reached for her cane and, after some effort, stood. She wasn't much of a painter, but it helped her feel peaceful. It was all about perspective.

* *

After waving goodbye to Ashley and her children, Rebecca entered her favored sunroom in the main lodge. On a table, the steward had fanned out recent issues of *Time* magazine like a deck of cards. She picked them up, one at a time, from left to right. The first cover featured a photograph, shot at night, that captured Rebecca from outside a window as she lay in a hospital room at Mass General, hooked to an IV drip. PRESIDENT SURVIVES ASSASSINATION ATTEMPT read the headline. An enterprising photographer had launched a mini-drone outside the hospital, which managed to transmit one image to his computer before a Secret Service helicopter discovered the device and shot it down. *Time* paid five million dollars for a one-week, North American exclusive. The next cover, an illustration, depicted Special Force soldiers in comic book fashion, rappelling from helicopters into a suspected Native Force training camp. The headline read ARMY AIRBORNE ASSAULTS IDAHO TERRORIST TRAINING CAMPS. The third cover's graphic, assembled in DaguerreMagix-X, displayed a split image of two fused faces, John Spencer, and Merewether Tree, below the words WHO KNOWS WHAT EVIL LURKS IN THE MINDS OF MEN? In the next, Attorney General Harriet Ogden's likeness appeared in a woodman's costume, chopping at a tree labeled CONGRESS. Rebecca, portrayed as a construction worker, wore a hard-hat, her red hair spilling out, as she leaned on Ogden's shoulder, a chainsaw in hand. ALL CLEAR? said the title encased in a pop art balloon. The next one she didn't find funny. The headline read COURT TO LOSE SUPREME, and it portrayed Rebecca and Ogden straddling a missile, with the projectile aimed at the Supreme Court building. After the advanced copy choppered to Camp David, she had chewed out *Time*'s editors in a conference call for their abysmal taste. This week's *Time* cover read READY TO RUMBLE, blazed in type over Rebecca's forehead. The editors had cropped a determined image of her looking straight into the camera, her eyes filling nearly the entire width of the cover. Inside her left iris, ghost typed, stood a single word, REFORM? The other eye, in a similar font, bore the ominous words, COUP D' ETAT?

Chapter 69

Home of Caleb and Camille Toussaint
Alexandria, Virginia

Caleb and Camille Toussaint had just finished a long-time favorite meal—Cajun Court bouillon. The Toussaints liked their rituals: their living room filled with the lingering savory smells of creole tomato sauce, its roux built out of bacon fat garnished with fresh tarragon and rosemary.

Like passengers on a luxury cruise liner the couple dressed in a suit and silk dress for their date-night dinner.

Toussaint began to tidy the table, taking off his jacket, and throwing on an apron, personalized to read "Top Secret Chef in Training."

After finishing her glass of wine, Camille got up from the table and came behind her husband, wrapping her arms around him as he loaded the dishwasher.

"Sweetie, I am going upstairs to take a shower and get ready for bed."

"Sounds like an excellent plan to me."

"Here's the thing," Camille said, a coy teasing tone in her voice. "Here's the thing," she repeated now giggling.

"Honey, with a woman like you, a guy like me would never need a 'Here's the thing' kind of pill. When I do, please take me directly to the nursing home. I'll be up . . ."

Toussaint's security phone rang before he could finish his sentence. Camille sighed and proceeded upstairs.

"Director Toussaint, it is Agent Aronson. I'm the night duty officer tonight at Camp David. A heads up. Marine One is taking off from Camp David in thirty minutes. Red Striker is due to land on the south lawn within the hour."

"She wasn't scheduled to come in until tomorrow for her press conference."

"You know how she is; she gave us only a few minutes notice."

"Do you know why she changed her plans?"

"We don't. She has been a whirlwind all afternoon — one hour with the physical therapist, then with the trainer she fast-walked and slow-jogged for a half an hour on a treadmill and was all smiles after that. Then she went into the secure video conferencing room for about two hours and came tearing out of there, very agitated, pacing about and saying she needed to be back at the White House as soon as possible."

"This is impossible."

"No, it gets worse. She wants to go for a jog from the White House to the Washington Monument precisely at three a.m.; Madam President requested a screened security area set up on the south side of the monument. What should we do?"

"Maybe Congress should change the law, and I could put her in protective custody. Secret Service can only advise the president. We can't stop her."

"So how do you want this handled?"

"Set up a decoy jogging team to go out with her body double ten minutes before she departs the White House. Send them to the Lincoln Memorial. Fill the sky with the Secret Service drones. Use the Kevlar running shields for the line-of-fire agents running beside the president."

"Anything else?"

"I am heading over there to talk her out of this."

* *

Rebecca reached the Washington Monument just after three a.m. She had jogged part of the way but ended up slowing to a walk for the last quarter of a mile.

Two folding chairs, with one already occupied by a thin elderly man wearing a rumpled gray suit, sat inside of a wall of Kevlar panels. He leaned on a walker with a wheelchair a few feet to his side. A battered fedora and a wide scarf partially obscured his face. At his feet stood a portable audio jammer, preventing any outsiders from hearing.

The man was a British spymaster, Robert St. John, the retired head of M1-6's Special Branch for Northern Ireland.

"Madam President, I am sorry to bring you out at this late hour, and to create this elaborate cover," St. John said, as he watched Rebecca rubbing her injured leg after she sat in the other folding chair. "How's your leg?"

"Healing, but slowly. The therapists want me to jog slowly a few times a week, but now I think that is too soon. Thanks for asking and for making the trip to Washington to see me."

"You don't need to thank me. I will tell you what I can. Perhaps it will help you."

St. John began a background narration outlining his duties as well as missions he had undertaken for M1-6.

"You can see in me one of the end results of all our Irish policy failures. I ended up partially paralyzed due to the good luck of an Irish bomb maker."

"I am sorry that you suffered for your service," Rebecca said.

"Madam President, there is no sorry in war. The Irish did terrible things, and the British did terrible things. It is best we get beyond an ugly time in history that scarred our country."

"You know something about my family."

"Yes, I will tell you what I can, but, if it ever comes up, I will deny ever meeting you. Is that understood? And what I reveal tonight can never be repeated, not even to your closest confidante. Understood?"

"Yes, you have my word."

"Your mother's father no doubt was an IRA operative. Like their best operatives, he slipped our intelligence net, at first. Your mother, perhaps reluctantly, supported Sinn Fein, the political arm of the Irish independence movement."

"Was she engaged in illegal activities?"

"Everyone in the north engaged in illegal activities. On all sides. We would have had to build a prison camp as big as your state of Montana to hold them all if we could have arrested them.

"We weren't after your mother, at first. Our first focus turned to your grandfather."

"What!"

"Yes, Merewether Tree, a little less than forty years ago, gave several million well-laundered dollars to Irish nationalist organizations."

"I don't understand; this sounds unreal and contrary to his professed beliefs."

"The British government made private protestations to the American government, but the Prime Minister, because of the Anglo-American relationship and your grandfather's power, wanted the whole matter treated with kid gloves. In any event, the donations suddenly stopped."

"So what was all this about?"

"That's when we looked more carefully at your mother."

"And?"

"You sure you want to hear all of this?"

"Go ahead."

"Your mother turned out to be certainly more than a Sinn Fein sympathizer. Our analysts believed that she acted as an agent for Irish nationalist interests, who had on occasion, sent their most attractive and intelligent daughters to America's finest universities seeking liaisons with children of the powerful."

"This is very unsettling."

"Well, it has a semi-happy ending."

"Which is?"

"Your grandfather's money was paid as a bribe to Sinn Fein, who, in exchange, decommissioned her from politics and told her to stay away from Ireland. We had an informant, a childhood friend of your mother to whom she confided that she loved your father and that she wanted to live in peace raising her children. She wanted out of the political strife that her father had forced her into. I take it her father was not a nice man."

Rebecca shuddered, and her eyes blinked rapidly.

"That's the whole story, or, at least, everything I know," St. John said, getting up to leave after shaking Rebecca's hand.

"Wait, what about this Dr. Ryan, who delivered my sister and I. We think he might have been murdered. What does that mean?"

"Oh, yes Dr. Ryan. Your maternal grandmother died giving birth to your mother in a British-run hospital, leaving her husband, Dillon McCauley, deeply embittered. As far as we can tell, Dr. Ryan, as a favor, attended to your mother's delivery. We believe his murder had to do with his plastic surgery activities but had nothing to do with your mother's delivery."

"I have to leave now," St. John said, abruptly hoisting himself from walker to wheelchair.

Rebecca climbed into the soundproof passenger compartment of a Secret Service SUV.

All the way back to the White House Rebecca wept uncontrollably.

Chapter 70

Press Conference
White House Press Briefing Room

"Good afternoon, ladies and gentlemen," Rebecca said the next day as she stood shakily behind the podium in the White House Press briefing room. Standing on her leg for prolonged periods caused her discomfort and her late night jog aggravated her wound. After returning from her three a.m. meeting at the Washington Monument she had spent an anguished, sleepless night. She struggled to contain her foul mood.

"Thank you for attending today's press conference. I have a brief statement, and then I'll take questions."

Reading from a written statement, Rebecca began, "I'm pleased to announce my nominee for the position vacant at the Supreme Court—Anders Hope Gaillard. Professor Gaillard, who holds the Thurgood Marshall Chair at Howard University Law School, is considered to be one of our country's most eminent constitutional scholars. His seminal legal work, *Three/Fifths: The Other Persons of the American Constitution*, narrates how slavery became embedded in the American Constitution and the legal struggle of over two hundred years to make the 'Other Persons' constitutionally whole. I believe he will make an excellent Supreme Court Justice. I'll take questions now. Yes, Mr. Lamm, we'll start with you."

"Thank you. As Dean of Washington's press corps, I would like to welcome you back." Applause broke out in the room.

"That's kind of you. But that's not a question."

"Madam President," Lamm continued, "first then, how are you feeling, and would you care to comment on the recent events in Boston?"

"I'll answer the second part first. If you're referring to the Red Sox's acquiring southpaw Willie Opala, it looks like that'd be a help to their pitching staff."

Laughter rippled the room, and the correspondents looked relieved that Rebecca seemed back in her game.

"And for the former part of your question, I feel fine. I'll be continuing with physical therapy and hope to play soccer again sometime . . ." Rebecca paused, "Next year for sure."

"That's terrific about the soccer," Lamm said, "but I'm referring to a more serious event, the assassination attempt by Rachel Reichle."

"Right, those events. There are national security issues involved here, and you can push all you want, but this is all I have to say on the matter: Reichle is allegedly a top echelon execution squad commander of Native Force. I've deemed her an unlawful combatant and the handling of her case will be carried out under special circumstances. Yes, Mr. Peskin."

"Could you define special circumstances?"

"She'll be subjected to extreme security considerations; she'll never be allowed to commingle with a general prison population. As soon as she's well enough, she'll be transferred to a military hospital or jail."

Hands shot up across the room.

"Yes, Mr. Messinger."

"It seems no secret that you had some direct role in defending your . . ."

Rebecca interrupted the questioner. "For legal reasons, I can't discuss the events you are referring to. I expect to be called as a prosecution witness, but I'll add that I look forward to seeing Ms. Reichle, in court. Can we move onto the next question?"

The room thundered with shouts, joined by raised hands.

"The next question can go to *Newsweek*, Mr. Smith?"

"Do you believe next week's special election, with ten Senate seats and fifty House seats being contested, will break the legislative gridlock that has paralyzed the American government for over four decades?"

"Yes, I'm hopeful. We've all seen the same polls; the American public is beyond fed up with the enrichment of some of their representatives.

I'm only disappointed that the events in Boston stopped my barnstorming the country for reform-minded candidates. Nevertheless, I've spent time videoconferencing for meetings and rallies. I hope every American will take the time to vote next week.

"Mr. Leavitt from *Time Magazine.* The next question is for you."

"Yesterday, at a news conference, the chairwoman of the House Oversight and Government Reform Committee said they would be announcing a schedule for hearings on Secret Service lapses relating to executive branch security. Sources tell me that they intend to issue subpoenas to, among others, Director Toussaint. Your reaction?"

"The chairwoman, with all due respect, seems more devoted to her never-ending campaign for the presidency and not too interested in legislation. During Sanchez-Smith's time in office, this same committee with this same chairwoman drastically cut Secret Service funding making it difficult for the Service to meet fully all of its obligations.

"No doubt, in Boston, I acted recklessly, but it was not a security lapse; that one is on me. I will fight any subpoenas issued to Director Toussaint, and I will see the chairwoman in court, if necessary, deciding how executive privilege trumps a fishing expedition subpoena.

"Next question. I see my second honeymoon with the press is as short as my first one. Let's get a tough question." Rebecca said, pointing to her nemesis Bob Daad, the Wolf Global correspondent. "Mr. Daad?"

"Yes, the Internet has been awash the last few days with this extraordinary cellphone footage of you confronting protestors after the Diaz funeral, and even facing them off as rocks were hurled in your direction."

"I've heard about his footage, but I have not personally reviewed it. But what is your question?"

"There are now three unexplained incidents which some are speculating might have presidential fingerprints on them — a president, with a background in military intelligence. First, the man who took the cellphone footage claims his house was burglarized, and only a laptop and his cellphone was taken. The burglars ignored more expensive items. Second, John Spencer has accused you of having operatives bug his home. Third, my network, Wolf Global, believes that Chinese hackers with ties to you disrupted their television and Internet transmissions on election night. Your response?"

Rebecca's face burst into a room-lighting smile. "I knew you wouldn't disappoint me today, Mr. Daad. Unfortunately, I don't know any Hollywood movie agents; else I would recommend you to peddle your lovely paranoid political thriller to them. Fiction sells."

She watched with pleasure as Daad's face went ghost white, and he began banging his fist on his notebook. "Madam President, I object to your treatment of me and my network. Stop being evasive."

"Next? Who's going to top Mr. Daad? Yes, Ms. Freymann from the *Huffington Post.*"

"Do you plan to indict your grandfather, Merewether Tree? He has been named as a person of interest in the matter of the D.C. Relief Act, currently being examined by federal grand juries in several states. And I'd like a follow-up."

"No more follow-ups today and this will be the last question," as the question sadly sobered up Rebecca. "Merewether Tree is a citizen to be treated no differently than any other citizen when it comes to the wheels of justice. I will not interfere with the attorney general. She advocates for the American people and is not the president's personal attorney.

"But . . . but . . ." out of character, Rebecca began to stammer. "His legal fate is in the hands of the attorney general; to be totally honest, depending on how it plays out, I would, if he is convicted, give consideration to a pardon." An imploring look crossed Rebecca's face, "He is an old man who is now alleged to have done some bad deeds, but I believe history might eventually credit him for doing some good deeds as well. And for better or worse, he is the only family I have."

Rebecca turned and wordlessly left the room.

The room erupted as the press began to shout after her like commodity brokers trading oil at the opening bell.

Chapter 71

Toussaint and Merewether Tree
Washington National Airport

Director Toussaint's red security phone began to beep loudly at his bedside shortly before three a.m.

"Sir, this is Agent Peters, the night officer. I was told to call you, but this is not a threat situation."

"What is it then?" Toussaint replied groggily.

"A 767 with hospital plane markings just touched down at Washington National."

"Why are you calling me about it?" Toussaint responded, his voice filling with irritation. His wife harrumphed in half-sleep and rolled away.

"Sir, the plane's manifest indicates it has on board two doctors, four nurses, and a passenger, retired U.S. Senator Merewether Tree."

"This is not a Secret Service issue."

"Senator Tree requests you come to his plane, now. He says it's urgent. He has information for you that he believes you will want to hear."

* *

In the main cabin of the 767, Merewether Tree lay in a hospital bed surrounded by an array of monitors. An oxygen mask pressed against his face. Toussaint approached Tree, who seemed to be napping like a cat with one eye open. Opening his other eye, his hand rose slowly as he made a small welcoming gesture with one hand and pulled off the oxygen mask with the other.

"Nurse, unhook these damn machines," Tree said, trying to pump volume into his weakened voice. "I have a visit from an old friend. Prop me up some more so I can talk to him."

"Good evening, Senator Tree."

"Call me Merewether. I'm not that sick, not yet, but they say I need all these nonsensical machines when I am flying."

"Why are you in Washington?"

"To talk to you."

"About what? You could have called."

"I needed to get some air," he cackled hysterically, pointing to a mask hanging near him. "Does my granddaughter know I am here?"

"Not yet. Unless you're here to assassinate her, or you have information about a world war starting before sunrise, then she is entitled to a night's sleep."

"God has me on his short list."

"For what?"

"Well, hopefully, to sit by his side soon, but to be truthful, it is not a sure thing."

"That's between you and your maker."

"I need a confessor."

"Do you want me to call a priest?"

"No, I want you to be my confessor."

"It's not part of my job description. But why me?"

"We have a great deal in common, and you're close to my granddaughter; she might believe you. Rebecca won't believe anything I say."

"Okay, Senator. Start your confession then with the truth about Allison. Rebecca is entitled to some peace. She is tormented about her twin."

"Well, you learned a bit of the truth when your goon squads staged that taxpayer-sponsored home invasion of my Hillock-Hill mansion."

"Government agents carrying legal warrants entered your home."

"Whatever. I am not contesting it. And be forewarned, I have beefed up my defenses if you decide to make a return visit."

"Cut to the chase, Senator. You got me out of bed. What do you have to tell me?"

"Before her third birthday, Allison started to throw terrible tantrums." Tree said, his head bobbing up and down. "They grew worse and worse, becoming violent. The doctors diagnosed it as a severe form of autism. They warned us that Rebecca could be the object of her anger."

"During what you call the home invasion," Toussaint said, trying to shake the sleep out of his eyes, "the cook Lu told Rebecca that Allison had been tied up and attacked Rebecca with a kitchen knife when she was freed."

"Lu is correct. We faced a harsh choice: to either build a private ward on the property for Allison, basically a padded cell with around-the-clock attendants, or institutionalize her. In the drawer of the table next to you is handwritten correspondence between myself and my wife about Allison's fate, which gives a full chronology of these events."

"But why didn't you tell Rebecca all this? She could have eventually found some peace with it."

"I'll get to that. I am not asking for any sympathy, but perhaps some understanding. When my son died, my only beloved child, I dedicated my life to building wealth and power as if that might heal my wounds."

"Senator Tree, how do you expect my sympathy or understanding? I too lost my precious only child," Toussaint said, his voice rising in anger. "If he had left children, my wife and I would have showered them with love. Where was your love for Rebecca? She needed you."

"Rebecca got love, plenty of love. Tough love."

"I'd call it extreme love, well beyond tough."

"Do you think she would now sit as president of the United States, do you think she would have had the successes in the world of business if she had been indulged?"

"You have your wounds, like me, from an accident in your son's case, from a senseless war in my boy's case, but your grandchild was innocent. She did nothing that deserved punishment."

"I did what I believed was right for her. You can't judge me. Leave that to history and my God."

"You have not finished the Allison story. I am losing patience with you, Senator. What happened to her?"

"She went to the home in Batesville, which you know about. Then a couple of years later, a lawyer reached out to us representing an anonymous party, a wealthy single woman, who wished to adopt her. My wife and I signed confidentiality papers through the lawyer. The legal agreements prohibited us from communicating with Allison, to seek out her adopted mother, or divulge any information about her condition. And as guardians, we signed away Rebecca's rights to seek out Allison as well."

"And Allison's gravesite?"

"We did all that before the adoption and then we were stuck with our lie. It was my wife's idea, but it was my doing. And the confidentiality agreement went in both directions, so the woman who adopted Allison was bound to silence as well. I had some of my people take care of the fake death certificate and the gravesite. If that is a crime, the statute of limitations has expired. At the time, I intended to make a run for the presidency. We needed closure on Allison. To be crass, she was politically inconvenient. My wife controlled a family fortune. She said it would not be available for my campaign if we didn't disappear Allison permanently. It's in the letters. But I share fully in the sin. I'm not proud of what I did."

"I wouldn't count on sitting at God's side."

"Yes, I know that now." Tree's eyes began to shake and his face quivered. "I hope to be reunited with my son on the other side. It's my only wish." A single tear dropped from Tree's face.

"Is Allison alive?"

"She might be."

"Stop playing with me, Senator Tree. If you don't give it to me, you can't expect God's forgiveness."

"Understood," Tree said.

"And even before you deal with God, you might have to deal with the attorney general who is looking at indicting you. So since I am your 'old friend,' I am telling you to give it all up now. You're out of time. You have only one move left, and it has to be the truth."

A strange look passed Tree's face, and he began coughing and trying to clear his throat. To Toussaint, Tree looked like a man who had been stuck for hours playing and losing at a slot machine and was now ready to bet his last dollar and make a final pull.

"Okay, my friend. After Rebecca's election, I hired a team of investigators to see what they could find out about Allison's adoption and what might have happened to her."

"Why?"

"I needed to leave my affairs in order. It's an obligation, isn't it? I felt guilty about it. I felt I had betrayed my son."

"You did.

"I know," Tree said weakly.

"And did your investigators find out anything?"

"Maybe. They came to visit me at my home two days ago with some information they believed relevant. I flew here to deliver it." Tree reached under his pillow to retrieve a frayed brown leather-bound volume. "Take this. It's a memoir. Follow the trail."

Chapter 72

Midnight fell at Camp David. Camille Toussaint and Rebecca talked in the Eisenhower study, a small room off the main dining room.

"When did you last hear from Caleb?" Rebecca asked.

"About an hour ago, he texted me. He said he was almost done."

"But he didn't tell you what was so urgent that it kept him working?"

"No, you look concerned," Camille said.

"It's my sister. And there's a lot of other disturbing stuff going on."

"Why don't you talk about it?"

"I wish I could. Because of the ongoing legal investigations, the AG has me gagged for the moment. But something's going on with the search for my sister. I can feel it. He's getting close to finding an answer, but he never tells me anything until he finishes a definable stage of his investigation."

"You're his boss. He'll do it differently if you want."

"No, he's right," Rebecca said. "I have a country to run. It's my first obligation."

Rebecca held out a bottle of Merlot. "Nightcap?" she asked her hand wavering.

"Yes, it's time to get a little tipsy."

"When are you and Caleb going on your vacation?"

"Next month. He's excited like a little kid. He'll only tell me we're going to Italy. It will be a second honeymoon."

Rebecca knew all about the trip to Italy. Caleb had promised at some point in the trip that he would talk to Camille about Rebecca's relationship with Jackson. She was anxious to finally have all her secrets in the open and hoped that Camille would accept it. Caleb was confident that she would.

Camille's phone vibrated. "Oh, that must be Caleb. He's inbound now," Camille said, as she read a text message.

Rebecca's messenger was next. *Becky, I'll be at Camp David within 45 minutes. Pack an overnight bag. We'll be leaving immediately. We've found Allison—she's alive, but not well. My thoughts and prayers are with you."*

Rebecca's eyes shut hard. A low moan rose from her throat; her body shook, and Camille put her arm around her. Rebecca put her right hand on her forehead. With fingers outstretched, she tried massaging the pain that throbbed in her lobes.

"Oh baby, it's going to be all right. What did he say?"

Rebecca, with her left hand, picked up the messenger and passed it to Camille.

"She's alive. That's amazing. You'll get to see her. God answered your prayer."

As tears now streamed down her face, she turned to Camille and managed a weak smile. "Would you pray with me before Caleb arrives?"

The women got down on their knees, praying silently.

Dear Father, in heaven, Rebecca prayed. *I know I've asked you for so much of late, and I thank you again for all your blessings, and for saving my life. I will cherish whatever time you will give me to share with my sister.*

Chapter 73

Aboard Marine One

Marine One lifted off from Camp David with Rebecca and Caleb Toussaint aboard.

"Your sister's primary care physician is standing by to update us and fill in the background of her medical care," Toussaint said, "but first the attorney general needs to speak to you urgently."

"Rebecca," Harriet Ogden said, talking on Marine One's video-conference system. "I've heard the news about your sister. I will be praying for both of you."

"Thank you. But I assume you are calling about other matters."

"Yes, before dawn tomorrow, unless you wish to object, FBI agents will be conducting sweeping raids across the country. We will be seizing files at William Tree's homes and offices and at an office in Washington D.C. belonging to Merewether Tree which we recently located. Also, agents will be conducting raids against John Spencer and his network of associates."

"I told you I would not interfere. I regret my comments at the last press conference about considering a pardon for Merewether."

"I understand, but this whole matter couldn't be more sensitive. I have prepared all the indictment papers except for Merewether Tree. I need your final thoughts about it."

Rebecca remembered sitting on her grandfather's lap when he was dressed as Santa, once a year for a few years—there was this magic with him. She also remembered the smell on his breath that she didn't recognize at the time as alcohol, perhaps the reason why he was so uncharacteristically kind? This was all too hard for her; she felt like a ship caught on rocks slowly but steadily being broken into pieces.

"Can we hold off on indicting Merewether Tree for a few days? I need to see Allison first. Could we revisit it then? He might be a monster, but he is the only father figure that I've known."

"I understand," Ogden said. "We'll talk when you are ready."

* *

A few minutes later, Allison Tree's physician Takeo Nakashita appeared on the videoconference screen. He had a full head of pure white hair and wore a white doctor's coat that hung on a bone thin frame.

"Good evening, Madam President, I have been Andrea Cabell's doctor for the past ten years. From the information we have received from the Secret Service, we now believe that she is your sister Allison Tree, but we will need to take a DNA sample from you to confirm that with certainty."

"Of course," Rebecca replied, as she wrote down notes on a tablet computer she carried. Her hands shook as she struggled to maintain composure.

"Where would you like me to start?"

"In the beginning. Please, take your time, and leave out no details."

"Alma Cabell, a very wealthy woman, adopted Andrea, or Allison when she was seven. She spared no expense for Allison's care."

"Dr. Nakashita, please, you can call her Andrea. That's how you know her, and I can see that you would feel more comfortable with that."

"Thank you. About ten years ago, Ms. Cabell became terminally ill, and used her money to establish this hospital here in Rosslyn, Virginia now called Cabell Memorial as an endowed facility to treat children with critical illnesses. Additionally, she built a private ward, on the top floor, for Andrea's lifetime care, if she came to need it."

"Wait, Rosslyn is right next to Arlington. How close to the Potomac is your hospital?" Rebecca asked.

"We are right on the Potomac. From the top floor, Andrea's floor, there is a splendid panoramic view of most of Washington, all the monuments, and," Dr. Nakashita paused, "the White House."

Rebecca's stomach churned, and her legs felt like jelly, as she considered the divine or maybe diabolic plan placing the twins within a mile of each other.

Recovering, she asked, "What do you know about Allison, I mean Andrea's adoption?"

"Not much. I'll have to jump the chronology a bit here. When Alma died, Andrea's health began to deteriorate, the details of which I'll get to in a moment. We hired investigators to see if we could find her birth mother or siblings."

"And did you find a trail?" Rebecca asked. Her eyes clenched as she now had to fight back tears.

"We knew where she came from, an institution in Batesville, Arkansas. But the institution, with all its records, had burned down over twenty years ago. The investigators found some of its staff scattered around Arkansas, mainly retired. The material pieced together remains very sketchy."

"Tell me what you found."

"We believe that the director at Batesville ran an unregulated private clinic within the facility. We learned this from second-hand accounts, from staff that worked in the public part of the hospital. In the private part, they thought a few children lived as patients, no more than four at any one time. Occasionally, perhaps a few times a year, a limousine might arrive and disgorge a passenger or two who would go in a door which led into the private clinic."

"Doctor, can you hold on one moment?" Rebecca took a deep sigh, looked at Toussaint, and mouthed nearly silently to him, "How did you find her?"

"A few days ago," Toussaint said, speaking softly. "Private investigators hired by your grandfather found a copy of a self-published memoir, the story of a boy-child who recounted his life in this doctor's private institution, which he described as a high-class, well-run prison for the disappeared children of the rich and powerful."

"Wait, are you telling me that Merewether only learned about this memoir a few days ago."

"We spoke to the investigative agency. I believe it to be the truth. They're not going to risk lying to federal agents."

"Alright. Keep going then."

"In the book, the writer describes a girl with freckles who we thought could be Allison. We tracked him down yesterday. He lives from inherited wealth as a recluse on a private island off the coast of Maine. He has no TV or Internet, nor does he read newspapers, but spends his time reading classical works in Greek and Latin. In any event, he spoke to our agents and remembered the woman who adopted Allison, and fortunately, he remembered her name. The rest was easy."

Nearly in a whisper, Rebecca said, "Run Alma Cabell's name through your database."

Goosebumps covered Rebecca's arms as she tried to fight off the chill racing through her body. The image of a child in an institution overpowered her. Rebecca had left the reality of evidence and entered a realm of feelings. *Did the child wait expectantly for a visitor, a family member to come?*

Turning back to him, she said, "Doctor, I don't understand one thing. Why didn't you go public with Andrea's story?"

"We wanted to, but Alma Cabell's will and the endowment for the hospital has covenants that restricted us from doing so. It's a bit complicated, but we will make all that material available to you."

Toussaint waved his hand to get Rebecca's attention. "Could you hold on a minute, Doctor?"

"Yes."

"Alma Cabell, is her married name," Toussaint said, looking at data coming in from the federal databases. "She is Alma Cabell nee Atkins."

"Atkins? . . . Atkins? . . . Atkins v. Tree! It must be a relative of the hardscrabble miner who fought Merewether Tree for mineral rights."

This was totally crazy, Rebecca thought to herself. The adoption of Allison was perhaps a way to settle a score for injustices that Atkins the miner received. But in this case, the motivation was to settle a score by doing a good deed and giving Allison the loving care that her own family most likely would have denied her.

"Alright," Rebecca said, shaking her head in full disbelief. "What's Andrea's condition now?"

"When her adopted mother died, Andrea went into a deep and severe depression. She stopped talking, wouldn't get out of bed, and refused to eat. The executor of Ms. Cabell's estate brought her here, where she has occupied the top floor private ward for ten years now."

"And she never came out of her depression?" Rebecca asked as she ground her teeth.

Did she ever look out her hospital window? Did Allison think about the color of the sky? Would she have any memory that she even had a sister?

"It has been in and out. We used some psychotropic drugs but sparingly. We've had better luck with visual stimulation techniques."

"Like what?"

"She likes birds, a lot. So we keep songbirds in her room. It's unpredictable. Some days she'll become lucid, especially if we've introduced a new songbird that she's never heard before, and she'll talk a bit, and sometimes we could coax her out of bed. Occasionally she was well enough for small excursions, and we would take her in a wheelchair to the Smithsonian. She responded very well to the dinosaur exhibits."

She sounds so much like me.

"And her physical health at this point?" Rebecca asked as a small ray of hope re-infused her.

"Unfortunately, it has been deteriorating steadily the last three years."

"What's wrong with her?"

"All her primary body organs—her heart, her liver, her kidneys— are severely weakened."

"But can't these organs be rejuvenated by stem cell therapy?"

"Yes, and no. Yes, in theory, but no, in practice."

"Why?"

"We could inject her with generic stem cells, but her auto-immune system is not strong enough. She would need to have transplants from a closely matched genotype."

"But doctor, I'm her twin. Why can't you harvest from me?"

Take my cells. I've got plenty.

"You're the president of the United States. I'm a doctor, not a politician, and in any event, ethically I cannot make that suggestion to any patient's relative."

"You're not suggesting anything. I understand what you're saying. You've made no inducement. Of course, I intend to be the donor."

Chapter 74

Cabell Memorial Hospital
Rosslyn, Virginia

Glass display cases stood against a wall filled with exotic stuffed animals. Outside the hospital bed area, plushed bears, gorillas, giraffes, and lions scattered randomly about the floor. In ornate cages stood a half a dozen species of rare songbirds. A warbler and a mockingbird began to chirp when Rebecca and Toussaint entered the top floor room.

Rebecca had never seen a hospital room so large. A panoramic view swept over the Potomac, past Theodore Roosevelt Island onto a stunning view of Washington D.C. with the Lincoln Memorial in the foreground and the Washington Monument in the background. She noticed that the roof of the White House completed the frame.

Connected to tubes and monitors, Allison Tree, re-named in adoption Andrea Cabell, lay passively in a hospital bed. Trembling from head to toe, Rebecca tiptoed toward the bed. Allison's eyes were closed, her breathing raspy and shallow. She was conscious but not alert. Rebecca shook as she took in the resemblance, one only she would notice. She appeared twice Rebecca's weight and looked thirty years older, her eyes puffy with a face deeply wrinkled. She had lost most of her hair.

Tears decanted from Rebecca's eyes as she reached out to touch her sister. She ran her fingers across Allison's cheeks and bent toward her face, her locket dangling between them. She didn't want anything in her way, so she rotated the locket to the back of her neck, tucking it under her shirt. Rebecca smiled through her tears; faded, nearly indiscernible freckles covered Allison's face.

"Ally, it's Becky here. I've been looking for you everywhere for years.

I lost you. I'm so sorry I didn't find you sooner. But I'm here now."

She looked around the room at Allison's stuffed animal companions. "Do you remember all the great trips we took together as kids?"

Rebecca recounted her own imaginary childhood flights of fancy to Allison in a hushed voice. "Do you remember when we went down the Serengeti, and we had to defend ourselves against the lion? We called him Leo, and he's sitting right there. And look, George the Giraffe is visiting you tonight as well. Do you remember the frogs we collected in Equatorial Guinea? Do you know that some of the species we collected later became extinct? The Explorer's Club honored you at a special dinner for preserving the last of a species. And later they named a previously undiscovered dwarf frog after you. Allison Tree's name is in all the biology textbooks; children all over the world read about your contributions to science. I bet you didn't know that."

Rebecca paused as she tried to gather her thoughts.

Allison was dressed in fresh, neatly pressed white pajamas imprinted with images of green, blue and yellow parakeets. Rebecca slowly ran her right-hand finger over a deeply etched wrinkle under Allison's left eye and with her left hand she combed out a remaining patch of hair.

"When you feel better, we'll take a trip to the Arabian Desert . . . we always wanted to go there together. We'll go on safari, the desert is beautiful, there are endless giant sand dunes, rising hundreds of feet, and then falling abruptly. We can wear these cute white robes like Bedouins. We'll jump off the sand dunes, and roll down together. You can't get hurt. I promise. It's like living in a giant sandbox.

"We can go when the annual meteor shower, the Lyrids, appear and lie on our backs watching the night sky. I spoke to your nice doctor. He told me what a wonderful woman Alma Cabell was. I am so sorry she's not alive; I would have liked to thank her for taking such good care of you. The doctor says you're not so healthy now, but if you had a compatible bone marrow and kidney stem cell transplant . . . well, that could make you better. I am here now; we are going to start the transplants within a few days, and then before you know we can travel a bit. I love you, Ally."

Rebecca could feel her sister's hand contract slightly. She had no clue if it was a voluntary movement. As she looked into Allison's face, her eyes fluttered ever so slightly, her eyes opened momentarily, and her faded freckles flickered like far away stars.

Lyra . . . Vega . . . Draco . . . Hercules . . . Vulpecula . . .

Rebecca could swear she was smiling.

The End

www.ingramcontent.com/pod-product-compliance
Lightning Source LLC
Chambersburg PA
CBHW071222250626
47163CB00001B/66